The Tende

Wendy Perriam

Table of Contents

For Chester and Beau,
top dog and top cat,
and for their top-cop master,
DCC David Zinzan – VIPs all three.

Our interest's on the dangerous edge of things.
The honest thief, the tender murderer,
The superstitious atheist ...

Robert Browning, *Bishop Blougram's Apology*

PART ONE - 6th December 2012

CHAPTER 1

'Oh my God, *no!*'

Anthony lurched forward, as his entire unwanted, ill-advised breakfast projectiled into the toilet-bowl. He remained crouching on his haunches, hands clammy against the cold rebuke of the porcelain, his stomach reeling and pitching like a ship in a squall. And, every bit as suddenly, a second eruption followed, no less violent than the first.

His sense of desperation screwed up to breaking-point. Piers was expecting him *now*, for a private briefing before the all-important meeting with Oceanic Energy, and Piers had zero tolerance for the slightest deviation from split-second punctuality.

Spitting out the last dregs of vomit, he grimaced at the clotted, brownish mess and began frantically flushing the bowl, using wads of toilet-paper to wipe away any splashes. The stench was overwhelming and he dreaded the thought of someone else coming into this reeking cubicle – too much was at stake for him even to be *seen* as ill. But never mind that – he had to get to the boardroom, double-quick.

Hastily, he washed his face, rinsed his mouth, and removed a few flecks of vomit from his tie. A glance in the mirror showed his immaculate suit and oyster-coloured shirt, let down by the face above them: ashen skin, dark-circled eyes. He should have seen the gastroenterologist over a week ago, but had been forced to cancel his appointment, due to sheer pressure of work. No time now, though, to reflect on the state of his gut – what mattered was Oceanic. The company might be small fry compared with titans like BP; nonetheless, this deal was worth a cool two billion.

Despite his groggy state, he dashed towards the bank of lifts, his mind mulling over the outstanding problem: the five bids for a substantial part of Oceanic all unaccountably low: two citing the company's latest results; one blaming the state of the economy; another worried about the challenge of ramping up production, given the lack of export capacity; and the fifth daunted by the difficulties of foreign tax law.

'Anthony, you're late!'

Typical. An accusation before even a "hello". He rued the fact it was Piers who was chairing the meeting, rather than easy-going Thomas, the partner he usually worked with and the nearest he had to a friend at Forsythe Foster Clark. Oceanic had particularly requested Piers, on account of his in-depth knowledge as an oil-and-gas specialist, whereas Thomas was more of a generalist.

Muttering an apology, Anthony seated himself at the table, all but gagging at the cloying scent of lilies from the showy flower-arrangement in the corner. Removing his papers from his briefcase, he tried to ignore the still unruly spasms in his stomach and fix his attention on Piers' staccato voice: a series of gunshots reverberating through his head.

'Right, whatever happens, we mustn't alarm the client, so we need to thrash out any potential problems first, and then spend ten minutes running through the presentation. Where are we against our budget? Are we meeting our scope?"

Anthony swallowed. Privately, he was worried that the team hadn't done enough due diligence to justify their conclusions but, before he could articulate his concern, they were interrupted by the three other members of their team, Charlie, Jon and Gavin. Piers gave them no more acknowledgement than a curt nod of his head and an angry glance at his watch. The trio were early, not late, but in his present tetchy mood, Piers might judge that equally unacceptable. Having recently moved back to England from an exceptionally high-paying job in New York, Piers clearly resented his fall in wealth and status. Not that he lacked either now, Anthony reflected, noting the hand-made shirt, designer suit, and Italian calfskin shoes. The man inside them was thin – thin-faced, thin-lipped and as lean as a fasting greyhound, despite the Michelin-starred restaurants he still patronised with enviable frequency.

Having given Piers a brief resumé of the problems with the specialist teams, Anthony then turned to Jon, a tall, tow-headed Scot, and the youngest person present. 'Jon, have you put through all those changes we agreed last night?'

Jon nodded, then shook his head, as if to contradict himself. 'Yes, but I'm afraid the figures don't tie up with the last financial statements.'

'Bloody hell!' Piers snapped, while Anthony suppressed a no-less-anxious groan.

'Look, it wasn't for lack of effort. I stayed up half the night.'

'Join the club!' Gavin put in, his air of patent exhaustion testifying to his lack of sleep.

'Okay, okay,' Piers interjected, tapping his fingers irritably on the table. 'Long hours are simply part of the job, so if you can't take the heat, get out of the bloody kitchen!'

"Long hours" was putting it mildly, Anthony didn't say. He had barely been back home this week, obliged to snatch naps at work, grab a shower in the company bathroom, send out for meals when time allowed, although they were often left uneaten. No wonder Deborah was scathing. 'You never seem to be here. And, as for sex, forget it! *You* have – that's blindingly obvious.'

He shut his eyes, as if to block out the domestic problems – worse than the work ones, in some ways. The vital thing was to get through the meeting with Oceanic, due to start in a matter of minutes, pacify their team and, most crucial of all, regain their confidence. And, after that, perhaps he could take life at a slightly slower pace, book another appointment with the gastroenterologist – maybe even bed his wife.

*

'Frankly, Anthony, your report completely misses the point. In fact, to be brutally honest, it's not worth the paper it's written on. It tells me more than I need to know about half-a-dozen Far Eastern countries, but skates over the fundamental problem of a falling oil price.'

Oceanic's Chief Executive Officer, Clive, could rival Piers in aggression. Indeed, before Anthony could defend himself, Clive was on the attack – again.

'And even the tax-risk you grossly over-estimate,' he barked, with near contempt.

Anthony kept his own voice rigidly controlled. 'I assure you the tax risk has been carefully thought through. If you turn to page three—'

Clearly Clive had no intention of so doing. 'The only way,' he interrupted, 'you can arrive at the figure of a hundred-million dollars is by including every cent of revenue for the last fifteen years, without any deduction for the corresponding expenses. That's totally unrealistic, if not an insult to my intelligence.'

Anthony struggled to maintain his determinedly unruffled tone. 'But,' he pointed out, 'the short time-line you afforded us severely limited the amount of work we could do. Our findings are as robust as humanly possible, given a mere four weeks. With more time, we could have refined our conclusions, but you kept stressing how urgent it was to finalize the sale. Surely you remember that conversation?'

'I'm hardly likely to forget it! But what you didn't tell me was that your report would actually scare bidders away!'

'Look, I suggest we all calm down,' interjected Jake, the corporate lawyer – a slim, sleek ex-Etonian, with a laser-sharp mind and a taste in arty ties. 'If we don't come to a sensible position on this, we're in danger of losing credibility with the potential buyers, and that would completely undermine our negotiating position—"

Shit, thought Anthony, he must be worried about the deal collapsing. His eyes strayed briefly around the circle of tense faces – everybody fraught; the clean lines and quiet colours of the boardroom contradicted by the almost palpable air of hostility and agitation. Having chimed in dutifully, in support of Jake's position, it was the Corporate Finance Officer who now cut him off mid-sentence.

'And another thing – your people have applied an extreme and inflexible interpretation of the law, which the Chinese tax authorities have never actually taken. In fact, I'm forced to conclude that we were seriously mistaken in opting to deal with FFC at all. You're supposed to be the best in the business and, when you pitched for the job, you certainly weren't shy about your capabilities, but all I can say is—'

As Anthony opened his mouth to interrupt in his turn, he was overtaken by another disconcerting wave of nausea, rising unstoppably from his belly to his throat, and intensified by the reek of Clive's obstreperously pungent aftershave. Not even daring to excuse himself, he sprang to his feet, made a dash for the door and ran full pelt to the gents, failing to reach the cubicle in time. Horrified by the stinking sludge spattering the floor, he fetched an unused toilet-roll and began feverishly clearing up. Having eaten almost nothing all week, the task demanded energy he simply didn't possess. This morning's half a croissant he'd only forced down in a futile bid to give himself strength. Strength!

Once the floor was more or less clean, he rested on the toilet-seat a moment before fumbling for his mobile and sending a brief text to Jon. 'Please tell Piers I've just thrown up, but hang on – I'll be back.'

Within less than sixty seconds, there was an answering text from Jon. 'Piers says go home, for fuck's sake! The meeting's going badly enough as it is, without you puking over everyone. Take a taxi and get the hell out – *now*!'

Anthony stared morosely at the ash-grey marbled floor. He couldn't go home; his partnership was at stake. Although partnerships weren't confirmed till June, he knew he was in the running from the hints he'd already received. Indeed, with his fortieth birthday only seven weeks away, he had no wish to wait much longer for the advancement that had been his goal since he'd first joined FFC as an ambitious twenty-one-year-old, just down from Cambridge. But now he had blown his chances at a stroke. Oceanic might assume he couldn't handle the stress and had suffered some sort of breakdown, rather than believing he was ill. How else to explain such an unprecedented exit from a meeting, and one so shamefully undignified? He *had* to go back, even if it demanded his last remaining ounce of willpower.

He waited a scant five minutes, still hunkered on the toilet-seat, sucking a peppermint to mask the foul taste in his mouth, even slapping his cheeks to put some colour in them. Then he reached for his phone to text Jon again, saying he felt much better and could return to the meeting right away.

As if in mockery, yet another squall of nausea sent him staggering to his knees above the toilet-bowl and forced him to admit defeat, although he hardly dared tell Jon that he had changed his mind again, knowing he'd be judged as hopelessly indecisive. But what option did he have but to sneak off home and hide his pitiful condition? So, stumbling from the gents, he took the mirrored lift to the imposing ground-floor atrium, deliberately avoiding his reflection. His briefcase was still in the boardroom, his overcoat in his office, but no way would he retrieve them and risk being seen in his dishevelled state.

Instead, he crept out of the building like a criminal, slinking past the security guard and only forcing a smile for the elegant receptionists. Hailing an empty taxi, he collapsed onto the seat, wincing at every jolt and barely glancing at the self-important Shard, or the graceful church spires, now dwarfed and overwhelmed by the towering steel-and-glass structures that seemed to hem them in. Yet, as the cab swung over London Bridge, he did notice the low, lowering clouds, laden with as yet unfallen snow and reflected in the tea-coloured Thames – the murky water and leaden sky both matching his sombre mood.

Had he acted too precipitately, he wondered? He was actually feeling a fraction better and, since there was probably nothing left in his stomach to sick up, he might just be able to function if he asked the driver to turn round and take him back. Yet how could he text Jon again? The guy would be maddened by such continual chopping and changing and, as for Piers, he would incur his full-fired wrath. Indeed, he could hardly believe his present vacillatory state. Normally, he could stick to a decision and follow it through, without veering all over the place. But his mind had been affected by the ever-mounting pressures of late, as had his usual schedule. His gym sessions and weekly squash match with Thomas, even the odd movie or meal out with Deborah – all had been swept aside. At least his boss was aware of his zeal and – Oceanic apart – of the strong client-relationships he had successfully built and fostered over the course of many years. In the normal run of things, that would mean more brownie points for his longed-for partnership, except any hope of that now was just a fading dream.

He stared wretchedly out of the window at a couple of Lycra-clad joggers pounding the pavement, their breath puffing clouds of steam as they negotiated past a group of camera-laden tourists and two well-heeled women emerging from Femme Fashion with designer bags and self-satisfied expressions. People at leisure – a concept he'd forgotten.

Why was he shivering so violently? True, it was the coldest early December in decades – the temperature outside a Siberian minus three – yet the cab itself was fuggily warm. What was wrong with him, for heaven's sake?

'You okay?' the driver asked, a swarthy chap with one gold earring and a patchy scurf of beard.

'Yes, fine.'

'Well, you don't look fine to me, guv.'

Anthony ignored the comment, fixing his gaze on the two miniature Spanish dolls dangling from the dashboard, their spiralling, zigzag motion reflecting the commotion not just in his stomach but in his head. He had disgraced himself in front of his own team – worse, in front of the whole panoply of the Oceanic top brass, as well as their high-powered retinue of legal and investment advisors. Such people were bound to tittle-tattle; word would get around that Anthony Beaumont was unwell, unreliable.

He gave a great shuddering sigh, aware he had no choice but to accept the situation. The taxi was already turning into Newman Street, so he would be home in less than ten minutes and, whatever the cock-up he'd made, his overwhelming desire was simply to go to bed and rest.

CHAPTER 2

As he alighted outside Clarence Court, a woman with a baby darted over to claim the cab. Why were there so many damned babies in London nowadays? Three years ago, they hadn't existed – not for him, at least.

With a shrug, he paid the driver and stepped into the foyer of his Marylebone apartment block, greeted obsequiously, as always, by the Armenian concierge. Alighting from the lift, he walked the length of the corridor, with its striking zebra-patterned wallpaper and matching black-and-white prints, and, stopping outside their flat, was surprised to realise Deborah had failed to double-lock the door. No doubt she had left in a tearing rush for her 7.30 breakfast meeting. They had rung each other briefly last night, since he hadn't had time to pop home, and she'd told him how keyed up she was about the exceptionally fussy client. When it came to long hours and stress, Advertising was no less demanding than Corporate Finance.

As he stepped into the hall, he was startled by a sudden noise. Not a break-in, he prayed, on top of all the rest. He stood a moment, listening. Deborah never got home till eight or nine at night and right now it was barely 11.30 in the morning. Anyway, he could hear a male voice, coming from the bedroom. The pricey stuff he had in there would be perfect swag for burglars. Without considering his safety, he burst in through the door, ready to confront the intruders – only to reel back in disbelief. His wife was lying stark naked in the king-size marital bed, clamped to some unknown fellow clothed only in his body-hair.

All three froze for a second, before the couple sprang apart and leapt to their feet, Deborah grabbing the duvet and trying desperately to cover herself.

'Wh-what the hell's going on?' Anthony could scarcely speak from fury. The hirsute bear of a stranger was now standing solid and rugged in front of him – a younger, fitter, taller man than he, and sickeningly virile with that jet-black pelt trumpeting his testosterone. 'Who the fuck are you?' he demanded. 'And what in Christ's name are you doing here?'

'I'd have thought it was bleeding obvious, mate!' The guy fixed him with an arrogant stare. 'I wouldn't *be* in your bed if you could give your wife what she wants.'

Anthony flinched, as from a body-blow. Enraged, he turned on Deborah. 'So you've been telling all and sundry about our private affairs?'

'Oh, for pity's sake, Anthony, Craig isn't "all and sundry".'

What was *that* supposed to mean? How well did she know the shit? Had the liaison been going on for months, all those stressful meetings she'd described really sessions in the sack? Everything about the brute incensed him: his burly, bragging size and dark, dramatic colouring (making *him*, the cuckold, seem pallid and anaemic), that insolent Estuary voice daring to call him "mate", the vulgarly ostentatious gold chain entangled in his chest-hair, the hair itself – all the more infuriating when Deborah made him wax his own timid bit of fuzz. But most galling of all was the fact he hadn't even bothered to cover himself. Was he deliberately displaying his long, thick, vaunting cock, to prove how well-endowed he was?

Deborah's voice was rising – defensive, even shrill. 'Anyway, what do you expect? I'm desperate for a child, and I'm not getting any younger, and soon it'll be too late. We've talked for bloody years, but talking gets us nowhere, so it's action I need now. If you can't give me a baby and refuse to use a sperm donor, then you're more or less driven me to …'

'What the devil do you mean, Debs?' Craig interjected, swinging round to confront her. 'You told me you were on the pill.'

'Well, I—'

'… said you were so frustrated, all you wanted was a damned good fuck. Okay, I was happy to oblige, but if you imagine you can help yourself to my sperm!'

Anthony clenched his fist into a tight and painful ball. So his wife had deceived them both; let this upstart assume she was panting for his cock; allowed *him* to think she was a loyal and faithful wife.

'You told me over and over your old man couldn't get it up, so—'

Incandescent with rage, Anthony lunged towards the greasy stud, yelling at his wife, 'You want action? I'll give you action! I'll fucking *kill* the bloke!' And, with that, he raised his fist and punched the bastard full-force in the face.

Craig lost his balance and teetered for a moment, so Anthony took his chance and kicked him in the groin. Craig suddenly keeled over, hitting his head on the sharp corner of the bedside cabinet, before falling, hard, against the solid oak-wood floor. He lay there, moaning, eyes half-shut, apparently unable to get up. Anthony watched, aghast, as blood gushed from the back of his head, trickled across the polished wood and began seeping into the white sheepskin rug. His nakedness seemed all the more blatant, with his broad-shouldered, six-foot-plus body spread-eagled on the floor and his preening genitals in full view. Nonetheless, he was utterly appalled by the strength of his own blow, a blow evidenced by the reddening mark incriminating his knuckles. Okay, so he had threatened the lout, but only in the red mist of a rage.

'Anthony, what the hell have you done?' Deborah rushed over to Craig, who remained alarmingly unresponsive to her cries.

He himself stood paralysed, unable to shift his eyes from the accusing bloodstain, inexorably deepening and spreading beneath Craig's head.

Suddenly, Deborah darted over to the dressing table, grabbed her mobile and dialled 999 for an ambulance, her voice frenzied with fear and shock.

As the call continued, she became increasingly agitated, presumably because the person she was speaking to was pressing for more details. And, once she'd rung off, she told him in a shaky tone, 'The emergency operator said she's going to summon the police as well.'

No, he thought, not the police! He was tempted to make a bolt for it but, incapable of action, he remained leaning against the wall, for support.

Deborah, for her part, was swathing Craig in the duvet and, having flung on the clothes she'd left strewn beside the bed, knelt beside her lover and started soothing and consoling him, begging him to speak.

He shielded his eyes from the pair of them, detesting their obvious intimacy, which made him feel an intruder in his own home. No, worse than an intruder – an aggressor, an assailant. After what seemed like hours of curdled guilt and horror, a ring at the door forced him to kick-start his inoperative body and stumble into the hall, to let in the two paramedics. Not stopping to introduce themselves, they simply followed him into the bedroom, the younger one immediately crouching beside Craig and checking his vital signs.

Having asked Deborah his name, he said in a calm, measured tone, 'Hello, Craig, I'm Barry. Can you hear me?'

Since Craig's only response was a muffled groan, Barry inserted a tube down his throat, Craig gasping and choking in protest. Anthony could hardly bear to listen to the harshly guttural sounds – or to Deborah's panicked babbling, as she repeated over and over, 'Oh, this is so terrible! It can't be happening. I can't believe it. Is he going to be okay?'

'I'm afraid we can't tell yet,' Barry said, continuing to busy himself with further medical procedures.

The other paramedic, Len, a small-boned man who seemed swamped by his green overalls, now turned to Anthony and asked, 'Are there any other casualties?'

Anthony shook his head, not trusting his own voice.

'Can you tell me what happened, please?'

He let Deborah explain, although all her normal clarity had vanished and, when Barry asked Craig's date of birth, address and medical history, she seemed at a total loss. He snatched at this speck of hope. Maybe she *didn't* know Craig well. Perhaps today was just a one-off. Except how the hell would that help? His violence and her infidelity were now stark, unavoidable facts.

He was jolted back from his train of thought when he heard Len on the phone. 'Can you confirm that the police are on their way?'

Deborah was right. This couldn't be happening. Never before had he been involved with the law, never before laid a finger on anyone, not even as a kid. The police belonged in television dramas, not here in his elegant flat.

Yet, within minutes, it seemed, they were at the door, two officers who somehow looked more menacing than any he had ever seen.

'We have a male casualty,' Barry explained. 'He appears to have a head-wound and I can't get a response, so I reckon it's serious. We're going to take him straight to hospital.'

After a further brief exchange, Len went down to fetch the stretcher and Craig was carried out, ominously pale and all but motionless.

The older officer, a small, sinewy man with cold blue eyes, now turned to him and Deborah.

'I'm PC Frank Irwin,' he said. 'And this is my colleague, Martin Renshaw. Could you please both give me your names and tell me exactly what happened.'

Again, Anthony left his wife to speak.

'I'm Deborah Beaumont. And this is my husband, Anthony. He came home early from work and … and got into a fight with Craig.'

'And who's Craig?'

'Oh, er … an acquaintance of mine.'

Anthony all but spat. So his wife went to bed with mere acquaintances. How many might there be, for Christ's sake? Had she amassed enough sperm to father a tribe? He was torn between wanting the bastard dead and desperately hoping he'd revive.

Frank now asked him to come with him to the bathroom, so he could give his own version of events. The officer, in his military-type ballistic jacket and with his Taser, baton and handcuffs, looked completely out of place against the tranquil dove-grey décor. He, too, craved body-armour, as Frank began drilling against the would-be shield of his reticence with a series of intrusive questions. He answered briefly, curtly, with as little detail as possible, but Frank persisted with the interrogation, until finally he blurted out, 'Okay, I admit it. When I saw my wife in bed with that … that scum, I just went wild and punched and kicked him.'

Frank immediately changed his tone to a more formal and officious one. 'Anthony Beaumont, based on what you just said, I have reasonable grounds to believe you may have committed an offence, so I am arresting you on suspicion of grievous bodily harm.'

As he spelled out the caution, Anthony was too stunned to do anything but stare down at the swirly marble floor, which seemed to echo the nauseous churning in his stomach. Frank then ordered him to empty his pockets, before frisking him for possible weapons. 'I'm going to have to handcuff you, sir. Put your hands to the front, please.'

The "sir" seemed offensively ironical. How could he be "sir", yet under arrest?

The full horror of his situation was underlined still further when Frank radioed on his walkie-talkie for transport for 'one prisoner back to the station'.

Prisoner! An hour ago, he'd been a respected Director in one of the top accountancy firms; now he was a criminal. And, when the other officer,

Martin, who'd been questioning Deborah in the bedroom, emerged into the hall and also started radioing the station, every word seemed a further accusation.

'It's quite a nasty assault. According to the hospital, the victim is breathing, but only semi-conscious, so this is one for the CID. Can you get them down here, please? I'll stay and preserve the crime scene until they arrive.'

And, within minutes, he was being marched out of the flat, the handcuffs ratcheted tight round his wrist – cold, restrictive and unutterably mortifying. Frank gripped him by the arm and steered him into the lift, as if he planned to pull free and escape – impossible whilst under such restraint.

As they exited the foyer, the concierge stared in astonishment and there were more humiliating stares from a well-heeled female resident just entering the building. Outside in the street, the cold December air seemed to slap him in the face, and he recoiled from the cluster of people gawking at the police van, double-parked, with blue lights flashing. Some of his near neighbours might be part of that group, or a local tradesman or shopkeeper – people who knew him as a high-principled, successful man. Yet, when Frank opened the back doors of the van and bundled him in to what appeared to be a cramped, claustrophobic dog-cage, he became instantly the lowest of the low.

As he felt the van jerk into motion, his senses were working overtime and he saw, again, the congealing pool of blood dyeing the pristine rug a shameful scarlet; heard Craig's moans of pain, smelt his rancid sweat. Frantic to distract himself, he peered out through the windows in the back doors of the van, but the fact he was facing backwards only increased his distress, as if everything in front of him – his fate, his future, his life from this day on – was shrouded in uncertainty and darkness.

Yet, all too soon, they arrived at the back yard of the police station, where Frank unlocked the back doors and marched him into the custody suite.

'Hi, Sarge!' he said, nodding at the plump, balding man behind the desk.

'How-do, Frank. I'm just finishing with another prisoner. Take a seat and I'll be with you in a tick.

Frank led him over to a long wooden bench, set against a stained and pitted wall. He glanced, appalled, at its occupants: a haggard-looking drunk; a black kid effing and blinding; a skeletally thin wreck of a man, babbling to himself; and a massive-breasted woman in black fishnet tights and clingy leopard top, her face a mask of lurid make-up. This was a hidden world, one he had never penetrated, where vice and crime were legion, and people out of control. In a daze, he squeezed himself into the small space beside the drunk, his nausea rekindling as he inhaled the stink of sweat and booze. Never before had he mixed with such types or been in such an oppressive place: four CCTV cameras mounted on the ceiling, chilling notices about terrorist offences, and an air of tension and hopelessness combined.

If the drive in the van had seemed short, now hours appeared to pass as he sat listening to expletives, crazed effusions, and a non-stop harangue from the woman, cursing all men – those present in particular.

'Right, bring him over, Frank,' Ian called, at last.

He was escorted to the desk, where his handcuffs were removed and he was subjected to another barrage of questions. Once his replies had been entered into the computer, the Sergeant looked up and said, 'You're entitled to have someone informed of your arrest. Is there anyone you want to phone?'

Who, for pity's sake? His irreproachable parents would be scandalised to learn that their only son – a model citizen not guilty of even a minor driving offence – was now totally disgraced. And, as for his colleagues at FFC, how could he admit that one five-second act of violence meant he would never be permitted to set foot in the place again?

He suddenly longed to speak to Deborah – his life-companion for the last eleven years – but that was out of the question. According to Frank, Martin had arranged for her to stay with her friend Isabel, since the Marylebone flat was now sealed off, awaiting the forensics. Isabel was a gossip and would take enormous relish in telling anyone and everyone about Deborah's husband's arrest.

With a maelstrom of conflicting emotions, he tried to imagine what his wife might be feeling. If she was in love with Craig, she could well be prostrate with grief. Or had she simply used the fellow as a handy supply of sperm? And what about her own job? No way could she deal with clients tomorrow in such a state of distress.

'I asked if you'd like to phone someone,' Ian said impatiently, still waiting for a reply.

'No,' he said, tersely.

'You're also entitled to speak to a legal representative – either your own solicitor, or I can arrange one from the Duty Solicitor scheme.'

His own solicitor, the suave and silky Sebastian, was a commercial lawyer and didn't deal with criminal cases. Sebastian was also a fellow member of his squash club and occasional dinner-party guest, so impossible to confess his dire predicament and change their whole relationship. Indeed, it struck him as ironic that, despite the plethora of lawyers he encountered in his professional life – corporate, contract, competition- and tax- lawyers – there wasn't a single one he could call on now

'Well,' Ian prompted, 'shall I phone the Duty Solicitor?'

'Yes.' Monosyllables were safer, with his voice so impotent.

'Okay, Frank, can you search him'

Again, he was instructed to empty his pockets and, as he handed over his wedding ring, his wallet, credit cards and driver's licence, his iPhone and his Patek Philippe watch – a gift from Deborah to celebrate his directorship – the essentials of his normal, ordered, cushioned life vanished at a stroke. Then, once Ian had recorded all his possessions in detail, and put them into a sealed plastic bag, he was taken to the cells, each one with a small whiteboard outside with the prisoner's name and offence scrawled in felt-tip pen: "Patel, burglary"; "Simmons, begging"; "Beaumont, assault". He shuddered to see his own name, and at the daunting sounds issuing from inside: inmates banging on their doors and yelling, 'Let me out!' 'Let me out!'; others moaning or swearing. But the worst sound of all was the slam of his own cell-door as Frank him led him into a claustrophobic hell-hole, bare except for a padded bench and an unsavoury-looking toilet.

'I need you to undress,' Frank said, pulling on a pair of latex gloves. 'Start with your shoes and socks, okay, then your jacket, shirt and trousers, and finally your underwear.'

His first instinct was to refuse. He was damned if he'd strip naked in front of this callous stranger. But, since refusal wasn't an option, he complied as slowly as possible, feeling more and more humiliated as each stylish item of clothing was deposited in a separate brown paper

27

bag, like rubbish for the dump. In return, he was given a cheap and nasty polo-shirt and tracksuit-bottoms, a pair of bargain-basement plimsolls, and some flimsy socks and underwear in a grubby shade of grey. Dressed in such gear, he seemed to lose his very identity and become a different person.

Back at the custody desk, all the brown bags and their contents were entered on his record, then he was locked up in his cell again, to await a medical examination. Once on his own, he experienced a surge of blinding, choking panic. Desperate to regain control, he forced himself to sit on the stained, blue-mattressed bench and try to calm his breathing. But his sense of confinement screwed tighter still when he realised that the tiny window didn't even open and its glass was opaque, as if forbidding even a view. "Outside" had disappeared. His world now measured nine feet by fourteen, and all he could see was pock-marked walls, a scuffed and dirty floor, and a couple of graffiti scribbled in lurching capitals: "HELP ME, GOD!' 'FUCK ALL SCREWS!"

'Yes, help me, God,' he muttered, although he had never had a God, despite the relentless chapel-going at Pembridge, his strictly traditional Church of England school. And, since 11.30 this morning, not only did he lack a God – he had no job, no home, no wife, no prospects, no future.

CHAPTER 3

He swung round at the jangle of keys to see a man in a white shirt and black trousers opening his cell door. Any interruption was welcome, in dispelling, even momentarily, his solitary confinement.

'Hi, mate! I'm Graham, the Detention Officer. The doctor's ready to see you now.'

He was led into a small interview room, where a grey-haired, distinguished-looking man rose from his desk to greet him. 'Good afternoon, Mr Beaumont. I'm Dr Alex Wilson, the Forensic Medical Examiner. I'll need to examine you and take some blood and urine samples. I hope that's all right with you?'

He all but wept at being treated with old-fashioned courtesy and by a man not in uniform but wearing a dark pinstriped suit. And, however galling it was having his bruised knuckles inspected and being asked to take down his tracksuit-bottoms and pee into a beaker in full view of Dr Wilson, the man's gracious manner made it just about tolerable. Even another round of questions – his medical history, current medications, the last time he'd taken drugs or pills or alcohol, how he was feeling, physically and mentally – were asked in a more gracious fashion than any previously. Deliberately, he didn't mention his panic or his recent bouts of vomiting, fearing he might be detained still longer or sent for additional checks.

Back in his cell, its restriction seemed the more intense after his brief respite with the doctor. And the contrast with his airy, spacious flat, and his office with its floor-to-ceiling windows, struck him with full force. At work, he enjoyed an impressive view of a swathe of teeming London, including a sweep of river, a soaring arc of sky and, within little more than a stone's-throw, the gleaming flamboyance of the Shard. But now he'd become a lowly creature cowering in its burrow.

Thoughts of work only fuelled his anxiety. He had lost all sense of time, but the Oceanic meeting must have long since ended – although not the recriminations, he suspected. His colleagues might be thinking that he had simply lost his nerve and feigned illness as an excuse. And they were bound to be annoyed that he'd disrupted the proceedings, risked Oceanic's contempt, and forced Piers to step in as chief spokesman when he lacked the detailed, in-depth knowledge he himself had been expected to provide. And his absence would have affected the rest of the team adversely, increased the pressures on them, even resulted in certain matters being deferred. Yet if they could blame him for a gastric bug clearly beyond his control, how the hell would they react were they to see him now?

In an effort to distract himself he started counting out loud, but, however hard he tried to focus on numbers, his mind was all over the place, veering from Craig to Deborah to Oceanic, then back to his own unspeakable situation.

'Duty solicitor's here!' the Detention Officer shouted through his door, after what seemed like hours. 'The interview rooms are all busy, so she's going to see you in your cell.'

In walked Graham, followed by a blowsy-looking woman in laddered tights, shoes worn down at heel, and a shiny navy suit that strained across her hips. Her blonded hair was dark at the roots and badly in need of a trim.

'You … you're the Duty Solicitor?' he stammered.

'That's right – Betty Jones,' she said, extending a friendly hand. 'Very glad to meet you, Mr Beaumont.'

'I was expecting … someone else.' To put it bluntly, a smartly attired professional like Sebastian.

'Women's brains are every bit as good as men's!' She flashed him a smile, to remove any sting from the comment.

But, since his sense of shock was nothing to do with her gender, he stood in silence, trying not to notice her nicotine-stained fingers.

'Any chance of a cup of tea before you go?' she asked Graham.

'No probs! How many sugars?'

'Three for me, please.'

Before Anthony could state his own preference, the door was slammed firmly shut.

'Do sit down, Mr Beaumont.' Betty patted the bench where she was already perched, now minus her navy suit-jacket. The tight blouse beneath outlined her large, mumsie breasts and revealed a deep V of ageing, mottled skin. He averted his eyes as they sat side by side, although no way could he avoid her cloying scent of carnation and cigarettes.

'First, we need to complete a few formal procedures, okay?'

She was interrupted by Graham, returning with two polystyrene cups. There was nowhere to put them except the floor, where Ms Jones had already parked her cheapo bag, bulging with books and papers.

While the tea was cooling, she dealt with a raft of preliminary procedures and helped him fill in a legal aid form. At first, surprised that high earners like him should actually be entitled to it, surprise gave way to worry when he learned he would have to make a sizable contribution, and that his wife would need to complete a similar form. Deborah would be justifiably aggrieved at having to forfeit a large chunk of their joint savings and, anyway, might refuse to fill in the form from motives of spite or vengeance. However, apart from those deep anxieties, he was impressed by Betty's efficiency and thoroughness, even dared to hope that her unprepossessing appearance might conceal a sharp legal mind.

'Right,' she said, passing him his cup, 'now that's all out of the way, let's get down to serious business. The CID have given me a brief outline of events, but I need to hear in your own words a detailed account of everything that happened.'

'Er, where should I start, Ms Jones?' he asked, gagging on his first mouthful of tea – liquid sugar, more like.

'Begin at the beginning and take as much time as you want. I'm Mrs, not Ms, by the way, but please do call me Betty. And is it okay if I call you Anthony?'

He nodded, although reluctantly, preferring to retain some measure of formality.

'But first I want to assure you that anything you say is completely confidential and will never go beyond this room, unless I have your permission. I also want you to know that I'm here to help you, Anthony. I'm on your side, a hundred per cent, and I intend to do everything in my power to build up a favourable case.'

Whatever his reservations, he warmed to this positive stance and to her kindly, reassuring tone. Wasn't it unfair to judge her by her south London accent and lamentable attire, before he'd even given her a chance?

'What I suggest is that, first, you explain why you came home early from work today and perhaps fill me in a bit about your job.'

He cleared his throat. As a child, his parents had stressed it was extremely bad form to broadcast one's woes or, worse, appear egoistical, so he had never been used to confiding in people or talking about personal matters. However, once he'd begun to speak, he was aware that Betty was listening intently, her full attention focused on his every word. That sort of listening was rare, almost like a gift, and encouraged him to open up – although not enough for Betty, who was now probing for more of the general background, more about himself.

Despite his distaste for self-disclosure, he knew that, if he didn't explain his failure to conceive and his family's abhorrence of any type of failure, Betty couldn't and wouldn't understand his crime. 'What you need to bear in mind, Ms Sm— … Betty, is that I was never allowed to fail, not even at kindergarten, let alone at public school. I *had* to achieve and come top – not just in academic subjects, but in everything I did. My parents were both high-fliers and continually pushed me to reach their own daunting standards. It was the same at Cambridge, where I just missed getting a First – a serious disappointment for them. Fortunately, they more or less forgave me when I was taken on by FFC straight from university and achieved the highest marks for my accountancy exams. And I continued to do well, thank God – secondment to FFC's New York office just a few years' later and, back in London, a director by the age of thirty-four. So, you see …' Playing for time, he gulped another mouthful of now cold and scummy tea, '… when I couldn't give my wife a child, it was the first real, appalling failure of my life. Mind you, it took us a while to realise there *was* a problem and that it wasn't simply due to our constant stress and busyness. But, with every birthday, Deborah got more anxious and, finally, in desperation, she began buying all these fertility gadgets and restricting our sex to just the one small window of her ovulation time.' He was acutely embarrassed by having to spell out such intimate details, which he had never discussed with a single soul before.

'Do go on,' Betty urged, giving him a sympathetic pat on the arm. 'And please feel free to say anything you want. I shan't be shocked, I assure you. People's sex-lives are simply part of my job.'

Although still feeling distinctly awkward – and also uncomfortably hot in the small, stifling cell – he forced himself to elaborate. 'It meant I had to perform to order, as a sort of mechanical baby-machine, tied to a rigid timetable, which, of course, killed any notion of pleasure or spontaneity. We both got more and more tense, and nothing was, er … happening anyway, so Deborah lost patience and insisted we go for fertility tests. *She* was fine – ovaries, womb, fallopian tubes, all functioning perfectly – but when *I* was tested, my sperm was found to be almost non-existent. That was a crushing blow, I can tell you. And, when I read that most normal guys can produce enough sperm in a just one ejaculation to fertilise every female in Europe, I felt a total freak in comparison. And she made it painfully clear that, if I was firing blanks, I was no longer particularly welcome in the bedroom. We still did it occasionally, but I could tell it was just a duty for her and that made me – you know – limp. So now I'd become not just infertile but impotent as well – a complete and utter washout.'

'Not at all,' Betty said. 'The whole thing's understandable and must have been terribly hard for you.'

Her soothing, kindly voice was like balm on a throbbing wound and made it slightly easier to continue. 'Well, eventually Deborah got this bee in her bonnet about using a sperm donor. At first, she suggested we just ask one of our friends, but I detested the very thought! Imagine them coming to dinner and knowing your kid was *theirs*! They might even lay claim to it, at some point, for heaven's sake! So then she went online and found hundreds of sites where you picked a donor and paid for his sperm at the checkout, as if you were buying a pack of batteries or something. It seemed so dreadfully soulless and I was also worried that the child might try to trace its natural father and forge a bond with him and I'd be – well, pushed out. But, any objection I made, Deborah had an answer to it, and the next thing I knew she'd booked flights to Copenhagen.'

'I've lost you, Anthony. Why Copenhagen?'

'Because the law's different in Denmark, so donors can choose to remain anonymous, unlike here in England. But, when I started looking into it, I discovered that some of those Danish donors had fathered as many as five-hundred babies. I suppose that's why it's called the sperm capital of the world!' he added, with a short bark of a laugh. 'Anyway, I cancelled the flights there and then, told Deborah it just wasn't on that our child should have so many random siblings, scattered all over the world.'

'Do you realise, Anthony,' Betty said, encouragingly, 'there's mitigation in this whole account? First, the fact that, when you came home early, you were feeling so seriously unwell, which can easily be corroborated by your colleagues. Okay, it's no excuse, but it does give reasons for you acting completely out of character. Next, the provocation on your wife's part by her resorting to adultery and, most definitely the mounting pressures on you to accept a method of conception you considered totally alien.'

Intent as he was on his story, he tried to drain his already empty cup. 'Well, actually, things became still *more* fraught when Deborah told her parents, despite our agreement not to breathe a word to anyone. Of course, as I feared, it only made things worse. Her mother was really opposed to the notion and felt her grandchildren might well be resentful when they grew up to discover they'd been conceived in a petri-dish, rather than through loving sex.'

'And *your* parents?'

'Oh, no way would I have told them! They'd have seen it as another failure and were bound to agonise about whether the donor was brilliant and successful enough to father any grandchild of theirs. And that's another thing – unlike the English system, the Danish clinics give loads of information about every donor on their books. Deborah saw that as a plus, because it meant we could choose a cultured, intellectual Alpha-male. But, to be honest, I felt daunted by the thought of such a paragon – who'd be super-fertile, on top of everything else.' All at once, he saw Craig in his mind again: that brawny, boastful stud, flaunting his potent nakedness. 'In fact, that's exactly how Craig struck me, so when he implied I couldn't get it up, it was too damned close to the bone, and I … just … just …'

To his horror, he felt tears pricking at his eyes – instantly blinked them back, straining every muscle not to give way to some demeaning display of emotion. Sensing his struggle, Betty laid her hand gently on his shoulder – a fatal gesture, since it snapped his iron control and suddenly the tears were spilling over and streaming down his cheeks unchecked. Worse, he began actually sobbing, his shoulders shaking, his whole body convulsed, his breath coming in short, painful gasps. Mortified, he tried frantically to stop, aware of what a sight he must look, with his snotty, contorted face and swollen, red-rimmed eyes. 'I'm so … so *sorry*,' he choked out, forcing his fractured voice to come up with excuses for his humiliating lapse – he was in a state of shock, agitated, sleep-deprived – but the excuses themselves were soon stifled by further anguished sobs.

Yet, far from recoiling, Betty's comforting arm had slipped around his shoulders and her nicotine-smelling handkerchief was gently mopping his face. 'It's all right, pet,' she murmured. 'Just let it all out. It's good for you to cry, love.'

Good for him? He'd been brought up *never* to cry. Tears made you less of a man, even when you were tiny. And "pet" and "love" were startling words, and truly extraordinary issuing from the mouth of a solicitor. Sebastian would no more use them to his clients than sport a hearts-and-flowers tattoo. Yet, three decades ago, when lying cold and sleepless at his prep-school, determined to be brave despite his crushing sense of abandonment, he had created a fantasy mother – a sweet, indulgent one, like Betty, to help him through the long, dark, shivery nights. And, yes, she *had* called him "pet" and "sweetheart", endearments totally outlawed in his normal waking life, but which suppressed the noise of the twelve other boys snoring and snuffling around him. And he'd endowed her with large, soft, comfy breasts, unlike his stick-thin real mother, who had bones instead of curves and was so vanishingly busy, she had told him briskly when he'd begged to go to day-school, that she couldn't cope with a child at home, on top of all the pressures of her job. In any case, both his parents had boarded themselves, and both championed the system as the best way of instilling discipline and self-reliance.

Discipline, for God's sake, when, to his eternal shame, he was blubbing still! He hadn't cried since the age of eight when he'd broken his ankle just before an important race his father expected him to win. He must have reverted to childhood – a major aberration for a man of almost forty. In fact, incredible as it seemed, he was actually resting his head against Betty's ample chest, as if he were back at school with that imaginary mother whose warm, consoling breasts banished fear and loneliness. Was he cracking up entirely?

'Better?' Betty asked, when, finally, the sobs shuddered to a halt.

Although profoundly embarrassed by his outburst, he did, in fact, feel some measure of relief from the tightly ratcheted tension of the last horrendous hours. 'I'm terribly sorry,' he repeated, the words still indistinct.

'Anthony, there's nothing to be sorry about. You're bound to feel emotional with all this going on, and when you're ill and exhausted, but, as I said, I intend to fight your corner so we need to stay positive, however hard it is.'

'But won't I go to prison?' The very thought brought him close to breakdown.

'Well, I'd say it's unlikely, based on what I know so far, but of course I don't have all the facts yet.'

Prompted by sheer fatigue, he let out a groaning sigh. 'If only I could just go home ...'

'I'm afraid that's out of the question. You're not free to go anywhere, especially if Craig's injury turns out to be serious.'

'But it *is* serious. The paramedics said so.'

'Yes, but he's in one of the best hospitals in the whole of the UK, with state-of-the-art facilities. And he was taken there pretty damn quick, which can make a world of difference. I've seen doctors do amazing things, in my time, pet, even when the outlook was pretty dire. Besides, once he's feeling even slightly better, he might well decide he doesn't want to press charges – I mean, considering the compromising circumstances. He's married, you see, with three kids.'

Anthony stared at her, incredulous. He'd assumed that Craig was single, the sort of footloose guy who screwed around, helped himself to other men's wives. 'How do you know?' he asked.

'The police managed to trace his address and sent a local constable round there to explain the situation to his wife. But she had the three children with her, so, before she could dash to the hospital, she had to arrange to leave them with a neighbour. They were all under five, the constable said, one still a babe-in-arms.'

Anthony swallowed hard, trying to remove the boulder-sized rock of guilt now obstructing his throat. Those three children's father was gravely injured, might suffer long-term brain-damage and be unable to play any further part in their lives. And the wife would suffer, too, with an invalid on her hands, instead of a functioning breadwinner. But he couldn't deal with such atrocious guilt. He had always been a *good* person, respected and esteemed – beyond reproach, in short. And, anyway, hadn't Craig brought it on himself? Any normal red-blooded male was bound to react impulsively when subject to such galling provocation. And Deborah herself was guilty as all hell. How dare she betray him, lie through her back teeth, help herself to some chancer's sperm, then broadcast the fact his own was deficient?

Anger was less poisonous than guilt – and he had every reason to be beside himself with fury. Just the sense of being completely in the dark, with no idea who her hateful lover was, or how long she'd been shagging him, was unbearably humiliating. Where and when had she met the lecherous bloke? Were they close in ways other than in bed? All those evenings she was "working late", had she actually been gadding with him to dinners, theatres, parties? All he knew was the shyster's name – Craig Stefanelli – which sounded half Italian and half Scottish and thus suspiciously fake.

He suddenly realised Betty was talking to him and that he must have missed much of what she'd said.

'But, look,' she added, apparently unaware of his inattention, 'the last thing I want is to raise false hopes, especially when things are so uncertain. We just have to wait and see and—'

All at once, her phone beeped and, having extracted it from her bag and read the incoming text, she sprang nimbly to her feet. 'I'm afraid I have to shoot off now and deal with a couple of shoplifters. Don't worry – I'll be back. Meanwhile, try to keep as calm as possible, okay?'

'Okay.' The fact he could assent to any level of calmness, given the turmoil in his mind, was due to her alone – her kindness and support. Even after she had gone, he could still smell traces of her fags-and-carnation scent, overlaying the smell of old pee seeping from the toilet. That itself was a mercy and had the added bonus of allowing him to retain something of her presence, whilst trying desperately to banish those of Deborah, Craig, and Craig's family.

A banishment utterly imperative, to save himself from madness.

CHAPTER 4

'There's a detective here to see you,' a deep, foreign voice shouted through his cell door.

Before Anthony could get up from the bench, a thick-set, sandy-haired man erupted into the room.

'Good afternoon, Mr Beaumont, I'm DC Bob MacArthur. I'm attached to the local CID and I've just returned from St Mary's Hospital. Craig Stefanelli was pronounced dead at 15.03, so this has now become a murder investigation.'

Despite the heat of the cell, Anthony felt himself go icy cold all over, as if he, too, had become a corpse.

The DC continued in the same brusque, officious fashion. 'Anthony Beaumont, you are under arrest for murder. You do not have to say anything, but it may harm your defence if ...'

He was now spelling out the caution, but Anthony's mind had stuck on the one word "murder". He had *killed* a man, his wife's lover, a father of three. No. Impossible.

Such was his state of shock, he barely took in anything further until the slam of the cell-door made him realise that the DC had left. Once alone, he began pacing round and round the small, confining space, like a lion in a cramped cage. If only he *were* a lion, a creature that didn't think, didn't feel extremes of guilt, wasn't faced with the intolerable consciousness of his whole life closing down.

Soon, he was dizzy from the frantic circling, yet couldn't seem to stop. Action, however futile, was preferable to endless speculation.

All at once, the same, unfamiliar foreign voice shouted through the door, 'Would you like some food, mate?'

Food, at such a time?

'We have these frozen ready-meals – shepherd's pie, lasagne or spaghetti Bolognese.'

'No, thanks,' he tried to say, but his voice had rusted up.

'Or, if you prefer a sandwich, there's ham, cheese or tuna mayonnaise.'

'Nothing, thanks.' Again, the words stuck in his throat.

'Well, how about tea or coffee or a cold drink?'

'*No!*' he yelled, the sudden furious shout jolting him as much as the man. What appalling rudeness, when the poor chap was only trying to help. But, presumably, murderers didn't have manners.

After another aching stretch of time, Betty reappeared, again doing her best to reassure him, despite her long, exhausting stint on duty. 'Okay, Anthony, we're in a different ball-game now, but we'll work our way through this together, so, whatever you do, love, don't give up hope.'

However, the upbeat voice and the arm around his shoulder couldn't help this time. And, when she informed him that the Homicide Team had now taken over from the CID, the word "homicide", like "murder", seemed branded on his forehead, the letters biting through to the bone beneath.

'And they want to interview you tonight, Anthony, but it's getting late, and I have to say you look dead-beat, so don't agree, love, unless you feel well enough.'

He had never felt less well: hands clammy, heart pounding, iron band clamped tightly round his chest, starving and yet nauseous, and so short of sleep he felt completely spaced out.

'I'm fine,' he said. One thing was certain: he would never again be fine.

'Good man! Although I must impress upon you, pet, that this is the most important interview you'll ever face in your life. It'll affect your entire future, so you need to be absolutely clear about what you're going to say before you step into the interview room. I'll be there, too, but *you'll* be the one answering all the questions, so what I suggest is that we run through your spiel together, here and now, and use it as a rehearsal.'

'Okay.' What else could he do but agree, having lost all self-determination?

Betty ran her hand through her already dishevelled hair. 'The crucial thing to stress is that you never intended to do Craig serious harm. Spell out what a shock it was to find a strange man in the marital bed, and how that made you act on impulse in an unthinking, jealous rage. And be sure to explain the whole infertility thing and how crappy it made you feel during those months and months of conflict with your wife. And don't forget the work pressures and …'

He wanted to close his ears to this recap of the last stressful hours – indeed years. Yet, once she left his cell, he made a supreme effort to recall every detail of her advice and continued going over it until he was escorted to the interview room.

Despite his apprehension, it was a relief to be out of his cell. This room was only small and somewhat bleak, but it was neat, clean and professional-looking, with a desk and comfortable chairs.

'Right,' said DC Bernard Hopkins, the smaller of the two-man team, impeccably dressed, with crisply cut dark hair, 'it's a legal requirement that this interview is recorded, Okay?'

Anthony nodded, attempting to unclench his fists, relax the screwed-up tension in his face.

'And once the tape-recorder has started, we are obliged to follow a set of formal words.'

Again, he nodded his assent, watching the DC remove the cellophane wrappers from the tapes and insert them into the large, cumbersome recorder.

'So, if you're ready, Mr Beaumont, I'll switch on the machine.' The DC cleared his throat before proceeding, his voice now louder and more formal as he spelled out his name and rank and that of the DS, stated the date, time and location of the interview, then repeated the caution and asked Anthony to state his own full name.

'Anthony Christopher Beaumont.' The name of a good, upstanding citizen and thus no longer *his* name.

'And now please state your address.'

And no longer his address, since he knew he could never return to the scene of his crime.

'And state your date of birth, please.'

Only seven weeks to his fortieth. He and Deborah had planned a big birthday bash …

Once the preliminaries were over, the DC asked for a full and detailed account of exactly what happened when he returned early from work that morning.

Although he could hardly bear to reprise the painful events, he was very much aware of Betty's reassuring presence, silently encouraging him whenever he met her eyes. And that gave him the strength to endure, even to make a case for himself and sound responsible, reliable.

Nonetheless, when, at last, the interrogation was over and he was taken back to his cell, he felt so completely drained he just slumped on the bench, head in hands. And, when Betty eventually reappeared, he had no idea whether fifteen minutes had passed or several hours. Without his watch and phone, he was totally disorientated, cut off from reality and living in some unregulated world.

'The CPS are making their decision now,' she told him, 'and I'm afraid you'll need to steel yourself, because it's highly likely you'll be charged with murder, Anthony.'

This time, he didn't react. There was no outrage or emotion left. Arrested for murder, charged with murder, these were now simple facts – yet still somehow incomprehensible.

'You'll be kept here in custody overnight, then taken to court in the morning. I just wish I could stay longer now, but I have to see another client. However, if anyone wants to interview you again, insist that I'm present, okay? They can call me on my mobile.'

Interview him again? He had no shred of strength or voice left.

'And, if you do get charged, I'll see you in court in the morning. And don't forget, love, I intend to do everything in my power in your defence.'

The minute she'd left, he slumped back on the bed and closed his eyes against the relentless glare of the light. There was no hope of sleep – not even room to stretch out – so he curled up in the foetal position and prepared for the longest, loneliest night of his whole life.

CHAPTER 5

'All rise.'

As the Usher's voice resounded through the court, Anthony was jerked to his feet by the Dock Officer. He watched in trepidation as three magistrates trooped in and seated themselves on the Bench, an elderly man in the centre, flanked by two younger women. But who were all those other people? Surely they couldn't be here for *his* case (the first on the list this morning), but for subsequent defendants. Having never set foot in a courtroom before, he felt totally out of his depth and, when he spotted DC Bernard Hopkins and recalled yesterday's grilling by him, his nervousness intensified. However, he kept his eyes on Betty, as a familiar, supportive presence, relieved to see her looking considerably smarter, in a better-fitting suit, with her hair swept back in a neat coiffure. He, in contrast, was still wearing his deplorable blue gear, now covered in clingy shreds of fleece from the blanket they had given him last night – a fleece that seemed to adhere to everything, including his hair. Worse still, he had cuts on his face from the useless plastic razor supplied at the police station, and feared he might even smell, after his tepid 6am shower, and with no clean underpants available.

The Dock Officer had barely pushed him back into his seat when, moments later, he was instructed to stand again.

'Is you name Anthony Christopher Beaumont?' an imposing black-gowned official asked.

He was embarrassed to confirm his name when he cut such a sorry figure. He had particularly asked to wear his suit for this hearing, only to be told that, if it was needed by the forensics, it would be examined in court and taken as an exhibit to the trial and, in any case, would be a total write-off, ruined by harsh chemicals.

When he was requested, next, to confirm his address and date of birth, the latter seemed utterly wrong. He had aged decades in a matter of hours; was no longer a man in his prime, but a decrepit, washed-up pensioner.

The Prosecutor now took centre-stage, a scraggy little man with thinning hair, who gave a brief outline of the case, insisting that the defendant had punched Craig Stefanelli with deliberate intent to kill. Anthony was so enraged he was tempted to burst out of the dock and confront the treacherous bloke. Of course, Betty immediately refuted the allegation, but was cut off after only a couple of sentences. Was this *justice*, he seethed, longing to take some part himself and put the record straight? He was used to being the one in charge, the one who made important decisions and treated with respect. Now he was a dumb, degraded puppet.

A brief discussion ensued between Betty, the chief magistrate and the Prosecutor, concerning the various papers each required, and, although Anthony tried to follow it, his mind suddenly veered off to his parents. They lived miles away, thank God, and rarely phoned or emailed, but sooner or later they would learn the terrible truth. He could well imagine their shock and incredulity were they to know that, late last night, he'd had his DNA and fingerprints taken, to be entered in the Criminal Records Bureau. His mother in particular would obsess about the horrifying prospect of anyone in their upstanding circle discovering the ineradicable shame he had brought upon the family.

'Mr Beaumont, please stand up.'

Aware that the magistrate was addressing him, he forced his mind back to the proceedings, cursing his lack of focus.

'Your case will be committed to the Central Criminal Court, to be heard on 12 December, 2012. Meanwhile, you will be remanded in custody.'

The phrase was so horrific, he swayed on his feet, as if about to faint. Sent to prison after a mere ten minutes in court! He'd begged Betty to apply for bail but, apparently, it wasn't permitted for murder cases in any magistrates' court and, although a Crown Court Judge had the power to grant it, she considered even that unlikely. It seemed a travesty, a scandal that he should be banged up before any proper case had been made against him. His resentment increased when he noticed the three magistrates now whispering amongst themselves. Their whispering excluded him, like an unpopular schoolboy shut out from his classmates' intrigues. And, since they were only jumped-up laypeople, probably seeking brownie points as worthies and do-gooders, what right had they to sit in judgment on him anyway?

'Right, let's go back down, Mr Beaumont.' The Dock Officer grabbed his arm and led him out of the court.

"Back down" only added to his sense of desolation, since it meant returning to the cells and, if he had thought the police cell obnoxious, the court holding cells were infinitely worse. He'd already spent a couple of hours there, before the court convened, and heard every scream, sob, curse and wail reverberating through the walls from adjoining prisoners. One man was so hysterical, he must have been withdrawing from heroin or crack-cocaine, and, when he eventually attacked his gaoler, still more pandemonium ensued.

Yet he would rather spend all *day* there than be transferred to prison. The very thought of custody brought a surge of choking panic – locked up in some filthy gaol with no vestige of control, no self-determination, no choice of companions, no say in his own life. He didn't even know which prison it would be. He might be shipped halfway across the country to some benighted place, hundreds of miles from everyone and everything he knew.

As the Dock Officer took him down in the lift and marched him towards the cells, he had never felt less alone, despite the hollering and yelling already audible. There was not a soul he could confide in – not his colleagues or his so-called friends, let alone his parents. And, worst of all, his wife was now completely cut off from him. Without his phone, he couldn't ring or text her and, in any case, she would probably never want to contact him again. Yet word was bound to spread about his crime, either through her or Isabel. It might even be reported in the press, for pity's sake! "City toff in the slammer!", or some other juicy little titbit in the *Standard*. The scandal the disgrace, the utter degradation …

The Dock Officer ushered him into a cell, a different one from last time, but every bit as cramped and smelly. 'Serve your time and keep your head down,' was his last curt advice before he slammed the door.

'*No*, Anthony muttered through gritted teeth. 'I'm damned if I'll submit.'

CHAPTER 6

'Tony, are you a fucking fraggle, for fuck's sake?'

What in God's name was a "fraggle"? Wiser not to ask, Anthony decided, since his six-foot-six hunk of a cellmate, inappropriately named Shorty, seemed in a state of constant manic rage. Even throughout the whole of last night, the guy had kept shouting in his sleep and, having woken himself, would let out streams of expletives and start inveighing against the screws, the cops, his "fucking useless lawyers" and Fate itself. Perched as he'd been on the narrow top bunk, he had felt totally at the bruiser's mercy – and he was still cowering on his bunk as the guy now prowled below in the dangerously small space, alternating prison slang with curses.

'I'm *talking* to you, Tony! Are you a sodding fraggle?'

'No, I'm not. I'm …' The sentence petered out. Everything he was belonged in the past tense. He *had* been a successful director at Forsythe, Foster, Clarke; *had* been a man of blameless character in a long and stable marriage; *had* been a dutiful son. Now he was just a prison number, his identity reduced to a string of digits. As for any future, he might be coffined in this hideous place for decades – unless he topped himself.

'Well, you're a fucking public school cunt, that's for sure. But I'm a fucking *yob*, Tone, so you'd better fucking well get used to it!'

Anthony murmured something anodyne, determined to avoid any confrontation with a twenty-stone sociopath. He knew little about prison, except the danger from fellow inmates of assault or rape – or both. Much to his relief, Shorty fell into a brooding silence, although there was still the deafening reggae music thundering from the adjoining cell, and the frequent slamming of cell doors in the corridor outside. But at least his cellmate appeared to have lost interest in him and had thrown himself on the lower bunk in an attitude of exhaustion and despair.

The respite was short-lived. Within minutes, he had catapulted up again and resumed his former raging, his ire now directed against some officer called Hodgkinson, who, apparently, had no other aim in life but to harass and torment every inmate he encountered and Shorty in particular.

'He's a fucking psycho, Tony, and the other screws are every bit as bad – ignorant arseholes with piss-poor training. They're so bloody useless they wouldn't get a job stacking shelves in Tesco's. Yet they strut about the landings like the toughest guys to ever walk the earth. So, if the Governor orders them to stick their riot-helmets on and crack a few skulls open, they can get away with murder. And they *enjoy* the mayhem, believe me. It's a thrill for them to roll around the floor with us poor sods and leave us bruised and bleeding.'

'Awful,' Anthony grunted, trying to sound concerned, although the officers he had met so far had struck him less as brutish than as inefficient, ignorant, overworked and barely in control of the simmering cauldron of violence and unrest that this prison appeared to be.

'Hodgkinson's the worst, no question. He's a fucking dog, who'd kill you just for looking at him. I'd like to kick him in his Niagaras until he screams for mercy.'

Anthony glanced down at the livid scar on the man's acne-pitted face, and his massive, muscly arms tattooed with daggers, skulls and looping coils of barbed wire. If this gangster switched his resentment from Hodgkinson to his "public-school cunt" of a cellmate, anything might happen. His desperation to empty his bladder only increased his fear. The shit-encrusted toilet was abhorrent in itself, but no way could he use it in front of someone else, when it had neither curtain nor partition to allow a modicum of privacy. How long could he hang on, though? Would they be let out of their cells soon? Like a foreigner in an alien land, he had no idea how the whole confusing system worked. He had been promised an induction, but it had never actually materialised, nor had he been put on the Induction Wing, which, as far as he could gather, was essential for first-time prisoners, giving them time to adjust and at least marginally quieter surroundings. But, according to Shorty, most of the normal procedures shut down at weekends, and it had been his bad luck to arrive in this hell-hole late on Friday evening

Already, his confinement seemed to have lasted an eternity, yet it was still only Saturday. He was partly to blame for refusing the chance to escape his cell when it was unlocked for breakfast and lunch (or dinner, as the latter was called here). But, being strongly disinclined to mingle with the crowd of drug-addicts, bullies and thugs he had seen on his arrival, he had deliberately remained where he was, glad at least to be on his own, once Shorty had barged out for what he termed his "munchies".

The guy returned to tell him he was a "fucking stupid arsehole", since missing meals was a reportable offence. However, no one had taken action; the chronic understaffing working in his favour, perhaps. Now, though, he was ravenous, his stomach a great gaping hole, growling for some sustenance. Yet, for all he knew, there might never be a next meal. Adrift without a phone or watch, and no one willing to explain the prison timetable, he was forced simply to exist from hour to hour, with no clue as to what might happen next. Shorty, for his part, was more concerned with vengeance than with food, and was actually hitting out at the walls now, in a toxic mix of fury and frustration.

'They're scumbags, Tony, the whole fucking lot of them, but Hodgkinson's a mental case – everybody knows that. If I could lay my fucking hands on a gun, I'd blow his fucking brains out!'

Was Shorty a mental case himself, Anthony wondered nervously, noting the ape-like grimaces contorting the fellow's face as he continued his frantic pacing, his aggressive voice hammering through the cell as forcibly as his blows against the wall? He, in contrast, had to maintain the strictest control, since *two* angry men, confined in a space fourteen feet by eight, might result in a bloodbath. Yet just thinking of the last twenty-four hours surely gave him equal grounds for rage: being transported here in a "sweatbox"; locked into a compartment resembling a cross between a coffin and a cubicle in a public lavatory. An actual lavatory would, in fact, have been a bonus, because one of his fellow detainees must have been caught short on the journey, filling the sweatbox with the sudden sickening reek of diarrhoea. Those fellow prisoners might have been out of sight, but their noise was inescapable – a violent eruption of banging, thumping and yelling of obscenities, as the van lurched and jolted on its way to … *where*? No one had bothered to inform them which gaol they were actually headed for, although the eventual sight of Wandsworth's grim Victorian exterior did nothing to allay his horror; indeed, it seemed the very essence of menace, as did the serried ranks of searchlights and the beetling walls beyond, topped with razor-wire.

Inside was just as ominous, especially when caged up again, this time in a large communal cell, cheek by jowl with some two dozen other prisoners who resembled feral beasts. And, even when released, there seemed no sense of order or efficiency, only endless waits, duplicated form-filling and pointless encounters with various prison officers, who, in the main, were neither welcoming nor civil.

But all that was of nothing compared with the humiliation of the strip-search. Ordered to strip naked and bend over, he'd maintained the mortifying position for a sadistic length of time, until podgy, clumsy fingers suddenly gate-crashed into his anus, appearing positively to relish the resultant pain and discomfort. And, when, at last, he was taken to his cell, he seemed to be living through a nightmare, led deeper and deeper into unending incarceration, each heavy door clanging shut behind him, every lock snapping cruelly shut.

The memory was so upsetting, he tried to imagine being at home with Deborah, enjoying a normal Saturday evening, relaxing on their luxurious white leather sofa, sharing a bottle of good claret and some exquisite nibbles from *La Fromagerie*, with Schubert playing softly on the sound-system. But such thoughts were still more painful, because every time Deborah entered his consciousness, Craig came in her wake, the pair now cemented inexorably together and bringing in their train sex, betrayal, violence, death …

A sudden jangling of keys outside interrupted the flood-tide and, seconds later, the door swung open and an unseen voice barked, 'Tea!'

Immediately, Shorty stopped his tirade, snatched his plate and cutlery and charged out of the cell.

The minute he was on his own, Anthony clambered down from the bunk. However foul the lavatory, he had no choice but to use it, his torrent of urine as strong as his relief. Fastidiously, he washed his hands in the equally filthy, plug-less sink, then grabbed his own plastic plate, smeary and discoloured, and the plastic knife and fork that looked too feeble to tackle so much as a blancmange, and dared to venture out.

The sight of the main wing, though, was as much of a shock as it had been yesterday: cell door after cell door stretching down the bleak, graffitied corridors; landing after landing, veering up beneath high and echoing ceilings, no colour but the eternal grey. And he felt still more daunted when he joined the queue for the servery; fights already breaking out as a few chancers pushed and jostled in an attempt to barge in, out of turn. Hesitantly, he tagged on the end of the line, trying to keep his expression inscrutable, to prevent any overtures.

Fat chance. The young, crew-cut lad in front of him immediately turned round and asked, 'Just arrived, have you, mate?'

Anthony gave the briefest of nods.

'Welcome to hell!' the guy continued, flashing him a smile. 'And Wanno's the worst, if you really want to know. It's a screws' nick, as you'll soon find out. But don't worry – you'll get used to it. I'm Ronnie, by the way.'

'Anthony.'

'Hi, Tony. Great to meet you!'

Here, he was called Tony automatically, but the name felt wrong for him, seeming to belong to someone less uptight, more outgoing and gregarious. But he *was* uptight and had never been gregarious, despite boarding school and Cambridge. Even in the cradle, he had been called by his full, formal name, just as his mother was always Cecilia, never Cissy or Cec, and his father William, never Bill or Will. His family believed in the tiny extra effort required to give a name its proper weight, and deplored such sloppy abbreviations as "veggies", "telly", "cardy". And, as soon as he could speak, they had taught him to call them Mother and Father, rather than Mummy and Daddy. "Tony" for them would have been an abomination and, certainly, it didn't seem to fit him – any more than did his clothes. Prisoners on remand were allowed to wear their own clothes, but, since he possessed nothing save the blue fleece police monstrosity, he had been given the standard grey tracksuit most inmates seemed to wear – although one clearly picked at random, since it was several sizes too large, the top swamping him completely and the trousers far too loose around the waist. Belts were forbidden in prison – a handy means of suicide – so he had constantly to hitch them up, along with the pair of underpants, which seemed designed to fit a giant. He envied Ronnie his smart, tight-fitting jeans, stylish top and Nike trainers.

'You done bird before, mate?' the lad enquired, as they inched along together, the queue moving frustratingly slowly.

'No,' said Anthony, tersely.

Undeterred, Ronnie confided that he was 'doing a two for drug-dealing.' 'But, that's nothing,' he added, 'compared with the six I done before.'

Anthony refrained from comment. If he was expected to share details of his own offence or the length of his own sentence, well, he fucking well refused, to borrow Shorty's terms. Fortunately, another guy approached – a dreadlocked Jamaican, wearing one gold earring and a string of coloured beads – and started hectoring Ronnie about an unpaid debt. To Anthony's relief, their dispute continued for some while, although he was aware of wary glances from other inmates in the queue, checking him out like suspicious used-car salesmen.

When, at last, they reached the servery and their names were ticked off the list, the Jamaican was given the last lone jacket potato, its wrinkled skin burnt black on top, while Ronnie received two of four remaining fritters, plus a hard lump of cabbage floating in greyish water. Supplies of all dishes were clearly running low, save for some patently cheese-less macaroni cheese, so Anthony requested the same as Ronnie, minus the cabbage.

'Sorry, no fritters left, bruv.'

'But what about those two?' Anthony asked, pointing to the pair of rock-hard, grey-brown discs.

'They're reserved,' was the reply. 'And, anyways, you're down for the Chef's Choice.'

Chef's Choice sounded promising – until the reality appeared: a small packet of cheese-and-onion crisps and a lemon mousse well past its sell-by date. Well, if nothing else, such scanty provisions wouldn't pose a problem for his plastic cutlery.

Before returning to his cell, he accosted one of the officers patrolling the wing, his arms garishly tattooed, as if he, too, were a prisoner, yet his belt weighed down with keys and chains. 'Look, I'd like a single cell, please. I'm on remand, so I'm pretty sure I'm entitled to one. And, in any case, I'm sharing with a psychopath and could be in danger of my life.'

The officer gave a sarcastic snarl. 'I'd have thought a posho like you might have better manners, Bowman. Don't you know that you address officers as "sir"?'

'I'm sorry, sir, I didn't know. And my name's Beaumont, not Bowman.'

'That's what I said, so watch your bloody tongue, Bowman. And, as for a single cell, this isn't the Ritz, you know. I suppose you'll be demanding room-service next!'

Anthony seethed in silence. The screw clearly resented his accent and the rumoured belief that he was a "fucking millionaire" – a rumour totally untrue but sparked by a miniscule item in the *Metro*. The journalist in question, clearly wanting to point the finger at what he saw as a felonious fat cat, had deliberately blurred the distinction between flamboyantly wealthy investment bankers and more risk-averse and modestly living accountants such as *he* was. Okay, he couldn't deny his high salary, or his privileged upbringing, but he wasn't hauling in the obscenely large bonuses the tabloids so loved to condemn. Maybe Shorty had been deliberately chosen as his cellmate, as an extra punishment to put the "posho" down a peg. So he must never, ever mention the fact that his distant ancestor, Robert de Beaumont, had come over from Normandy in 1066 and fought alongside the Conqueror, to be rewarded with vast tracts of land. However, distinguished his family might be, officers and prisoners alike would detest and deride such distinction.

Having no choice but to return to his cell, he found Shorty hunkered in the only chair and hogging the one small table. He appeared to have been given double rations – although neither of the two congealing brownish messes bore any resemblance to normal food. A boxing championship was in full swing on the television, the excitable commentary half-drowned by Shorty's shouted expletives and encouragements. His cell-mate had excluded him entirely, allowing him no physical space – even the lower bunk was piled with clutter and piles of porn magazines – so he was forced to clamber up to his top-bunk perch again.

He ripped open the bag of crisps with unnecessary force, biting into each crisp as if crumbling Shorty to dust, along with the whole inefficient establishment. It was still only afternoon, yet this totally inadequate "tea" (supper) was meant to keep him going till Sunday morning, when they would be unlocked again for breakfast – or so he had learned from Ronnie, who had tried to engage him in a chat again. He had also asked the time and, on discovering it was not yet five, the empty hours and his empty belly seemed all but unendurable. As for any prospect of sleep, that was out of the question. Had Shorty been a Buddhist monk who had taken a vow of silence, that wouldn't solve the problem of the few clearly out-of-control prisoners, who had been yelling to each other from their windows, even well into the early hours. The cacophony of banter, insults and gibberish had then prompted other inmates to start shrieking 'Shut the fuck *up*!', some kicking their cell doors in protest and thus adding to the general pandemonium.

His personal discomfort seemed minor in comparison, although the lumpy mattress made his hips and shoulders ache, the cement-hard pillow and coarse-grained pillowcase smarted against his razor-sore face, and the one, thin, threadbare blanket did little to assuage the damp coldness of the cell. Their bedlinen at home was fine Egyptian cotton; their micro-quilted mattress luxuriously soft; their duvet pure goose-down, cocooning them in warmth. But worst of all the sleep-destroyers was the turmoil in his head, which meant the minute he lay down, guilt, remorse, self-pity, fury, terror, began cascading through his mind in disorienting succession. How ironical it was that the only release from such torment would be sleep itself.

He blew up the empty crisp packet and smashed it between his hands, the resultant feeble bang no match for the uproar on television. The crowd was enraged by the referee declaring that the Frenchman was the winner, rather than the British favourite. Shorty had bet three chocolate bars on the Brit, and his near-hysteria at the outcome all but overpowered the storm of boos, catcalls and furious accusations from the huge television audience.

Anthony yanked the lid off the lemon mousse, the pot so small it would have failed to satisfy an ant. He barely tasted the urine-yellow pap – if it *had* any taste – because all at once he had come to a decision, despite the uproar that made it difficult to think. Indeed, it was because of that very uproar – and all the other aggravations – that what he had to do was suddenly crystal-clear: ignore Betty's advice about not applying for bail at his Preliminary Hearing this Monday. He was due to appear at the Central Criminal Court, where he would meet his junior barrister, Edmund Hall – one highly recommended by Betty's firm of solicitors.

He and Betty had discussed the issue of bail in the holding-cell of the magistrates' court, while awaiting his transfer to prison. 'They're not likely to grant it anyway,' she'd warned him. 'But if you wait until the next Crown Court hearing on January 23, Edmund will have had more time to study the papers, by then, and so can prepare a more detailed and convincing case.'

He hadn't known at that point, though, how impossible it would prove to survive in prison until January 23 – another endless forty-seven days. Even surviving until this coming Monday would take courage and resilience he wasn't sure he possessed, so, however great Betty's expertise, he intended to instruct Mr Hall to apply for bail forthwith. Admittedly there were problems. With his deep-seated reluctance to involve any of his colleagues or acquaintances, who in heaven's name could he ask to stand surety for him, or give an address that would satisfy the court? But if Edmund was as impressive as Betty claimed, surely he could come up with solutions.

Just at that moment, Shorty kicked back his chair and lurched over to the lavatory, where he proceeded to empty his bowels explosively and publicly, the noise aggravated by the echoing metal toilet bowl. Anthony shut his eyes in distaste at the noise and the stench, yet they only strengthened his resolve to succeed in his one overriding aim: to escape this living hell by Monday evening at the latest.

CHAPTER 7

Marched into the interview room by a small, officious officer, Anthony glanced around, to try to get his bearings. The room was little bigger than a Portakabin, but the fact it was neat and clean was a blessing in itself, as was the large wire-meshed window looking out on the corridor. He'd heard from a lifer in the lunch queue that the window was only there so that inmates could be spied on when their lawyers visited; nonetheless the extra light and sense of space lifted his spirits a fraction.

He swung round at the sound of the key turned firmly in the lock. The officer had already departed, without saying a single word, simply ensuring he couldn't escape.

Moments later, Betty entered, through the door on the opposite side, that door also locked by another officer escorting her. She greeted him with a warm and welcoming smile – rare in this place of scowls and snarls. 'So how's it going?' she asked, having put down her clutch of carrier bags.

He refrained from saying that prison life was as unspeakable as ever. Betty was so supportive, the least he could do was not complain. Judging by her baggage, she had probably fitted in this visit after a stint of Christmas shopping and could well be feeling tired.

Once she had seated herself opposite him at the table, she immediately broached the subject of bail. 'I know you were upset, love, about Edmund dissuading you from applying at this early stage. But, as he explained, he's not permitted to make more than one application, so he didn't want to spoil your chances by acting too precipitately before he'd had time to consider all the facts.'

'Yes,' Anthony said, resignedly, 'he made things perfectly clear. And, however desperate I am for my freedom, I'm not fool enough to ignore his professional advice.' In truth, he'd found Edmund somewhat dominant and pompous, and nothing like as sympathetic as Betty. Yet why should any barrister need cottonwool clouds of clucking compassion, rather than self-belief and steely determination?

Keen to change the subject, he asked Betty if she had managed to get hold of Deborah, although the situation with his wife was every bit as fraught as that of bail

'Well, yes, but ...'

The "but" induced instant disappointment.

'I'm afraid she wouldn't allow me access to the flat, although I did explain your urgent need to get some of your own clothes.'

Never mind his clothes – it was Deborah's attitude towards him that was weighing on his mind. If she was so angry and resentful she wouldn't even allow his solicitor to fetch a few garments for him, then his feeble hope of an eventual reconciliation was already dashed, it appeared.

'I did try, pet, honestly. I said, if she didn't want *me* to go, could she possibly fetch the things herself and I'd make sure they were handed over to you, but she refused that, too, I'm sorry to say. But then I realised that a return to the flat might be just too painful for her, so I suggested that one of her friends might go instead, but, again, she wouldn't hear of it.'

His wife must already have decided to sue for a divorce, he thought with a sense of racking isolation. From now on, she and all her friends would shun him as someone unstable, violent, beyond the pale; eleven years of marriage chucked onto the rubbish-heap.

'Actually, I do need to talk to you about Deborah,' Betty said, getting up for a moment to fetch her stack of carrier bags, 'but let's sort out the issue of the clothes first. Since I drew a blank with getting hold of your own stuff, I took the liberty of buying you a few things myself. They're only basic Marks and Spencer and I had to guess your size, so I'm afraid they may not even fit, but at least they'll be an improvement on what you're wearing now.' Rummaging in the largest bag, she withdrew a pair of smart blue-denim jeans, a couple of slate-grey sweatshirts, a warm and serviceable fleece in matching grey, and three packs each of underpants and socks.

He was astonished by her kindness, as well as deeply moved. Surely it was beyond the remit of most normal lawyers to go shopping for their clients. Yet she'd had the sensitivity to understand that, clad in his baggy "pyjamas", which continually threatened to fall down and reveal his thin, cheap, greyish, chest-high underpants, he felt a total buffoon. And, since he was forced to wash that sole pair of pants in the small, dirty, plug-less sink and put them on next morning, still damp, it was a definite bonus to have so many spares.

'And,' Betty said, reaching for two more bags, 'some other bits and pieces that prisoners tend to find useful.' She unpacked a notebook and three biros, a giant pack of toilet rolls, a bar of luxury soap and tube of Colgate toothpaste, a couple of paperback books, and a large assortment of chocolate bars. 'You probably don't eat chocolate, but it's a very handy currency in prison, to pay for favours or swap with other goodies.'

He struggled for the words to thank her. Here, on the table, were all the things he'd craved: not just decent clothes, but replacements for the harsh but ineffective prison soap and toothpaste, as well as reading and writing materials, to distract his reeling mind and make his usual "to-do" list – however futile that might be here. Admittedly, given the inadequate food and his horror at "performing" in front of someone else, he doubted he would need the toilet rolls – at least not for their proper purpose – but they would provide the perfect stand-in for Kleenex, paper napkins, and even for stuffing into his over-large and continually slipping plimsolls. Prison toilet rolls were rationed to one weekly, and Shorty had been bellyaching about having to use pages of the *Sun*.

'By the way, Anthony, don't worry about these biros being confiscated. The authorities are very strict about which biros they permit, because sometimes they're used to smuggle drugs into the prison. But these transparent ones are fine.'

She had thought of everything, yet he still hadn't said a word of thanks. In truth, he was fighting a quite ludicrous urge to press himself against her ripe maternal breasts, emphasised by the fuzzy turquoise sweater. But, having lost control already in her presence, it would be fatal to repeat the experience, or he might crack the whole careful carapace he had spent all his life maintaining. His parents had never gone in for displays of affection or emotion (let alone called him "love" or "pet") and, as for boarding-school, toughness was essential there, along with the cultivation of an undemonstrative detachment, even from the age of seven.

At last, he found his voice, now torn between gratitude and guilt. 'These things are absolutely perfect, Betty. You couldn't have chosen better if I'd written you my own personal wish-list! But I wouldn't dream of accepting them without repaying you and, unfortunately, I don't see how that's possible. Prisoners aren't allowed to handle cash, so the two tenners I had in my wallet will be put on my prison account, and thus not the slightest use to *you*. And, anyway, twenty quid would be nowhere near enough.'

'You keep it, Anthony,' Betty said, with a laugh. 'You'll need every penny for more important things than squaring up with me!'

'Yes, that's another worry. You see, apart from my debt to you, I need to top up my prison account just for day-to-day living, which means transferring money from my bank. But God knows how I do that, when I'm stuck here out of touch. And soon I'll also need to pay my legal-aid contributions, but *how*?'

Betty flicked a stray tendril of hair from her eyes. 'Maybe you should discuss it with an officer.'

'Fat chance! They're far too busy and seem to have it in for me, in any case.'

'Well, how about Probation, then?'

'Equally impossible – at least judging by last Thursday, when the offender manager, as she called herself, came to see me, armed with a whole bunch of files. But – would you believe – mine wasn't there! She rifled through them for ages, becoming more and more flustered, and finally admitted it might have been sent to the wrong prison by mistake. So she dashed off in a spin, promising she'd get back to me in a day or two, but I haven't heard a word.'

'Typical!' Betty gave a theatrical sigh. 'But try not to worry, pet. You can certainly access your bank from prison, either personally or through a Third Party Mandate. You'll have to do everything by post, of course, rather than online, and you'll need to inform them of your change of address. I can help there by writing a formal letter confirming your present whereabouts, but let's leave all that for later, Okay? Our time today is limited and we need to get down to legal matters, rather than financial ones.'

'Yes, but what about the money I owe you?'

'Anthony, you don't owe me a thing, so not another word about repayment. Just accept the stuff as a Christmas present.'

So she had braved the crowds of Christmas shoppers – *and* the recent snow – not for her friends and family, as he had naturally assumed, but simply to ameliorate his existence here.

'But,' she said, extracting a pen and a shorthand pad from her well-worn but capacious hold-all, 'there is a crucial matter we do need to discuss. You see, when I spoke to Deborah on the phone, she told me something rather troubling.'

He tensed. What in God's name had his wife confided – unflattering details about his character, or – worse – his sexual inadequacies?

'Of course, it's too soon for me to have read her Witness Statement and it wasn't included in the MG5.'

'In *what*?'

'Sorry, love. The cops are as bad as us legals when it comes to abbreviations. It stands for Manual of Guidance and it's a brief summary of evidence drawn up by the police. But, if Deborah's speaking the truth, then what she told me will be a crucial part of her Witness Statement, which undoubtedly will complicate our case.'

He felt himself flushing with anxiety, uncertainty. Whatever his wife's peccadillos, he had never, ever, caught her out in a lie. 'So what did she say?' he hardly dared to ask.

'That, just before you hit Craig, you shouted out "I'm going to fucking kill you!" I have to say, Anthony, that came as a bit of a shock. I mean, it does seem quite extraordinary that you failed to mention such an important fact in the account you gave to me, or in your interview with the Homicide Team. I also know you very rarely swear, so I questioned Deborah more closely, but she assured me she was quoting your exact words.'

He hid his head in his hands, unable to meet Betty's eyes; still finding it near-impossible to accept he could have uttered so violent and intemperate a phrase. He must have simply blanked it out, erased it from his memory as too damning, too discreditable. Yet, were he to admit it now, Betty would assume that he had deliberately misled her, given her a false account, to depict himself in a more favourable light.

'So *did* you say that, Anthony, or is Deborah mistaken?'

'No, she's not mistaken,' he mumbled, resisting the urge to justify himself. Too easy and irresponsible to say he hadn't meant it, that it had been an impulsive, irrational expression of his fury; a reaction to his profound sense of shock – all completely true, in fact, but who would ever believe him? He remained doubled over the table, deeply ashamed of having exacerbated Betty's already onerous task.

Yet, far from blaming him, he felt her hand on his shoulder, heard her reassuring voice. 'Don't worry, pet, we'll simply have to work around it. Okay, it's a challenge, but challenge is part of any lawyer's job. And let me assure you, I don't intend to let anything or anyone to get in my way of preparing the best possible defence.'

Her tone was so resolute, he made an effort to co-operate. This messy, overweight woman, with her vinyl handbag and nicotine breath (whose clothes and accent Deborah would deplore, especially the "vulgar" turquoise sweater), was his champion, his only hope. She could easily have wasted time on justified but futile recriminations; instead, she spent the next half-hour outlining various strategies to take account of this new piece of evidence and, soon, he felt himself drawn in, until they were working on his case together, which was restorative in itself. He was so used to being busy at work, sorting out complex projects, the idleness of prison had reduced him to an empty shell.

'Okay,' she said finally, with a brief glance at her watch, 'It's been a very useful session, love, but our time is almost up and, before I go, I want to hear how you *are* – and the truth, please, not just "fine".'

'Well,' he said, hesitantly, 'I suppose the worst thing is being banged up so long – twenty-two hours at a stretch, this last weekend. All the simple things I used to take for granted, like moving from room to room, or popping out to Starbucks for a coffee, or just a breath of air, seem infinitely precious now. Some prisoners have jobs, or go to Education, or the library or the gym, but because I'm on remand, I don't qualify for those – at least as far as I can gather in this maddeningly Kafkaesque system. But, if I'm honest, Betty, I can't just blame the system. I don't actually have the heart to find out what I *can* do and what I can't, so, most of the time, I'm sitting slumped on my bed, staring at four walls.'

'But I thought you had to go out, if only to collect your meals?'

'Yes, we do, but I always head straight back to my cell. Admittedly, that means more time with my cell-mate. In fact, I can't tell you what a relief it is to be here with you, rather than cooped up with that foul-mouthed lout.'

'So why don't you go to Exercise? Remand prisoners are entitled to that and it would be an escape from your cellmate.'

'Maybe so, but it keeps getting cancelled on account of the lousy weather.'

'Well, just stay out on the wing after meals, then you can socialise a bit. That's why it's called "Association" and most prisoners seem to enjoy the chance of getting to know other people.'

He had deliberately avoided Association. Those "other people" were rapists, fraudsters, murderers – all the more impossible now he, too, was a murderer.

'And have you talked to one of the Listeners yet? They're trained by the Samaritans, but, because they're prisoners themselves, they can be wonderfully supportive.'

That very link with the Samaritans had caused him to rebuff the two Listeners who'd approached him. No one in his family ever sought – or needed – help from quasi-therapists; it would be considered a deep source of shame.

'You could even go to chapel. It doesn't matter whether you believe or not. Just see it as another way of getting out of your cell and enjoying a bit of company. The Christmas carol service is bound to be booked solid, if only because of the free mince pies on offer, but why not put your name down for an ordinary Sunday service?'

'Yes, perhaps I will,' he said, aware that he had rejected all her suggestions, so far. Indeed, even the thought of Christmas here filled him with the deepest dread.

'Christmas is always difficult,' she said, as if tuning in to his thoughts. 'And with so many staff absent on home-leave, I imagine lots of normal activities will be cancelled. So try to get out *before* then, as much as you possibly can. And make an effort to be friendly and strike up conversations. Some of your fellow inmates are actually very worthwhile people, you know, whatever your initial impressions may be.'

The faint note of rebuke in her voice didn't escape his notice. He *did* put a division between himself and other prisoners, considered himself almost a different species – a stance they naturally resented and which only put their backs up. But he could hardly admit his attitude to Betty, so it was almost a relief to hear the noise of a key in the lock and see an officer appear on Betty's side of the room, to escort her out of the prison.

He said his farewells, repeated his thanks, then returned to sit at the table, expecting another officer to unlock his side of the room. No one came, however, so he dared to hope that, given the general inefficiency, he might have been forgotten. If he was left here for a while, he could relish the peace and solitude, the all-too-welcome respite from Shorty's racket, stinks and rants – and most vital of all – try to halt his despairing ruminations.

Some hope! Within minutes of Betty's departure, Deborah and Edmund both burst into his mind, one demanding a divorce, the other spelling out the reasons why, even at the *next* hearing, bail might be withheld. And, along with thoughts of bail, all the frustration and deficiencies of the Preliminary Hearing itself seemed to be re-enacted in his head – the indignity of appearing in shapeless prison garb, instead of a decent suit; the endless hanging about in yet another fetid cell, before and after the proceedings, contrasted with the brevity of his actual time in court. His entire future was at stake, yet his case had been dispatched in a few mockingly inadequate minutes. Up until last Monday, the Old Bailey had been an impressive historic building; now it was a place of terror and disquiet.

But, he thought, with a sense of utter wretchedness, terror and disquiet would rule his life here on.

CHAPTER 8

'Right on, preacher!'

'Hallelujah!'

'Praise the Lord!'

To Anthony's embarrassment, exuberant cries from the largely Afro-Caribbean congregation continually punctuated the sermon. Indeed, his ecstatic black neighbour could hardly contain his fervour, rocking his body from side to side and occasionally flinging both arms in the air. Anthony, his space invaded, already regretted Betty's suggestion that he attend a prison service. His sole experience of church – the tepid C of E school services – had left him completely unprepared for such happy-clappy, rackety devotion. Yet, while some of those present obviously believed in their own direct line to the deity, others were deviously whispering amongst themselves, perhaps conducting nefarious drug-deals, despite the intimidating number of officers lining the chapel walls. Earlier in the proceedings, a raucously amplified rock-band had made the whole building vibrate, and the reek of rancid sweat and sickly hair-oil curdling the packed space seemed a far cry from the more traditional smells of candle-wax and incense.

'Father, I have sinned against heaven and against you. I am no longer worthy to be called your …'

The preacher's words suddenly jolted him back to the sermon – the parable of the Prodigal Son. That he did remember from school, except there it had never had such painful relevance. Far from killing the fatted calf in his honour, his own father might well have decided to permanently disown him. Yet, with Christmas only two days off, he felt distinctly uneasy about letting the festive season come and go without making one more effort to contact his parents – all the more so since he and Deborah were due to spend Christmas Day with them. Yet they had failed to respond to his letter explaining the situation – the one letter with a free postage stamp he'd been allowed here on arrival. So, although he dreaded the thought of speaking to them, he felt honour-bound to use his one free phone call – also granted on arrival, in the form of emergency credit on his PIN – to apologise for having wrecked their lives. Fortunately, their number had been approved by the prison authorities, although not his wife's, alas, since they feared he might intimidate her as chief prosecution witness. And, of course, Deborah might have already spoken to his parents, which made him still more nervous; nonetheless, he was determined to do his duty and ring them later today.

A burst of applause greeted the end of the sermon, with further rapt cries of 'Hallelujah!' 'Praise the Lord!' He bowed his head and clasped his hands, hoping, hypocritically, that this uninhibited gathering of bible-bashers might imagine he'd been deeply moved by the Spirit of their Lord. Indeed, some omniscient god would be extremely welcome, in dictating the right conciliatory words when his furious mother or contemptuous father picked up the receiver and heard the voice of their worse-than-prodigal son.

As the congregation exited the chapel, every member was subjected to a search before returning to their cells. Anthony noticed, to his annoyance, that whereas most of the other inmates received just a perfunctory pat-down, his going-over was more thorough altogether – hardly any wonder when it was conducted by the Welsh screw, Bryn Llewellyn, who appeared to have it in for him.

'Why the Gestapo tactics?' he objected, all but spitting out the obligatory 'sir!'

'Who the hell do you think you *are*, Beaufort?' the officer snapped, drawing himself up to his full, pathetic five-foot-five.

'Well, I'm not Beaufort, for a start. My name's Beaumont, as I've told you lot continually.'

'Don't be so bloody insolent! You're not at Eton now, I'll have you know, so don't imagine you can beat the system.'

What system, Anthony fumed? There was no management or order in this whole chaotic institution. However, being desperate to move cells, he deliberately adopted a less hostile tone in explaining the request. 'You see, it's impossible to sleep, sir, where I am, because of the noise from other prisoners yelling out of their windows half the night.'

'Well, buy some bloody earplugs, then!' the screw retorted, giving him a last vicious shove, part of the "search", no doubt. Now they had mislabelled him an Etonian, they were clearly out to deflate him at every opportunity.

And 'bloody earplugs' would certainly have helped when, on re-entering his cell, he was greeted not only by the blaring of the television but by a frenetic gasping and panting. Shorty was sprawled on his bunk, trouserless and wanking, the bed shaking and rattling so wildly, it added to the din. Face screwed up in a grimace, hand pistoning furiously up and down his cock, the uncouth bloke continued to gasp and moan, apparently totally unfazed by the intrusion. Anthony remained skulking by the door, uneasily reflecting on his own inhibition, compared to such excess. Had Deborah always found him too reserved, he wondered, wretchedly, and resorted to Craig not on account of his potency, but for his sheer unadulterated passion?

And, as the breathless panting cresecendoed, suddenly it was *Craig* who was wanking on the bunk, *Craig* who finally exploded with a great snorting yowl, an arc of semen spurting over his chest, *Craig* lying back with a self-satisfied air, as if the rapturous applause from the television audience was directed at him personally

Except Craig was dead, for Christ's sake! And, quick as the thought, Deborah's cocksure lover disappeared, to be replaced by a dismembered corpse lying on a mortuary slab.

Nauseated, he sagged down onto the chair. Whatever happened, he must fix his mind on more mundane concerns. The chair itself would do – still the only chair, since all his requests for a second one had been frustrated. And, of course, Shorty didn't care a jot that his cellmate was forced to eat standing up, or clamber with his greasy plate to the cramped space of the top bunk. Nor had the selfish shit ever once consulted him about the choice of television programmes, but subjected him to the sort of cheesy talent show now in its hysterical finale, the audience going into overdrive as they cheered and clapped the successful contestant.

He jerked to his feet and stood right in front of the door, as if willing it to open. The minute they were unlocked for Association, he would be out like a shot – not just to make the phone call to his parents, but to put as much distance as possible between himself and this gross lout. Fortunately, his ordeal would soon be over since Shorty was being transferred tomorrow to another prison, and all he could say was 'Good riddance!' and 'Thank God!'

As he ventured out on the wing, he was struck again by the palpable air of barely contained violence. As usual, groups of different nationalities were clustered together, excluding everyone who didn't speak their languages. Not that he wanted to be sociable and, indeed, tensed in annoyance as a bull-necked skinhead sidled up to him. 'Are you a newbie?' he asked.

Anthony gave an uncommunicative nod. The word "HATE", tattooed across the base of the fellow's stubby fingers, didn't exactly encourage friendly chat.

'Hi! I'm Leroy.' The man lowered his voice, edged a little closer. 'Want to buy any gear?'

'I beg your pardon?'

'I said, do you want to score?'

'I'm sorry, I don't follow.'

'In that case, you're a fucking idiot!' Leroy turned on his heel and walked off, muttering audibly, 'Stupid bloody cunt!'

Stupid bloody cunt or not, Anthony had no intention of getting involved with drugs. Some of his acquaintances in the worlds of banking and advertising regularly snorted cocaine, but neither he nor Deborah had ever succumbed. Here, though, he would have to be on his guard, because, according to Shorty, drugs were rife in every British gaol, half the inmates being crackheads or heroin addicts, and many officers turning a blind eye to the constant dealing and smuggling going on in their midst, or even taking part in it themselves.

Warily, he made his way to the public phones at the far end of the wing, conscious of hostile stares. And there was no respite from the noise, especially round the pool table, where a group of prisoners were yelling out advice and commentary. Just as he was trying to squeeze past, the game came to an end and the defeated player flung his cue down on the table with such a volley of expletives he seemed on the verge of assaulting his opponent. Every situation here seemed a trigger-point for fisticuffs, even the most trivial things. Just yesterday, in the breakfast queue, one inmate given a smaller sausage than the prisoner ahead of him immediately went into action, kicking the fellow in the groin and trying to wrest away his plate with brute force. An officer had intervened, of course, but here there were fewer staff and Anthony felt distinctly vulnerable as he joined the long queue for the phones.

Once again, there was tension, some prisoners jostling and pushing, others complaining volubly about the endless wait. And, once again, the system was at fault. Why only four phones for so large a contingent of prisoners? He longed to be in charge, not only to increase the number, but to institute a proper booking system, to avoid such inefficient queues. For his own part, he felt slightly demeaned by having to use a public phone at all. One of the worst of his deprivations was being parted from his iPhone, which cut him off from all his contacts, most sources of information, and from access to the outside world.

He was also continually worried about the number of emails that would be piling up inexorably. His normal practice was to email back immediately, but people would now assume he'd become slipshod and disorganised and, as the weeks went by, the stream of unanswered messages would become an avalanche. As for his work computer, that would have been wiped by now and allocated to someone else. Rumours were bound to circulate, however, and the firm would almost certainly lose business as a result of the taint he had laid on it. LinkedIn was another problem – again messages accumulating, all awaiting his response. At least he didn't need to bother with either Facebook or Twitter, having deactivated both accounts a year ago, owing to his increasingly pressured life.

'Hi, mate! I'm Vince.' The man in front turned round to introduce himself. 'Just arrived, have you?'

'Sixteen days ago,' he replied, barely able to believe that his eternity of punishment had, in fact, lasted little more than a fortnight.

'Is this your first time in?'

Anthony nodded, his gaze riveted by the crisscrossing of livid red scars braceleting the fellow's skinny arms.

'I see you're looking at me scars, mate. Don't worry– I don't do violent. I done 'em on myself. I hear voices, see – hoped I'd get psyched off, but they just give me pills and stuff. I'm okay on the pills, mate, except they fuck me head up.'

Was anyone at Wandsworth even halfway normal, Anthony wondered? Perhaps this guy was schizophrenic, rather than simply a self-harmer. At least he seemed reasonably peaceable, in contrast to virulent Shorty.

'This nick ain't as bad as some,' Vince continued, raking his hand through his unkempt greasy hair He then proceeded to give details of various abuses and atrocities he'd experienced at Belmarsh, Brixton and Wormwood Scrubs.

'Lord! It sounds horrific,' Anthony put in, deciding to respond to Vince's overtures, if only to keep his mind off the ordeal of the phone call. The queue was barely moving and the longer he stood here doing nothing more than shuffle forward the odd pace or two, the more his apprehension built about speaking to his parents.

'Yeah, I'm an old hand,' Vince confided. 'I done a four, a three, and three twos. This one's only a year, with just six-and-a-half weeks left. Mind you, I'm chuffed I'll be inside for Christmas – it's a shit time to be released. Anyway, as I said, I know the ropes, so take my advice, okay? Don't give no one nothing. If they come cadging for burn or food, just say no, straight out.'

'Okay, will do.'

'Avoid Oshoba like the plague. He'd slit your throat for half an ounce of burn. And watch out for the nonces. They're utter scum, so keep your distance.'

'Right, I'll remember. Thanks.'

He continued to engage with Vince, although only superficially, since a good half of his mind was still imagining his parents' reproaches. Would they speak to him at all, or simply cut him off? Did he face a future of total isolation, with no family, no wife, no colleagues, only mental cases like Vince for company?

Finally, after the fellow had given him the lowdown on cell searches, bullying, drug tests – both mandatory and voluntary – and the 'useless prick' who ran the bricklaying course, they reached the head of the queue. Vince shot off to use the one free phone, while Anthony kept a sharp eye on the other three, determined not to let some chancer push in front of him.

Yet, once he was actually keying in the PIN number, his resolution faltered, partly because of the warning notice that all phone calls were recorded, and partly because of the lack of privacy. The phones were so close together, those on either side of him could easily listen in and the thought of people overhearing his stream of abject apologies truly was anathema. Besides, the endeavour now seemed futile. Did he really expect his high-principled parents to forgive him, let alone to sympathise?

Nonetheless, he hung grimly on as their number rang and rang. That was odd in itself, since it was part of their general efficiency to ensure they never missed a call and that all important messages were recorded. So perhaps they had decided not to switch on the answerphone, deliberately to avoid any chance of contact with him. Or had they gone away, to escape the scandal his crime was bound to have provoked in their law-abiding Sussex village?

The bleak ring-tone, shrilling on and on, was depressing in itself. Eventually he put down the receiver and tried his mother's mobile, instead, despite the fact that any calls to a mobile would gobble up his precious credit as if he were phoning Sydney or New York.

All at once, he heard his mother's voice – or at least her recorded message. But, instead of enunciating the contrite words he had been rehearsing half the morning, he stood paralysed with dread. Apart from anything else, speaking to a machine meant that, if he sounded defensive and self-pitying rather than truly repentant, his message would be preserved on tape, for his parents to deplore.

As he finally succeeded in blurting out his name, the line suddenly went dead. His credit must have already run out, which meant he couldn't make any more calls until he had topped it up. That was bound to be a rigmarole – maybe even impossible with so many staff on leave, so the problem of his parents would hover like a black cloud over Christmas.

Miserably, he slouched away from the phones, to be hailed by Vince, now lounging against the wall. 'Want to come to my cell for a cuppa?' he suggested.

'Perhaps some other time.' Despite his refusal Anthony was genuinely heartened by the offer. Indeed, it allowed him a gleam of hope that his new cellmate might be not another vicious Shorty clone, but a guy like Vince – disturbed, maybe, but basically congenial. And the deeply etched frown – more or less permanent since the moment he'd arrived here – softened at least a little at the thought of sharing his space with someone more humane.

CHAPTER 9

'Would … you … like … my … lunch?' Anthony spoke slowly and clearly, with pauses between each well-enunciated word.

But, as with all his previous overtures, his new cellmate shook his head in total bafflement. Although a huge improvement on Shorty, the man spoke not a single word of English and that presented problems in itself. However, there was no mistaking his insatiable hunger and, since his arrival last night, he'd been sucking sweets and munching crisps in an obsessional, driven manner, with little sign of enjoyment. He had also stowed away, in his grime-encrusted locker, large quantities of food from God knew where, most of it looking disgustingly old and germy.

Anthony pushed his plate across the small, Formica-topped table they were sharing and signalled to Constan to help himself. At least the gesture was understood, since the lad immediately tipped the contents onto his own plate with an expression of famished concentration. Although how anyone could eat it was beyond Anthony's comprehension. The thin slice of turkey-roll originated, it seemed, from a chemical-processing plant rather than from any recognisable bird. No better were the rock-hard roast potatoes and the greyish mess of squishy Brussel sprouts, all anointed with viscous gravy and starred with pockmarks of congealing fat. Yet Constan devoured both meals in a matter of minutes, the feeding frenzy punctuated by explosive trumpetings into the lengths of kitchen roll he was using as handkerchiefs.

Anthony had been tempted to retreat to his top bunk, not only to avoid catching that stinker of a cold, but to distance himself from the slurping and crunching noises now only inches from his ear. Yet it had felt wrong on Christmas Day, of all days, not to make some small attempt to be friendly, even at the cost of an unwelcome and uncomfortable proximity. At least they had two chairs now, but any chance of sociability was thwarted by the lack of conversation. He didn't even know this poor fellow's Christian name and referred to him as Constan merely as an abbreviation of his surname Constaninscu, displayed on the cell door – Romanian, he guessed.

In the enforced, uneasy silence his mind kept stealing back to former Christmases: he and Deborah at his parents' house, celebrating in luxurious style, with free-range goose, potatoes roasted to perfection in the goose fat, honey-glazed parsnips and sprouts cooked *al dente* with chestnuts and bacon lardons. Never mind the food, though – it was the normality he craved, to be enjoying Christmas Day as a man with a loving wife and high-powered job, in charge of his own life and time, free to go for a stroll after lunch, or pour himself a whisky after a companionable game of chess. As it was, there was no prospect of activity beyond a brief respite at four, when inmates would be unlocked for "tea". After that, all cell doors would be shut at five and not re-opened until Boxing Day – an equally cheerless and unfestive day, no doubt. The term "banged up" was apt, in that the slam of the cell door had a panic-inducing finality, cutting him off from the outside world.

Once Constan had swallowed the last sprout, Anthony offered him his Christmas pudding – a small brown square swamped by lumpy custard, sadly different from his mother's brandy-soaked confection, rich with fruit and nuts. Yet Constan found no fault with it, all but snapping his plastic spoon in his zeal to scrape up every morsel. How could a Christmas pudding be square, Anthony wondered, as he reached for his goody-bag – the Governor's Christmas gift to every inmate? Having reserved the apple, the orange and the packet of crisps for his own lunch, he offloaded the rest to Constan, who got up to stow the booty in his locker, first withdrawing a chunk of unwrapped and visibly ancient-looking meat pie. As he proceeded to eat it, between further sneezes and nose-blowings, it struck Anthony that perhaps he was genuinely starving – maybe a refugee or asylum-seeker cut off, until his imprisonment, from normal supplies of food. Certainly, he looked skeletal; the bones of his face seeming to push through his pasty skin and scarcely an ounce of flesh on his coat-hanger-frame.

Having run out of kitchen roll, he now blew his nose on his fingers and used the (unwashed) hand to eat. Anthony gave silent thanks that he'd agreed to the Hepatitis B jab offered on arrival – an injection he'd initially refused until the nurse said, casually, 'But suppose you get into a fight and your cellmate slashes your face with broken glass?'

Little risk of violence from Constan, who seemed completely harmless, just vulnerable and wretched. The risk of illness was greater, though, in that the two of them were obliged to eat, sleep and excrete in this one tiny, fetid space where the unlidded, stinking lavatory was only inches from the table. He himself had barely contributed to that stink and indeed doubted if his bowels would ever function normally again, given the worse-than-inadequate diet and the disgusting state of the toilets on the wing. And, judging by the way his jeans were hanging on him, he had also lost a fair amount of weight, and had developed both dandruff and a skin-rash. Just as well the one small mirror he and Constan shared was so old and scratched he could make out little more than the pale blur of his face.

Constan suddenly got up, abandoning the last piece of pie, and sank down onto his bunk, lying face to the wall. Hearing the sound of anguished weeping, Anthony glanced across and saw the lad's whole body racked with sobs. What the hell should he do? Any words of comfort would come over as gibberish and, anyway, the slightest show of compassion threatened his own protective shell. Indeed, Constan's uncontrolled distress was bringing back the suicidal thoughts he had harboured yesterday. What was there to live for, when he'd lost everything that gave existence meaning, point and value? Such thoughts had been sparked by an actual suicide on B-Wing: one of the remand prisoners had hanged himself with a rope of twisted bedsheets and, until the corpse was removed and an initial report drafted, the entire prison had been put on lockdown. As the leaden hours of Christmas Eve ticked by, Anthony had found himself envying the dead man for no other reason than he was released from consciousness. His own thoughts were unendurable: Craig again – first, shagging Deborah, his tongue halfway down her throat, her legs wrapped round his rugged, hairy body, his cock thrusting and thwacking as they climaxed in mutual ecstasy. Then, mere seconds later, Craig prone and horribly injured and bleeding onto the rug, and his own senseless, high-cost violence that must have kiboshed Christmas for Craig's wife and three young kids. And, worst of all, his desperate longing for Deborah: her touch, her smell, her presence, their shared bed and home and life. He kept wondering where she was – with her parents, or with his, or still with Isabel? And was she even thinking of him, or had erased him from her life already, as if pressing a "delete" button?

Perhaps Constan was also weeping for his wife, or maybe mourning his lost home and country? Awkwardly, he edged towards the bunk and gave the fellow a tentative pat on the shoulder. Far from consoling him, however, Constan started howling even louder, until he was gasping and fighting for breath, as if in the throes of a panic-attack. Anthony stood rigid – angry with his own impotence and also with the authorities. Couldn't they lay on some sort of counsellor, for pity's sake, or at least an interpreter, so that this fellow could communicate?

Then, all at once, the outburst stopped as suddenly as it had started, and Constan struggled up from his prone position and fell to his knees in the tiny space between the table and his bunk. Having closed his eyes and clasped his hands, he began praying in a low, muttered tone, the words sounding utterly alien. Anthony backed towards the door, longing more than ever for the blessing of a single cell. Praying, weeping, defecating – all were highly intimate and he felt a crass intruder witnessing these aspects of Constan's private life.

To his huge relief, however, the lad appeared to have regained control, as he finally made the sign of the cross and got up from his knees. He even grabbed his goody-bag and ripped open a packet of custard creams, so, presumably, the prayer session had restored his ravenous appetite.

Anthony joined him at the table again, refused the offer of a biscuit, but decided to eat his own orange and apple for lunch. The "special treat" Christmas breakfast of grease-soaked fried bread, cold baked beans and sausage from some unidentifiable beast had been fit only for the bin. His plastic knife couldn't cope with cutting an apple, so he bit into it instead, revealing mouldy black flesh inside, surely symbolic of his present situation.

'For God's sake,' he muttered, annoyed at such empty conceits. He should be making an attempt to "man up", the phrase used at his prep-school, to teach seven-year-olds that real men didn't cry, or feel sorry for themselves, or miss their mummies, or shirk challenging situations. This most challenging of all situations would undoubtedly involve a large amount of waiting: waiting for milestones in his court case and for key people to play their parts. Normally, it was he who kept others waiting, but, like it or not, he was no longer a highly paid director in a top accountancy firm but one of almost nineteen-hundred prisoners in an utterly undistinguished gaol. So, instead of deploring the time as "endless", he must draw up a survival plan and divide it into manageable chunks. The first, obviously, must be the four weeks until his Plea and Case Management Hearing – although if he were granted bail on that occasion he would have no need of the plan, at least not till after his trial.

By coincidence, his fortieth birthday was the next day after the hearing, so if he were released from prison that in itself would be a cause for celebration. There was still the problem of obtaining an address to satisfy the bail requirements – an issue that prompted yet another worry – the sky-high rent he was still paying on his Marylebone flat. After what had happened there, neither he nor Deborah was ever likely to return, yet how could they terminate a joint lease when they were forbidden to communicate?

He forced his mind away from Deborah and back to the bail requirements. Perhaps he'd be allowed to stay in a hotel or rent a temporary bedsit. Even the most basic pad would seem Ritzy compared to this place, he thought, glancing at the graffiti on the wall, a scrawled tangle of pain, fury and revenge, revealed only after Shorty had removed his busty pin-ups. "Fuck the fuckers!" "Help! I'm losing it." "All cops are bastards!" "Speed kills – stick to grass."

He gave silent thanks that at least he wasn't addicted to either speed or grass. Nor had he ever resorted to porn, like Shorty, or used food, as Constan did, as a comfort or a crutch. Indeed, he decided to postpone his lunch and give priority to drawing up a timetable to help him cope whether out of prison, or – God forbid – still here. And, using one of Betty's pens and pads, he became so absorbed in the task that Constan's biscuit chomping and barley-sugar crunching faded to a mercifully tolerable descant.

CHAPTER 10

Anthony inhaled his first fresh air for weeks as if it were an elixir, then stood with his face to the late-January sun, jolted by its brightness after the long period of sleet and snow. One thing he'd learned of late was that tiny pleasures, once taken for granted – light, sunshine, the breeze on one's face – could be ridiculously important. Yet, however much he relished this brief escape from the oppressively gloomy building, there was no denying the equal grimness of the exercise yard: high fences on three sides, topped with razor-wire, the fourth side blocked by the beetling red-brick structure of the wing, which resembled a three-decked man-of-war. And the usual prison greyness was echoed by the flocks of tatty pigeons flustering around, or flying in short hopeless bursts, as if they, too, were doomed to captivity.

'Excuse me,' said a timid voice.

He swung round to see a small, slim, youngish man, his peat-brown hair contrasting with intense blue eyes.

'You're Tony, aren't you?' the fellow asked

Anthony nodded, warily. The yard was full of aggressive types, some shouting insults to other inmates, others charging round and round the restricted space with the sort of force and vehemence that suggested inner violence. However, this guy looked safe enough. Indeed, he was blushing as he spoke, his voice tentative, uncertain. 'I know you're clever and everything … I mean, they said you been to Cambridge.'

Who had said, Anthony wondered? The only time he'd mentioned Cambridge was after completing an education test so absurdly elementary a pre-school child could have romped through it in minutes. 'The cat sat on the m_t. Fill in the blank'. Prison-level literacy, presumably, moving swiftly on to maths: 'How much time is there between ten-fifteen and twelve noon?'

'I'm Darren,' the man continued, still sounding diffident. 'And … and I want to ask you a favour.'

'Go ahead.'

'I need to write a letter to me girlfriend, but ...' he lowered his voice in obvious embarrassment, '... I can't read or write, see, so I wondered if you'd do it for me?'

Anthony tried to conceal his shock. Darren didn't look far off thirty, so how in heaven's name had he managed for so many years without basic literacy? 'Well, yes, okay,' he said, 'if you tell me what you want to say. Shall we do a circuit or two together, then you can explain?'

They set off around the perimeter fence, dodging groups of inmates smoking with an intensity little short of addiction, one or two even swooping down to pick up fag-ends amidst the pigeon crap. Never before had Anthony seen so many smokers gathered in one place. Nor had he heard so many different languages, each nationality sticking together in its exclusive little clique.

'You won't tell no one, will you?' Darren whispered.

'I wouldn't dream of it.' In truth, there was no one to tell. He and Constan were still co-existing in mutual silence and, as for making friends here, he deliberately avoided it. Even in his pre-gaol life, when colleagues and clients took up most of his time, there had been little scope for close, demanding friendships. And, once his crime was public knowledge, all his clients would be scandalised and his colleagues and acquaintances shun him altogether.

'I grew up in care, see, and never done much education. The other kids taught me how to bunk off school, and no one was that bothered to make me do homework and stuff.'

'But what happened to your parents?' Anthony enquired, screwing up his face in distaste at the drifts of litter blowing across the filthy concrete yard.

'Oh, me mum done a runner ages ago and I never knew me dad. The home weren't that bad, if I'm honest. I didn't even want to leave, but they turf you out at sixteen and then you're on your own. It's like they simply dump you in some crappy hostel or bedsit, with other mixed-up kids who just hang around boozing or smoking pot. And, if you're in a hostel, there's these dodgy older blokes, mostly off their heads with drink or drugs. It's worse for the girls, though. One girl I knew was shoved out of the home at barely fifteen-and-a-half and sent to a B&B, which never ought to happen and where she got abused non-stop. Them men don't use no condoms, see, so their victims land up pregnant, like as not. And you can bet your bottom dollar them kids are taken into care, same as their poor mums.'

Anthony realised to his discomfiture that these were the sort of women he had condemned, in the past, as feckless and irresponsible. If he came across such stories in the paper, he'd quickly move on to another page, preferring to ignore what he had then regarded as an alien type of existence.

Darren kicked an empty Coke can out of his way. 'When you live in them sort of places, see, you don't have no one around to help you get your head together. I didn't know nothing about cooking or cleaning, so I just lived on chips and stuff. My teeth was bleeding and everything, but we didn't have no dentist.'

Involuntarily, Anthony put a hand to his mouth. His own teeth were bleeding, but, throughout his privileged life, he had enjoyed the blessings of highly nutritious food and top-notch private dentistry.

'They're meant to tell you how to manage money.' Darren gave a hollow laugh. 'Well, I didn't *have* no money – couldn't get no work, see, which is why I started nicking stuff. At first I was lucky and got away with it, but then I met this Nigerian bloke – Chidima he were called – and we done these jobs together, bigger jobs, like breaking into jewellers' shops. He made me do the risky stuff, so soon I landed up in trouble and, since then, I been banged up more times than I can count. Burglary was me job, see, and the trouble with bang-up is you learn to do it better here. Other prisoners tell you the best sort of stuff to nick, and how to offload the gear and everything. And we swap tips about not getting caught.' This time, Darren's laugh was rueful. 'I didn't learn *those* too good, though.'

Anthony shook his head in shame at his own blinkered ignorance. He had read about prison as a "college of crime" but, before today, it had been just words.

'And there's loads of gang members on our wing,' Darren continued, apparently glad to explain the complexities of prison life. 'Some still do business with their mates outside, or run these criminal rackets from their cells – you know, on their mobiles.'

'But I thought mobiles were forbidden,' Anthony said, confused.

'You must be joking, mate! It's like Carphone Warehouse in here! And some screws are happy to turn a blind eye, if the gangster makes it worth their while.' Darren made a gesture of transferring banknotes from his pocket to his open palm. 'But listen, Tony, don't get the wrong idea. I was never in no gang. I wanted to go straight, see, but without no job or nothing, I was forced back to me old ways. The discharge grant don't last no time at all and, soon, I couldn't even feed meself and started raiding dustbins. Prison's better than starving, innit? There's folks I know who see it as just free board and lodging. And I weren't far off thinking that meself – until I met Carol-Ann, that is.'

'Your girlfriend?' Anthony interjected.

'Yeah. I don't deserve her. But I only got done this time because I nicked the cash to buy her a ring – a gold one she'd really set her heart on. That's why I need to write the letter – to ask her not to give up on me and to promise I'll change me ways once I'm out of here.'

Anthony freed himself from a stray sheet of the *Mirror* entangled round his foot. 'But surely she knows you can't write?'

'No, she don't. And she *mustn't*.' Darren's voice was fierce.

A burly black man lounging against the fence suddenly stepped forward to accost them. 'Tony's a wanker, Darren – too fucking posh for the likes of us. The fucking creep looks down his nose at everyone, so why the fuck are you talking to him?'

Although he himself ignored the gibe, he noticed Darren tense in alarm and immediately clam up. 'Tell you what,' he suggested, once they were safely past their tormentor, 'when exercise is over, let's find somewhere more private to talk.'

'You could come to me cell,' Darren offered. 'At least it'll be warm. It's perishing out here.'

The guy was shivering, Anthony realised, from fear perhaps, as well as cold. Despite the bold stare of the sun, there was no heat or strength in it.

'We'll be on our own there, because today is me pad-mate's birthday, see, so he won't be in no hurry to leave his pool game.'

'Well, that's a coincidence,' Anthony blurted out. 'It's *my* birthday, too!' Immediately he regretted the admission, having vowed not to tell a soul.

'Great! I'll make you a hot drink, mate, and we'll do a toast and everything.' Darren's face relaxed into a smile. 'Happy birthday, Tony!'

Hardly happy, Anthony reflected, trying not to think of the glitzy dinner he and Deborah had planned to celebrate the start of a whole new era, with his partnership assured. Now, his fortieth seemed more an end than a beginning: the end of his youth, the end of any worthwhile life. 'I'm afraid it didn't start too well,' he admitted, surprised to find himself confiding in this unlikely fellow. 'I was in court yesterday, hoping to get bail, but …' he shrugged, '… no luck.'

The Prosecution had argued that, as a wealthy man with no children and no community ties, he could easily flee the country, with the added risk that he might contact his wife and try to persuade her to alter her evidence. Worse, his plea of not guilty to murder had been rejected as unacceptable – a crushing blow, since he was now facing a trial that might result in life imprisonment. The prospect induced such extremes of panic, he had been struggling to suppress it, since he simply couldn't function if he looked ahead to so bleak and barren a future. Indeed, he shouldn't even be thinking about the hearing, when the whole day had been a write-off – like his suit. Although he'd managed to gain possession of the garment, if only for the duration of the trial, it was so crumpled and even smelly, he'd felt ashamed to have to appear in it in court.

'Shit! I'm sorry, Tony.'

And his companion *sounded* sorry, the blue eyes clouding over, the expressively mobile face registering genuine sympathy. Nonetheless, Anthony resolved to say nothing more about his personal circumstances, let alone about his crime. In this vindictive rumour-mill, every tiny thing could be magnified, distorted and passed on to all and sundry, so, from now until the end of exercise, he must encourage Darren to do the talking.

*

'Your cell's so clean!' Anthony exclaimed, gazing at the neat and tidy space: no piles of clutter, no grime-encrusted surfaces, even the lavatory smelling fresh.

'That's Ricky,' Darren said. 'He's a bit OCD, to tell the truth, for ever mopping and scrubbing – can't bear so much as a speck of dust.'

'But how does he get cleaning materials?' Anthony asked, as Darren filled the kettle from an unnaturally gleaming sink. 'When I asked for some bleach, I was told it was forbidden, in case prisoners drank it, to do away with themselves.' And, indeed, had *he* obtained some, he might have swallowed the whole bottle, as the easiest way out.

'It aint just that,' Darren told him. 'Some dealers add powdered bleach to heroin. The skag goes further, see, and the pusher rakes in more dough.'

Anthony stored away this piece of information in his ever-expanding prison "glossary". 'Forget heroin! They wouldn't even give me basic washing-up liquid. The screw just said, "Get real!"'

'Well, Ricky works as a wing-cleaner, so he helps himself to stuff. To be honest, though, all that clearing up really gets on me nerves. He even made me take down me pictures of Carol-Ann, because I'd stuck them up with toothpaste, see, and he said they looked a mess.'

'You should have stood your ground,' Anthony remarked, although secretly craving a cellmate with such a sense of order. Constan left a tide of litter: empty Coke cans and crisp packets, discarded chocolate wrappers, instant-noodle pots.

'You don't know Ricky! It's less hassle to give in.' Withdrawing a photo from the back pocket of his jeans, Darren passed it across the table. 'That's Carol-Ann,' he said, proudly.

Anthony studied the bottle-bleached blonde, with her pouty mouth and blue-mascared lashes. 'She's pretty,' he murmured, trying to overlook the atrocious fake leopard top.

'Yeah, a stunner! I'm dead lucky. Let's leave her picture here on the table and it'll help us with the letter. But what d'you want to drink, mate? I got tea, coffee, Bovril and— That's another thing,' he added, interrupting himself, 'I can't fill in them lists they give us to order stuff from canteen. They're just double-Dutch to me. And the weekly menus are worse still, so unless Ricky helps ...'

'And does he? Anthony prompted, noting Darren had broken off.

'Sometimes,' Darren said. 'But he always makes a song and dance about it and complains I'm effing ignorant. He's right – I *am*. But he don't realise I feel like shit – I mean, all them prison forms and notices and stuff that make no sense to me.'

Only now could Anthony begin to grasp what illiteracy must mean in daily life: so many tasks impossible; so many avenues permanently closed off. According to his parents, he could read at three and, by five, was writing his own stories, even putting together a child's version of his father's *Daily Telegraph*.

'Kettle's boiled,' Darren announced. 'Fancy a hot chocolate, Tony?'

'I'd prefer a coffee, if that's okay.'

The coffee proved far superior to the dishwater-weak prison brew, and was served in a proper china cup – a definite advance on his usual smeary plastic mug. However, the irony wasn't lost on him that, as one of the wealthiest inmates, with savings and investments, he was actually one of the poorest when it came to his prison account. He might be able to fill in his canteen-sheet, but, unlike Darren, could afford almost nothing on the long list of products, which ranged from Coco Pops, luncheon meat, Hamlet cigars and African Pride shampoo to toenail clippers, jelly babies and Fixodent Denture Cream. Having always been one of the "haves", he had now become a "have-not", and, although he had started the slow process of liaising with his bank, "slow" was the operative word. Not only did all communication have to be by snail-mail, but Barclays had demanded a letter from the prison Governor, which had engendered further long delays. Having never laid eyes on the Governor, he could hardly accost the big boss-man and insist the letter was written.

Admittedly, just by dint of being here, he did receive the princely sum of £2.50 a week – standard "bang-up pay" – but that wasn't enough to keep his phone-credit topped up, let alone afford the large supplies of food, tobacco and toiletries that many other prisoners seemed to buy. But of course *they* had loving friends and family to send them postal orders.

However, his present privations were chickenfeed compared with the raft of privileges lavished on him since the moment he'd drawn breath, a shaming contrast to Darren's lousy start in life. So, the least he could do was write Darren the best letter possible, put his heart and soul into the task. Of course, he would have to employ simple language (to prevent Carol-Ann suspecting it wasn't her boyfriend's handiwork), and ask Darren for personal details to add an authentic note, and for any particular sentiments he was keen to put across.

Once the guy had brought paper and an envelope, the words were soon flowing freely, as he imagined he was addressing them to Deborah, declaring his love, reminding her of their years together, and making an impassioned case for his loyalty, devotion and sheer unwavering determination to remain permanently out of trouble the minute he regained his freedom.

However, every thought of Deborah only seeded new anxieties, not just the personal, marital ones, but the matter of their flat. As an efficient, organised person, he yearned to terminate the lease and rid himself of a crushing financial burden, yet that flat was his only home, a cherished place he and his wife had chosen and furnished together at a time when their life was still blessed, their love still sound and strong. Nonetheless, he would have to confront the problem, perhaps by asking Betty's assistance. If she contacted his wife, on his behalf, she could find out if Deborah agreed to give up the flat and, if the answer was yes, maybe suggest that Deborah's parents help expedite the process, or even …

'Are you okay, mate?' Darren asked, still hovering by his side.

He nodded, guiltily aware of his lapse of concentration, which Darren had obviously noticed. 'I just need to polish it a bit,' he said, picking up his pen again.

He spent some time working on the draft, shortening his sentences and removing over-complicated words, before writing the whole thing out again on a second sheet of paper and, finally, reading it to Darren.

'It's brilliant!' the fellow enthused, reaching for the letter and gazing at it in mingled awe and delight. 'Only trouble is, she'll be expecting letters as good as this every week.'

'Don't worry. I'll write as many as you like. I'm so used to being busy, it'll suit me to have a project.'

An idea began forming in his mind. Why didn't he teach this guy to read and write? If he mapped out a basic literacy scheme, with regular lessons and simple weekly assignments, he could make a lasting difference to Darren's life. And it would give him a purpose, too – help fill the empty days until his trial on 22 April. Those daunting three months weighed heavy on his spirits, with no prospect of a prison job while he was still on remand, and the enforced silence every evening after lock-up. In truth, there was something appealing about Darren's very diffidence, his submission to his bossy cellmate for the sake of a quiet life, his apparent lack of bitterness or rage about growing up in care. Perhaps he could even learn something in his turn– not how to read and write, but to be more accepting, less angry with the world.

*

Just as Anthony was returning to his cell with "tea" – a so-called Chinese stir-fry, glued together in one viscous lump – Darren appeared at the door.

'Okay if I come in, Tony?'

'Yes, course.' Anthony gave silent thanks that Constan was still in the servery queue, rather than on his knees, muttering incomprehensible prayers. Of late, he seemed to be storming heaven with worrying frequency.

'I just brought you a couple of things, mate.' Darren handed over a bottle of kitchen cleaner and a stiff brown envelope. 'For your birthday, see, and to say ta very much for the letter.'

'That's incredibly kind,' Anthony said with unfeigned pleasure. In the absence of Deborah's usual luxurious birthday gifts, this bottle of "Elbow Grease" seemed ludicrously precious. And it would certainly come in handy, since now he could do a Ricky and sanitise his cell. 'And what's this?' he asked, as he unsealed the flap on the envelope.

'A Black Cats calendar. Sorry it's not new. One of me mates sent it to me for Christmas. But black cats mean luck, you see, so I felt you could do with it.'

Again, Anthony felt deeply touched, and, again, the gift would prove extremely useful. Never mind luck (mentioned by Darren several times, he'd noticed) – he could use it as a diary and tick off each day before his trial, just as he had done at prep-school, ticking off the aching stretch of time before the end of term.

'And I *do* wish you luck, mate,' Darren added, shyly.

'And I you.' Anthony's voice was choked. Today's encounter with Darren was the first genuinely friendly overture he had yet received in all his seven weeks in prison. Damn it, he thought, however great a struggle it proves, I'll do my utmost to ensure that, by the end of April, Darren will be writing his *own* letters.

CHAPTER 11

'Get up, Bowerman. Court today!'

Anthony winced at the bellowed wake-up call – totally unnecessary, since, although he wasn't Bowerman, *up* he most certainly was. Sleep had proved impossible last night, with the first day of his trial looming this very morning. And the sweltering heat hadn't helped – an unprecedented late-April heatwave coinciding with an over-exuberant prison boiler.

Before the officer could disappear, Anthony begged him in a placatory tone, liberally sprinkled with 'sirs', if he could possibly have a shower.

'Not a dog's chance, Bowerman! It's far too early and we're short of staff. You should have had one yesterday.'

'I did, sir. But last night was so hot and sticky, sir, I'm literally dripping with sweat, and I'm due at the Old Bailey today, sir.'

It required several more entreaties – and 'sirs'- before the officer relented. 'Okay,' he muttered, tetchily, 'but you'll have to be step on it. Five minutes max, Okay?'

Grabbing his soap and towel before any change of mind, Anthony tried to match the fellow's breakneck pace. Apart from their echoing footsteps, the prison seemed eerily quiet at this hour, without its usual bustle and bedlam. Even the normal conflicting smells of sweat, bleach, testosterone and cooking were noticeably less pronounced. However, the stench that assaulted their nostrils once they reached the shower-room was so chokingly foul the officer jerked to a halt with an irate exclamation.

'Bloody hell! Some bastard's shat in the shower!'

Anthony wrinkled his nose in disgust. 'Can you please take me to another shower then, sir?'

'For Christ's sake, Bowerman! My day doesn't revolve round *you*. This is an emergency and needs sorting out double-quick. If you want to wash, what's wrong with your bloody sink?'

'Well, to start with, it doesn't have a plug. I've put in three applications, sir, but—'

'I've told you before,' the officer cut in, 'you have a serious attitude problem and the sooner you address it the better for us all.'

As he marched him swiftly back along the corridor, Anthony fought an urge to take to his heels and run – to escape this constant harassment, escape his trial today, escape prison altogether. He wasn't sure how long he could endure without cracking up, or losing the control he tried so desperately to maintain. But, all too soon, the cell door slammed behind him and he was forced to console himself with the thought that prison showers were useless anyway – the tepid trickle of water, the floor awash with other inmates' grimy suds, the one thin towel that had to last a week. At home, he had a power-shower, a profusion of soft, thick, bath-sheets and a range of luxurious toiletries. Betty's Imperial Leather soap had long ago run out, so he was back to the gritty prison issue that barely lathered, yet still inflamed his skin.

Resignedly, he washed and shaved in the inadequate conditions, ignoring his bleeding gums, as usual. At least his new cellmate hadn't woken. Slasher, a heroin addict, had crashed out in a semi-coma last night, after hours of coughing, snorting and puking throughout the previous two days. Constan had been an angel in comparison, but the poor, silent compulsive eater had been transferred to High Down in Surrey. In a holding prison like this, inmates were constantly on the move, although Darren was still here, thank God, and the literacy lessons still going full steam ahead.

He glanced across at Slasher, lying dead to the world in the lower bunk. Granted his sleep was drug-induced, but its sheer depth and duration were truly enviable, since sleep was the only way to be "out" of prison. He longed to be like those inmates who could sleep away the entire weekend, or had spent the whole of the Easter break comatose in bed.

He had no wish to disturb his cellmate, whose name might indicate a frightening propensity for violence – and he wasn't thinking solely of his own safety from attack, but also of Slasher's need of a lie-in, if not a permanent rest-cure, on account of his pitiful condition. So he dressed as quietly as he could in his suit, white shirt and best shoes. Frankly, he'd been surprised that the clothes had turned up on time when most of his other applications for possessions or permissions had been ignored, or overlooked, or were still waiting to be processed. Admittedly, the shoes were sorely in need of polish, and the suit and shirt were badly creased, with an ineradicable prison smell on them, but at least he wouldn't look a total disaster in court.

It was a relief to wear supportive leather footwear after four-and-a-half months of slopping around in grubby, gaping plimsolls. There was as much a hierarchy in gaol as in the world outside – everyone needed someone to look down on – and such bargain-basement plimsolls were considered seriously uncool, here, if not downright uncouth. However, attired in his Jermyn-Street glad-rags, the outfit only served as a bitter reminder of his former successful life. The suit itself had cost little short of a grand, whereas it had been a struggle last week to afford the smallest size deodorant – a necessity for his court appearances in such uncomfortable heat. And he'd been desperate about the state of his hair, since the appointment he'd booked with the free prison hairdressing service had been unaccountably cancelled. True, there were also prisoner-barbers, the best of them, he'd heard, being a lifer called Rod MacCrindle, but Rod charged two tins of tuna for a haircut – way beyond his present resources, being still a comparative pauper. The long, frustrating saga with Barclays had reached a new impasse and, although the Governor had written to them a whole six weeks ago, there had been no response from the bank. Darren suspected that Barclays *had* replied, but their letter was being deliberately withheld by a bolshie officer – a common practice, apparently, among screws who enjoyed inflicting petty punishments.

'But don't fret about your hair,' the lad had urged. 'You take my appointment.'

Providentially, Darren had booked a slot with the prison hairdresser just three days before the trial. 'You go for it, mate, for God's sake! I can get me mop chopped any time, but if you don't get a haircut, you'll have to turn up in court looking like Russell Brand!' In point of fact, his hair had been cut so short he felt very nearly scalped, but better that than resembling an out-of-control firebrand.

He deliberately kept his mind on Darren, as far preferable to thinking about the trial and its attendant images of a hostile jury, or his barristers failing to withstand the onslaught of the Prosecution. Admittedly the Junior, Edmund Hall, had already showed himself reassuringly tough in his handling of the previous hearing, but his QC had been called away to another case, that day, so he hadn't yet seen him in action. True the man had seemed impressive on the one occasion they'd met so far, and, of course, Betty had nothing but praise for him. However, in his present nerve-wracked state, he was doubting even Betty's judgement, doubting every damned thing, including the justice system itself. In any case, what hope was there of avoiding thoughts of the trial with the cat calendar stuck up on the wall and all the pre-trial days crossed off? And the fact he'd be seeing Deborah today was so unnerving in itself he'd spent much of last night agonising about how he'd react when she was ushered into the court. It would be their first contact since early December – a contact he both craved and dreaded. They had never been apart so long in all their years together, and the next time he encountered her might well be in the divorce court.

Desperate for distraction, he went to his locker to fetch his breakfast provisions – a plastic bag containing a mini-pack of cereal, one stale roll and a blackened banana, given to him last night since he'd be leaving too early to queue up at the servery. As he reached for the bag, he noticed a small, white envelope on the floor, half-hidden under the locker. Inside was a Good Luck card, complete with shamrock, horseshoe and yet another black cat, but what caught his eye was the hand-written message:

"Good luck for tomorrer, Anteny, from yor new best mate, Darren."

The guy must have slipped it under the door before lock-up yesterday evening and, in the tiny space of the cell, it had all but vanished under the locker, unseen until this moment – the perfect moment, in truth, since he was about to leave for court. Although he was no closer to trusting to luck (despite Darren's many tales of black cats bringing good fortune from Sidcup to Singapore to Sydney), it couldn't be denied that Darren's kindness and decency were a stroke of luck in themselves. Nor had the presents stopped. He even owned a watch now: Darren's spare one – admittedly a cheap and tinny thing, but of inestimable value in that it had banished his confusion and lack of control at having no idea of the time.

Having strapped it on, he re-read the card again, with a definite sense of pride. The writing was beautifully neat and the spelling mistakes were surely excusable, given the intractable nature of English spelling. What was truly impressive was that Darren could now read most of the items on the weekly menus, including tricky ones like "Vegetarian Fritters" (leftover potatoes, soggy with gravy and fried in rancid oil) and

"Tropical Coleslaw" (limp cabbage awash in salad cream, with the lucky-dip of one pineapple chunk for every dozen inmates). Darren's courage and persistence in tackling the Herculean task of learning to read and write at the age of twenty-eight, and also in overcoming his embarrassment at being what he called "pig-ignorant", had proved a valuable lesson in itself. And he had to rival that courage today, however daunting the trial might be.

Darren had other virtues, too, including being trustworthy, in that he'd not divulged to anyone that "Tony" was on a murder charge. Many prisoners did freely admit their crimes (even violent and obnoxious ones), although often with the proviso that they'd been "stitched up" or "sold down the river" and no way was the offence their fault. But *he* had remained tight-lipped, confiding only in Darren, who clearly had integrity.

Carefully, he tucked the card into the inside pocket of his suit and sat waiting for the officer to take him down to reception. And, when the chap appeared, Anthony seemed to hear not his bullying voice but Darren calling out encouragingly, 'Good luck, me new best mate!'

CHAPTER 12

Anthony was led into the dock, where the officer released his handcuffs and then stood on guard beside him, just as he had this morning. How intimidating that morning session had seemed, not to mention interminable, the pace so slow he had longed for a fast-forward button, so that all the onerous days of the trial would be over in five minutes. However, there was no guarantee that, when it ended, he wouldn't be feeling considerably worse, facing a sentence so long, better to kill himself and be done with it.

He already felt weak and empty, unable to eat a morsel during the lunch-break. Not only had the noise from adjoining cells been more than usually disorienting, but those damning phrases from the Prosecution's speech continued to swirl like poisons in his stomach:

'Mr Beaumont left work early on the day of the assault with the express intention of killing the deceased – a calculated decision to rid himself of his rival … This cold-blooded, callous act was clearly thought out in advance and planned with deliberate precision …'

It had required all his self-control not to bellow an objection at such a travesty of the facts, but so shameful a lapse would have totally contravened the quiet and measured demeanour of the court. He might be cracking up inside with terror, rage, despair, but the barristers never so much as raised their voices, let alone lost their composure. Indeed, the formal robes, formal language and this elegantly proportioned wood-panelled court reminded him of his old Cambridge college. Yet the civility and ostentation seemed to him, standing in the dock, like elaborate icing on a putrefying cake. And, in the eyes of most of those present, *he* would be deemed the putrefaction, no better than the long successive scum of murderers, rapists, fraudsters and thieves who had stood here over the decades.

He ran a finger round the inside of his collar, sweltering in his winter suit. His mind suddenly veered off to his wardrobeful of light-weight suits, his cashmere jerseys and stack of freshly laundered shirts; and then to all his other possessions – the state-of-the-art music system, the ultra-powerful laptop, the coffee-machine that made every conceivable type and strength of brew – all now packed into crates and put in storage. Betty had finally managed, with the help of Deborah's parents, to terminate the lease on the flat, going far beyond the call of duty in personally supervising the safe transfer of his belongings. Yet, despite his debt of gratitude to her, he felt an aching sense of loss at having forfeited his home.

But why, in God's name, was he preoccupied with shirts and coffee-machines, when his entire concentration should be on the trial? He glanced anxiously at his QC, Nigel Spencer-Soames, hoping the heat wouldn't similarly distract him, since he must be distinctly uncomfortable in his heavy gown and wig. The two opposing barristers were markedly different in their appearance: Spencer-Soames tall, sleek, pale, dark-haired; the Prosecution short and stout, with a gingerish thatch atop his ruddy face. But the one who meant most to him was – again – Betty, who had demonstrated repeatedly her loyalty and kindness. Throughout the formidable morning session, she had given him silent support simply by her presence; a presence he valued all the more, knowing she could ill afford, in any sense, this time away from her normal job. As if reading his mind, she caught his eye and smiled encouragingly, aware of his nervous state.

'All rise!' the usher commanded, and Anthony was jerked to his feet by the dock officer as the judge – a balding, shrivelled little man, who seemed too puny for the power invested in him – strode in and took his seat. Nor did the jury inspire great confidence. Several of them had been fidgeting and yawning this morning, and one overweight female had drunk an inordinate amount of water, continually filling and refilling her glass, as if more concerned with assuaging her unnatural thirst than with listening to the evidence. And an elderly Asian man had actually nodded off, his heavy breathing an embarrassment to everyone until the usher intervened and woke him up.

All such thoughts were instantly banished by the sight of Deborah being led into the witness box – that moment he had been fearing, dreading, craving, during the last endless, anguished weeks. Yet nothing had prepared him for the dramatic change in her. His slender, willowy wife, with her normally flat and well-toned stomach, now had a bulging belly. True the bulge was only slight, but the fact itself was so devastating, he missed every word of the oath she was swearing, and failed to hear the Prosecution's words as he put his initial questions to her. How could he have been so obtuse in not having realised she might be pregnant, when she had resorted to Craig only for his sperm? Or had he deliberately blocked out the possibility as too painful, too unbearable, another odious complication in the whole chaotic tangle?

He couldn't drag his eyes away from her newly rounded form. This could have been *his* baby – his by law, if not genetically – had he only agreed to a sperm-donor. Now the child was fatherless. Yet Deborah looked radiant, despite the tragic circumstances of the child's conception. Had her intense longing for a baby cancelled out the horror of Craig's death, the horror of his own hapless fate? For all he knew, she might already have another lover, who had persuaded her to put Craig's demise behind her – maybe one of her Bohemian advertising colleagues who wouldn't object to taking on another man's child. Or perhaps, he thought, with still more agitation, the child wasn't Craig's at all. She could have been so desperate to conceive she had slept with several different men. And she did look maddeningly fuckable, for God's sake, with her fuller breasts and swelling belly; her long, slim legs set off to perfection in elegant high heels, her dark glossy hair swept up in a chignon. Often, in the past, that mane of hair, loosened from its clips, had swept across his naked body, tickling and flicking on his shoulders as she straddled him in bed.

The memory sparked such rage and jealousy, it was if an electric current was rippling through his body, mingled with a laser-beam of lust. His life might be in ruins, but he still itched to bed his wife, to put his mark upon her, tell the world she was *his,* and his alone, and warn all the other bastards to back off. Instead, that alien bulge was telling all and sundry that she'd been screwing around, betraying him, and was now carrying some gross, aberrant love-child.

His mind was in such turmoil, the proceedings continued to pass him by, his whole attention fixated on the pregnancy and his own failure to foresee it. And not until the Prosecution's questions focused more directly on the events preceding the assault was he jolted back to what was going on in court: could Mrs Beaumont kindly give some indication of her husband's mood and demeanour in the months leading up to the incident.

Deborah wasted no time in giving details, apparently unfazed by the pomp and protocol of the court. 'He became increasingly irritable and sometimes downright unreasonable. And his work pressures increased so hugely, he was very rarely there for me. And, even when he *was* at home, he was often snappy and distracted, even boorish. But what upset me most was that our sex-life became non-existent, yet he refused point-blank to consider using a sperm-donor.'

A downright lie! He had spent abhorrent hours researching the whole issue, poring over the profiles of those preening studs who flaunted their mortifying potency by offering their sperm to sterile, mothballed men like him.

'To be honest, it was a major blow, because we'd both always wanted children – or so I thought. I mean, we discussed the issue in detail before we were even engaged. But, once we were married, Anthony showed little interest and kept coming up with different reasons why a baby wouldn't suit our lifestyle.'

Totally unfair! It was *she* who'd come up with the reasons, because, hungry for wealth and status, she'd been determined to put her career before motherhood.

'I was very patient at first and tried to see things from his viewpoint, but, when I reached my mid-thirties, my biological clock became the overriding issue and I knew that if I didn't take action soon, I'd be permanently childless. Yet Anthony didn't – or wouldn't – realise how much the matter meant to me.'

How *dare* she misrepresent the facts so blatantly! They had spent stressful years trying to conceive, timing every act of sex with the precision of a rocket-launch, cutting down on alcohol, swallowing special vitamins, gearing their life to the process of conception. Admittedly, he had delayed a longish while before agreeing to consult a specialist or go for specific tests, and that must have been frustrating for his wife. But he'd eventually relented, swallowed his pride and submitted – only to have to face the shaming truth about his defective sperm.

As he replayed the whole wretched saga in his mind, his concentration was once more shot to pieces while he struggled to reconcile his view of the marriage as happy and successful with Deborah's depiction of it as an unendurable ordeal. He had obviously failed in every respect: as a husband; as a lover; as a father; as a stud. There was no hope of any future with his wife – no hope of any future, full-stop.

He was only hauled back to the proceedings when he heard the Prosecution asking Deborah to give her own account of the day of the crime. Again, she answered without hesitation.

'Well, the whole thing was suspicious, because my husband *never* comes home early. I mean, it's often well past eight or nine at night, so you can imagine what a shock it was when he burst into the flat mid-morning and started acting like a madman. He seemed more like a wild animal than a rational human being and actually threatened to kill Craig before he'd so much as …'

Anthony clenched his fists with such force his nails left deep red weals in his palms. He'd been ill, for Christ's sake, barely able to stand, let alone rampaging like an animal. He wanted to grab her by the shoulders and shake some sense into her, yet screened as he was by toughened Perspex and guarded by a court official, he couldn't so much as touch the hem of her dress, was forbidden to lay a finger on his wife of eleven years.

He slumped back in his seat, feeling a tide of desolation. What was the use of paying expensive lawyers to defend him when the Prosecution was determined to depict him as a savage beast intent on calculated murder? He would face a lifetime in gaol – except it wouldn't be a life, only a living death.

Suddenly, he noticed a change in the Prosecution's voice. The former confident, self-satisfied tone was now tactfully unobtrusive, gentler altogether. 'Mrs Beaumont, I hope you don't mind me asking, but are you pregnant?'

'Yes,' Deborah replied, with obvious satisfaction.

'And how long have you been pregnant?'

'Almost twenty weeks.'

As if rocket-propelled, Mr Spencer-Soames sprang to his feet and addressed the judge directly. 'My Lord, a point of law has arisen.'

Then, all at once, and with no explanation, the usher began leading the jury out of the court. Anthony watched in bafflement as the twelve members gathered up their possessions before being herded out of the room. What in God's name was going on?

Hoping for elucidation, he focused his attention on the judge, but all his Lordship said was, 'Mrs Beaumont, will you kindly wait outside.'

The minute she had left the court, Spencer-Soames pressed home his point. 'My Lord, I cannot see the relevance of the Prosecution's line of questioning. None of this has been disclosed to the defence and may prove highly prejudicial to the defendant.'

The judge did nothing more than look across at the Prosecution with a quizzical expression and then invite him to speak.

'Since Mrs Beaumont has confirmed that she is pregnant,' the Prosecution responded, 'it could be *more* prejudicial for the defendant were the jury to speculate about the father of her child.'

The judge cleared his throat, as if to give himself a moment's pause, before declaring: 'This evidence could clearly be relevant, not least to the motive for the attack on the deceased. The Defence needs time to consider this new fact, so the court should be adjourned for the police to take a witness statement.' And, with that, he swept out of the court.

Before Anthony could make sense of the adjournment, he was immediately handcuffed and escorted down the steep spiral stairs that led from the dock to the cells, a tangle of questions still tormenting his mind. How long would the court be adjourned? How soon could the police take a witness statement? Would he have to face another intolerable stretch of time in prison before proceedings resumed? Why had nobody explained the situation?

The answer was obvious. As a cold-blooded, callous murderer, he deserved no explanation.

CHAPTER 13

'I can't believe your trial's still dragging on.' Darren paused to shovel in some chicken curry, an unnaturally bright yellow concoction, with no trace of any chicken. 'I ain't seen you since last Saturday and you told me then the trial was stopped or something, but that was a whole week ago. You must be knackered, mate!'

Anthony nodded in assent 'But I haven't been neglecting you, Darren. There's simply no chance of seeing anyone when I leave so early in the morning and get back here so late.'

'I weren't complaining, mate. I were just worried about what's going on and how you feel and everything.'

Anthony tried to stop his elbow knocking into Darren's at the small uncomfortable table they were sharing. 'Well, it's a strain, I have to say. The adjournment itself lasted only a day, but now it's the jury that's holding things up. They've been out for five whole days, and twice they've asked for extra time, so obviously they're having trouble coming to a decision. There's probably one recalcitrant member who ...'

'What's recal ....?'

Although Darren stumbled over the word, Anthony took pride in his pupil's eagerness to widen his vocabulary. About to say "refractory", he settled for a more colloquial explanation, always on his guard not to make Darren feel inadequate.

'My barrister suspects,' he continued, 'that one of the twelve might be an out-and-out feminist – the sort who regard marriage as rape and hate all men's guts on principle. And, if that's the case, she may be taking the stance that, in order to conceive, my wife was perfectly entitled to have as many affairs as she chose. But if the other jury members strongly disagree, that would explain the long delay.'

'Shit! I'm glad I never had no jury. Every trial I been through were over and done with in less than fifteen minutes!'

'The trouble is, while they're arguing the toss, I'm cooped up in the basement cells for endless hours each day, with no idea what's going on, or how long the process will last.' The court itself might be daunting, but it was a haven of tranquillity compared with the bestial uproar of those cells, some of his fellow prisoners reminding him of Slasher in their howls of fury or screams of panic. And the long confinement gave him far too much time to think, as he replayed in his mind every detail of the trial: Deborah's brilliant handling of her cross-examination, which put his own inept performance to shame; the hideous memories sparked by the two police officers who had arrived on the day of the crime; the continual regurgitation of the evidence, each word hammering home his guilt despite the valiant efforts of his QC. Then the judge's summing up, which had seemed troublingly ambivalent, affording no clue as to how the jury might decide. And, worst of all, the unbearable suspense of awaiting their verdict, not knowing if he would become a lifer, like the many he had seen here – so habituated to prison they probably couldn't function in any other environment. Some had missing teeth, or scars, or broken bones, testifying to their former years in some brutish Category A gaol.

'I wish you'd share this grub, mate.' Darren mopped his plate with a flabby slice of greyish-looking bread. 'Pardon me for saying, but you're beginning to look like one of them Belsen victims. And don't tell me you ain't hungry after that crappy tea we had – vegetarian sausage roll, for fuck sake!'

Yes, something of an oxymoron, Anthony reflected, and so utterly revolting he'd been tempted to flush it down the lavatory.

'I'm dead lucky to have this second tea and to have Eric as a mate. He's a servery-worker, see, so he can save me leftovers. Ricky never wants to eat twice of an evening – and, anyways, he's playing pool – so there's plenty here for you, Tony, if you've changed your mind.'

'Thanks, but no thanks.' The strong smell of spice curdling with the reek of Ricky's disinfectant was enough to turn his stomach and, anyway, the curry had been hanging around for the two or three hours since teatime and now looked cold and congealing. What he did appreciate however, was this chance to talk to Darren in the privacy of the latter's cell, rather than venturing out on the wing for Association with a gang of noisy inmates. Much to his surprise, when he was normally so reticent, he had found himself confiding to Darren even the most intimate matters of the trial, including his dud sperm.

'Did *you* want kids?' he asked now, keen to shift attention from his loss of appetite. Food like sleep, was a necessity of life, yet both eating and sleeping had become near-impossible.

'Yeah. Dozens! When you grow up in care, see, you have these dreams about big, happy families. I used to lay on me bed and imagine being dad to a whole football team of kids. But it didn't happen, did it? One of me girlfriends wouldn't have nothing more to do with me once I was banged up and another—' He broke off, as if the memories were too raw. 'And, to be honest, Tony, after all them years inside, I'd be rubbish as a dad. I mean, I've made a right mess of me life. Sometimes, I think I was *born* bad.'

'No one's born bad,' Darren.'

'Well, why did me mum piss off, then? And why was I in all them prisons up and down the country?'

'Well, as far as your mother's concerned, she had problems with drugs, you said, so the fact she left was nothing to do with you. And, as for prison, you got off to a bad start, with everything stacked against you. I'm not saying you didn't do wrong, but none of it was basically your fault.' He winced as Darren removed a piece of gristle from his mouth. His own vegetarian sausage roll had also contained a few choice morsels of gristle, along with lumps of cold potato. 'In fact, in my opinion you've done jolly well to survive at all, without succumbing to drugs, like your mother, or making illegal hooch in your cell, like those guys you were telling me about. And you're holding down a job here and—'

'Only a crap job in the laundry.'

'Don't keep belittling yourself. Clean clothes are important, Darren. When I last got clean sheets, it definitely lifted my spirits a bit, and how often can we say that in here?'

Darren leaned across the table and gave him an awkward pat on the arm. 'D'you realise, Tony, you're the only person who's ever seen me good points, and that means a hell of a lot. I never had no dad, see, never had no one who'd sit me down and say, "Listen, son, let's work this out together." But you've helped me with a load of stuff. And though you're really posh, mate, you don't look down on me or nothing.'

Anthony forbore to say that, in his former life, he wouldn't have given Darren so much as the time of day. Indeed, he had never mixed socially with anyone who earned less than fifty grand a year – not that such well-heeled acquaintances had ever become his intimates. Friendship for him had always taken second place to ambition, achievement and constant competition with his peers, which made it essential to conceal any hint of weakness or vulnerability. Even at school, his parents had vetted his friends, discouraging any who failed to reach their own exacting standards. So his unburdening to Darren, and the bond developing between them, was totally unprecedented.

It also made him increasingly aware of how he had accepted it as his natural right to be born to great prosperity and privilege. While Darren was learning how to break into shops, to nick a few porn mags or sherbet-dabs, he was being taught Latin, Greek and French, higher calculus, and the refinements of classical tragedy at a school that cost thirty grand a year. And, far from being "born bad", to use Darren's distressing phrase, he had been presented with a model of goodness almost from the cradle, encouraged to develop every civic and moral virtue and to strive for perfection in every area of life. He had been miserable at school, however, on account of the constant pressure from top-flight academic staff and single-minded housemasters – whose overriding aim was to make every boy excel – which had often left him longing to be simply left alone, to indulge in idle daydreaming. And his parents, of course, had added to the strain, his father in particular insisting on non-stop effort and success, loving him, apparently, only when he was "good".

And they hadn't changed their stance, it seemed, since they were still fielding his phone calls and ignoring his letters, presumably on the grounds that no son of theirs could possibly be contacting them from prison. And, as for Deborah's parents, along with all Craig's family, they would regard him as irredeemably evil, although his conversations with Darren had left him increasingly unsure what goodness or badness meant – perhaps basically a matter of genes or circumstances, in the same way as good and bad luck.

'There's something I want to ask you, Tony.' Darren was now tackling a bowl of glutinous sludge that resembled wallpaper-paste – rice pudding, possibly. 'And I need you to be honest, mate. Okay?'

'Okay, I'll do my best.'

Darren paused, embarrassed, before finally blurting out, 'D'you think I could ever make it as a dad? See, I'd love to have a kid with Carol-Ann, but when I imagine settling down with her, me mind just goes a blank. Thing is, Tony, I've moved around so much these last ten or fifteen years – you know, from one nick to another, or someone's lousy sofa to another, I've never put down roots. And now I'm so screwed up, I feel I don't belong in prison or on the outside neither.'

'That's probably because you've never had a proper home.' Anthony felt far from qualified to advise anyone on parenthood. However, from what he'd gleaned from reading Carol-Ann's letters, she seemed reasonably loyal and loving and, anyway, it would be cruel to dash Darren's hopes. 'But maybe, with Carol-Ann, you *will* have a home, if you make a real effort to go straight this time. I'd strongly suggest, though, waiting a while before you have a kid. But,' he added, tentatively, 'if things go well between you, I can't see any reason why you shouldn't start over again.'

Easy to say that to Darren, but what about *his* life? Would *he* ever have the chance to start anew? He certainly shared Darren's sense of not belonging anywhere – neither in gaol, nor back at his job. Of course, he would be emphatically forbidden ever to set foot again at FFC, yet amidst all the other trauma, thoughts of work continued to torment him: uncompleted tasks; deadlines long passed; abandoned projects; indignant clients. Who had taken over his role? Were his colleagues still tittle-tattling, or had they chosen to draw a veil over his heinous act? What had happened with Oceanic?

Darren stirred a dollop of jam into his rice pudding, turning it a sickly pink. 'Well, she's certainly over the moon with them letters you wrote.'

'*We* wrote,' Anthony corrected. 'The last two you did almost on your own.'

'Only 'cause you told me what to say. I'd never have thought of all them romantic things meself.'

He could hardly tell Darren that, in each and every letter, he had been addressing Deborah, along with Carol-Ann – a totally futile exercise in the present situation. His wife's air of confident radiance at the trial had showed him a steely side of her he had never even suspected. She appeared to be coping perfectly well, despite the horror of her lover's death, whereas *he* was still assailed by grotesque images of Craig's bumptious sperm exploding into her: shooting into her cervix, racing up to her womb, dashing along her fallopian tubes with sheer, brazen insolence. It was obvious she had no further need or use for him, yet the prospect of a divorce was unutterably painful and would, of course, bring more worrying expense when his legal-aid bill was already proving a burden. And, from all he'd heard, divorce courts were extremely hard on men, invariably favouring wives over husbands and dunning the latter for every penny they possessed.

Darren washed down his pudding with a can of Coke. 'When we write the next letter, Tony, d'you think we should ask her straight out how she feels about having kids?'

'No, probably best to save that for after your release. As I said, try to concentrate on *her* first and build up a strong relationship.' However crap he might be as counsellor, Anthony felt a certain pleasure in the role, if only because it proved that someone needed him. And, if nothing else, the literacy lessons would certainly be beneficial for any children Darren might go on to have.

'Bang-up!' an officer bawled, from outside the open door. Everyone back to their cells.'

'We'll discuss it later, Darren, Okay?' Anthony rose slowly to his feet, reluctant to leave this clean, tidy, unthreatening space, and return to the unpredictable Slasher. The guy had started blackmailing him with threats of violence if he didn't shell out money for drugs, apparently believing his cellmate had piles of ready cash just waiting to be used to purchase smack.

'Wait a second, mate.' Darren went over to his locker, bringing out a small toy cat, its black fur worn thin in places and one green glass eye missing. 'It's me lucky mascot, Tony,' he said, pushing it into Anthony's hand. 'I had it when I first went into care. Okay, it didn't work that good for me, but it may help you through your trial, mate. So good luck for tomorrow, Tony – or however long the whole thing lasts. I'll be thinking of you, mate.'

'Thanks,' Anthony said, tersely. Now *he* was the one struggling to find adequate words. This limp, thin, balding cat was hardly likely to bring him luck, but the fact that Darren had entrusted it to him was ridiculously consoling.

CHAPTER 14

As Anthony was led into the dock of an entirely different courtroom to the one he'd been in every day, so far, he felt instantly disorientated. This room was larger and more modern, and its new, confusing layout meant his barristers were sitting in a different part of the court and seemed much further away. Betty, for her part, was no longer within smiling distance – not that he felt like smiling. Indeed, knowing at any moment the jury would pronounce their verdict, he was screwed to breaking-point. He already feared the worst, even wondered if this change of courtroom might be an unlucky omen.

Such superstitious nonsense must be due to Darren and, shameful to admit, he had actually stuffed the lucky-cat mascot into the pocket of his suit this morning and only removed it because of the unsightly bulge it made. Was he losing his basic common sense and reason, cracking up completely?

He continued to glance around the court, in a bid to get his bearings, his gaze moving from the jury box to the public gallery above. In the previous courtroom, he'd been unable to see the gallery without turning round in his seat – and had deliberately never done so for fear of spotting prurient voyeurs. Here, however, it was in full, unavoidable view and all at once, to his horror, he suddenly noticed Piers, his former boss at FFC, sitting right in the front row. What in God's name was he doing here, away from work on weekday morning? Had he come to gloat or jeer, or out of sadistic curiosity to discover more about the useless colleague who had dumped him in the shit with Oceanic, maybe hoping that the pest would be convicted as a murderer? But why did he give a damn what Piers thought when Piers belonged in the past and it was his whole future that was at stake?

'All rise!'

Anthony's attention was jolted back to the proceedings as the judge entered the court, followed closely by the jury. He could hardly bear to look at that motley crew of twelve now his fate lay in their hands, and was aware that he was shivering, noticeably and violently. This courtroom was air-conditioned and distinctly on the chilly side, in contrast to the previous one, but his tremulous state was in no way due to the cold.

Once the twelve had settled themselves and stowed away their bags, the Clerk of the Court swivelled round to face him and commanded, in a ringing voice, 'Will the defendant please stand.'

As Anthony rose to his feet a second time, it required a determined effort to keep still. Lava-streams of heat seemed to be searing through his body, conflicting with the shudders of Arctic cold.

'Will the foreman please stand,' the clerk requested next, now turning to face the jury.

The elderly Asian struggled to his feet – the man who had fallen asleep in the course of the trial, not just once but three times. Why, Anthony agonised, should the jury choose a foreman who had clearly missed much of the proceedings?

'Please restrict yourself,' the clerk instructed the fellow, 'to answering my question yes or no. Have you reached a verdict on which you all agree?'

At the foreman's guttural 'Yes', Anthony's hot-and-cold sensations intensified so greatly, it was as if he were in an ice-box and a sauna both at once.

A hush fell on the court as the clerk proceeded to ask, 'Do you find the defendant, Anthony Christopher Beaumont, guilty or not guilty of murder?'

Time had slowed for Anthony to an extraordinary degree, hours crawling and lumbering past, before the foreman replied, 'Not guilty.'

'And is that the verdict of you all?' the clerk continued.

'Yes.'

'Thank you. Please sit down.'

As the Asian obeyed, the judge said, in a kindly tone, 'You, too, may sit, Mr Beaumont.'

Anthony reeled back into his seat. He couldn't take in what he'd heard, couldn't even believe it. Surely, if it were true, he would be feeling overpowering relief, a tide of soaring gratitude. He'd been spared a life-sentence, spared the stigma of being branded a murderer until he, too, went to the grave. His barristers must be delighted, Betty overjoyed, yet *he* was more concerned with his physical sensations – the racing heart, the dizzy, spaced-out feeling clouding his whole mind. The only relief he felt was at being safely seated, which meant he wouldn't keel over in a faint and thus disgrace himself in front of the whole court – in front of Piers, for God's sake.

He was distracted by the noise of someone entering the court – an unknown woman with a baby in her arms and two small boys, barely more than three or four years old, clinging to her skirt. Once they were seated, the Prosecution rose to his feet and, having acknowledged them with a smile, then addressed the judge. 'I have a statement from the victim's widow, Mrs Hazel Stefanelli, which I now intend to read out.'

As Anthony stared at the small, pale, scraggy woman, with her limp, fairish hair and face devoid of make-up, his jealousy and fury suddenly reignited. No wonder Craig had found Deborah a turn-on – her stunning figure and dark, dramatic colouring so much more alluring than this pallid wraith of a wife. And no wonder Deborah had chosen Craig as a sperm-donor, when he had fathered three children on Hazel within a mere five years or less.

But why was he giving way to jealous rage, when he should be rejoicing in the all-important verdict? He feared he must be heading for a breakdown, unable to feel any normal emotion, unable to control the turbulent state of his body, or to concentrate on Mrs Stefanelli's statement. The Prosecution's boomingly confident voice seemed unsettlingly at odds with the woman's own shrinking self-consciousness, as she tried to shield her boys from the scrutiny of the court, the smaller one hiding his face in her lap.

'Craig was the sole breadwinner, so, since his death, it's been a constant struggle to make ends meet, however much I scrimp and save. I can't take a job myself, because my youngest is only six months' old and the boys aren't yet at school. But the financial problems are only part of it – the emotional ones are infinitely worse. I've scarcely slept a wink these last four-and-a-half months, on account of the shock and grief. And Tim and Toby have been really badly affected. Tim's started wetting the bed again, and Toby has these dreadful nightmares and wakes screaming with terror night after night.'

Anthony craved to hide his face, as the younger boy was doing, block his ears, refuse to listen, refuse to accept any guilt or responsibility for these four shattered lives. Yet, he knew, from Darren, that the absence of a father could affect a child profoundly and long-term. Darren's cellmate, Ricky, had also grown up fatherless and, according to Darren, was still bitter about the havoc it had wrought throughout his life.

'They're too young to understand *how* their father died,' the Prosecution continued, with again that jarring mismatch between his self-assured voice and the simple, colloquial words written by the widow herself. 'But when they're old enough to ask, I'm already worried sick about what to say and how on earth I can explain adultery and murder. You see, despite his lapse, I still love Craig to bits and would hate to damn him in the children's eyes. In fact, every night I pray to God to bring my husband back – only to realise every night what a futile prayer that is.'

As the Prosecution concluded, Spencer-Soames sprang to his feet and embarked on a Plea of Mitigation. 'Mr Beaumont has lost his wife, his job, his home, his former status and unblemished reputation, and will henceforward be regarded with abhorrence in society. Thus he has already been punished severely, as well as already serving four-and-a-half months in custody. It should count in his favour that he pleaded guilty to manslaughter at the earliest opportunity, accepted blame and responsibility right from the ...'

Anthony had to remind himself that it was *him* the QC was discussing, not some fictional character. His frightening sense of disassociation made him feel he was watching a play – a passive spectator rather than the lynchpin of the trial. Yet every word now spoken was of overwhelming import in that it could well reduce his sentence. He should be feeling triumph that, whatever else transpired, he had undoubtedly been spared a life-sentence, so why was he more focused on the fact that *any* sentence seemed totally unbearable? The answer was obvious: because he lacked the resilience to return to that oppressive gaol, to give up all autonomy again, all hope of normal existence.

'Mr Beaumont, please stand,' the judge instructed.

He could hardly believe that his body was still functioning, or how his shaky legs could support him, when his mind was in such turmoil.

The judge removed his glasses and rubbed his eyes a second. 'I've listened closely to what your barrister has said. You are a man of previously impeccable character and you accepted your guilt at a very early stage, as Mr Spencer-Soames has pointed out. I give you full credit for that and also for the fact that, in the course of your trial, you have made it obvious that you deeply regret your actions and have expressed true sorrow and remorse ...'

All at once, Anthony seemed to return to his full faculties, even dared to hope. The judge was sounding positive, taking a stance quite different from the condemnatory one he'd both dreaded and expected. Clearly, his Lordship had been persuaded by the QC's favourable words, so there was actually a fairish chance the might consider four-and-a-half months in custody to be sufficient punishment for an unpremeditated crime. Indeed, "crime" was the wrong word. In Darren's terminology, what had happened was simply an extremely unlucky turn of events.

As if echoing his thoughts, the judge asserted, genially, 'This offence was basically an unfortunate accident. You are *not* an evil or violent man, Mr Beaumont. In fact, you are someone held in high esteem by your associates and neighbours.'

Anthony experienced a surge of new strength flowing into his body, as if he'd had a blood-transfusion. He felt himself stand straighter, shoulders no longer slumped. He might walk from this court a free man, find a new job, a new flat.

The judge paused a second, to make a slight adjustment to his wig. 'However,' he continued, his tone noticeably more sombre, 'there can be no denying, Mr Beaumont, that you have taken a man's life and done so in a fit of jealous rage, thus depriving a woman of her breadwinner and leaving three young children fatherless. Mr Stefanelli was innocent, yet he has forfeited his life. Mrs Stefanelli has lost her husband, as well as her financial and emotional security. And her baby daughter and two young sons have lost not just their father but all hope of a normal family life.'

Anthony's new spark of hope fizzled out like a firework, the former fleeting burst of light and colour now an empty, blackened shell.

'You alone, Mr Beaumont, are responsible for this family's trauma, and, in the interests of justice, you must be punished for it. You will go to prison for forty months, reduced from sixty months, on account of your guilty plea.'

Anthony felt himself sway on his feet, the whole court blurring before his eyes into a grey and ghostly wasteland, as the judge pronounced his final, fateful words:

'Take him down.'

PART TWO - 29th August 2013

CHAPTER 15

'Beaumont, are you up?'

Miss Naylor, his favourite officer, opened his cell door. She was not only plump and pretty, she always got his name right.

'We'll be moving you as soon as we've got the remand prisoners off to the Bailey. So strip your bed and pack your things and I'll be back around 9.30am, okay?'

'I've already packed,' he told her, glancing at his "luggage": one large plastic bag, stamped HMP, and barely three-quarters full. It was hard to believe that his life had been reduced to these few pathetic possessions, compared with the vast array he had previously owned. Even his school trunk had always burst at the seams with expensive paraphernalia.

As Miss Naylor left, locking him in again, his mind flashed back to the designer cases he and Deborah had crammed with beachwear, sportswear, eveningwear and all the latest "must-have" gadgets, when packing for some exotic holiday.

He kept vowing not to think of his wife but, with her baby due in less than a fortnight, that was more or less impossible. She would be huge by now, flaunting her smug belly and newly voluptuous breasts. For all he knew, she might have already given birth. Due-dates were notoriously unreliable and, in any case, babies could be premature. He pictured her cradling the new-born infant, a mother at last, fulfilled and self-sufficient. He knew from talking to fellow prisoners that the bond between a mother and child could be the strongest of all possible ties, surpassing that between spouses and lovers. But, he wondered, bitterly, who had helped her through her labour – some dashing young creative she had shacked up with in the last few months, who was bound to be creative in the sack, far more thrillingly imaginative than her stolidly dull accountant husband.

He yanked off his clammy bed-sheets and the one thin, grubby blanket with unnecessary force, kicking at the tangled heap of bedding, only to slump down at the table, aware of his own futility. Instead of taking out his fury on the bed, he should be making an effort to do normal, calming things to try to reduce the stress of his imminent transfer to Elmley. So, mindfully and slowly, he opened his breakfast-pack and tipped the cereal into his smeary plastic bowl. Cooked breakfasts at Wandsworth had recently been stopped – no real loss, considering the bullet-hard eggs and grease-soaked fried bread. Not that the alternative was much better: one flabby bread roll and a tiny sachet of cornflakes or powdered oats, both tasting like pappy cardboard.

As he ate his flakes, he ran through the pros and cons of the move, as he had been doing for the last twenty-four hours, when they had first sprung the news on him. The greatest loss would be this single cell, a larger cell on a quieter wing, which meant he could eat and sleep in comparative peace, with no violence, ranting tirades or blaring television. He would also lose his job as junior toilet-cleaner – hardly high-end employment, but at least it earned him a wage and got him out of his cell. On the other hand, he might secure a better job at Elmley, in the library, perhaps, or even as a healthcare orderly. And, from all he'd heard, Elmley was a definite advance on Wandsworth – less chaotic and with fewer disruptive remand prisoners.

He jumped at a shout through the door. 'It's Troy, mate – just come to say goodbye.'

Troy had taken Darren's place as pupil, after Darren's release, a month earlier. The two men weren't that dissimilar, having both grown up in care and both missed out on education.

'Thanks for all you've done,' Troy added. 'I'm going to miss our lessons.'

'Well, write to me at Elmley,' Anthony shouted back, detesting the humiliation of being caged up like an animal and forced to communicate in this barbarous fashion. 'I promise to reply.'

'But I'm still rubbish at writing, Tone, so my letters will be full of mistakes.'

'Don't worry. I can correct the mistakes on the page, if you like, and send them back to you, so we can continue the lessons long-distance.'

'Ta, mate – sounds great!'

It was far from pure altruism on his part, more a question of his basic sanity. If he didn't have a project, he knew he couldn't endure the aching stretch of prison life still in front of him, but be tempted simply to cut his throat and be done with it.

'Bye then and good luck!'

Anthony returned to his breakfast, opening the minuscule carton of strawberry-jam-that-had-never-seen-a-strawberry and spreading it on his roll. It was pointless to waste any more time weighing up the pros and cons of his transfer when he had no say in the matter. Here, he did what he was told, with no vestige of control.

But, he wondered suddenly, had he *ever* had control? From the moment he was born, his parents had mapped out his life: the "right" schools, the "right" hobbies, the "right" Cambridge college (Trinity), the "right" career and colleagues. Sometimes, as a boy, he had dared mention his desire to sail round the world, or train as an actor, or join the SAS, but his father – one of the most prestigious fund-managers in the City – had immediately cracked down on such notions as woolly-headed and impractical and, instead, steered him into a safe, high-status career. Even his wife had been chosen for him. Deborah, the well-born, highly educated daughter of his mother's closest friend, was considered far more suitable than the flaky girl he happened to be in love with. Why, he fumed, ripping off a piece of roll, had he never rebelled, never questioned his parents' values or insisted on striking out on his own, but had passively allowed them to suppress his natural instincts and all his spontaneity, even the chance of genuine leisure? "Play" for them meant competitive sports: winning and achieving, making them proud – again. And, since his letters were still unanswered and his phone messages ignored, presumably they had cut him off irrevocably, now that he could no longer reflect credit on them, but only shame and stigma.

Abandoning his breakfast, he rummaged in the HMP bag for Darren's letters, the two sent since his release. Darren didn't see him as a failure and a disappointment, but as a brilliant teacher and faithful friend.

"Hello Antheny, hows things? Im alrite – no, Im more than alrite becos I feel a different person now. Im not a bricktop no more, but someone who can read and rite. Ive pined yor letters to the wall, so I feel yor watching over me ..."

The thought, however sentimental, did contain some truth. He wrote to Darren every other day, feeling an inexplicable urge to act as some sort of mentor and try, long-distance, to keep his "mate" out of temptation and help him change his life. The letters themselves he saw as a positive sign, since paper, envelopes and stamps would all eat into the meagre wage Darren was paid for his part-time, low-grade job. Nonetheless, Darren must consider it worthwhile. The paper was cheap and flimsy, the spelling still atrocious, and, at this very moment, Anthony ached to give him some spelling lessons, maybe even tackle apostrophes, but knew he mustn't go too fast and risk wrecking his pupil's new, shaky self-belief.

The second letter had arrived only yesterday and given him real pleasure.

"Grate news Tony! Ive moved in with Carol-Ann. Probashun had to chek her out and ask her loads of questions, like did she have another feller who might cut up ruff if I was there. Bloody cheek – of course she dont! Anyway, Im saving up me pennys, so I can bring her on a visit. I cant wait for you to see her, mate!"

Darren's "pennys" were unlikely to cover the long, expensive journey to the Isle of Sheppey, so his natural inclination was to write back straight away and say he'd finance the trip for the pair of them. Fortunately, his prison account was far less pitiful since, way back in mid-May, he'd finally re-established contact with his bank. Indeed, his finances were more healthy altogether because he no longer had to pay a crippling rent. He had also cancelled his iPhone contract, although not for financial reasons – the cost was chickenfeed – but because it was patently futile to pay for a phone he couldn't use. The accumulating unanswered emails continued to worry him, but they were a minor anxiety compared with the burden of his hefty legal-aid contributions and the constant uncertainty about how he would earn a living in the future, let alone fork out for what was bound to be a punitively expensive divorce.

Again, he forced his thoughts from Deborah and back to Darren's letter, although with his transport arriving any second, he resisted the urge of embarking on a reply. Wiser to spend the last few minutes trying to quell his agitation. In his present nervous state, *any* move seemed threatening – not just all the upheaval, but his fears about a new regime. At least he knew his way around here, had made some friends and started going to the gym and library. But ahead lay … what? … nothing but a dark ocean of uncertainty.

*

'Sorry, Beaumont, but there's been a bit of a delay with your transport.'

'A bit of a delay' was a major understatement. Miss Naylor had said 9.30am and it was now past noon, and he had been hanging around for hours in this stuffy, airless cell, with no word until this moment about any possible hitch. He held his peace, however, having learned the hard way not to alienate the officers, and especially not Miss Naylor. Females were thin on the ground and he derived a secret thrill just looking at her breasts.

'It should be here by 1.30pm, but not before, I'm afraid. Still, you're just about in time for dinner, so if you'd like to go and grab some food …'

As he followed her out on the wing, they both stopped in their tracks at the sight of a sallow, swarthy man repeatedly banging his forehead against the concrete wall, with alarming force and impact. Miss Naylor swiftly radioed for help and, the minute a second officer arrived, the pair of them rushed over to restrain him, but not before Anthony had glimpsed the man's anguished expression and bruised and bloodied face. The intense late-August heat seemed to have galvanised the self-harmers. Just last week, a lad of barely twenty had cut off his own finger, and prisoner-on-prisoner attacks seemed to increase by the day. Maybe Elmley would be a good move, in that respect, at least. Because Wandsworth was notorious for its violence, he lived in a state of constant jumpy apprehension whenever he ventured out of his cell.

Indeed, he made his way to the servery with his usual extreme caution, on his guard to spot the thugs and bullies before they could target him, although no one approached him, in point of fact, except easy-going Mark, a man on a fraud charge, to whom he'd been giving financial advice.

'Anthony, I thought you'd gone!'

Anthony explained the postponement, falling into step beside him.

'Bad luck for you, but, selfishly, I'm glad, because I could I do with a few more ideas about sources of venture capital. I'm pretty sure my new project could succeed, so long as I have backers.'

Now that word had got around about Anthony's skills, several other prisoners had been asking him for business tips, or ways to pay less tax, or generally sort out their finances. Frankly, he was glad to be some use and, as he and Mark queued for lunch, he drew on his long experience to advise the younger man. The busier he was, the less prone to panic and despair.

Returning to his cell with his baguette, he was aware how much he'd miss Mark, a highly intelligent entrepreneur he could talk to as an equal, and the only inmate who ever used his full name, Anthony. However, he still kept up his guard with him, because, like all those he consorted with, Mark had no knowledge of his specific offence. He'd been hoping, since his trial, that if the manslaughter conviction did somehow leak out, people would assume he'd been done for drunk-driving or involvement in a pub brawl, both far less open to prurient speculation than having knocked off his wife's lover.

Having booted Craig from his mind, he ate as quickly as he could, so as to finish before his transport arrived. Ham or cheese baguettes were now the standard lunch fare, hot dinners having gone the way of cooked breakfasts. As he chewed the tough and tasteless bread, he wondered if all prison food would soon end up as the cold picnic type, if only to save money – not that they'd been over-spending even on the former regime of three hot meals a day. He'd been informed by Mohammed, a lifer who worked in the kitchen, that the total daily cost of feeding each prisoner was only £1.90 – roughly half the price of a cup of coffee in Starbucks.

One-thirty came and went with no sign of his transport and, even when another hour had crawled by and Miss Naylor opened his door again, it was only to announce a further delay. Deliberately, he detained her, craving a bit of company and some distraction from his ever-circling thoughts.

'That guy we saw, Miss Naylor, banging his head – is he okay?'

'Yes, he was taken straight to hospital and, frankly, he's better off there. His English is so basic, I reckon he feels very much alone.'

His own sense of isolation was bad enough, so how much worse for these hopeless, hapless foreigners. Despite the overcrowding and the swarms of people everywhere, there were so few inmates he felt any sort of bond with, which is why he would miss Mark so much and – even more so – Darren. The latter's lucky-cat mascot was still his secret companion, although he was forced to keep it well hidden to avoid being taunted or even attacked for being seen with a toy.

'Don't you sometimes fear for your own safety, Miss Naylor?' he dared to ask, emboldened by the fact she seemed willing to chat for a minute.

'You bet! I've seen it all in my time. Two years ago, I was punched to the ground and had to have eleven stitches in my arm. And a colleague of mine was kicked in the head and was off sick for a good six months. I've known officers suffer broken legs, broken ribs, concussion – you name it! And most of us have had excrement flung in our faces.'

'But how do you stay so ... so *sane*?'

Her only reply was a laugh. 'Sorry, Beaumont, I have to dash. But I promise to be back the minute I hear about your transport.'

He mused on her courage during the next long, frustrating wait, unable to comprehend why anyone should choose so dangerous and ill-paid a job. As time ticked on, however, he became increasingly dispirited, his usual resentment at having no phone, or being unable to enquire what the hell was going on, rising to an infuriating pitch. The deprivation seemed all the more unfair in that Darren's claim that many prisoners did, in fact, have mobiles, despite the prohibition, had been confirmed by several dozen other inmates. Mark had even told him that some notorious gangsters used their phones to mastermind highly complex criminal networks from within their cells, in light of which the official ban on email and the internet seemed all the more futile, if not antediluvian. While the rest of the world had gone digital, the prison system remained locked in the age of the quill pen, regardless of the financial cost and blatant inefficiency of such obscurantism.

He began pacing up and down, but the cramped dimensions of his cell allowed him little scope to work off his annoyance. Had they forgotten him altogether, he wondered, or collected the wrong prisoner by mistake? Either was quite possible in this inept establishment.

In fact, it wasn't till 4.40pm that he heard the sound of a key in the lock and an officer appeared, not Miss Naylor, who presumably had gone off-duty by now, but the shifty little Mancunian, Mr Peters.

'Sorry, Beaufort, your transport's been cancelled.'

'Cancelled, sir? But why?'

'Could be any number of reasons,' Peters gave a casual shrug.

'So will I be going tomorrow, sir, or some other day this week?'

'Couldn't say.' A second shrug. 'And no point speculating. Just unpack your things, Beaufort, and re-make your bed – and do it double-quick.'

'Okay, sir,' he said, silently seething at this whole wasted, stressful day. No way was it okay, but, whatever else he had learned here in the last few months, it was how to hold his tongue.

CHAPTER 16

'I like the snazzy haircut,' Doug remarked, emerging from the neighbouring cell. 'Off to breakfast at the Ritz – again?'

'I'm off to clean the lavatories.' Anthony's riposte was sharp, the Ritz joke having worn thin long ago.

'Come off it, mate! Hair gel and a restyle just to clean the bleeding bogs?'

'Well, if you really want to know, my wife's visiting this afternoon.' Since the visit would soon be common knowledge, given the general nosiness and gossip, why bother to conceal it?

'I thought you never had no visits.'

'Not many.' The last thing Anthony wanted was any prying questions. Deborah's letter to him, requesting a visit, had been shock enough in itself, still more the news she intended to bring the baby with her: Jonathan Henry Charles, born six weeks ago. Why, he agonised, should the hapless infant have to meet the man who had killed his father? The only possible reason, he'd concluded, was that she had decided to flaunt her status as a single mother and dun him for more money in the divorce. Applying for a Visiting Order had proved quite a rigmarole and, during the long, frustrating process, he'd kept hoping she would change her mind. And, when told by the Booked Visits team that he had to supply full details not just of his wife but also of the baby, including its birth certificate, his anxiety and guilt redoubled. Deborah was instructed to send the certificate directly to the prison, so he had no idea whom she had named on it as father – Craig, or some other feckless bloke? Or had she simply left the space a blank? And while he waited an age for the visit to be officially approved, his apprehension mounted by the day.

'Well, if your missus ain't been before, I hope you've warned her she'll be searched – and I mean the whole bleeding Colditz rigmarole – sniffer dogs, metal detectors, mouth inspection, probes beneath her tongue ...'

'Sorry, Doug, must dash, or I'll be late for my job!'

His job was crucial, not just for the wage and his new status as an Enhanced Prisoner, which itself brought certain privileges, but because simple physical tasks helped calm the churning maelstrom of his mind. Indeed, he attacked the first toilet-bowl with the greatest application, trying to shift his thoughts from Deborah to the step-by-step procedure they had taught him on the Induction Course. It had struck him at the time as ludicrously over-detailed: "*Take the Harpic in your left hand and take the long-handled brush in your right hand. Using circular movements of the brush, scrub in a clockwise direction, sprinkling more Harpic with each...*" Now, however, he welcomed the precise instructions set out in the cleaning manual – Bible-thick and complete with coloured diagrams – since, again it proved a useful form of distraction. Even his usual disgust at having to scrape encrusted faeces from the bowl hardly registered today, with the ordeal of having to see Deborah's fatherless and illegitimate child.

A chunky, dark-skinned man suddenly breezed in to the shower-room. 'Hi!' he said. 'I'm Manuel. One of my mates on B-wing told me he always comes over to piss in *your* bogs, because they're the cleanest in the effing gaff. So I thought I'd give 'em a try, as a change from our filthy dirty ones.'

'Help yourself,' Anthony said, pleased he was doing something right. On the first day of the Induction Course, the Welsh screw, Bryn Llewellyn, had taunted, 'I don't expect you ever saw a mop at Eton. They're for cleaning floors, Beaufort, not for leaning on.'

Although he had told them ad infinitum that he hadn't been to Eton, they clearly preferred to believe it and, anyway, how could he make a case for not being a "toff", when the Pembridge fees were even higher than the Eton ones and the school equally prestigious? What he must never, ever admit to anyone was that in the entire course of his life he had never cleaned a lavatory or, indeed, done any sort of housework. At school, at home and even in his adult life with Deborah, there had always been "menials" to take care of all the chores and only now did the word "menials" give him pause for thought. If he used it in this environment, he would be resented even more – and with reason, he had to concede.

'Yeah, five-star bogs, no question,' Manuel quipped, as he sauntered out, still zipping up his flies.

Anthony tackled the next toilet-bowl with the same perfectionist zeal. There were a dozen in all, along with twelve showers and twelve urinals, twenty wash-basins and all the floors, the latter often puddled with urine – or worse. But, however stomach-turning the job, and however shocking his descent from high-paid director to skivvy earning nine pounds a week, he nonetheless gave thanks for his employment. If nothing else, it would keep him busy until he had to face his wife this afternoon – or should he say his *ex*-wife?

*

'Table fourteen, Beaumont. And keep facing the front. If you turn your head and look round, we may be forced to terminate the visit.'

'Right, sir,' Anthony said, although all he wanted at this moment was just such a termination. The main Visits Hall was daunting, with the usual ubiquitous CCTV and the rows and rows of tables packed close together, each with four chairs – a red chair for the prisoner, most now occupied, and three blue ones for the visitors, all empty as yet. The atmosphere was electric – prisoners visibly on edge; officers ready to swoop on the slightest infringement of the rules – the tension increasing still further as the first visitors came in.

Anthony gripped the edge of the table, which was bolted to his chair, with a gap between prisoner and visitor, to prevent the passing of any contraband. He glanced nervously around – difficult without turning his head – at the crowd of women and children swarming through the door, an exotic species from the outside world, with their casual chatter and colourful clothes. Unable to see Deborah in the crush, he watched enviously as other wives and girlfriends darted over to their prisoner-relatives and eagerly embraced them. He had not the slightest notion of how he should greet Deborah – with a smile, a snarl, a hang-dog expression?

But where *was* she, for God's sake? Almost all the blue chairs were now occupied and the prisoner at the table directly in front of him was already deep in conversation with an attractive red-head and two small girls.

He shifted in his seat, uncomfortably aware of the scrutiny from the bald and burly officer positioned on a raised platform only yards away. Perhaps the baby had been taken ill, or there'd been some problem with Deborah's transport…

He continued to survey the hall, attempting to check every dark-haired woman, in case, unsure of her bearings, she had made for the wrong table. Maybe she had come and gone, unable to cope with her first experience of a gaol, or perhaps she had simply failed to recognise him from the far end of this cavernous room. His hair looked different, for one thing, with its fancy cut and uncharacteristic gel, and the humiliating tabard all prisoners were obliged to wear for visits was a far cry from the stylish clothes she was used to seeing him in. All his efforts to appear presentable had been kyboshed at a stroke when forced to put on that grubby scarlet "bib". And the aftershave he'd ordered from Canteen not only smelled unpleasant, but had cost £4.99 – admittedly a piddling sum compared with his usual brand, but more than half of what he earned for a whole week's graft in the shower-rooms. If Deborah had decided not to come, he could have saved the money for a jar of decent coffee and, far more importantly, saved himself a whole insomniac night.

Then, all at once, he spotted her, weaving her way to his table, at this very moment, with a bundle in her arms. He stared in shock at her haggard face and dark-circled eyes, an unnerving, startling contrast to the radiant Deborah of the trial. She looked older altogether and, although dressed in her usual elegant fashion, her silk blouse was stained with baby-sick and slobber. All he could see of the baby was a thatch of thick black hair, dark against the white froth of the shawl – *Craig's* hair, *Craig's* colouring.

Tongue-tied, he rose to greet her, formally and awkwardly, as if they were strangers to each other – true, in one sense, as both their lives had been utterly transformed since the first week of December: she now a mother; he a convicted prisoner. There was no need for him to speak, however, because she herself launched into a furious rant, her voice rising in distress.

'Anthony, I can't *believe* how I've been treated here! You'd think I was a criminal myself, what with their brutish little officers ordering me about and subjecting me to metal detectors – and worse. There's no part of my anatomy they haven't poked and prodded, and this really savage-looking sniffer-dog crouched slavering at my feet, as if I had a stash of heroin secreted in my bra. But the most appalling thing of all was they put Jonathan through an X-ray machine! That's an outrage, don't you think? I mean, for all I know, it may have done him some permanent damage. Then his nappy had to be taken off and searched, and they handled him so roughly it was all I could do not to march straight out and dash off a formal letter of complaint to the Governor.'

Clearly Doug had been right about the Colditz measures, which, indeed, he had experienced himself: his crotch frisked, his anus examined and a whole raft of other mortifying procedures before being permitted to enter this hall. However, as he was about to sympathise, Deborah sank down at the table and resumed her tirade.

'And I've been hanging around for literally hours. The system's totally useless, with long delays at every stage, first on the prison steps, where we were all herded together like refugees, then a long queue for checking in and an even longer queue to be searched. And, before I was actually called, I waited so bloody long, Jonathan started screaming with hunger and I had to give him his bottle. They told me I could leave him in the crèche, but God knows what would have happened to him there! The noise in the Visitors' Centre was quite unbearable – other babies yelling their heads off, children bashing each other or fighting over toys, visitors shouting at officers, officers bellowing back—'

Suddenly, she burst into tears, two officers watching closely, alert for any trouble. 'I'm sorry, Anthony,' she sobbed, 'it's not just today – these last nine months have been indescribably *awful*. My whole pregnancy was a nightmare. I had this really dreadful nausea. I don't mean just morning sickness, but violent vomiting, throwing up every ten minutes, night and day, almost until my due-date. I couldn't move from the loo, couldn't do a single thing except puke. I lost a huge amount of weight and couldn't even drink water without throwing it up straight away. In fact, several times they admitted me to hospital and put me on a drip.'

Horrified, he stammered, 'B-but,' you looked so *well* at the trial, absolutely glowing with health.'

'Oh, that was simply make-up – concealer, foundation, rouge, blusher – the whole damn works. I've been staying with my parents all this time, and Mummy insisted I shouldn't appear at the trial looking so frightfully ill. In fact, I only managed to make it to the court at all because the doctor put me on steroids. Anthony, you can't imagine how miraculous they were! I could actually go out and function fairly normally, at least for a few days. I begged the doctor to let me stay on them for the rest of the pregnancy, but he refused point-blank, in case they harmed the baby.

I have to confess at that point I was desperate – as most women *are* with this condition. I heard of one poor soul who vomited so violently she ruptured her oesophagus and had to be rushed to A&E. And some women actually choose to terminate their pregnancies rather than endure another day of throwing up.'

He couldn't take it in. He had imagined her delighting in her pregnancy, blooming and burgeoning with health, as expectant mothers often seemed to do, and with energy to spare for some new, young, dashing lover.

'And the labour itself was unspeakable – thirty-five hours of excruciating pain. I was left alone for great long stretches and, frankly, scared to death. You see, because I'd been so ill, I hadn't had a chance to do pre-natal exercises or prepare in any way whatever.'

'But surely there was someone with you?' he asked. He had pictured an adoring birth-attendant – Deborah's new hands-on man, competent, devoted, totally unfazed by blood or pain, and without his own secret dread of having to be part of such an intimate, if not lurid, process.

'Well, Mummy was meant to be there, of course, and I have to say she's been a tower of strength. She just couldn't have done more, but, would you believe, she developed a severe bronchial infection the very day before the birth. She was ill for a good month, so obviously she couldn't help with the baby and I had to ring an agency and try to get hold of a nanny at short notice. The girl they sent was useless and …' She paused for breath, interrupting herself by switching subjects. '… and then, on top of everything else, I went down with mastitis, and my boobs are still so sore and inflamed, there's no way I can breastfeed Jonathan.'

As if on cue, Jonathan started wailing, until Deborah shoved a dummy in his mouth – a dummy, for heaven's sake – something they had both abhorred in their innocent pre-baby days, and vowed they would never use for any child of theirs. However, it not only calmed the infant, it seemed to pacify his wife as well.

'Forgive me moaning on like this,' she said, in a far less frantic tone of voice, even managing a weak smile. 'I haven't asked you how *you* are, which is unforgivable. And to be perfectly honest, you don't look good at all. You've lost a huge amount of weight. And what's that awful rash on your face?'

He shrugged. 'Prison's not exactly a health-spa! The food is total crap, to start with, and there's so little fresh air or exercise.'

'I'm sorry, Anthony. It must be totally ghastly, yet here I am making things worse still. I never intended to offload like this. In fact, I was determined to be calm, just give you a brief account of all I've been through, introduce you to Jonathan and ...' Again, she broke off, this time to mop a trail of baby-dribble from her blouse. 'But the last two hours drove me almost insane. I just don't know how you bear it, darling.'

The 'darling' was a shock. Had it slipped out from force of habit, or did she still feel something for him?

'I mean, the whole place is so grim and dirty and totally unwelcoming. Of course, I had no idea what to expect, but nothing as ... as uncouth as this.'

'You get used to it,' he lied, refusing to admit the extremes of desolation he experienced so often. Rather than dwell on his mortifying privations, he contented himself with telling her the bare minimum.

'But don't you find the disorganisation utterly frustrating? I mean, when I first decided to visit, I tried to phone, to check out the procedure, and had to hang on for simply hours. I was passed from pillar to post, yet no one even bothered to be civil, let alone try to help. Then they put me on hold for literally forty-two minutes – I timed it on my watch – but, after all that waste of time, I was suddenly cut off. I can hardly credit how downright inefficient the whole system seems to be.'

Anthony's attention was still on her second sentence: '... when I first decided to visit'. But *why* she'd decided to visit was still far from clear. The tirade he'd been expecting had been directed not at him, but at the prison, and she hadn't yet broached the subject of divorce, nor even shown any traces of hostility. Perhaps she was so shattered by her experiences today, she had lost track of what she had come for. Yet, now that she had got things off her chest, she still made no attempt to return to her agenda. In fact, she seemed totally exhausted, slumped in her seat and trying to soothe the grizzling infant on her lap.

The silence grew oppressive, as if, again, they were two strangers, desperately trying to find topics of conversation. The people around them, in contrast, were all chatting away, and children in the play-area laughing, fighting, arguing. There were other noises, too: the thud of feet or click-clack of heels as visitors went to the snack-bar, to fetch drinks or crisps or chocolate. All this evidence of normality made him feel still more isolated and, despite the stress of the situation, he was also troublingly aware of his own long-suppressed sexuality. Deborah might look tired and worn but, with her curvaceous figure and fuller breasts, she continued to be frustratingly desirable. In this prison setting, however, his lustful itch for her was totally inappropriate, so, ignoring it, he forced himself to speak.

'I, er, wondered, Deborah, about your plans for the … the future.'

'Well, the first thing I need to do,' she said, seeming relieved he had broken the silence, 'is move out from my parents' place. It really isn't fair on them for me to stay there any longer. Mummy's at her wits' end. She hasn't really recovered from her bronchial thing, yet the minute she was out of bed, she began helping me with Jonathan, even doing most of the night-feeds, bless her heart. And that's pretty decent, don't you think? I mean, considering he's Craig child and the whole business of his conception, she could have been incredibly judgmental or even washed her hands of me, yet she's a really devoted grandma. But, as well as all her other problems, she's very worried about *your* mother.'

'*My* mother?' he asked, mystified.

Deborah paused a moment, biting her lip and frowning. 'Actually she didn't want me to tell you, but I insisted you had to know.'

'Know what? I'm sorry, but I've no idea what you're talking about.' He noticed she was avoiding his eyes, as *he* was avoiding looking at the baby. His first brief glance had been more than enough, arousing a potent cocktail of pity, shame, guilt and distaste.

Another hesitation, before she suddenly blurted out, 'I'm afraid to say she has pancreatic cancer.'

He stared at her in shock and disbelief. His mother had always been remarkably healthy, still worked full-time at the age of sixty-seven, even filled her so-called leisure hours with a dozen different exemplary pursuits. 'Cancer?' he echoed. 'Surely not? And why on earth wouldn't she want to tell me?'

'It's not exactly easy trying to communicate with prisoners,' Deborah retorted, sharply.

'Come off it, Deborah! She could have written me a letter, or left a message with the Governor. And, anyway, I've been trying to contact *her* ever since I first arrived here. She never answered my letters, though, or picked up when I—'

'Look, you don't know half of it!' Deborah interrupted 'When you first landed up in custody, both your parents were paralysed with shock. They simply didn't know what to do – whether to support you or, frankly, let you stew. As you know very well, your father isn't brilliant when it comes to emotional matters, so he left the decision to your mother, who agonised for simply ages. And that took a tremendous toll on her health. All the years I've known her, I've never seen her in such a state. She wasn't eating or sleeping and she even resigned from her job. She couldn't concentrate on work, you see, so she felt it wasn't fair to carry on. But, with all that spare time on her hands, she only worried *more*. And it wasn't only you, it was me, as well, of course – the fact I was pregnant with—'

She broke off, swallowed her words, quickly skated over whatever she had meant to say. 'That was another great shock, especially for someone like your mother, who's so high-minded. And, since she's always been very fond of me, she must have felt terribly torn. In fact, I wouldn't be surprised if all that stress is the reason she got cancer.'

He couldn't take it in. The mother he knew was always in control, invariably decisive and on top of situations, never prone to fear or worry. Thus he'd assumed it had been an easy decision for his parents simply to cut him off once he had disgraced them. 'So when was the cancer diagnosed?' he asked.

'A couple of months ago.' Deborah jiggled the increasingly fractious baby on her lap. 'She became seriously ill with what at first we thought was jaundice, lost masses of weight and felt terribly weak and tired. She kept saying it was nothing, but when she finally agreed to have tests and scans and things, they found she had stage-three cancer, which was a complete bolt from the blue for us as well as her. The doctor didn't want to operate. Apparently, the surgery is risky and he didn't think she was fit enough to withstand it. But he started her on chemo, which he said would help relieve the symptoms and might possibly shrink the cancer.'

'So what's the … the prognosis?' he hardly dared to ask, noting that ominous 'possibly'.

'Not good.'

A sudden chill went through his body, despite the fug of the room. As a child, he had regarded both his parents as immortal and, even now, his mother seemed imperishable, an ineradicable presence towering over his life.

'Unfortunately, when she was first diagnosed, I was so ill myself I couldn't do a thing to help, but Mummy was quite wonderful. She supported Cecilia through the chemo sessions and kept an eye on your father and cooked for him and made sure he was okay. I've visited several times myself now, which was jolly awkward at first – you know, because of the whole Craig thing – but, actually, we mostly talk about *you*, which appears to be her main concern. I've been insisting you should know about her illness, but she wouldn't hear of it until just last week; said she didn't want to make things even worse for you when you already had so much on your plate.'

He fidgeted in the uncomfortably cramped seat. His mother's new concern for him, her strong desire to protect him, still struck him as out of character. But perhaps it wasn't new. Had he always been so obsessed with himself he had never really known her?

'Beaumont, keep facing the front!' the screw nearest to him bawled.

He was embarrassed to be so rudely rebuked in public – and for nothing more than moving his head a fraction – but Deborah took no notice, absorbed as she was in the saga of his mother.

'In one way, though, the cancer's freed her, if only in that she's been forced to focus on herself, just to get through the demanding treatments. However, *my* mother says she's still extremely anxious and keeps bringing the subject back to you, even when she can barely get the words out. She's in a hospice now, you see, and heavily sedated. And, as for your poor father, I'm not sure he can cope with losing his wife as well as his son.'

'He hasn't lost me,' he struggled to say, although aware of his shaming ignorance of all his mother's suffering, not to mention Deborah's, so fixated on his own ordeal, he had spared little time for them, except to bridle at their imagined displeasure. 'Is there anything I can do?' he offered.

'Hardly,' she said, tartly. 'Not from prison. And, anyway, we need to discuss the whole situation – you know, what happens to your father if Cecelia doesn't … pull through – but it's such a big subject we don't really have the time now. I'll come back, of course, when you're allowed another visit, but on this occasion there's something else we have to talk about – the reason I'm here, in fact.'

Still reeling from shock, he felt unable to deal with yet more unwelcome news. And it didn't help having to discuss such intimate matters in a crowded public place, with eagle-eyed officers watching his every move, and the baby a constant source of guilt and distress. It was whimpering now, pathetically – a desolate sound that seemed to express the horror of its conception.

Deborah did her best to settle it more comfortably, plugging it into its dummy again and rocking it on her lap. 'You asked about my future,' she said, 'and that's the very thing we need to address. You see, I'd planned to return to work once I'd recovered from the birth and all those months and months of vomiting. But, to be perfectly honest, I was unprepared for what having a baby actually means – the constant crying and broken nights and the huge responsibility of caring for such a tiny scrap. And I have to admit Jonathan wasn't the only one howling. I kept bursting into tears myself, on account of the stupidest things. I suppose it was post-natal depression, and I'm not over it even now. Most of my friends aren't mothers, so they can't really understand and, anyway, they're far too busy to help. I envy them in a way – you know, their total involvement in work. Compared with them, I feel almost downgraded, with no targets to meet or campaigns to plan and no high-status job– no job at all, except baby-minder and bottle-washer. And, of course, *they're* still slim and stylish, whereas I'm having to come to terms with my leaking breasts and bulgy stomach. So, all things considered, it's becoming increasingly obvious that I need to change my life. And, since I'm determined to give Mummy a break, I'll have to find a new flat and sort out all my stuff and get my brain into gear for when I go back to work. The problem is I'm not sure I can cope with all that stress at once.'

He tried to drag his thoughts from his mother's possible demise and focus on his wife. 'Couldn't you get another nanny – a decent one, this time?'

'Oh, it's so much hassle, Anthony, interviewing candidates and taking up their references. And, even then, you can't be sure the girl will be any damned use. But …' Again, she paused, this time looking noticeably awkward, '… I've had another idea. It may sound … well, peculiar, but it came to me quite recently, now I'm seeing much more of your parents and realising how strong their marriage is. Even with all this going on, they're totally there for each other and utterly supportive and I though how fantastic it would be to have that sort of mutual understanding and to live in peace, rather than full of anger and resentment. My parents are the same, of course, but it struck me only the only the other day what a huge achievement it is to clock up thirty or forty years together, and not give up and opt for divorce, as so many of our age-group do.'

He gazed at her, confounded. Wasn't *she* about to press for a divorce?

As if answering him, she continued, 'Don't get me wrong, Anthony. I was determined on divorce right up until Jonathan was born. I felt utter fury towards you, if you really want to know, and the only reason I didn't start proceedings months and months ago was that I was too damned ill to stir from my sick-bed, let alone start consulting lawyers. But then something happened that I really can't explain. Maybe it's due to motherhood, but there are other factors, too, like your father's terrible grief at the prospect of facing life on his own, or even Mummy's sheer decency and kindness. Those things set me thinking and I started remembering all the good things about our marriage and realising (spelled with an s) what a waste it would be to chuck away everything we had together. And I've even began to see that what happened to Craig was more an unfortunate accident than deliberate murder on your part.'

'For pity's sake!' he exclaimed, barely able to credit her admission. 'At the trial you insisted it was murder, and that's what dumped me in the shit. If you'd only taken your present stance, you could have spared me all this ghastly time in prison, rather than ruining my whole—'

He stopped in mid-sentence, as an officer darted over to the adjoining table, where a prisoner was leaning across to kiss his wife.

'What's going on?' Deborah whispered as another two screws joined the first one and a noisy altercation broke out.

'That's the way drugs can be passed,' Anthony whispered back, 'from mouth to mouth. And drugs are absolutely rife here, despite all their efforts to crack down.'

An uneasy silence was rippling out from the area as other prisoners and visitors sat staring at the couple and clearly trying to eavesdrop, despite the efforts of the staff going from table to table, encouraging people to ignore the incident and continue with their visits. However, most eyes were still riveted on the woman as she was escorted off the scene, and on the guilty prisoner, marched out of the hall by a second officer – to the Segregation Unit, from what Anthony had overheard.

Deborah was looking distinctly chastened, as if fearing a similar expulsion. And, when she finally spoke again, it was still in a low murmur. 'Anthony, I want you to know, before we discuss things any further, that I'm desperately sorry about what you've had to go through. I vaguely imagined that prison was like boarding school, but just this one short visit has shown me how naïve that was.'

'Well,' he shrugged, 'both systems have a strict timetable and very little self-determination.' In point of fact, school had afforded even less freedom than gaol, in that every hour was programmed with brain-expanding lessons or purposeful activities. The overwhelming difference, though, was that his Pembridge contemporaries had been top-drawer and highly intelligent, with not a foul-mouthed duffer in sight. And the staff had been exceptionally well-qualified, in contrast to prison officers, who did a laughably inadequate six-week training.

'Things have been grim for both of us, darling,' Deborah continued, in a conciliatory tone. 'But that doesn't mean we can't start again. In fact, that's my new idea – we'll find a flat for the three of us and, once we've settled in and got things straight, I can go back to my job. I mean, now you have a prison record, you're highly unlikely to get any sort of work, whereas I can earn enough to keep us in some style while you stay at home and look after Jonathan.'

'Deborah, you're out of your mind!' Did she really think an apology and another inappropriate 'darling' could make him accept such a preposterous idea? 'How the hell can I look after a child whose father I've killed? Every minute I spent with him would bring back appalling memories, not to mention intolerable guilt. And what in God's name do we tell him when he's old enough to find out about Craig?'

'He doesn't need to find out.'

'And you really think we could keep it from him, when so many other people know and when it's been the subject of a public court case?' Perhaps his wife was suffering not merely from post-natal depression but from full-blown post-natal psychosis. 'Suppose Hazel's children decide they want to contact their half-brother when they're older?'

Deborah frowned for a moment, as if such basic problems had simply not occurred to her. Then her face relaxed. 'That's okay,' she said, 'we'll go abroad. I can probably get a transfer to one of Maddison Carruthers' branches overseas, then we can start a completely new life in New York or Dubai or wherever.'

'Of course we can't! You're forgetting you're on Facebook and Twitter. However far you go these days, social media can always track you down.'

'We'll have to change our names, then.'

Had his wife gone stark staring mad? Next, she'd be suggesting they change their entire appearance, undergo plastic surgery and total body re-shaping. Besides, she was missing the point. 'Look, wherever we go, we'll still be living with a child who's bound to ask questions at some point.'

'Why should he, if we pass you off as his father?'

'That's out of the question. I won't stand for such deception.'

'Well, in that case, we'll have to tell him we used a sperm-donor. I did actually put that on his birth certificate, and the people who do use donors normally explain to the child at some point, so it's not really a big deal. The clinics even give clients guidance as to what to say and when.'

'He's bound to find out about Craig when he's older and then he'll loathe and detest me and our precarious "family" will simply fall apart. And, anyway, I don't want to be a house-husband. You seem to be writing off my chances of any sort of role beyond that of nursery-maid.'

'Anthony you're kidding yourself if you really think you can get a decent job, least of all in finance, when you're legally obliged to tell any potential employer about your criminal record.'

'And you're kidding yourself if you imagine I'd be content to piddle around at home changing nappies and preparing feeding bottles. You just talked about feeling downgraded, but what am *I* meant to feel when I'm stuck at home doing the chores while you return to your high-powered career and queen it over me?'

Another baby in the hall had started shrieking, the horrendous noise amplifying his own distress. And a little boy in the play-area was taunting a bigger child, the two indignant voices rising to a hurting pitch.

'That's totally unfair! We need money, Anthony, and I'm the only one who can earn it now.'

'Look here, Deborah, this whole discussion is not only ludicrous, it's completely theoretical. Perhaps it's slipped your mind, but I shan't be released till August next year. That's a good ten months away, so what do you intend to do between now and then, I'd like to know?'

'Ten months? Are you sure?'

Noting her crestfallen expression, he hoped the whole inane discussion could now be terminated as premature, impractical and a recipe for disaster. Clearly, she had lost her usual discernment; her "inspired" idea mere wishful thinking.

'I thought a prisoner like you would be released early automatically, for good behaviour or whatever they call it.'

'Well, you thought completely wrong. There's not a dog's chance of my getting out before then. And you're bound to change your mind in those ten months. In fact, I suspect your sudden transition from hating my guts to wanting to shack up with me will prove extremely short-lived. It's probably just a matter of your hormones.'

'Don't be so bloody patronising!' Her raised voice alarmed the baby, its former bleating cries now crescendoing to full-blown howls.

'Okay, that was unfair. But I suspect hormones play some part in it, combined with all the stress, of course. You've been telling me how awful these last months were – your pregnancy and labour, and my mother's cancer, and both our sets of parents having to come to terms with an illegitimate grandchild. And you said yourself you still had post-natal depression, which I assume makes it hard to think straight. Besides, the whole disruption of living with a baby must be a total shock, when neither of us has ever had to consider anyone but ourselves.'

'Yes, that's exactly it. There is someone else to consider now – an innocent, fatherless child. I'm offering you the chance to make up for your crime by coming back and being Jonathan's father.'

'For God's sake, Deborah. You just said it wasn't a crime, but an "unfortunate accident". And I'm not Jonathan's father and can't be in a million years!'

The baby's wails were now resounding through the room and the officer nearest them came striding over to investigate. 'Is everything all right between you two?

'Yes, fine,' Anthony muttered, praying that neither he nor Deborah would be ordered to leave the room before he'd finally convinced her that her fantasy of rose-tinted family harmony was totally irrational. However, the minute the officer had moved out of earshot, she returned to the attack.

'You owe *me* something, as well as Jonathan. You've probably conveniently forgotten, but I had to put up with a hell of a lot in the marriage. You were always so dominant, for one thing, and made all the important decisions. You chose our very first flat, remember, with barely any reference to me. It was right in the City, only minutes from your work, but bloody miles from mine. You even chose our honeymoon, for God's sake! You were so set on the Maldives, again you hardly bothered to consult me.'

'Deborah, that was eleven bloody years ago!'

'So what?'

'Well, if you intend going back a whole decade and more and start raking up every petty grievance since then, I can do the same and dredge up just as many grudges.'

'Okay, forget the early years. But your refusal to use a sperm-donor was another example of the way you overrule me. And yet none of this would have happened if you'd only—'

'I didn't refuse,' he cut in. 'But I have absolutely no intention of starting on that subject again. "If onlys" are quite pointless. It's what happens next that matters.'

'Which is exactly what I'm trying to address. I've come up with a solution which you won't so much as consider.'

'A solution for you, maybe – and a highly convenient one. You get your built-in nanny and go back to your high-status job and snazzy office, leaving me holding the baby – literally – with no prospect of any future at all.'

'But you haven't any future. You've blown it, Anthony, and at least I'm offering you the chance of a different sort of life, with no financial worries or—'

'I don't want that sort of life – being some sort of skivvy, wholly dependent on your largesse. Besides, how can I bring up a child when I feel nothing but distaste for it? If you really want to know, I'm not sure if I ever wanted children.'

'So you totally misled me' – Deborah's voice was icy – 'from the very first year we met?'

'No, at that stage, I knew nothing about kids.' He was so agitated he could feel his eyelids twitching, every muscle in his body taut. This visit was veering out of control, which was frightening in itself.

'Yet you agreed we'd start a family.'

'Well, yes, at some point,' he conceded, making a determined effort to moderate his voice. 'It just seemed the natural next step. But, from what I've seen since then, kids are hugely disruptive. Look at Thomas and Beth! Thomas confided to me once, in a rare unguarded moment, that life had never been the same since Alicia was born. Beth went completely off sex and continued to push him away for ages after the birth. And he found the baby a terrible strain and said he was constantly looking forward to the next stage being over and done with, whether it was breastfeeding, or the drag of Alicia sleeping in their bed and screaming half the night, or her tantrums or teething or bouts of colic. He told me he began counting the days until she started school; and now she *is* at school, he's probably looking forward to when she leaves home.'

'Anthony, I've never heard anything so totally negative!'

'I'm sorry, but the statistics bear me out. Marital happiness plunges way, way down once the kids are born and only climbs back again when they're grown up and out of your hair.'

'So all the time we were trying for a baby, you were simply stringing me along and never actually wanted one at all?'

'It's not as simple as that. In prison there's a huge amount of time to think and I've been reflecting on things I used to take for granted, like the sort of hothouse life we both led, where every step was laid down in an inevitable progression – first school, then university, then professional qualifications and a creditable career. Then marriage, promotion and eventually – yes – children, then *their* school and university, *their* careers and promotions, and *their* success, of course. Success was our watchword, the reason we put up with all the pressures and never had a minute to ourselves. But recently I've had a chance to reconsider the whole concept.'

Deborah would never understand how Darren's achievement in learning to read and write could actually be viewed as greater than his own Cambridge degree, given their relative advantages – or lack of them. And what about Miss Naylor? Her dangerous, uncongenial prison-officer job earned her only the tiniest fraction of what his former colleagues raked in, including those who arranged highly questionable tax-avoidance schemes. Although he dreaded the very thought of divorce, he couldn't escape the fact that he had moved beyond his wife, no longer shared her values, had started meeting completely different types of people and been forced to question all his suppositions. Besides, he wasn't ready to settle yet for any new way of life until he had rethought his whole existence. Whatever the horrors of prison, there were certain jolting advantages in being free from responsibilities, job pressures and family ties. The punishing hours he'd worked at FFC, and the firm's expectation that directors should be contactable more or less 24/7, now seemed a burden too far.

'The trouble with you, Anthony,' Deborah accused, unwrapping the overheated baby from its cocooning shawl, 'is that you're completely and utterly selfish. You imagine the world revolves round you and you alone.'

'So why the hell do you want me back, then' – his voice was rising again – 'if I'm so dominant and selfish and a total waste of space? Because you're desperate, that's why. You told me yourself you can't cope and that you envy your workmates and feel inferior. No wonder when you're on your own, with no job, no man, and a kid you can't handle and probably wish you'd never had.'

'How dare you say such a thing!'

His casual shrug disguised the extremes of turmoil he was feeling – including anger with himself. How unbelievably obtuse he'd been in assuming he could stay married without the damning presence of the baby. Yet only now had it occurred to him that he'd been clinging to a fantasy by removing the child from the equation – a repeat of his blind folly in not realising his wife might be pregnant as a result of her affair. In both instances, he had rearranged the facts to suit his own convenience, while accusing Deborah of doing much the same. Yet, with the baby only a couple of feet away, he could no longer deny its overwhelming reality.

Appalled at his misjudgement, he turned on Deborah again. 'You're only angry because it's true. Jonathan is obviously unhappy. He's been wailing and caterwauling ever since you first arrived. You only have to look at him to see how thoroughly miserable he is.' He forced himself to do just that, gazing at the infant's swollen scarlet face, the strings of spittle webbing its toothless mouth, the Craig-black hair stubbling its scalp – living proof of his wife's betrayal and of his own humiliation. Its eyes had disappeared into slits of screwed-up fury as its bellowing intensified and, suddenly, he, too, ignited in equal fury and frustration – fury not just at his blindness, but with the whole hopeless situation. 'Far from being the brat's father,' he yelled, springing to his feet, 'I never want to see him in my life again!'

'And I never want to see *you* again, you ungrateful, brutish, hypocritical shit!' Deborah also leapt up, turned on her heel and began stumbling and sobbing her way between the tables to the exit.

As one officer rushed to restrain her, another headed grimly towards his table.

'Right, that's your visit over, Beaumont! Stay here until I can get you taken back to the wing.'

'But can't I just go now, sir?'

'I said sit there! Are you deaf? You and your wife have already caused more than enough disturbance, so sit down and shut up!'

Wretchedly, he subsided in his seat, unwilling to watch other visitors enjoying their time together, nor to reflect further on his stupidity, prompted, as he saw now, by his horror of divorce. Had he really imagined that, if he and Deborah stayed together, she would put the child up for adoption, or offload it on to her mother, leaving the pair of them free of all entanglements, free of the terrible past? Yet, to be perfectly honest, that that was what he craved: a return to happy coupledom and some magical annihilation of not just the last eleven months, but all those wasted years trying for a baby and arguing about methods of conception. And, because of such delusion, he had lost all chance of a rapprochement and any hope of future visits which, from all he'd heard, could be the very lifeline that kept prisoners sane and grounded.

So should he have agreed to her idea, despite his overwhelming reservations? At least it would have secured him some sort of future – a place to live, security, cash to pay the bills – and, vastly more important, a return to an intelligent, beautiful partner who knew him through and through, and to the status and companionship of marriage?

Except it wouldn't be companionship. If the past was any guide, he would barely see his wife, once she had returned to her former twelve-hour working days and mega-levels of stress. Long ago, they had stopped sitting down to dinner together or going out for anything save work-related functions.

His mind continued frantically to search for other possible solutions. If he couldn't face moving in with her, perhaps he could continue to see her *minus* the baby, if only on an occasional basis. That way, he could salvage some part of their relationship – the intellectual and sexual, maybe. He couldn't deny how much he craved her body, even after her adultery and all the argument and aggravation. Or was he back in never-never land, imagining she would welcome his advances now they had parted as implacable foes?

He was aware of guilt seeping into his body, like some noxious virus. His wife had made him see not only his own faults – self-deception, dominance, complete and utter selfishness – but how many innocent lives his crime had affected: his mother's cancer; his father's impending widowhood; *her* parents faced with a grandchild whose father had been killed by their own son-in-law; and Deborah herself – ill, alone, vulnerable and sleepless. He had accused her of being desperate, but shouldn't he have shown her more compassion? The very fact he felt isolated and deflated, now that she had left, only proved the bond between them.

Head in his hands, he shut his eyes, lost in a fog of confusion, indecision. He had no idea what to think, whether he had taken the right line, or bungled the whole visit. One thing alone was clear: he would have to live with this racking uncertainty for the next ten poisonous months, since, as he had pointed out himself, he was trapped here till next August. There was still another Christmas to endure, another totally unfestive New Year's Eve, another mocking springtime, with nature budding and burgeoning outside, while his internal system registered bleak winter.

'Right, Beaumont, come with me. And look sharp about it, please!'

He opened his eyes, saw a podgy, bull-necked officer looming over him, and slowly lumbered to his feet.

'Step on it, I said! I haven't got all day.'

He had no choice but to be marched back to his cell – no longer his precious single cell, but one shared with a bed-wetting maniac, a repellent fellow, whose urine-soaked sheets stunk the place out, night and day. And, as they approached the cell door – and the all-pervasive stink – he let out a groan of utter desolation.

PART THREE - 22nd August 2014

CHAPTER 17

The glare, the heat, the sheer sense of space …

Anthony stopped a moment, just to take it in. The sky seemed vast, the world bigger altogether, the vista almost frighteningly untrammelled. And here, outside, on one of the hottest days of the summer, the sun beat down relentlessly, making all the colours brighter, sharper, overbearing.

Free. He rolled the word round his mouth like an expensive chocolate truffle, surprised at its bitter aftertaste. Having crossed off every snail-paced day till this long-awaited moment, why wasn't he feeling gloriously liberated, instead of strangely daunted by the absence of razor-wire-topped walls, barred gates and surly officers?

The barrage of farewells from earlier this morning was still replaying in his head:

'Chin up, Tony. You show 'em, mate!'

'Give her one for me, Tone!'

'Send us a postcard from Biarritz!'

'Give me love to Soho, mate.'

'Best of luck, Posho – and don't you dare come back!'

Ironic that, without those fellow inmates he had so often longed to escape, he felt isolated, denuded, now totally on his own and facing a future that had neither shape nor solidity. The guy in the adjoining cell, Abdallah, had also been released today and was returning to his wife and kids and to a familiar home and street. *His* new home, in contrast, was some tawdry bed and breakfast place in an unknown part of London, which Yasmine, the prison probation officer, had helped him book on her computer. The whole session had been such a rush, he'd had no chance to check the place online in any sort of detail, and doubted if it had much to recommend it except its name, The Haven. And even that "home" was provisional, since first it had to be vetted by another probation officer who worked in the specific area – a woman called Barbara Banks, who would be supervising his case during his twenty months on licence. But what if she *didn't* approve it? Would his bed be a sheet of cardboard in a doorway? He wasn't seeing her till four, which meant everything was uncertain for the next five hours or more and, with so much time to kill, the day stretched ahead alarmingly, without his usual strict timetable, or any purpose or activity.

At least he wasn't encumbered by heavy luggage. One black bin-bag, mercifully light, now constituted his entire worldly goods, since he had given away most of his prison stuff to his former mates still in custody. Even his designer suit was now Abdallah's property. The guy had been delighted, saying his missus wouldn't recognise him in such expensive gear. Frankly, he was glad to be rid of it, since the fabric seemed imprinted with horrendous memories of his crime and of the nerve-wracking court hearings, whereas, clad in his Mark & Spencer jeans, he was reminded of Betty's kindness. Remarkably, she had continued to stay in touch, sending him a brief note or card every couple of months, including one for this all-important day.

He dawdled down Alma Terrace, still not knowing what to do or where to go, yet anxiously aware of the many tasks ahead of him, including finding a new flat and job, retrieving all his former possessions from storage, visiting his recently widowed father and taking flowers to his mother's grave. He needed time to adjust, however, before tackling such big undertakings and emotionally draining obligations.

As he halted at a busier road, he was struck by the noise of the traffic – not just the stream of cars, but an ambulance with a shrieking siren, and a huge shuddering lorry clanking and rattling past. And the roar of a low-flying plane overhead added to the sense of a vigorous, impatient world, putting his own lassitude to shame. He was tired from nothing more than the complicated release procedures: a stack of forms to sign; countless prison departments to visit; and myriad check-out rituals to complete. Even getting out of the place had been a palaver in itself – the daunting succession of doors and gates to be unlocked, the long wait in the holding-cell while the screws did still more paperwork – before he was finally escorted to the main prison gate by, unpropitiously, the Welshman, Bryn Llewellyn, who had failed to soften towards him, unlike most of the other officers.

It was still not yet 11am, according to Darren's watch, which, cheap and basic as it was, he favoured above his Patek Philippe – returned today, along with all the other possessions removed at the police station, another lifetime ago. Strange as it might seem, Darren was now the nearest he had to a friend, and he and Carol-Ann had twice visited him in gaol, Darren touchingly proud of his improving literacy skills.

'I can read the *Sun* now, mate,' he'd confided, while Carol-Ann was queuing at the visitors' snack bar. 'Well, bits of it, at least. And I can tell you, Tony, I feel dead chuffed when people see me with a newspaper, like I'm a proper educated bloke!'

And he shared that pride himself, since, when he'd first started the postal learning-course, a year ago, after Darren's release, he'd secretly harboured doubts about his 'pupil's' cooperation. Yet Darren had never failed to send back each assignment for comment and corrections. So, he had vowed, there and then, while they were still sitting in the Visits Hall, that, once he had access to the shops, he would buy the lad some simple but beguiling books, in the hope of weaning him off the *Sun* onto more nourishing reading matter. However, books would have to wait until he had bought more crucial items – an up-to-date Oyster card and a new iPhone to replace his old one. Although the latter had been returned by the prison, the battery was dead and the contract long since terminated, and, without a phone and a travel-pass, he was seriously adrift.

Indeed, crossing the street when the green light showed, he felt like a foreigner in London, recently arrived from some remote, outlandish region, with different customs and a more feral race of men. So, seeing an expanse of green ahead on the other side of the road, he decided to hide away there until he found the courage for formidable tasks like braving the shops, or facing the noise and exposure of the tube. Besides, any green space was welcome on this sweltering day, as was the chance to savour those now exotic rarities – trees, grass, flowers and birds.

He quickened his pace, as he set off down the path, only to realise that his access was barred by a long stretch of black metal railings. Prison bars and railings were too similar for comfort, yet, when he came upon an open stretch of parkland, his relief was tempered by the same ridiculous dread of being unsupervised and unconfined. This was Wandsworth Common, presumably, and already fairly crowded, although it was hard to match the mood of indulgent enjoyment that befitted the start of the late-August Bank Holiday weekend. Half-naked bodies glistening with sun-oil were reclining on the grass, couples kissing and entwined, children kicking balls around, families picnicking in happy little groups, a manic dog tearing round in circles, as if to express its sheer joy in life.

For his part, he remained in the shelter of the trees, not only to evade the fierce stare of the sun, but from a natural instinct to conceal himself, now that the word "CRIMINAL" was branded on his forehead, marking him out as a dangerous man to be avoided and excoriated. He had come to see that the biggest difference between people wasn't class, wealth, or privilege, but whether one was good or "evil"- to use the word favoured by Darren's *Sun*. Once, he had regarded such evildoers as an entirely different species, as remote from him as was a Rolls Royce from a clapped-out bike. How cringe-worthily condescending that view seemed, now that he personally had joined the clapped-out-bike brigade and, like them, would need to suppress his shameful past for the remainder of his life. Not easy when he was legally obliged to disclose his conviction to any potential employers.

It was Yasmine who had spelled that out, along with the many other restrictions as to where and how he could live post-gaol, and the other galling curbs on his so-called freedom, galloping through the information with the same inefficient haste as when booking his accommodation. He was meant to have seen her three months ago, instead of just two days, but that earlier session had been unaccountably cancelled, and thus she'd had an inordinate amount of ground to cover in one brief window of time, and a mere forty-eight hours before his release. There was an upside, however, in that at such short notice, all the probation hostels were full – a lucky escape judging by Darren's tales of such places, with their strict 10pm curfews, unsympathetic staff, bans on all booze, and distressingly high number of junkies and psychotics.

Once he'd explained to Yasmine that he had no friends or relatives to stay with (his father too grief-stricken and real friends in short supply), she seemed concerned about his apparent homelessness. But that very concern, combined with sheer pressure of time, had probably worked in his favour, since she had acceded with little opposition to his request for lodgings in the Seven Sisters area. Although he had never set foot there, he remembered Darren saying that he had liked it best of the many places he'd touched down in when homeless and forced to sofa-surf. As far as *he* was concerned, however, the important thing was its postcode, suitably far away from his former haunts. No way could he return to

Marylebone, since gossip would have spread and people were bound to point the finger at this murderer in their midst. Even more impossible to set foot in the City and run the risk of encountering FFC employees, who would look askance at the savage brute who had dishonoured the prestigious firm. None of his former colleagues lived as far out as N17, so it would definitely be safer. Even the thought of encountering Piers or Thomas just as he was emerging from the probation office suffused him with a surge of shame.

Yet, even if he moved to John O'Groats, he couldn't escape the sense of his own guilt. Indeed, as he passed a mother sitting on a bench with her three children, he was inexorably reminded of Hazel's shattered life. He moved hastily past them, only to come upon a bikini-clad girl, her skin a glistening golden-brown, her voluptuous curves on display. Never before, had he been so aware of women – another unknown species for the last twenty months, apart from the few female screws, who, with the exception of Miss Naylor, were plain and unappealing. However, gorgeous girls were now everywhere, revealing expanses of bare flesh, in their shorts, crop-tops and tantalising miniskirts. In gaol, he had tried his best to suppress his sex-drive and, although such restraint was no longer necessary, the urge itself was clearly redundant when there seemed little hope of future relationships. Any sort of intimacy would, sooner or later, involve confession of his crime and, since he had never been the type for one-night stands, he was probably doomed to perpetual celibacy.

Seeking distraction from such thoughts, he watched two squirrels shinning up a tree-trunk with enviable agility, and a raggedy black crow raucously crowing on a bench, as if claiming possession of its perch. Then, having passed a thicket of smaller trees and brambly undergrowth, he reached a junction of paths and, seeing a pond ahead of him rippling in the sunlight, crossed the grass towards it. Two smugly magnificent swans were gliding serenely along, flatfooted geese paddling in the shallows, coots diving down and popping back up in jerky little bursts of black and white. Most were in pairs, he noticed, as most humans were in families or couples. It was beginning to dawn on him, with increasing desolation, that not only would he fail to find another mate, but he would remain a permanent outsider and pariah.

'For God's sake, count your blessings,' he muttered. Most newly released prisoners had none of his resources – certainly not the wherewithal to pay for a B&B and, later, shell out a month's rent in advance for a reasonably salubrious flat. As far as he could gather, most left prison with little cash beyond the standard discharge grant of £46, and thus found life outside infinitely more difficult. Bits and pieces of their tragic tales, lodged now in his mind indelibly, should provide the perfect antidote to self-pity: those buggered in their children's homes, yet forced to put up with it to avoid a beating; those on heroin by age thirteen and homeless at sixteen, joining gangs and dealing drugs in a bid to gain respect. One guy he remembered in particular who said, by the time he was released, his six-month-old daughter would have kids of her own – maybe even grand-kids, all of whom would be total strangers to him.

His former ignorance of existences like those was now a source of shame, as was his failure to see that inequality extended far beyond wealth and privilege to genes, brain-cells, health, environment and life-chances. If *he* had been born on a sink-estate, to a druggie mother and an absentee father, and forced to join a gang for any sense of belonging and security, he, too, might have ended up as a serial offender. He had assumed, with blinkered arrogance, that what he hadn't personally experienced was either unimportant or non-existent.

Suddenly, he tensed. *Deborah!* Standing with her back to him on the other side of the pond. Even from this distance, he recognised her elegant hairstyle, swept up in a chignon, her slender figure outlined by her clingy summer dress. He stood in an agony of indecision, debating whether to approach her or not, torn between a deep longing for some contact and a very real fear of rebuff. She had remained implacably out of touch since her prison visit ten months ago, so he had no idea what she was thinking, where she was living and whether she had decided on divorce. But, if the latter, why had she left it so long before instructing her solicitor to apprise him of the fact? She had even failed to inform him of his mother's death in April, although she would have known full-well how much the news would distress him. It was his father who had written – a brief, grief-stricken letter, giving details of the funeral and saying he hoped the prison would permit him to attend.

Coward that he was, he hadn't attended, unable to face the prospect of seeing his all-powerful mother crammed into a coffin. Yet such dereliction of duty had induced tremendous guilt, so wasn't this the perfect chance to apologise to Deborah and hope she would convey his remorse to his father?

Nervously he ventured round the pond, skirting past a man with his young son, the two dark heads bent towards the water as the child threw bread for the ducks while the father looked on dotingly. Did his own lack of interest in being a father mean something was basically wrong with him, or was it more a fear of failure – an unthinkable word in his family? Yet failure seemed worryingly probable when so much was expected of a contemporary dad: to be present at a brutal, bloody birth; to take paternity leave and risk letting down his boss; to get up at night and do his fair share of the feeds, solely responsible for a tiny, vulnerable infant, who might choke or shriek or vomit.

Disturbed by his obvious inadequacies, he hurried on, along a boardwalk, where he temporarily lost sight of the far side of the pond. Suppose Deborah had already gone and he had missed this one felicitous chance? He began to run full pelt until the vista opened up again and he could see the elegant figure once more. But, as he drew closer, he realised, with a pang, that it wasn't his wife at all. Whatever the problems between them, and however hurtful her criticisms, it was still all but unendurable for his wife of nearly a dozen years to have become a missing person. Yet how stupid to imagine she would be wandering alone on Wandsworth Common, of all places. She would have found a nanny by now and returned to her former job and, from what he knew of Maddison Carruthers, they were highly unlikely to give her the Friday off, even at the start of a Bank Holiday weekend. He could see her in his mind, closeted in her office with some hunk of a fellow employee, who, oozing sex from every pore, was already ogling her cleavage, even daring to run his hands up her long, tanned, shapely legs, creeping disgustingly closer to …

He strode away from the pond in a fury – fury more with himself than with the fictitious lover. Why the hell was he being so self-punishing and negative on the day he had awaited with such fierce anticipation? Okay, there were problems, but at least he was no longer confined in a cramped and dingy cell, eating yet another stale baguette with an uncongenial cellmate, or having to clean shit-encrusted toilets. Instead, he actually had the chance, for once, to enjoy the simple things he had missed for the last twenty months. There would be hassle enough with probation this afternoon, so, until then, couldn't he just bloody well relax?

Deliberately slowing his pace to a leisurely stroll, he took his time finding a suitably secluded spot, then, lying back on the grass, he closed his eyes and allowed the beneficent sun to paint a little healthy colour onto his prison-pasty skin.

CHAPTER 18

He strode down Landsdowne Road from the Probation Office with a growing sense of dejection, as he tried to absorb all that Barbara Banks had told him. The woman had proved disconcertingly different from the worthy, dowdy, inefficient Yasmine, being a brisk, tough-minded character, smartly dressed and following a well-organised agenda. True, she had repeated the whole rigmarole of probing personal questions already put to him by Yasmine, about his lifestyle, attitudes, relationships (nil), and the likelihood of him re-offending (also nil, since nothing would induce him to risk another stint in gaol), and had also spelled out all the Licence Conditions again. What she had particularly stressed, though, was that his obligation to disclose his offence when applying for a job would be operative for a full ten years and, for any job involving key financial responsibility, it would remain in place for the rest of his life. Ten years was bad enough – he'd be fifty-one by then, almost ready for the scrapheap – but, if he had harboured any dreams of returning to the world of corporate finance, they had been shattered at a stroke. Barbara had actually used the phrase "going from hero to zero", since there was little chance, it seemed, of any but the most menial kind of jobs. Indeed, many employers would reject him even for those, regarding him as over-qualified, unlikely to knuckle down to lowly tasks or mix easily with run-of-the-mill employees.

He kicked out at a loose paving-stone, displacing his resentment. It struck him as, frankly, demeaning to have to sign up at a Job Centre and book an appointment with an Education, Training and Employment Officer, for pity's sake! He had completed his education twenty years ago, then trained at one of the most prestigious accountancy firms worldwide, yet Barbara appeared singularly unimpressed by either his Cambridge degree or his former high position, and suggested only servile jobs, such as barman, waiter or shop-assistant. Admittedly, toilet-cleaner was even more lowly, but prison jobs were *sui generis* and, once released, he had hoped for something more challenging. Besides, all Barbara's suggestions involved the public and thus ran counter to his instinctive desire to hide himself away. If someone he knew happened to swan in for a coffee at his new place of work, he would die with shame at being seen mopping greasy tables, or clad in a long white apron, rushing to and fro with cappuccinos.

He paused a moment, only now aware of his surroundings. He was in some featureless no-man's-land, strangely silent and totally deserted, despite the serried rows of red-brick terraced houses, interspersed with cheap and ugly council flats. It was as if the whole street had been evacuated and he was the only person left. But, as he turned on to the High Road, he was jolted by the contrast: streams of double-decker buses swooshing and panting past, groups of kids shouting and fighting in the street, swarthy men hollering to each other from the doorways of their open-fronted displays of fruit and vegetables. The rows of houses were now replaced by rows of dingy shops and unhygienic-looking cafés offering jerk-chicken or kebabs at knock-down prices. Everyone looked poor: obese and down-at-heel women munching bags of chips, as they waddled along, sweating in the heat; doddery old men on sticks; another man bent double by the load of dirty sacking on his back; tarty young girls in fake leopard skin and equally fake bling. The shops themselves reflected the same poverty: pawnshops; betting shops; run-down charity shops; some boarded up and covered in graffiti. The entire area seemed alien and, despite the press of people, he still felt achingly alone.

He'd been surprised to learn from Barbara that this was Tottenham, not Seven Sisters, although she appeared to think there was no great difference between the two. Yet surely the notorious Tottenham riots put the place in a different category – those savage eruptions of violence that had monopolised the news in 1985 and again in 2011. So, when Barbara pointed out The Haven on the map, he was alarmed to see it was less than half a mile from the infamous Broadwater Farm Estate. But, since she had officially vetted the place on his behalf, he had no choice but to head there, although he resolved to buy some food first. Apparently, The Haven had no dining room, and provided only a basic breakfast-pack. Certainly, he didn't fancy any of these local low-grade cafés and had no desire to eat in public, anyway, so probably best to eat his meals in his room.

He trudged on down the High Road, in search of a supermarket, unable to stop his mind from swooping back to elegant, villagey Marylebone, with its air of privileged wealth – a world away from this blighted urban sprawl. Indeed, noticing a fabrics stall selling nylon sheets priced at £1.99 each he recalled the exquisitely tasteful boutique where Deborah had always bought her bedlinen – hand-embroidered Egyptian cotton, costing a cool £200 a pair. The contrasts were everywhere: the shabby café he was passing, its grimy window plastered with special offers – egg and chips, £1.50, all-day breakfast, £3.50; the City restaurants where he had wined and dined important clients, boasted rather different fare – quail braised in Cointreau, with a redcurrant coulis, pan-fried sea-bream with samphire and saffron sauce. He stopped a moment to peer inside at a group of workmen in sweaty vests and hobnailed boots, and tried to picture a sleek, black-coated sommelier explaining the various vintages of champagne to them, or droves of obsequious waiters flambéing crepes suzettes at the plastic-topped table, with its HP sauce bottles and plates of greasy chips.

As he walked on, however, he was uncomfortably aware of the sheer pretention of all that bowing and scraping, that over-dramatic presentation of over-priced and "fashionable" food. He no longer belonged in that milieu, but where he *did* belong was much more open to question. His job, his fate, his future, all were cobweb-frail.

Spotting a newsagent, he went in to grab a copy of *The Times*. A daily paper would be something of a luxury, since all his efforts to order one in prison had foundered in the usual bureaucratic snarl-up, and he'd been forced to resort to the noisy prison library and read a well-thumbed copy of some red-top. About to walk out with the paper, he realised to his horror that he was so unused to handling cash, he'd clean forgotten to pay and, although he rushed straight back with his wallet, he continued feeling deeply anxious. If he were had up for shoplifting, he might land back in gaol on the very day of his release.

And the sight of a policeman just outside the shop only increased his anxiety. Was the cop about to nab him for just a fleeting oversight? No – the guy walked on, leaving Anthony aware that his view of the police as a neutral, unthreatening force, with no bearing on him personally, had disappeared for ever.

Tramping on, past further rows of small, dark, foreign shops, with their restricted range of goods, he eventually reached a supermarket, only to find it had the opposite problems: too large, too bright, and with such a huge variety of produce he felt paralysed with indecision. And the glaring neon lights seemed to expose him to the other shoppers as a criminal just out of prison and therefore dangerous. Suppressing such thoughts, he found himself a trolley, feeling very much a novice, since, shameful as it sounded, he had rarely done any food shopping in the past. He and Deborah preferred to send out for stuff, or rely on Ocado to deliver a weekly order and, if they needed to entertain at home, several local restaurants had been happy to supply a selection of their elaborate signature dishes. Recalling the steep price of such a personal service induced a surge of guilt on behalf of those he had left behind in gaol, who gorged on instant noodles (often heated – dangerously – in the kettles in their cells), bacon-flavoured crisps, tinned peaches in syrup, and the ubiquitous Twix and Mars bars. Still caught between the two worlds, he was uncertain what to buy. Although now free to eat healthy, upmarket fare, it was actually prison comfort-food he craved: mushy peas and beans on toast – both impossible without a saucepan or a toaster.

He stood blocking the aisle, jostled by purposeful people, their trolleys already half-full. Chastened by their example, he finally settled for a wedge of Gorgonzola, a selection of exotic fruits, a jar of venison terrine, a bottle of Cabernet Sauvignon, several pots of instant noodles, two Twix bars and a jumbo-sized bag of crisps, thus steering a middle course between his two opposing lifestyles. He also remembered to buy a glass for the wine, some basic crockery and cutlery, a couple of Tupperware containers and a roll of kitchen-towel. Then he went to pick out a phone and, bemused by the huge range, simply grabbed a cheap pay-as-you-go model – a far cry from his former iPhone with all its bells and whistles.

As he queued to pay he glanced at the headlines in *The Times*, in an attempt to quell his nervousness at handling money and using credit cards again. He could hardly believe how once ingrained and automatic skills could vanish in less than two years.

Emerging, at last, from the air-conditioned store, he was engulfed in clammy heat once more and, now that he had a heavy bag to carry, decided to take a bus. Buses had been as rare in his life as supermarkets – tubes were quicker, taxis more convenient.

'Glorious weather!' remarked the voluptuous black woman he squeezed himself beside, rolls of her flesh overlapping his seat.

'Glorious' was hardly the word he'd use for the now oppressively high temperatures, or, indeed, for his general situation, but he gave her a friendly smile. Thus encouraged, she continued to chatter, switching from her daughter's chronic asthma to the ambitious plans for the new Tottenham Hotspur stadium which, she claimed, could transform the entire area, a claim he strongly doubted.

'Sorry, this is my stop,' he said, interrupting her account of last night's television drama, and ungluing his thigh from her hot and sweaty one.

'Well, nice to talk to you, sweetheart. And be sure to take care of yourself.'

This woman was a total stranger and probably called everybody "sweetheart". Nonetheless, her affectionate tone was definitely consoling and provided a crumb or two of comfort as he made his reluctant way to his new "home".

Once the door was shut, the room seemed little bigger than his cell, the only furniture being the narrow bed and one small chair. A few rusty metal hangers on the door constituted his "wardrobe" and, in the absence of any floor-space the television was mounted on the otherwise bare wall. What the room lacked in size, however, it made up for in garish colour. The acid-yellow curtains were patterned with unlikely-looking blue poppies, the pea-green bedcover was inset with turquoise bands, and the thin, threadbare carpet boasted an eye-catching confusion of purple whirls and spirals.

Unpacking was clearly superfluous, since there was nowhere to put anything except the narrow space between bed and wall, and the tiny bedside locker, whose cheap veneer was peeling off and stained. He assembled his new phone, though, relieved to see that its battery was more or less fully charged. As for his food, he was glad he hadn't bought too much as it would soon turn rancid in the stifling heat. Depositing it on the bed, he pushed at the grimy window only to find it jammed. He dared not hammer it too hard for fear of annoying fellow residents, and had no intention of asking help from the landlord – a cadaverous cold fish of a bloke who had left him with a deep sense of unease, heightened by the fact that the place was so weirdly quiet. After Darren's accounts of B&Bs, he had expected constant noise and disruption from an unruly mob of young druggies or old soaks, yet, even when he strained his ears, he couldn't hear a sound. How ironic that in gaol he had longed to escape the din of slamming cell doors, blaring televisions and brain-addling ghetto-blasters, yet now found this eerie silence even more disturbing.

Since the only view was an expanse of brick wall, he turned back from the window and rummaged in his black bin-bag for Darren's black-cat mascot. He was struck by the fact that, despite the huge gulf in their backgrounds, he was currently sharing Darren's experience of being homeless and jobless – with one overriding difference: his "mate" had none of his resources, financial or otherwise. It must be infinitely harder for an illiterate lad to cope, and one so short of cash he would be forced to live from hand to mouth. Tenderly, he placed the black cat on the pillow, put Betty and Darren's latest cards on top of the bedside locker, then poured himself a glass of wine before opening the crisps and the terrine. He used one to scoop up the other, eating ravenously, since his last meal had been the scanty prison breakfast some eleven hours ago.

However, once he'd finished his first course, he made an effort to slow down, savouring the claret – a truly welcome indulgence after twenty months of enforced teetotalism. Indeed, already he felt dizzy and light-headed, as if he were a young teen again, reeling after his first glass of champagne. Worried about its effect, he put down the glass and instead tackled the mango, cutting it into manageably small pieces. And, as a final treat, he couldn't resist a Mars bar – such a common form of currency at Wandsworth, Troy had "paid" him in Mars bars for his reading lessons, and Mark for financial advice. To be honest, he was missing both men and, in a bid to dispel his growing sense of isolation, reached for his new phone. But who could he ring, for God's sake? Mark and Troy were forbidden to take phone calls, Deborah might slam the phone down, he couldn't face his father's grief, and Darren was spending the Bank Holiday weekend with Carol-Ann's parents in Clacton. And, as for his casual acquaintances, all their numbers were stored on his now defunct iPhone and, anyway, why should they want to hear from him? With so much time to think in prison, he'd become aware that he'd probably always been lonely, even from early childhood, with no aunts, uncles, siblings, cousins or close friends – a troubling insight, since the word "lonely" had implications of wimpishness and failure, concepts despised by both his parents and his school. Marriage had brought companionship, of course, but soon, his and Deborah's mega-busy lifestyles meant they saw little of each other, except in bed.

No! Thoughts of his wife were forbidden, so, seeking distraction, he got up to switch on the television, only to find it was broken. Resisting the urge to complain, he slumped on to the small, hard chair and unfolded his copy of *The Times*. Yet even that proved futile. He was too on edge to concentrate on the rebels in Ukraine, or the latest instalment in the Goldman Sachs debacle. He snatched up his phone again, deciding to utilise this stretch of empty time by sorting through his avalanche of missed emails. Yet, within minutes of downloading the app, he was overcome by exhaustion. How ironical it seemed that, having counted the days till his release for the last endless twenty months, the outside world, with its noise, confusion and endless stimulation had proved so challenging and draining. Perhaps he should simply settle down to sleep, despite the fact it wasn't fully dark yet.

He undressed swiftly, cleared the bed of all his supper debris, then slipped between the slimy nylon sheets. Yet barely had he closed his eyes, when a rollercoaster-rush of panic switch-backed through his body. His heart was thumping, stomach churning, his very identity melting and dissolving like sugar in hot tea.

He sat up in a sweat, terrified of losing control, and switched on the overhead light to dispel the murky twilight. But now that he could see more clearly, the blue poppies on the curtains seemed to be jeering and grimacing at him, which intensified his fear. Was he heading for a breakdown, going mad, for God's sake? Certainly, the continuing eerie silence was heightening his racking sense of aloneness, so chokingly oppressive it felt as if all other human life had been annihilated, including Deborah, Darren, his father, Barbara Banks, the landlord …

He sprang out of bed to ground himself, but the walls were closing in on him in some claustrophobic nightmare, and he could see Craig's bleeding body sprawled unconscious on the floor. He lunged for the wine, started glugging from the bottle. He *had* to escape, couldn't spend another night in this unspeakable place, must get up at dawn tomorrow and start looking for a flat, a job – any sort of job – just to prevent himself from cracking up. There were still hours to go till dawn, though, and nights passed slower than did days, so how would he endure the endless stretch of nothingness in between?

All of a sudden he choked on a mouthful of wine and began spluttering and coughing – a merciful accident, in fact, since only at that moment did he become aware of his own appalling behaviour in resorting to the bottle and indulging in such craven negativity. He'd been brought up to be strong and self-reliant, to avoid the slightest shred of weakness or incompetence, yet here he was collapsing into an ignominious wreck, rather than rejoicing in the fact that he was out of prison at last, and free to plan the rest of his life. Ramming the bottle back on the locker, he snatched up a pen and one of Betty's notebooks and took them over to the chair. No chance of sleeping, but at least he could quash the panic by to drawing up a timetable, setting specific dates for each of his future goals. September was already looming, the month when schoolchildren and students either started afresh, or returned to their former structured routines. He resolved to do the same, restore to his existence some much-needed regularity and a basic sense of purpose.

And, as he began jotting down the various tasks, neatly and coherently, the very act of ordering his life brought with it the first glimmerings of calmness and composure and – above all – of control.

CHAPTER 19

'Congratulations, Anthony,' Nenita said, shyly, one of the few of his fellow-workers who spoke English. Leaning over, she spelled out the words on his certificate: 'CLEANER OF THE MONTH AWARD'.

He'd been ridiculously pleased to receive it, not on account of the £30 gift-voucher (peanuts to him, but a fortune for some of his workmates), but because, at this juncture of his life, even small achievements brought a certain satisfaction, and he did try to do his job to the highest possible standard. Indeed, he'd been told by his delighted boss that never before in the history of the company had any employee won the award for his very first month of work.

As the others followed him out of the building, they smiled their own congratulations, before heading for their various bus-stops and tube stations. Most were too tired to talk, some too pressingly busy, with second jobs or large demanding families. One or two might chat when they first arrived in the evening, and also during their thirty-minute break, but the lack of a common language prevented any general conversation. From what he could gather, the group comprised a mini United Nations: Columbians, Filipinos, Romanians, Lithuanians and a few whose nationality still eluded him. The lack of sociability suited him, in truth, allowing him to remain anonymous and affording him much-needed time to think. Although grateful for this job – grateful for *any* job – it could only be a stop-gap while he searched for something better and worked out his future direction.

Walking on to the main road, he found himself totting up the string of rejections he'd received in the last month. All the positions offered by the Job Centre, or spotted in the Situations Vacant columns, were either barred to him, beyond his capabilities, or in other ways unsuitable: school caretaker, financial controller, 'superstar barista', dental hygienist, classic-car restoration technician, laser-hair-removal specialist … Never before, had he actually had to *look* for work. Each stage in his advancement had always been conveniently laid out for him, along with "useful" contacts to smooth his path. But he was now just one of some nine million people with criminal or spent convictions – most of them with none of his advantages – struggling against the odds to persuade employers to give them a chance.

He paused a moment to glance up at the sky, the former murky-darkness beginning to lighten into a tentative grey dawn, although a lingering slice of moon grinned from between the clouds. It was distinctly chilly at this hour of the morning and he was shivering in his uniform – his own stupid fault for not having brought a coat. But then September, and even October, had been exceptionally mild so far, as if summer refused to yield to autumn, despite the browning leaves and dying flowers. Only now, at the very tail-end of the month, was there a definite hint of winter in the air.

For all his four weeks in the job, he still wasn't used to working nights, so, once aboard his bus, he tried to doze off, taking advantage of the welcome peace that characterised this morning bus, as against those on his outward, evening journey, with their raucous drunks, snogging couples, and giggly teens out on the town, often with an infernal racket leaking from their earphones.

Dozing proved impossible, though, with so much on his mind – Deborah most prominently. Despite pumping his father for news of her, all he'd managed to discover was that she'd found a new flat with room for a live-in nanny, and had returned to work full time. What she was feeling, however, and how she was actually coping remained a total mystery. His father had been strangely reticent, refusing even to give him her current address. Had she deliberately sworn him to silence about some new man in her life? But, if so, why no divorce proceedings? He'd been dreading a letter from her solicitor, not only during his final stretch in gaol, but in the last three weeks since visiting his father, whom he'd asked to give her *his* address. But not a single word from her, neither olive branch nor further hostilities. Every time he thought of her – a good hundred times each day – he experienced an acutely painful longing to undo her traumatic prison visit, undo the last two years, or go back even further to the blessed era when they hadn't started trying to conceive, but were perfectly content with and by themselves.

Besides the wife-shaped hole in his life, there was also a gaping space where his mother had once been, despite the fact they had never been close emotionally. The bouquet he'd put on her grave only exacerbated his sense of loss, the lush vitality of the exotic blooms contrasting with the corpse beneath, mouldering into dust.

Alighting from the first bus, he waited for the second, accustomed now to the tedious journey – nothing in comparison with the two-hour treks each way some of his fellow workers endured, living as they did far-out. From what he could gather from Nenita, many were forced to choose between buying food or heating their homes, and some lived in appalling conditions, crammed half a dozen to one small room. Yet, through nothing more than a mere accident of birth, *he* had been able to move into a pristine-clean apartment block only just completed – a welcome contrast to the cramped and gruesome Haven; no risk of going hungry or shivering through the winter on account of handing over a hefty deposit and a month's rent in advance.

And, despite his lowly occupation, his working environment was even more amenable than his large, light, modern flat: a block of forty offices, again a new-build, with huge plate-glass windows and stylish décor. His aim was to keep the place as spotless as FFC – not difficult with Fabuclean's state-of-the-art equipment and extremely thorough training, a world away from the one-day farce of his so-called "instruction" in prison toilet-cleaning, armed only with an ancient broom and ragged mop. Admittedly it was mortifying being paid less than the minimum wage, and having to clock in and out, but the relief of being taken on at all silenced such objections. Many firms had refused point-blank to consider him, whereas Fabuclean, although tough on security, seemed more concerned to crack down on illegals with no work permits than on those with criminal convictions. And it was a relief to be in a job were the only computers were those he had to clean, rather than subject to his former barrage of emails. Even his personal emails were now far fewer than before because when he had finally steeled himself to download the 562 unanswered messages on his now dead iPhone, he'd been struck by how much time he'd wasted replying to such stuff, and also how much junk-mail had accumulated. Having ruthlessly pruned and unsubscribed, he had made the whole business more manageable and, although at some point, he would invest in a new iPhone, he felt no great sense of urgency about it – surprisingly.

The second bus-ride was shorter and once he reached his stop he was about to head for his flat, as usual, but stood hesitant a minute outside the small, anonymous café a few paces along the road. Having not yet been out for a single meal, he'd been tempted to try it out before or after work, but his persistent sense of being a "leper" always held him back. Today, however, he was determined to treat himself to breakfast, to celebrate his award; celebrate the fact he'd found a job in a mere five weeks – a rare accomplishment, according to Barbara, as was finding a flat in a little under a fortnight. She had also praised him for doing all the spadework himself, without expecting her to "spoon-feed" him.

She had played her part, of course, by completing, with commendable speed, all the official checks and vetting required. Now she called him a "success-story" – surely a tad ironic in light of his low-grade work, but she probably meant in comparison to some of the hopeless-looking clients he'd seen in the Probation Office waiting room: young lads in ragged jeans and hoodies, huddled over Coke-cans; older, ravaged men muttering to themselves; aggressive types, wearing scars like medals. And the pile of leaflets available, offering help and advice on drug addiction, alcoholism, unemployment, domestic violence and homelessness, all made him grateful for his own relative advantages.

Before entering the café, he popped into the newsagent to buy the *Financial Times*, his attention riveted by a screaming tabloid headline: *"MURDERERS AND RAPISTS REVEL IN THE LIFE OF RILEY!"* Reading on, he fumed at the misrepresentation of convicted criminals enjoying a whole raft of perks and privileges, all funded by the taxpayer. He was uncomfortably aware, though, that he had once taken that line himself, used words like "scroungers" and "the criminal class", without the slightest inkling of who such people were or how they lived.

Nervously, he pushed open the café door. The place was almost empty, but the three workmen at the window table nodded a friendly greeting, presumably accepting him as a humble fellow-worker, since he was in his cleaner's uniform. At first, he'd been highly embarrassed by the black nylon two-piece, with its lurid purple stripe, and "FABUCLEAN" stencilled on the back, especially as the company insisted that all cleaning staff wear it to and from work.

He ordered the full English, enjoying the freedom to ask for what he wanted, rather than having to put up with what was sloshed into his plastic dish – often a completely different item from the one he'd ticked on the prison menu. Once the plate was brought to him, though, overflowing with eggs, bacon, sausages, baked beans, fried bread and black pudding, he was relieved that Deborah couldn't see it. On the rare occasions they'd had time to sit down for breakfast together, she had insisted on a healthy repast of organic yogurt, wheat-germ, chia seeds and blueberries. Again, he dislodged her from his mind, distracting himself by leafing through the *FT*, hoping the workmen wouldn't realise that the distinctive pink newspaper was an unlikely choice for a cleaner. However, all the things that had once seemed so compelling – quantitative easing, government debt, reflationary fiscal policy, the growth in China's economy, the surprising fall in oil prices – only served to remind him that his high salary and prestigious job had come at an exacting price in terms of time and leisure. That never-ending busyness was almost a form of prison in itself, with no freedom of soul or choice, no option beyond the need to achieve and conform.

Having paid the bill – an incredibly low £4.50, which included tea and toast – he gave the waitress a lavish tip, partly because of her cheery smile (so different from the surly mien of Hashim and Emeka, who worked at the prison servery), and partly to compensate for his lascivious thoughts, as he eyed up her legs and breasts. In his present celibate state, every halfway decent female reactivated his urge for sex. In truth, he sometimes felt so frustrated, he found himself fancying even frumpish Nenita. The problem was he'd been womanless so long, he feared he might have totally lost the knack – if he had ever had it. Deborah had criticised his selfishness and dominance but, for all he knew, she might also have found him boring and unadventurous in bed.

Having called goodbye to the men, he crossed the road and started walking towards his flat, shuffling through the fallen autumn leaves. His tree-lined street was surprisingly quiet, but it led off West Green Road, one of the most rundown parts of Seven Sisters, which, as Barbara had said, was little more salubrious than nearby Tottenham. But in his haste to escape The Haven at all costs, he hadn't had the time to explore other, more congenial places. Today, however, once he had snatched a few hours' sleep, he would set out on a recce, before clocking in again for tonight's long shift.

Suddenly, he heard the sound of pounding footsteps and saw a figure down the far end of the street, apparently racing towards him. A cop, he thought, in terror, come to apprehend him. He must have breached the terms of his licence, or Barbara had …

'Fool,' he muttered, as the figure drew nearer – as different from any sort of law-enforcement official as it was possible to be: a striking young woman in a pink fake-fur jacket and a frilly, floral-patterned party frock, winter and summer combined in her unusual outfit. Her hair was a tousled mass of curls in a gleaming conker colour and sprang up around her head as if it had a life of its own. But he saw to his dismay that tears were streaming down her cheeks and, as she panted to a stop beside him, her voice, too, was choked with emotion.

'There's a cat in the builders' skip,' she cried, obviously too het up to say hello or introduce herself. 'It's in this sort of cage thing, underneath a load of other stuff – old bricks and lumps of concrete and bits of broken-up furniture. I've been trying to shift it for ages, but I don't seem to have the strength.'

Only then did he notice that her hands were scratched and bleeding – tiny feminine hands, the nails varnished in a delicate pink. He fought a sudden crazy urge to take those hands in his and never let them go.

'The workmen aren't here yet,' she continued in the same frantic tone. 'In fact, there's no one around at all, which is why I'm begging *you* for help. I know it's an awful cheek, and you're probably frightfully busy or—'

'Not busy at all,' he said, cutting through her apologies. Of course I can help.' Indeed, so struck was he by her touching youth (little more than twenty, he'd guess) and her sheer girly prettiness, the strength of Hercules seemed already to be surging into his veins.

He followed her onto the demolition site, where they squeezed with difficulty through the "KEEP OUT" cordon, entering a wasteland of rubble and detritus.

'If you climb up on these two packing cases,' she said, 'you'll be level with the top of the skip and can lower yourself down inside. Luckily, the cases were lying nearby, so I dragged them over, to make a sort of step-ladder. But do be careful – they're terribly wobbly.'

Hardly had she instructed him when he was clambering up and scrambling down inside, bricks and concrete shifting perilously beneath his feet. As he peered at the hodge-podge of lumber in the battered metal skip, he spotted the cage halfway down, and the cat inside – a black cat.

Darren, he thought, and his lucky black-cat mascot! But here was a *real* black cat, and one that looked as thin and mangy as Darren's. Yet, only through so unprepossessing a creature had he chanced upon a girl for whom he felt an instant, indeed overwhelming attraction, so might this whole encounter turn out to be a lucky one?

Ashamed of so irrational a notion, yet determined to impress her, he began dislodging with superhuman speed all the dross piled on top of the cage, chucking it to one end of the skip. She had taken his place on the packing cases and was watching his every movement. 'Oh, Lord!' she cried. 'You're bleeding. Here, take my hankie and use it as a bandage.'

'It's nothing,' he assured her, although touched by her concern. 'The important thing is to free the cat. We don't know how long the poor thing's been trapped, so it might be at its last gasp.'

'Oh, don't say that! D'you think we're too late to save it?'

'It's okay– I'm almost there.' Heaving off the last few broken bricks, he seized hold of the wire cage, which, fortunately, was only halfway down the skip. Lifting it out with the utmost care, he then negotiated the tricky manoeuvre of climbing out of the skip, with the near-hysterical cat clawing wildly at its cage. The woman tried to steady him and, once he was safely back on terra firma, she flashed him a look of such gratitude he felt like the resurrected captain of the *Titanic*, reversing the course of history and rescuing one lone survivor from the perils of the deep. Although this, for her, was a crisis situation, he couldn't help but notice her eyes: so lustrously blue they combined every poetic cliché in the book: speedwell, azure, gentian, forget-me-not.

'We mustn't let it out,' she warned, 'or it'll run for its life and we'll never catch it again. I've fostered quite a few cats in my time and my last one was a rescue cat and as slippery as an eel.'

'So what *should* we do?' He cursed his ignorance of pets in general and cats in particular. 'I could help you take it home, if you like.'

'Oh, no. It has to be seen by a vet. It may have broken its leg, you see, or suffered internal injuries.' Her face clouded over and again his gaze was riveted by her full, generous mouth and endearingly pink-and-white complexion. She seemed like a princess in a fairy-tale and, despite the fact he knew nothing whatever about her, he resolved to be her prince – further proof of his wild irrationality.

'The problem is,' she frowned, studying the feline captive with mingled worry and affection, 'vets are dreadfully expensive. I'm still paying off the debt from Smokey's last illness.' She broke off for a moment, clearly recalling some painful memory. 'He ... he passed away three months ago and, by the end, he was in such a bad state I couldn't just stand by and let him die in agony. But the final vet's bill was crippling.'

'Don't worry – I can pay. In fact, I'm so involved in this whole thing now, I'd like to do my bit.'

'I wouldn't dream of it! Hold on, let me think. Maybe one of the free vet services would help – except last time I tried the PDSA they said you had to be on benefits to qualify, and the Blue Cross were even stricter about—'

'Look,' he interrupted, 'I absolutely insist on paying. We haven't time to waste on wild goose chases when every minute counts.' He had no idea, in fact, if time was of the essence, or even if the cat was seriously hurt. Perhaps its indignant protests were simply due to its long confinement, which he, more than anyone, could understand.

'But why should you, when I'm a total stranger?'

Because, he refrained from saying, I'll do anything for you – anything – so long as you don't disappear.

'I'm Mary, by the way,' she said, in the absence of an answer from him, 'which I should have told you ages ago. But I was just so relieved to see you that ....' In lieu of finishing the sentence, she gave him a radiant smile.

'And I'm Anthony,' he countered, the cat's yammering cries all but drowning his voice. 'Anthony Beaumont.'

'*My* surname's Sparrow,' she admitted, apologetically, 'a stupid name for someone as plump as me.'

'You're not plump. You're ...' Again, he couldn't voice the words that came to mind: "voluptuous" and "lust-inducing". Yet, despite her womanly curves, her petite build (scarcely five feet tall) and shy, sweet, artless manner did have something of the sparrow in them. And a northern sparrow, judging by her charmingly unsophisticated accent, with its slightly broad intonation. 'Okay, Mary, just show me the way to your regular vet and let's go!'

'It's a good bus-ride away and I came here on my bike, so—'

'We'll take a taxi then – waste less time getting this poor thing treated.' The 'poor thing' started whimpering again, as if in support of the plan.

'But a taxi may refuse to take him. He's peed his cage, so he *is* rather smelly.'

'Leave it with me. A lavish tip can work wonders.'

'But it'll cost you a fortune, on top of the basic fare.'

'Mary, not another word about expense! I suggest we walk down to the main road – we're bound to find a cab there. And if your bike's the fold-up kind, we can take it with us.'

'No, it doesn't fold, but I can lock it up on the High Road and, meanwhile, I'll strap the cage on the carrier.' She tried to console the creature as she fastened the straps securely, using such tender words of comfort, he longed to change places with it.

'You know,' she said, wheeling the bike as gently as she could so as not to bump or jolt the cat, 'it appals me just how cruel some people are. Fancy dumping this poor innocent kitty, leaving it to starve to death or die of hideous thirst … And it was obviously done deliberately – rammed so far down in the skip, and in a cage, of all things, so it couldn't possibly escape.'

'Thank God you happened to be around,' he said, again touched by her soft heart. 'Or do you live in this street?' Say *yes*, he begged her, silently, already imagining them as neighbours – soon becoming lovers.

She shook her head, a flush of embarrassment suffusing her face. 'You probably think I'm awful, trespassing on a private building site. But workmen often chuck out decent stuff from the flats they're tearing down, so I always check the local skips, to see what I can find. Last month, it was a kitchen stool and, the month before, an ironing board.'

He ached to buy her a whole new fitted kitchen, with ironing boards and stools galore. But now that they had turned onto the High Road and Mary was padlocking her bike, he must concentrate on flagging down a cab. Fortunately, it took him only minutes and, once he'd pressed a couple of bank notes into the driver's hand, there was no problem about the cat. However, hardly had they settled themselves inside when Mary let out a horrified gasp.

'Oh my God! I'm meant to be at work. With all the panic over the cat, it went clean out of my mind. But I'm terribly late already.'

'Can't you phone them?'

'It's not a "them", it's just one man – a solicitor. He's actually past retirement age, but he wanted to keep his hand in so he left his big firm and set up on his own. I work as his secretary and sort of general factotum.'

'But surely he'll understand.'

She shook her head, with a bounce of the copper curls. 'No, he'll hit the roof if I try to make out that rescuing a cat is more important than typing his contracts and stuff. I've had loads of time off already, you see, especially when Smokey was ill, and he's not even that keen on animals.'

'You'd better ring in sick, then.'

'Oh, no!' she said, sounding genuinely shocked, as if he'd suggested she *murder* her boss. 'I'd never lie to him – or anyone. He was really decent to take me on at all, when I'm not a proper legal secretary. I had to learn on the job and was pretty clueless at first, so I am truly in his debt.'

'Tell you what – I'll phone him. The man-to-man thing sometimes works much better.'

'Maybe,' she said, dubiously. 'But what about your work? Aren't you meant to be somewhere by now?'

He dodged the question, refusing to admit he worked nights. She must already think it odd that a mere cleaner in a cheapo uniform would have the wherewithal to pay for taxi-cabs and foot expensive vet's bills. And, apart from anything else, he cursed the fact he should be looking so deplorably unstylish when he yearned for her to find him at least reasonably attractive. Worse, he might even smell, having worked physically hard for eight hours and not yet had a shower. Fortunately, he wasn't the sweaty type and, anyway, the offices were cool at night, so he tried to suppress his fears. 'Just give me your boss's name and number, Mary, and let's see if we can sort this out.'

Adopting his most authorative tone, he informed Mr Edwardes (who sounded tetchily curt – annoyed no doubt that, in the absence of his secretary, he'd had to answer the phone himself) that Ms Sparrow had encountered an unexpected crisis and would not be in until tomorrow.

Once he'd rung off, Mary appeared exceptionally anxious, her voice rising to a wail. 'But how will I explain the "crisis", without telling him about the cat?'

Stumped for an answer, he gave silent thanks that, just at that moment, the cab drew up at Pets Are Our Passion. With any luck, they wouldn't have to hang around too long – certainly not long enough to justify a whole day's absence on Mary's part – but he was determined to stake his own claim. The cat might need her ministrations, Mr Edwardes insist on her secretarial help, but *his* need for her was burningly, desperately urgent.

CHAPTER 20

'Gosh, what a relief' – Mary gave a long, expressive sigh – 'to have left our kitty in such good hands.'

'I was surprised though,' Anthony put in, 'they decided to keep it overnight. But I suppose that gives them time to do everything that's needed, including another thorough check-up.' And give *him* time alone with Mary, without a wounded creature as rival for her attention.

'I just can't thank you enough for paying.' Mary gazed at him with such gratitude on their way out of the vet's, he might have raised the Siege of Mafeking single-handed. 'The bill was so steep, I still feel terribly guilty but, with the drip and the blood-tests and the various drugs and injections, it all mounted up alarmingly.'

'Don't mention it. I was just glad to help.'

'But, Anthony, I want you to know it's the most amazingly generous thing anyone's ever done for me!'

Inflating his tiny act of mercy into laurel-crowned munificence, the passion in her words was both ridiculous and thrilling.

'I wish I could invite you back to my place and cook you a slap-up lunch. It's the very least I could do in return, but I live worryingly close to Mr Edwardes' office and daren't take the risk of running into him.'

'Let me take you out for a meal, then.'

'But I'd like to do something for *you* and, anyway, I'd still be worried about my boss. I mean, suppose he happened to be lunching a client in the very place we chose?'

'Okay, I'll give you lunch in my flat. It won't be "slap-up", I'm afraid, but I do have eggs and cheese and all the basics.'

'But it's not fair for you to keep giving and me to keep taking.'

'Actually, you'd be doing me a favour. I've only lived in the place a few weeks and I've been really looking forward to having my first visitor.' Not exactly true, but the only thing that mattered at this moment was keeping this woman close. 'And, in any case, we have to go back for your bike, and where you left it is only five minutes from my pad.'

'Well, if you're really sure.'

He had never been more sure of anything and, having insisted on another taxi to whisk them down the High Road, he then wheeled Mary's bike the three streets to his apartment block.

'Wow!' she said. 'This is very swish. Thank goodness we came to your place, rather than my grungy little bedsit.'

As he pressed the buzzer and ushered her into the lift, he warmed to her trusting nature. Some women would be wary of going home with a total stranger, especially one with a criminal conviction – although that, he vowed, she must never, ever know.

'It's like a show-house!' she exclaimed, as she stood admiring his open-plan sitting room with the streamlined mini-kitchen at one end. 'I don't know how you keep it so immaculate. My place is full of clutter.'

'Well, I moved from a larger pad, so a lot of my stuff's still in storage. And, since I was thinking of moving again, there didn't seem much point in retrieving it yet.' Except he *wouldn't* move – not now. Being a mere mile or two from Mary seemed infinitely more important than living in a more congenial location.

As she unbuttoned her jacket, he had to force his eyes away from the tantalising outline of her breasts. 'You sit and relax and I'll make a start on the lunch.'

'No, let me do it, please. I can rustle up an omelette with the eggs and cheese you have, and, if you can dig out a few veggies, I can turn those into a nice hot soup. Forgive me saying, but you do look rather cold.'

'Actually, I would like to put on something warmer.' He jumped at the chance of changing out of his uniform, extremely relieved that Mary hadn't quizzed him about it. She never seemed to pry or probe or subject him to awkward questions – a definite point in her favour.

'Okay, just show me where things are and I'll get cracking with our lunch.'

'I'm afraid there's not so much as a carrot in the place.' He opened the drawers and cupboards and pointed out their contents. 'But I do have tinned soup, if that's any use.' Normally, he was so tired after work, he grabbed a quick snack, then crashed out on his bed, postponing his shower and a proper meal, until after he'd had some sleep. Today, though, he felt extraordinarily invigorated and strode into the en-suite bathroom for the quickest but most thorough shower of his life, still not quite accustomed to swapping the constipated, tepid trickle of the prison showers for this generously hot jet – not to mention a stack of fluffy bath-towels. A full-length mirror was also definitely a treat, in place of a small square of steel that showed nothing but the blurred top half of his face. Other things he could no longer take for granted were a door with a handle he could open from the inside, soft carpet underfoot, clean underwear each day, and a yielding, well-sprung, mattress. Ironically, he had found the bed *too* comfortable at first and had to adjust to its cushioned softness and to a luxurious goose-down pillow, rather than a brick-hard square. But, best of all was the end to imperious knocks at his door as a screw barged in with some barked command.

Once dry – and positively glowing – he doused himself with aftershave and changed into his new jeans and a slate-blue cashmere sweater. Emerging from the bedroom, he sniffed the air appreciatively. 'Something smells delicious!'

'That's the soufflé. I thought it would be nicer than an omelette. I've also tarted up one of your canned soups by adding a few bits and pieces I found in the fridge.'

How enchanting that she could cook – an increasingly rare accomplishment, judging by the high-powered females at FFC, some of whom actually boasted about never having used their wildly expensive ovens.

'The soup's almost ready, but the soufflé will be another fifteen minutes.'

'Perfect – just time for a drink.' He went to fetch a bottle of wine, noting with approval how artistically she had laid the table, the paper napkins folded into elaborate white swans.

'I envy you this dining-space,' she said, once they'd had their first glass and decamped from the sofa. 'My kitchen's little bigger than a cupboard, so I mostly eat sitting on my bed.'

As *he* had done at Wandsworth, he thought, hastily suppressing the image of his grimy prison cell. As far as Mary was concerned, his incarceration had never happened. 'You've certainly transformed this soup. It tastes nothing like boring old Heinz. Where did you learn to cook?'

'From my Mum, and very early on. As the oldest of seven children, I was expected to do my bit.'

'Seven!' he exclaimed. 'I'm an only child and aren't we usually said to be selfish and spoilt rotten?'

'More lonely, I'd guess, than spoilt, especially as you never had a pet. We had loads – not just dogs and cats, but guinea pigs and gerbils, even a parrot at one point.'

'So you'll definitely be keeping the cat when he comes back from the vet?'

'Goodness yes! If I don't offer him a home I dread to think what might happen. Anyway, since Smokey died, there's been a huge cat-shaped hole in my life.'

What about a *man*-shaped hole, he wondered? Did she have a partner, or was she …?

'Unless,' she said, looking up from her soup. '*You'd* like to keep the cat. That's only fair, in a way, since you were the one who rescued him and paid for all his treatment.'

'I'm afraid pets are totally forbidden in this block. They're so strict about it they even cavil at guide-dogs.'

'Well, that's a shame. But tell you what – let's call him Anthony, after you. It's high time we chose a name for him.'

He shook his head. Considering Mary's obsession with cats, it was imperative he kept a separate identity.

'What name would you prefer, then?'

Naming cats had never been one of his life-skills. 'What are cats normally called – Sooty? Sambo? Felix?'

'No, something more distinguished' Frowning for a moment, she suddenly exclaimed, 'I know – Anton! Still in your honour, but less of a mouthful for a cat. My second eldest sister is married to an Anton and he's absolutely lovely.'

'Fine,' he said, hoping now they had settled on a name, they could move to more important matters: Mary's sexual availability, for instance.

But, already, her expression had switched from radiant to doomy. 'I'm just so terribly worried about tomorrow. You see, I really ought to stay with Anton once I fetch him from the vet. I mean, he may be scared or shaky or still recovering from his treatment, yet I daren't take another day off. It's such a pity Mrs Murray-Wood's away.'

'Mrs Murray-Wood?'

'My landlady. She owns the whole house and just rents me out the basement, which is ideal for a cat because there's this flight of steps leading up to the garden. You see, soon after I first moved there, I found poor little Smokey wandering the streets, and realised he must have been abandoned. Mrs Murray-Wood's as much a cat-person as me and, since neither of us could bear the thought of him coming to any harm, she let me take him in and even arranged to have a cat-flap specially made. And she never minded keeping an eye on him while I was at work, so I didn't have to worry. What's so annoying is that she hardly ever goes anywhere, yet the very time I need her desperately, she's taken herself to Lyndhurst to visit an old friend. In the ordinary way, she'd bend over backwards to help. She's so mad about animals, she'd let Anton sleep in her bed with her and cosset him with delicate little invalid meals.'

As Anthony savoured his last spoonful of soup, he couldn't help imagining Deborah's distaste at the thought of unhygienic creatures sharing their owners' beds. Her family, like his, had strongly discouraged pets.

'So I'm at my wits' end, you see. I just can't afford to lose my job. Apart from anything else, I have to pay off Smokey's vet bill.'

'Actually, that's done. When the girl was taking my credit-card details, she mentioned the outstanding sum, so it seemed sensible to settle that, as well. I wasn't going to tell you, but—'

'Oh, Anthony …'

Mary's expression combined incredulity with the deepest gratitude. Her emotions were so transparent, written clearly on her face, he guessed she was incapable of any kind of guile or pretence.

'How can I ever thank you properly?'

Easily, he thought – just come into my bedroom and … Forcing his mind away from the beguiling prospect of her nakedness, he asked if she might now consider taking another day off. 'I'll come with you to the vet, of course, then I can stay with you and help look after the cat.' Which, with any luck, would be sedated, so he could look after her, instead.

'No, I just have to go in tomorrow. A VIP client is bringing along his accountant and other important bods and, if I'm not there to let them in and make them coffee, my boss will do his nut.'

'There's only one solution then – we'll collect the cat first thing, so you can get to work on time, then I'll stay on at your place and cat-sit till you're back.'

'But don't *you* work, Anthony?'

'I work nights,' he admitted, since she would have to know at some point, or he would tie himself in knots. 'But I don't leave until nine-thirty in the evening.'

'Oh, I'll be back long before that. But don't you need to sleep in the daytime? Although,' she added, as if answering her own question, 'you're more than welcome to sleep on my divan, so long as you keep an ear cocked for Anton and phone me at work if you're the slightest bit worried about him.'

'Of course,' he assured her. 'I'd do that automatically. I want you to trust me, Mary.' He felt guilty even using the word 'trust', whilst concealing so much from her. Besides, she herself was clearly far too trusting and, although he found that naiveté appealing, it could put her in real danger, as he knew from the many burglars he'd consorted with in gaol. To allow an almost-stranger access to her home was an open invitation for such thieves to fleece the joint. Okay, *he* was honourable, but suppose she let in some other guy – a rogue or even rapist? He longed to protect her and be there for her, but at least tomorrow's plan might be a vital step towards achieving that very goal

For her part, she was still fretting about the cat. 'I just hope he's not frightened by the fireworks, what with Diwali coming up and Halloween, and Guy Fawkes the following week. It's a very scary time for pets.'

Her sensitivity to any sort of suffering was so acute, he was tempted to disclose his own prison ordeal, just to bask in the salve of her sympathy. Except that would be quite insane. His overriding task was to try to win her affections, not lose them at a stroke.

'I'm still trying to think what I could do for *you*,' Mary said, as she cleared away the soup-bowls. 'Though I says it myself, I'm quite a dab hand at sewing, so if there's anything you'd like made – cushions for your sofa, maybe, or curtains, or a patchwork quilt, you only have to say. I make all my own clothes and stuff, so I have loads of fabrics squirrelled away.'

He was lost for words. No one had ever sewn for him. Forget cushions and curtains – his natural instinct was to choose something like a bathrobe – something worn close to his skin, which involved her taking his measurements. He completely missed her next words. They were in the bedroom together, the tape-measure cool against his naked chest, slipping lower as she moved it down to his waist, lower still to …

CHAPTER 21

Once Mary left for work the next morning, he sank into her one small armchair, exhausted not so much by lack of sleep, but by excitement and anticipation. He was actually *here* in her flat, trusted by her, needed by her, her cat named in his honour. The said cat had undergone a transformation, as if the vet had tended not simply to its (mostly minor) injuries, but changed its very temperament. Having steeled himself to cat-sit for a vicious, agitated creature, darting around hysterically and continually biting and scratching, he'd been astonished by the fact that Anton was proving little more trouble than Darren's mascot-cat and was now sound asleep right beside his chair. His mind jumped back to his early days at Wandsworth, when he, too, had been angry and aggressive, taking out his venom on inmates and officers alike. But captivity had that effect, of course, just as love and care worked wonders in the opposite direction. And, certainly, Mary had poured out love and care on both of them, taking trouble even with their beds. Anton's was a wicker basket, lined with soft layers of fabric and topped with a squashy velvet cushion, while she had made up the divan for him with clean rose-patterned sheets, then gone to fetch what she called her "special" counterpane – a striking, hand-made creation in a kaleidoscope of colours.

He glanced down at the sleeping cat, which looked completely different from the mangy mog of yesterday, the encrusted eyes now clean and clear, the fur no longer matted, and seeming twice as thick. Then, letting his gaze extend to the whole room, he again worried about her ingenuousness in allowing him to spend the day here on his own. Admittedly, there was very little to steal – she didn't even have a television, let alone a music-centre or any expensive gadgets – but, with Mrs Murray-Wood away, a burglar like the unreformed Darren could have ransacked the whole house.

Despite the lack of consumer goods, the place was still overcrowded, as she had warned, but only in a delightful way that reproached the bare austerity of his own flat. All the things she had retrieved from skips or hunted down in junk shops had been transformed by her artistic skills:

the armchair reupholstered in deep purple velveteen; the headboard of the divan padded with a length of matching fabric; the curtains a veritable poem of furbelows and frills. And, although she clearly favoured striking colours, the effect was glowingly harmonious, in contrast to The Haven's motley of discordant, clashing shades.

She had even enhanced the walls with two framed collages of photographs. He hadn't yet had time to study them, but got up now, to peer closely at each face. As far as he could tell, they all seemed to be her family, a work-worn but cheerful-looking woman presumably her mother, her five sisters and one much younger brother, still a child of only six or seven, and a chunky, balding man he took to be her dad. To his great relief, he could see no other man – certainly no one resembling a boyfriend, although felines featured prominently on the second, smaller collage. The large, ash-grey cat at the top he identified as Smokey, since there was a second, black-bordered photo of him, set up on a shelf, constituting a sort of memorial shrine, flanked as it was by two candles and a plaque reading "REST IN PEACE".

The sight engendered a certain distaste, albeit mixed with sympathy, so he turned on his heel and squeezed into the cupboard of a kitchen, following the promptings of his stomach. Mary hadn't had a minute to make breakfast this morning before setting off to work, what with all the frantic rush of fetching Anton from the vet in time. However, once she'd left his place yesterday evening, she had clearly done a huge amount – shopping, cooking, and spring-cleaning her whole pad. And, before dashing out, twenty minutes ago, she had explained the various dishes: ready-soaked muesli in the fridge, brimming with fruits and nuts; a shepherd's pie for lunch, topped with her own special mash of sweet potato, parsnip and carrot; some creamy creation for pudding, decorated with chocolate curls and toasted almond flakes; and a moist fish medley for Anton. She had also stocked up with croissants, yogurts, bananas, grapes and a variety of cat-treats, as if she were catering for her family of nine, plus a hungry tribe of felines.

And, not content with preparing such a feast, she had promised to be back in time to cook supper for him before he left for *his* work. Never before had he been so fussed and feted and, he had to say, he relished the experience. Indeed, reluctant to waste any "Mary-time" by having to go back home and change, he had even brought his uniform, explaining his job, briefly, as 'superintendent for a major contract cleaning firm'. He excused the lie on the grounds that, following his award, his boss had urged him to work his way up in the firm towards the rank of supervisor. And, although he'd assented to the boss's plan, now that he had Mary as his lode-star, things had changed dramatically and he intended to do his utmost to find a very different sort of job. He certainly hadn't lost his drive or his ambition and yearned to attain a top position, if only to impress this bewitching girl. Since his fall from grace, that was more or less impossible, but he might find freelance accountancy work for any tolerant individuals willing to accept his conviction, which most big companies would emphatically not do.

Taking his muesli and two croissants back to the main room, he found Anton on the point of waking up, his extravagant yawn displaying a surprisingly healthy-looking pink tongue.

'Who's a gorgeous brave boy, then?' he forced himself to say, copying Mary's cooing tone and using her vocabulary, despite his acute embarrassment at so doing. 'You're safe with us, little kitty. This is your new home.'

However foolish he felt, Mary had told him it was vital to overcome Anton's natural caution about the two virtual strangers who had come into his life. Preferring action to soppy talk, though, he went to fetch a second spoon and offered the cat a tiny taste of muesli, avoiding any fruits or nuts, but just the creamy residue at the bottom of the bowl. Anton seemed to relish it and was clearly ravenous, so, abandoning his own breakfast, Anthony popped back to the kitchen to warm up the fish stew and, stooping down to the level of the basket, fed milky pieces of cod to Anton, morsel by slow morsel. He should probably have put it in the cat-bowl in the kitchen, but he refused to be found wanting compared with Mrs Murray-Wood, so why not cosset the invalid with breakfast in bed? And, certainly, with every mouthful, Anton seemed less wary, no longer shrinking away or giving him suspicious glances from narrowed, green-slit eyes. Okay, it might be cupboard-love, but any love was acceptable in his bid to win Mary's affections.

Once the stew was finished, he dared tentatively to stroke the cat, still kneeling on the floor, to fondle his ears and chuck him under the chin, the way Mary had advised. And, since there was no objection, he went further still and lifted the creature gently on to his lap. At first the cat panicked, mewing in protest and clawing wildly at his jeans, so he quickly reverted to the baby-talk, barely able to believe that such sentimental billing and cooing could be issuing from his mouth. Yet there was no denying that the soothing words were having the desired effect, since Anton had now settled down and even curled himself on his namesake's lap, paddling around for a bit first, as if choosing the most comfortable position. Anthony dared not eat his croissants, for fear of disturbing the cat and, as for sleep, it would have to wait. So he sat rhythmically stroking Anton in what he hoped was a calming manner, whilst continuing the babble of sweet nothings.

Then, all at once, the cat began to purr – a deep rumbling sound that seemed almost too loud for its size. Mary had told him this morning that purring was unlikely until Anton felt totally safe with them and had fully recovered from his trauma, so his first instinct was to text her, knowing how thrilled she'd be. Not wanting to break the spell, however, he sat completely still, as the purring continued, emphatic now and confident.

And suddenly he realised, although still with some sense of embarrassment, that *he* was thrilled, as well – as thrilled as a proud new father witnessing his baby's first smile.

CHAPTER 22

'I told you, mate, *not* posh!' Darren glanced, intimidated, at the leather-bound menu and crisp white tablecloths.

'This isn't posh, Darren, I assure you. Just an ordinary Italian restaurant.'

'Well, your idea of ordinary ain't mine.' Darren attempted a grin, as he opened the menu. 'I mean, I can't make head or tail of this. It ain't English, by the looks of it. What the hell's *pappar* ...?' Daunted by the pronunciation, he let the word stutter to a stop.

'It's just a type of pasta.' Anthony cursed himself for making Darren ill at ease. He had actually chosen the place for the lad's convenience, because it was close to Charing Cross station, where the Lewisham train came in. Obviously, though, he hadn't yet dislodged his conditioning that, if you wined and dined a friend, you had to make some effort to impress. 'Look,' he added, reassuringly, 'the English version is written here, underneath – admittedly in very small print.' He spelled out the translation: 'Wide ribbons of pasta, with grass-fed chicken, shitake mushrooms and fresh basil.'

'Well, £13.99 for pasta's a bit steep, innit, even with all that fancy gubbins?'

'Please don't worry about the prices. I wanted to take you somewhere nice. It's such ages since we met, I felt we ought to splash out a bit.'

'But I'm the one asking you a favour, mate, so why should *you* splash out?'

'What is this mysterious favour,' Anthony asked, seizing on the change of subject.

'It ain't mysterious, just ...' Darren cleared his throat. 'You .... You may hate the whole idea, see, so I'd rather tell you later.'

'Okay, let's have a drink first.'

'Ta, mate. A pint of bitter.'

'I'm afraid they don't do bitter here, only lager. Shall I order you a bottle, or would you rather share a bottle of wine?'

'No fear! I know where I am with beer.'

'And why don't we order our food, as well, then we can settle down for a chat. What do you fancy, Darren?'

'I'll have that pasta thing. But don't ask me how to spell it!'

Anthony opted for pasta himself, deliberately avoiding the minefield of starters, most of which seemed unnecessarily exotic: wild-boar terrine, salami infused with fennel seeds, ewe's cheese with pears and rocket ...

'Hey, look at that Christmas tree!' Darren gestured to the back of the restaurant. 'It must be twelve-foot high.'

Anthony grimaced at the thought of Christmas, now less than a month away. Mary planned to spend it with her family, while his father had been invited to join Deborah at her parents' place, and, as for Darren, he, of course, would be with Carol-Ann. Only *he* seemed surplus to requirements and, with neither a religious faith nor young kids to give it point and purpose, it was hard to enter into the spirit of festivity. Still, at least he wouldn't be spending it in prison – a truly inestimable bonus.

'Darren, tell me more about your new job,' he urged once their drinks had arrived.

'Well, I'm still a bog-standard labourer, so all I do is sweeping up and stuff. But I did pass me Health and Safety test, which is the first step to promotion. So, once I've learnt some skills from the other blokes, I'm going to apply for my CSCS card ...' Seeing Anthony's puzzled expression, he added, '... a card that makes it, like, official that I'm safe to work on a building-site.'

'Sounds good, Darren. You're obviously making progress. But what's it like, that type of work?'

'Noisy!' Darren gave a sudden honking laugh. 'But they give us ear-muffs and all the other get-up – you know, hard hats and high-viz whatsits, and them boots with big steel toecaps. I reckon Carol-Ann fancies me in me tough-guy gear!'

'How *is* she?' Anthony took a sip of his wine, relishing, as usual, his escape from prison abstinence.

'Fantastic! I have to keep pinching meself to believe she's agreed to tie the knot. In fact, that's what this favour's about.'

'Well, go on – spit it out!'

Darren put his glass down, his anxious look returning. 'Promise to say no, mate, if you don't fancy the idea? You may think it's a bit of a cheek, see, or—'

He seemed relieved to be interrupted by the waiter, who appeared at that moment, with two extravagantly large plates. 'One *pappardelle* and one *tagliatelle ai Funghi Porcini. Buon appetito, signori!*'

'Crikey!' Darren muttered.

'*Parmigiana, Signori?*'

As Anthony nodded for them both, Darren watched in bemusement as the waiter grated a hail of yellow shavings onto both their plates.

'What *is* it?' he whispered.

'Just a type of cheese.' Again, he regretted his choice of restaurant, as another waiter glided over with a Doric column-sized pepper-mill. Apart from anything else, it had taken courage on his part to risk being spotted somewhere so central and "public" yet, three months into his release, he knew it was high time he made an effort to overcome that fear.

Having taken a first wary mouthful, Darren gave a vigorous nod of approval. 'Best pasta I've had in my life! Remember that stuff at Wandsworth – strands of spaghetti all stuck together like glue? It used to bung me up for days. Just think, Tony, we're both out of there and ain't never going back. That's something, isn't it?'

'I'd say! But never mind prison spaghetti – you were about to tell me the favour.'

Darren took a gulp of lager, as if to give himself courage, then blurted out in a rush, 'I want you to be my best man, Tony, and make a speech and everything? You're already my best *mate*, see, so it makes sense, don't it? And, anyways, Carol-Ann's parents are right snobs and don't think I'm good enough. But, if you said some of them nice things you said in your letters – like me being conscientious and meticu—, and all them other long words you taught me – I'm pretty sure they'd come round, especially with your nice posh voice and everything.' Again, he took refuge in his drink.

'I'd be really honoured Darren.' In truth, Anthony was forced to conceal his unease about such parental opposition, which had been news to him till now. He severely doubted whether long words and a posh voice would, or should, carry any weight, especially when uttered by a best man with a criminal conviction. Yet to refuse would be unforgivable. 'It'll actually be a first for me. I've never been anyone's best man. I'll have to start working on my jokes!'

'Never mind the jokes, Tony. I just need you to tell her family I'm basically okay.'

'You're much more than that, Darren, so I shan't let you down, I promise. But when's the wedding going to be?'

'Oh, not for ages. We need time, see, to save up. Weddings cost a bomb and Carol-Ann wants the whole shebang.'

Anthony paused a moment to sample his *tagliatelle*, the food matching the refinement of the ambience. 'Darren, do you mind if I give you a word of advice?'

'Mind, mate? 'Course not! There wouldn't *be* a wedding if it weren't for your advice. A girl like Carol-Ann would never get hitched to a right plonker who couldn't read or write. And, even when you and me was miles apart, you never gave up on me. I mean, all that trouble you took correcting me lessons by post, and them books you bought me last month, they was something else! But what means most of all, Tony, is you being there for me, like the dad I never had.'

Anthony gave a dismissive shrug, despite his pleasure in this bizarre form of fatherhood. 'Okay, Darren, all I want to say is try not to go mad and spend too much on the wedding. You're not earning that much, remember, and it's only one day, after all.' Hypocrite, he thought, recalling the huge cost of his and Deborah's wedding, even all those years ago.

'Yeah, but the most important day of Carol-Ann's life. And nowadays, everyone has big, expensive dos and I don't want her to think I'm a skinflint.'

'But surely her parents will be paying for most things?'

'Yeah, but not the rings, or her bouquet – or my gear, come to that. I can't be married in me jeans, mate!'

'I can easily lend you a suit. I have several rather snazzy ones and we're much the same size, so...'

'Oh, *Tony*!' Darren's face expressed his delight, and he began tucking into his pasta again, as if relief had restored his appetite.

'Borrow anything you want in fact if it'll stop you getting into debt again. You've been doing so well of late, and I'd hate to see you chucking all that progress down the drain.'

'I'll be good as gold – honest! But I want to hear your news now. It's all been me, me, me, so far, and I want to know why a brilliant bloke like you settled for such a crap job.'

'Frankly, it was all I could get. I hope it'll be just a stop-gap, but, if nothing else, it's made me see I'm not indispensable.'

'What's indispens—?'

'All-important, absolutely necessary. Which is what I felt I was to my former company. But that was simple arrogance. Someone else would have instantly taken over my desk and my computer and what I saw as my essential role. Yet I sacrificed my entire leisure-time to that company.'

'You must miss it, though – if only for all that dosh!'

'What I do miss is being part of a huge global corporation, which gave me respect and an entrée into almost every circle. And doing vital work that had an immediate impact on the economy. But the pressures were unrelenting. I was often up till the early hours trying to deal with the backlog and Deborah sometimes had to set an alarm to remind me to go to bed. And she complained I slept with my phone at night rather than with her!'

Darren grinned. 'Talking of which, tell me more about Mary.'

'She's completely and utterly perfect.' He tried to suppress his soppy smile at the mere mention of her name.

'It's weird, though, innit, you meeting her because of a black cat? I reckon me mascot brought you good luck.'

'Well, if that's the case, Mary's in your debt because she's besotted with the creature, showers love and devotion on it like a child with her best-beloved pet.'

'Well, you did say she were miles younger than you.'

'Not "miles",' he said, defensively.

'Nineteen years is quite a big gap. Ain't that a bit of a worry?'

'Why should it be?' Aware he sounded peeved (all the more so since he'd recently discovered that Mary's mother was exactly the same age as he was), he quickly moved on to Mary's other attributes. 'Age doesn't really come into it when she's so sweet and loving and kind.'

'But she don't have your fancy schooling, you said.'

'Well, no. But she has heaps of other talents. She can knit and sew and crochet and she's a really amazing cook and—'

'She don't sound nothing like Deborah,' Daren laughed. 'I remember you told me once your wife could barely boil an egg.'

It wasn't Mary's culinary skills, Anthony reflected, mopping up the last of his sauce, that made her so different from Deborah, but her whole attitude and temperament. She never argued with him, or put him down, or insisted on being right, but regarded him as clever, wise and knowledgeable. It was a heady new experience to bask in such approval and, indeed, only since he'd met her had he realised how critical and dominant his wife had often been.

'Well, they're certainly different physically,' he conceded, reaching for his phone. 'Here, let me show you her photo.' He couldn't resist running through all twenty pictures, the fond smile returning as he gazed at her unruly copper curls, a crazy contrast to Deborah's long straight hair, worn always neatly coiled. His eyes strayed to her figure – petite and yet voluptuous, the tantalizing breasts outlined beneath her clingy sweater – again an exciting contrast to his wife's slender elegance. 'She's just gorgeous, isn't she?'

'Yeah – a corker!'

'And she's so gentle and unaffected – a real country girl at heart. Her family live right up in the wilds of Lancashire. Her dad's a fencing contractor who supplies the local farms and suchlike. And Mary herself loves animals and nature and—'

'So what's she doing in London?'

'I suppose she must have moved down for her job. To be perfectly honest, I don't know that much about her yet. I've only known her a month.'

'Well, you be careful, mate. It's easy to go nuts about some girl the minute you're released from nick. You're like gagging for it, see, 'cause it's been so long since you got your leg over.'

'It was nothing like that,' he said, resentfully. Darren assumed his feelings were purely sexual, yet in point of fact he *hadn't* got his leg over. Besides, Mary wasn't 'some girl', but the most enchanting female he had ever encountered. 'I think I'm definitely falling in love with her.'

Darren still looked unconvinced, but gave a complicit grin. 'So do you plan to get hitched, like me?'

'I'm already married, Darren. And, quite apart from that, there's another huge problem standing in the way. You see, Probation insist I come clean about my time in gaol and tell Mary everything before I've any hope of moving in with her, let alone making it a permanent relationship. But doing that will destroy the whole thing, at a stroke.'

'It don't have to, Tony. Carol-Ann accepted me conviction and, if Mary's so kind and everything, she'll probably understand. And, anyways, that whole Craig thing was really a sort of accident. You didn't *mean* no harm.'

'She won't see it like that, though. She's a really moral person – brought up as a strict Roman Catholic. Which is another headache,' he added, deciding to open up. 'It may sound pathetic, with all your talk of leg-overs, but we haven't actually gone the whole way yet. We've kissed and cuddled, of course, yet she always stops me taking things further.'

'Yeah, because she's Catholic, mate. They're not allowed to shag around.'

'No, it isn't that. We've discussed religion, actually, and she says it means a lot to her, but she doesn't hold with all the rules, such as no divorce and no sex before marriage. I suspect it's more to do with her mother. The poor woman had nine successive pregnancies and although two ended in miscarriage, she still had seven children to bring up. And, apparently, the actual births took a huge toll on her health.'

'Well, that's a plus, ain't it – I mean if she ain't keen on having kids? Have you told her about your problem in that department?'

'God, no!' Because Mary thought so highly of him, he was extremely loth to tell her any of his faults and failings, let alone admit to firing blanks, or killing a father-of-three.

Darren forked in the last of his pasta, then sat back in his chair. 'D'you think she might have been abused or something – you know, as a child? That can make people dead-scared of having sex. And with all them cases we keep hearing about …'

'Lord! I never even thought of that.'

'Is everything all right, signori?' The waiter had sauntered over again.

'Yes, fine. And perhaps you could bring the menu, so we can order some dessert.'

With his mind in such turmoil, he was unable to focus on *tiramisu* or *pannacotta*. The very thought of Mary being raped or interfered with made his stomach churn with horror. 'But how on earth could I find out?'

he asked Darren, with a troubled frown. 'She's very shy and sort of ... innocent, so it would be out of the question even to ask her such a thing.'

'It sounds to me,' Darren declared, banging down his glass, 'that you both need a good long talk. I mean, it's all very well saying you're in love with her, but you just told me you hardly know her yet, so how can you be close? It's asking for trouble if you're both hiding loads of stuff.'

'There's not the slightest sign she's hiding anything. She seems perfectly happy and normal.'

'Yeah, but *you're* not being upfront, mate, so the sooner you tell her the truth the better – quite apart from Probation insisting.'

'But where in God's name do I start? And, anyway, we don't see that much of each other. By the time I've finished my night-shift, she's getting ready to leave for work. And, even when she's back, we don't have long together before *I* go off again. Besides, I have to be in my own flat a certain amount of the time, just to keep the authorities happy. And, even if I do confess, I shan't be allowed to move in with her until my probation officer's interviewed her and checked on the place and everything, which means we're talking months. We do have weekends, of course, but those are our best times, so I'd hate to spoil them with something that'll shock her to the core.'

'Well, in that case, mate, it ain't going to work. You'll be living a lie and that just ain't fair to her.'

Darren sounded so uncharacteristically sharp, Anthony put his head in his hands.

'Sorry, Tony, didn't mean to snap. It's just that I'm fond of you, see, so I want things to work out. But, listen, I got an idea. Why don't you take her on a day-trip to the sea? If you get right away from London, that'll help you relax. Me and Carol-Ann feel like different people when we're down at Clacton, what with the sea air and everything. In fact, I told her all me own baggage when we was walking on the beach and, though I was nervous as all hell, at least we had plenty of time to go over the whole thing and not be interrupted by the phone or work and stuff.'

'What can I get you, *signori?*'

Although annoyed by the waiter's intrusions, Anthony made an effort to explain *tiramisu* to Darren, since both *mascarpone* and *savoiardi* were untranslated on the menu.

'Yeah, sounds good. I'll have it, ta.'

Anthony settled for it, too, hardly caring what he chose. If he revealed his crime to Mary, he might as well wave goodbye to her now.

'Now, listen, Tony,' Darren said, crumpling his linen napkin into a ball, 'I've made loads of promises to *you* – sticking to me budget and doing me homework and stuff. But now it's your turn to promise *me* something – that you'll do what I suggest and take Mary down to Brighton or some such, then, once you're away from all the pressures, just bite the bullet and tell her about your time in nick.'

'I can't!'

'You *can*, mate. And here's something that may help.' Darren rummaged in his pocket and brought out a lucky-shamrock-keyring in a jolting shade of green. 'It's me new lucky mascot, even better than the cat – helped me get me new job and made me less shit-scared when I told Carol-Ann's mum I were marrying her daughter, so I reckon it'll bring you luck with Mary. But you need to take it with you to the beach and keep holding tight to it all the time you're 'fessing up.'

Anthony stared down at the shiny enamel trinket. How could anyone possibly believe that a four-leaved clover could persuade a sweetly virtuous girl like Mary to throw in her lot with a criminal? 'But you obviously need it yourself, Darren.'

'Not half as much as you do, mate! Go on, take it – and no more argument.'

In desperation and even a sort of anger, Anthony rammed it into his pocket.

'Great! And be sure to phone and let me know the minute you've had your talk. And make it soon, okay?'

CHAPTER 23

'I still can't believe this weather!' Mary exclaimed. 'Wall-to-wall sunshine in the first week of December! And doesn't it look beautiful glinting and shimmering on the waves?'

Anthony nodded, slipping his arm around her waist as they stood together on the beach, looking out at the sea. 'It's such a shame, though, that we have to leave so early. Can't I persuade you to change your mind?'

'No, honestly, I must get back for Mass – and for Anton, of course.'

'He'll be fine with Mrs Murray-Woods.' In his element, in fact: cossetted and cuddled and fed like a crown-prince. Add hyphen.)

'Yes, but I do need to spend some time with her after church. She's been really lonely since her husband died, and even the son hardly visits at all. His wife's expecting their first baby, you see, at the age of forty-two and had lots of ghastly problems with her pregnancy. And now she's near her due-date, they just have to stay close to the hospital.'

Half admiring, half annoyed, he reflected on Mary's assumption of the role of daughter-in-law. Typical of her kindness to provide comfort and companionship for someone completely unrelated to her.

'Besides,' she added, with an affectionate squeeze of his arm, 'it'll be dark in an hour, so we'd have to make a move in any case. The days are very short, remember, however sunny it may be.'

Darkness might actually help, he thought, with increasing desperation. Perhaps he would finally succeed in "confessing" if they went for a *second* walk on the beach and were no longer subjected to the full, judgemental stare of the sun.

They stood a few minutes' longer, listening to the rhythmic slap of the waves, followed by a slower, withdrawing whoosh as the water flounced back onto the shingle.

'Hark at those gulls!' Mary raised her voice above a sudden raucous screeching from a cluster of black-backs fighting over a discarded sandwich. 'I have a friend who lives in Eastbourne and she insists the

Eastbourne gulls are nothing like as noisy as these vulgar Brighton ones, but better-mannered altogether!'

He laughed, although in truth he felt more like weeping at the thought of losing this delightful girl. Today she looked particularly adorable, all muffled up in her fake-fur coat, a pink, woolly, pompomed hat and long, fuzzy matching scarf.

'I'm sorry to rush you, my sweet,' she said, with a quick look at her watch, 'but if we're going to catch the 3.35pm, we ought to set off for the station.'

No one had ever called him 'my sweet' before and, since it was hardly an apposite term for a criminal, it seemed even more impossible to reveal his true self, even under the cover of darkness. Darren had made this onerous task sound ridiculously simple, yet so far he'd failed ignominiously in even attempting it. There was still time, however, on the walk back to the station – not exactly the ideal setting, but at least he would have met the challenge before they actually left Brighton.

However, once they'd turned off the promenade and were walking up Queen's Road, he realised the street was too crowded to embark on so tricky a conversation and, what with dodging pushchairs and scatty kids on scooters, and stopping at each crossroad, he was forced to conclude that the idea was a non-starter. Wouldn't it be better to tell her on the train? He would have a whole hour then – as well as her undivided attention – and if they choose two seats on their own, as they'd done on the way down, they would be guaranteed a certain amount of privacy. This morning's journey had brought them closer, and, in face of her touchingly childlike excitement at this rare-for-her expedition, his agitation had actually dwindled a little. And, although bashful at first when he'd kissed her 'in public', as she called it, she had soon responded eagerly. Her hair smelled of summer-in-winter, her lips were sensuous, soft …

'You're very quiet,' she observed, giving him an anxious glance.

Not wanting to cast a pall on the day until he absolutely had to, he made an effort to chat about anodyne subjects until they reached the station, but, once they were walking through the train in search of seats, he was annoyed to see that many were already taken. This morning, they had set out really early, to make the most of the light and, because most people weren't yet up, the train had been near-empty. Mary had packed them a picnic breakfast of bacon rolls and hot chocolate, which they'd devoured in delicious seclusion. This train, however, was quite another matter – indeed, surprisingly noisy, considering it was only mid-afternoon. People were jabbering on their mobiles and fractious children fighting over computer games, while a couple of harassed mothers chipped in with threats and warnings, and a gaggle of teenage lads began a mock fight in the aisle. Eventually, he and Mary found two seats at a table for four, but opposite, not side by side, and with the other two seats occupied, which put the kybosh on any chance of a private conversation.

Mary dipped into her capacious holdall and brought out some home-made flapjacks and a flask of tea, still warm, this second picnic prompting more anguish than delight, since the more she indulged him, the more loath he was to face the prospect of the relationship ever ending.

'Are you okay, my sweet?' she asked, leaning towards him so she didn't need to raise her voice. 'Since we left the beach, you do seem rather down.'

'I'm just sad at the thought of leaving you. Do you have to go to that Mass?'

'Well, I've paid to have it said, you see, so I really ought to be there. And, in any case, it's my mother's birthday present – a special Mass celebrated in her honour. I do it every year and it's become a sort of tradition, one I wouldn't like to break.'

'But you said you're going to church again tomorrow. Couldn't *that* Mass be for your mother?'

'No. Tomorrow's the Feast of the Immaculate Conception, so it's a completely different thing.'

Although the Catholic Church struck him as bizarre, he was charmed by her devotion – another aspect of her simple, innate goodness, as was her loving duty to her mother. Presumably this Mass was a precious gift, which meant he shouldn't even try to talk her out of going, however strange a gift it might seem, compared with the Chanel scent or Hermes scarves he used to buy for *his* mother.

'Tell you what – once we're at Seven Sisters, I'll walk you back to your place and pop in for just a minute or two,'

'But that'll take you out of your way. Wouldn't you rather go straight home?'

Home was where Mary was. 'I just want to give Anton a quick cuddle,' he lied, depressingly aware that if he went straight home he would have to admit to total failure in his mission of disclosure. And, despite the fact he would have only an extremely short time at Mary's, it might actually be better to compress the whole complicated narrative into a short and succinct précis, rather than spell out every damning detail.

Leaning forward again across the table, Mary put her hand on his. 'Thank you, darling, for such a lovely day.'

'Darling' was new and special – 'darling' was important. But there would be no more 'darlings' after today, no more cuddling Anton, or kissing Mary.

'It's ages since I've been down to the sea. Sometimes, I forget it's even *there*! But just being on the beach today made me feel sort of ... spring-cleaned, as if the wind and the waves were scouring off all the London grime and polishing me to a shine!'

She *always* looked polished in her artistic, artless way, and now, after their energetic walk, her skin was glowing with youth and health. Another Immaculate Mary – sitting opposite a criminal.

She continued happily chatting and somehow he managed to get through the remainder of the journey by keeping part of his mind on their conversation, while another part struggled to condense the last two traumatic years into a manageably brief account. And, by the time they were back at her place, he was ready to blurt it out in one fell swoop, but barely had he opened his mouth when they were interrupted by Mrs Murray-Woods, with Anton in her arms.

'He's been such a good boy, my dears – not a squeak out of the little love! As I always say, he has a really beautiful nature.'

Any praise of her pet prompted Mary's radiant smile, and she was beaming as she thanked the old lady and handed her a present, having transferred the cat to him. 'Here's a souvenir from Brighton for you. I know you're keen on jigsaws and this one's called "Brighton Bound". She pointed to the picture on the front of the puzzle-box. "It shows one of the old Pullmans thundering out of Victoria down to the coast.'

'Oh, how lovely, dear! Thank you. It looks fiendishly difficult and, with eight-hundred pieces it should keep me nice and busy.'

'That's what I thought. But listen Mrs Murray-Woods, I'll come to see you later, as I promised, but I have to dash off to church now, and Anthony's just leaving.'

No, he *couldn't* leave. This was his last remaining chance to get things off his chest.

'Well, in that case, I'll take pussy back upstairs. I'm sure he'll appreciate a few more little cuddles.'

As Mary handed Anton back and the old lady made her slow way up the basement steps and on to the main house, he turned to face Mary, now determined to confess.

But no words came out, for Christ's sake! At this vital moment his voice had rusted up, as if he'd been struck dumb. Perhaps that was a blessing, though. Wasn't this the worst possible time, with Mary in a rush and unable to concentrate? Indeed, wouldn't it be selfish and unfair to make her feel torn between doing her duty by her mother and listening to his saga?

With a last, terse goodbye, he darted out of the room, took the basement steps two at a time and began hurtling along the street in a turmoil of shame and frustration, only lurching to a halt as he recalled Daren's words about never being close to Mary if he continued to deceive her. The lad had exacted only one promise from him – a promise he was about to break. He thrust his hand into his pocket and felt the hard, accusing outline of the shamrock, which, in obedience to his "mate" he'd been gripping throughout their walk on the beach – not just crazy superstition but a patently futile endeavour. Yet it wasn't too late, even now. With just a few inadequate minutes in hand, it was still better to get the thing over.

Impulsively, he rushed back to the house, all but colliding with Mary, who was coming up the steps as he was blundering down. 'Mary, listen!' he half-sobbed, half-shouted, 'there's something I *have* to tell you – something desperately important that may change everything between us.'

Mary looked seriously alarmed – as well she might when he was gripping both her hands, as if to keep her there by force.

'It won't take long – five minutes. And don't worry about church. If I call you a taxi, so—'

'Never mind church,' she cut in. 'You're clearly in a dreadful state, so come back in and sit down.'

Impossible to sit. Nor, this time, could he prepare or polish his words. So, standing up – one hand deep in his pocket, clutching the shamrock so tightly it cut into his skin – he recounted the whole saga in one headlong, breathless torrent, from the moment he'd found Craig in bed with Deborah, right up to the present. And only when he had gasped to a stop, did he collapse onto a chair, feeling extraordinarily exhausted and with no idea whether he'd been speaking for the five minutes he had promised, or for well over an hour.

Mary's face was a mask, her usual rosy cheeks now ashen pale. And even as he gazed at her imploringly, she failed to smile or soften, failed to say a single word in response to his agonised outpouring. The silence seemed to stretch beyond the bedsit, to Edmonton and Enfield, reach further still, to Milton Keynes and on to …

'I understand,' he said, at last, his voice now a shred, a rag. 'You're shocked, disgusted, never want to see me again. Don't worry – you won't have to. I'm leaving – now!'

As he turned his back and stumbled towards the door, he suddenly felt her hand on his shoulder, heard her voice sounding shaky and disjointed.

'I am shocked, yes – of course I'm shocked. B-but it's not that … It … It's …'

Her words stuttered to a halt and silence flooded in again, like a clammy, choking fog. Then, all at once, she whispered in an anguished tone, 'You say you understand, but, Anthony, you don't – you can't. You see, what you couldn't possibly know is that I … I've killed someone, too, so I'm just as much a murderer as you.'

CHAPTER 24

Anthony stared in astoundment. How, in heaven's name could this gentle sparrow be a hawk? Mary looked too innocent and ingenuous to have killed so much as a ladybird. How could you ever tell, though? In his previous life, people would never have imagined that *he* would have been capable of crime.

He and Mary were standing facing each other, like enemies. 'Let's sit down,' he said, leading her to the sofa, aware she was visibly trembling. 'Can you try to tell me about it?'

'No. I've never told a single soul – except for one close friend, who was involved in the whole thing.'

Two of them? Conspirators? The self-important clock was the only sound in the room now, its ponderous tick rebuking the silence. 'Mary, *I* told you everything and that was a hell of a risk, because, for all I know, you may hate me now.'

'Oh, Anthony, how could I? I feel desperately sad to think of you landing up in prison, when you never intended to kill anyone.'

Her words brought dizzying relief in that there was still the chance of a relationship – unless, of course, what *she* revealed proved so grotesque it changed his feelings for her. 'And the reason I told you was I knew it was wrong to let you go on thinking I was a normal, decent sort of bloke, and not give you the true picture. But the same applies to you. How can I know the real you if you're hiding something so important?'

'But where do I start?' Mary said, sounding fraught and still reluctant.

'At the beginning,' he suggested, with just a ghost of a smile.

She took in a great gasping breath, before speaking in a frayed, ragged voice. 'Well, there was this … this man called Ronald – my boss. I was working as his secretary in Ribchester and still living at home with the family. He was much older than me, but very sweet and supportive, and he took a lot of interest in my life. My father hadn't done that – not that I'm blaming him, of course. With seven kids to provide for, and a job with very long hours, he just didn't have the energy or time. And, anyway, there was always some younger child who needed his attention more than me. So I found myself staying late at the office, just to talk to Ronald, who actually seemed quite lonely. Then, one evening, he invited me out and, afterwards, we ... went back to his place. It was *my* fault, Anthony – I shouldn't have gone. But he said all these lovely things – how pretty I was and how good at my job – and I suppose I let myself be flattered. I'd also had a glass or two of wine, so things well ... sort of developed and somehow ...'

Mary's face invariably revealed her state of mind; once ashen pale, it was now suffused with a deep blush. She swallowed several times, as if clearing an obstruction in her throat. 'And ... and the result was I fell pregnant.'

He felt a surge of jealous rage towards this 'sweet', 'supportive' bastard, as well as extreme distaste for the subject of pregnancy – again.

'Although I was twenty by then, it was the first time I'd ever ... done it. You see, I'd been brought up to believe that sex outside marriage was a really serious sin. I no longer think that, actually, and the majority of Catholics are much more liberal nowadays, but not my parents, I assure you. They're only in their forties, so you might expect them to be less rigid, but they still insist on sticking to the strict letter of the Church's teaching. So, when I realised I was expecting, no way could I tell them. They'd have turfed me out of the house, there and then, if only to prevent me scandalising my younger sisters and brother.'

'But you told Ronald, I assume?'

'Oh, no! I didn't want to involve him, because I was the one who should have known better. He had no religion, you see, and probably thought I was on the pill. That's also a sin for Catholics, but I doubt he would have known that.'

Anthony tried to suppress another surge of anger. How dare she excuse some 'lonely', lascivious bloke who had clearly taken advantage of her innocence, plied her with drink and compliments, then laid his filthy paws on a virgin – a rare species, these days, for God's sake – yet still managed to escape scot-free? Darren had been right in his hunch about abuse.

'Having no one to tell made it worse. The baby seemed to be growing at a terrifying rate, although, in fact, it didn't show yet. But I knew I'd have to leave before it did – leave my home and job and the whole area. We live in this tiny village, you see, where everybody knows each other, so gossip and scandal would spread like wildfire. Well, I began to feel so frantic, I finally confided in Josie.'

'Josie?' Mary had mentioned several of her friends, but never a Josie.

'My best friend. I've known her since primary school and, even when she moved down to London to get a better job, we remained as close as ever – we were always on the phone to each other and she came back on regular visits. She's a Catholic, too, with equally strict parents, so she totally understood how shocked my parents would be. And, as for having an abortion, that was simply unthinkable. So she invited me to stay with her in London, and I have to say I did feel safer, living in a big, anonymous block, where people keep themselves to themselves. I told my parents she'd found me a job in her firm, with much higher pay than I'd ever get locally. Surprisingly, they didn't object. Maybe one less person in our small, overcrowded house was almost a relief and, anyway, I should have left home long ago. I felt awful, though, lying about the job, when actually I *couldn't* work.'

'Why not?' he asked, puzzled.

'Well, by that time I was beginning to show, and Josie said on no account must anyone realise I was pregnant. You see, we'd discussed the thing over and over and considered all the possibilities – me having the baby and bringing it up at Josie's place as a single mum on benefits, or having it adopted, or entrusting it to this friend of Josie's who was desperate for a child, but couldn't have one of her own. But all those options would have made it much more public and my parents might have found out.' Mary's frenetic tone made it seem as if she were reliving the whole dilemma.

'I just didn't know *what* to do, so I started Googling "unwanted babies" and loads of sites came up – some with horrendous stories of tiny babies dumped in rubbish-tips or even flushed down the toilet. And there was masses of really worrying stuff about the various ways the police can trace mothers who abandon babies. The very thought of being nabbed by the police made my blood run cold, yet I didn't want my child coming to the slightest harm. So, eventually, Josie came up with a plan: I'd give birth in her flat, with her on hand to help, then we'd leave the baby on her parish priest's doorstep. He's a really holy man, she said, who'd find it the best possible Catholic home. But, of course, we had to keep the whole thing strictly anonymous, leave an unsigned note and implore him never to try to search out the baby's mother. But, since we knew he might ignore that, from a sense of duty or something, we had to take every possible precaution. Josie stressed that no one must ever find a shred of evidence either on me or on the child.'

Mary let out a great, shuddering sigh. 'You've no idea, Anthony, how complicated it was, even just the letter. I had to type it on a computer, wearing latex gloves, and using a brand new pack of paper, and be sure not to lick the envelope. Josie did this research, you see, on all the methods the police use to track these mothers down. So, in order to get round them, she gave me detailed instructions about what I had to wear when I was delivering the baby to the priest's house – completely new clothes, and a hat to hide my hair so no one could identify its style and colour, and a coat with a big shawl-type collar to pull right up and blur any images that might be caught on CCTV. I even had to wear a face-mask, so as not to breathe over the baby. And Josie said I must avoid all public transport and keep to the side-streets, where there are fewer cameras anyway. And the minute I'd left the child on the step and was safely out of sight, I was to change my entire outfit and hide my face and hair again, with …'

'I'm sorry, Anthony—' she suddenly broke off. 'I must be boring you with all these footling details.'

'Boring me! Are you joking? For God's sake, carry on.'

'Well, Josie had also warned me that abandoned babies always make the headlines, so there'd be a big media campaign, and the police would start a public investigation and ask witnesses to come forward – you know, had anyone seen a woman carrying a suspicious-looking bundle in the priest's vicinity, or know a woman who'd recently given birth but no longer had the baby? I was so terrified, I barely went out at all, except to Mass each Sunday. I couldn't take Communion, of course, but it's another sin to miss Mass altogether and I didn't want to make things worse.'

He felt troubled by her obsession with sin – an unknown concept for most of his casually secular contemporaries, and surely unusual for someone of her age. It hadn't slipped his notice that she was missing Mass right now – another sin, presumably. Yet, whatever crime she might have committed, her essential nature was sinless, or so his instinct told him.

'Of course, I didn't go to Josie's church. In fact, I chose a different one each week, so there was no risk of people noticing a new "regular". And, fortunately, it was winter, so I could hide my bulge under a big, baggy coat. Apart from that, I just skulked indoors and Josie did all the shopping and stuff. Luckily, I managed to get a couple of jobs I could do at home, from her place, with no one needing to lay eyes on me – addressing envelopes and cold-calling for a double-glazing firm – so at least I could contribute a bit to the rent.'

As she paused for breath, Anthony jumped in. 'Mary, from all you've told me so far, I can't see any element of wrong. You did your best by Josie, you'd planned to leave your child with someone highly responsible, and you hadn't burdened your parents with the worry of your situation when they already had their hands full.'

'Wait a minute! You don't know the half of it. Things didn't go to plan, you see. The baby was due in early April and Josie had arranged to take that time off work, so she could help me through the birth and make sure I followed all her instructions afterwards. But my labour started almost four weeks early, when she was abroad on a business trip. I didn't dare to phone or email, in case the calls or texts or whatever could be traced. Besides, I couldn't drag her back when so much was at stake for her. She'd told me more than once that, if the trip went well, she was bound to get promoted and get a big pay-rise into the bargain.'

'So you gave birth all alone?' he asked, appalled.

She nodded. 'Yes. I was scared shitless the whole time, because I didn't really know what was happening to my body. Josie had read up the whole business, so she could act as midwife, and she kept urging me to read the books as well. But the briefest glance at them made me still more frightened, and I suppose I found it easier to pretend there wasn't going to *be* a birth.'

'Oh, Mary, I'm just so sorry for you.'

'Well, you won't be when you hear what happened next.'

Could she have suffocated the child the minute it was born? No, impossible.

'The labour seemed to go on for an eternity and I was in really dreadful pain. In fact, when the baby was finally born, I just couldn't believe how small he was, because all the time I was trying to push him out, he felt as big as a whale. And I looked at the poor little scrap, all red and crumpled and bald, and felt this sort of … horror. He seemed so miserable himself, and was whimpering and snuffling, as if he couldn't breathe. But the worst thing of all was that I didn't feel the slightest shred of love for him, so I must be truly wicked, because most mothers love their babies just by instinct.'

'Mary, you're the least wicked person I've ever met! Anyway, how could you *expect* to love a child who'd already caused you so much pain and grief?'

'You don't understand' – she sprang to her feet in obvious agitation – 'I didn't even feed him, although I had plenty of breast milk.' Her cheeks crimsoned again, at the mention of breast milk. 'Forgive me, Anthony. I shouldn't be telling you all this intimate stuff.'

Just as he was trying to reassure her, there was a tap at the door and Mrs Murray-Wood called out, 'I've brought Anton back, my dears.'

Mary rushed to let her in, looking still more embarrassed at the intrusion.

'Forgive me if I'm interrupting. I did try to ring first, Mary dear, but your phone was switched off, so I assumed you'd gone to church. But then I heard you talking from my sitting-room upstairs and I wasn't sure whether to bring pussy back or not.'

Mary's blush grew deeper, so Anthony filled in for her. 'Mary decided to miss Mass, as she wasn't feeling well, so I felt I ought to stay with her.'

'Oh, I'm sorry. What a shame! Are you a little better now, dear? Is there anything I can do?'

Just make yourself scarce, Anthony bit back, taking the cat from her arms and placing it on the sofa. 'She's fine now, Mrs Murray-Wood. It was just a dizzy spell.'

Mary was clearly making an effort to sound her normal, cheery self as she thanked the old lady for cat-sitting. 'Anthony will be going soon,' she added. 'We're just discussing …. various matters.'

'Don't worry. He can stay as long as he likes. I don't have rules about gentlemen callers.'

Once she'd returned upstairs, he joined Mary on the sofa. 'Don't let that interruption put you off. You just have to finish your story.'

He noted that, uncharacteristically, she hadn't put Anton on her lap and seemed distracted altogether. And, when she eventually spoke, it was with all the weariness and weakness she was actually describing. 'I felt so shattered after the birth, I just lay there on the floor and couldn't seem to rouse myself to do a single thing. There was all this mess on the carpet I knew I should clear up, but I was still having awful pains. I'd no idea why and there was nobody to ask, so I just took four Paracetamol and crawled into bed with the baby and tried to keep it warm. But I must have fallen asleep, because when I woke up – and this is the really awful bit …' As the sentence trailed away, she began sobbing inconsolably.

He put his arm around her, took both her hands in his. 'What happened, Mary? You must go on.'

'The baby was … was dead. I'd killed him – killed my own child.'

'Of course you hadn't, Mary! He was nearly a month premature and very small, you said, so his grip on life was probably very tenuous. He might well have died in any case.'

'You don't understand,' she repeated. 'I'd put myself first, don't you see? *My* pain, *my* exhaustion, *my* need for sleep. Any half-decent mother would have put her child first, however bad she might feel herself. If only I'd fed him, he'd still be alive, I'm sure.'

'You can't be sure. For all you know, he might have been damaged during your long labour, with no one there to help.'

'But that's my fault, too. I should have realised it might be dangerous giving birth alone, and taken myself to hospital the minute my contractions started. All I had to do was call an ambulance.'

'Yes, but then all the trouble you'd taken to try to hush the whole thing up would have been blown apart at a stroke.'

'Too bad. I ought to have simply put up with the consequences. But I was only thinking of me, me, me again – my need to keep the baby secret and escape my parents' anger. If Mum was ever to find out that I hadn't even baptised the child, she'd never forgive me, I swear! She lost two babies herself, both within hours of their birth, but when the midwife told her they were unlikely to survive, she baptised them herself – you know, to prevent them going to Limbo and never seeing God. Hardly anyone believes in Limbo these days, but for Mum the very thought was quite traumatic, because it would mean her being parted from those babies for all eternity, instead of them being reunited in Heaven, after *her* death. But you mustn't think she's weird. She's a really lovely person and far more unselfish than me. I mean, she calmly accepted all nine of her pregnancies, whatever the cost to her health. And so did Dad, despite the fact he had to work even harder to feed us all.'

Not so much unselfish, he thought, bitterly, but stupid and straitlaced, a narrow-minded, blinkered couple who refused to use contraception and allowed priests and popes to interfere with every aspect of their private life.

'Of course, I hadn't seen them for months and I'd had to keep making up excuses why I hadn't visited – how busy I was at work and how my boss kept cancelling any leave I was due. To be honest, I was earning such a pittance, I couldn't have afforded the train fare, anyway. But it turned out they had problems of their own – my brother was ill and Dad had been made redundant and was frantically trying to find another job. I was gutted to hear that, of course, but at least it meant they weren't too focused on me. And, even after it was over, I still kept away. I mean, how could I face them when I'd murdered my own baby?'

'You *hadn't*, Mary!' he all but shouted, in his effort to convince her. 'Infanticide involves a deliberate intention to kill, or some wilful act of negligence, whereas your baby died because it was too weak to live. Never for a moment did you intend to do away with it.'

All at once, she began crying again, stammering through her tears. 'I … I haven't told you how awful it was being alone in the flat with the … the corpse. I simply didn't know what to do, so, in the end, I decided to follow Josie's original plan and leave it on Father Michael's doorstep, with a different note, begging him to give the child a proper funeral. But, when I set out in the early hours, carrying the cold, lifeless little body wrapped up in layers of cardboard and brown paper to make it look like an innocent parcel, I felt that every person in the world was watching me, including God Himself. In fact, it was a terrible struggle to get there at all, because I was still bleeding quite a lot and I had to stuff this great thick towel up …'

Suddenly aware she was confiding appallingly intimate matters, her flush deepened even more and, to spare him further embarrassment, she mumbled something about how her very desperation gave her the strength to carry out the task, then rushed on with her story. 'Anyway, I rang the priest's bell really loud and long, so he'd be certain to wake up, then, once I'd left the letter and the …. the parcel, I took to my heels and fled. I destroyed all the clothes I'd worn and, of course I had to burn the towel, so nothing could incriminate me. There was no way I could escape, though, because the discovery was splashed all over the papers, just as if a live child had been found. And there was the same effort by the police to trace me, the same appeal for witnesses. I was absolutely petrified my cover would be blown, despite the fact I'd followed all Josie's instructions. So, within days of her returning from Frankfurt, I deliberately moved up here, to put myself at a safer distance from her West Acton flat.'

'But how did you find a new place, let alone pay for it?'

'Josie came up trumps again! She'd heard on the grapevine that a friend of a friend in the office had just moved out of this bedsit in Seven Sisters and that the owner of the house – our dear Mrs Murray-Wood – was looking for a replacement tenant. Apparently, she's always been happy to charge a lower rent to someone really responsible who's willing to do a bit of shopping for her, or give her a hand with the chores. Fortunately, once we met, we hit if off immediately and she said I could move in that very weekend. And because I told her I was trying to find a job and things were a bit tight till I'd succeeded, she even gave me three months' grace before I had to pay a penny. I promised to pay off the backlog as soon as my finances improved but, at that stage, she wouldn't hear of it – said I'd been so helpful in the interim she was actually in *my* debt.'

'Thank God', he murmured, *sotto voce*. Mary deserved a few favours, and was certainly sounding more upbeat.

'And another stroke of luck was finding Smokey. In fact, he proved a boon for all three of us because Smokey had a nice safe home, *she* felt useful and needed, caring for him when I was out at work, and for me it was a godsend because I could pour out all the love on Smokey I should have lavished on my baby.'

Aware that Mary had gone off on a tangent, he gently returned her to her story. 'But what about Josie? Did you tell her the baby had died?'

'Oh, I had to! There were posters up in her area by then, as part of the whole police campaign, and this great hoo-ha going on. But I made her promise never, ever to mention the whole ghastly thing again. I pretended I wanted to blank it out completely, although that was quite impossible since never a day goes by without my thinking about it. But I did keep it a total secret till this moment and—'

'I hope you don't regret telling me,' he cut in.

'No, I actually feel better, but just reliving it again brings back all the—'

She broke off with a shudder and he kept both his arms around her, trying to make them like a firewall, shielding her from any further pain. 'The one thing I understand, Mary, is how all-consuming guilt can be. But I have far more cause for guilt than you. I *wanted* to do Craig harm.'

'Not to kill him, though' – timidly, she sank into his embrace – 'and that's entirely different. Also, you were punished with the loss of your job and that awful long stretch in prison, whereas I got away with my crime.'

'Darling, it wasn't a crime. How many times must I tell you?'

'D'you mind if we don't discuss it any more? To be honest, Anthony, I feel completely shattered ...'

Her voice tailed off in exhaustion. Hardly surprising. The last hour or two had been unutterably draining for them both. 'Why don't you lie down and rest, and I'll stay around for a while, just to make sure you're okay? I shan't say another word, though, so if there's any chance you could get a bit of sleep ...'

To sleep in any comfort she would need to remove her bulky sweater and pleated tartan skirt but, if he suggested such a thing his intentions might sound dubious. Indeed, he couldn't deny how randy he felt as she stretched out on the divan, instantly joining her in fantasy – not just on the bed but *in* it. Anton, for his part, did, in fact, spring on to the bed, settling himself against his mistress's chest. Envious of such lechery when *he* was forced to remain on the sofa, he had little option but to rehearse the many obstacles standing in the way of any true intimacy with Mary. However liberal she might claim to be, her parents' abhorrence of sex outside marriage must have influenced her profoundly. Or perhaps her lapse with Ronald had put her off the whole business altogether and, of course, she was bound to fear falling pregnant again. That wasn't a problem in his particular case – one crumb of comfort, at least. And there was, undeniably, a powerful bond between them now, both burdened as they were with guilt and both forced to hide their pasts. And she must undoubtedly trust him, he realised, as he saw her eyes close and heard her breathing deepen, in allowing herself to fall asleep in his presence.

He dared not make the slightest sound or movement, for fear of waking her. Indeed, he felt annoyed with the heedless cars that droned past on the road outside. Mary mustn't be disturbed – that was paramount.

He still had a raging hard-on, though, and prurient images were still flooding into his mind, some prompted by her earlier mention of breast-feeding. As he, too, closed his eyes, he imagined her breasts enticingly full as he cupped them in his hands, his mouth moving slowly to her lips. And, as he parted her lips with his tongue, encountering no resistance, what had started as a tentative kiss gradually intensified, as her tongue, too, seemed to learn new sensuous skills. Driven half-wild, he began kissing her neck, her throat, her breasts, then dared to go still lower, aware of her breathing quickening, her excitement matching his. It was simple in his fantasy to change her from a shyly modest violet to a raging tornado of a vamp, and thus free himself from the need to take things slowly, or keep his touch gentle and considerate. Instead, he thrust deep into her with frenzied force and energy, thrilled to see she was equally worked up, hear her crying out in a great, gasping voice, 'Yes, go on, go *on*!' Needing no such prompting, he abandoned himself to full-flame coupling, his long, lonely, sex-starved months shrinking to the merest dream. And then, at the exact same moment, they exploded in the most tumultuous climax he had ever known in life – or fantasy.

CHAPTER 25

'I'm sorry, Mr Beaumont, but this isn't going to work. I don't mean just the business of your criminal conviction – although that *is* a risk, of course – but the fact you're wildly over-qualified for so basic a position.'

'Yes, you've made that clear, Mr Newman' – Anthony tried to keep his voice upbeat – 'but that's not a problem for me.' An Accounts Assistant was a definite improvement on disinfecting office toilets and scraping chewing gum off office chairs.

'Maybe so, but it could be a problem for my other staff. One or two are bound to feel uncomfortable with someone of your calibre doing such lowly work. And you'll be answerable to them, of course, which could make things still more awkward.'

'But there's no need for me to mention my experience.' He was determined to keep arguing his case, despite the fact there seemed scant chance of changing Mr Newman's mind.

'Even so, I fear you'll soon tire of doing routine tasks far below your natural abilities, and then up and leave us for a more high-powered job.'

Fat chance! Who was likely to employ him as a Finance Controller or indeed any prestigious accountancy job, when he couldn't get a footing on the lowest rung of the ladder? His disappointment was all the greater because it was Betty who had supplied this contact. He had taken her out for a drink, last week, to beg her help in finding him more amenable employment, and she had given him the details of this small Soho advertising agency – promising in itself, since he knew the ad-world through and through, if only from Deborah's eighteen years in the business. Then, obliging as ever, Betty had even spoken to Mr Newman in person, to vouch for his integrity and skills, so again he'd had reason to hope.

It was now clear, however, that any further argument would only alienate Mr Newman, who, in any case, was rising to his feet to signify that the interview was over. Having thanked him for his time, Anthony mooched out of the overheated building into the rebuking slap of the cold December air, which seemed to emphasise his deep-seated sense of failure. He even resented the busy, purposeful people rushing past him in Frith Street, all probably high achievers. Okay, he *had* a job – and one he still performed to the most exacting standard – but, for Mary's sake, he needed something better. He was also keen to end his inconvenient night-shifts, which he felt were partly to blame for the fact he still hadn't got his leg over, to use Darren's terminology. Sometimes Mary wasn't back from Mr Edwardes till seven or even eight, which gave them a pitifully short time, before he left for *his* job, for the sort of gentle, slow-paced, unthreatening sex essential to win her trust, whereas, with normal daytime work, he could stay at her place at least until the early hours. Any chance of spending a night there, though, or moving in with her, still depended on Probation.

Whatever the problems, just the thought of Mary was invariably consoling and, recalling her motherly advice not to go too long without food, he decided to grab a bite to eat. He could also put the lunch-hour to good use by continuing his job search. The pubs he passed appeared to be in Christmas overdrive, so he settled for a quiet café further up towards Tottenham Court Road and, having ordered an expresso and a wrap, he logged on to the recruitment sites he had book-marked on his phone, this time deliberately avoiding all accountancy jobs. Soon, however, he felt his usual frustration at the morass of unsuitable vacancies: sales assistant with 'a passion for fashion'; parking attendant; motorcycle food-delivery courier; vertical lift engineer; care-worker in an old people's home; car mechanic; florist. Were florists ever male, he wondered – although, even if they were, he doubted he'd find much job satisfaction in arranging lilies with maidenhair fern. And, as for working with the elderly, he drew the line at wiping the withered bottoms of nonagenarians.

After twenty fruitless minutes, he switched off his phone and decided to head home to catch up on sleep. He paid the bill and made his way to the underground, suddenly changing his mind en route and altering course for Harrods. Mary had told him yesterday that she had never set foot in so exclusive a shop – hardly surprising when she made her clothes from offcuts picked up cheap, and bought most other stuff from charity shops – so he had hatched a plan to buy her a Harrods Christmas present.

He found the store ablaze with festive lights, but, now that his own Christmas plans were finalised, he no longer felt dejected by all the seasonal hype. Having resigned himself to spending Christmas alone while Mary was with her family up North, everything had changed with Mrs Murray-Wood's recent announcement that she would be breaking her usual habit of staying home over Christmas, which had sent Mary into a tailspin of anxiety about leaving Anton on his own. Eager to help, he had resorted to Probation and begged Barbara's permission to cat-sit at Mary's over the Christmas period (fortunately, all Fabuclean employees had been given that time off). Mary's unalloyed relief when this permission was finally granted was ample compensation for his unconventional Christmas. And he certainly wouldn't be lonely or hungry, as Mary had promised a lavish Christmas feast and frequent phone calls during her absence.

Heartened by the prospect, he entered the great lighted ship of the store, all but colliding with a tall man coming out. Christ, *no*, he thought, staring in surprise and embarrassment at his former colleague Thomas, who seemed equally ill-at-ease, both of them doubtless recalling the sudden break, two years ago, in their long association.

'Good God!' exclaimed Thomas. 'What are *you* doing here?'

'And what are *you* doing here?' Anthony countered, adopting the same jocular tone. 'Shouldn't you be slaving at the coalface on a weekday afternoon?'

'I'm on paternity leave. Beth gave birth to twins three weeks ago, and today she sent me on a shopping expedition to buy a heated cot-blanket, of all things!' He indicated the embossed green Harrods bag.

'Congratulation, Thomas! Boys or girls, or one of each?'

'Both girls, which means I'm now seriously outnumbered – the only male in a household of four females, or five, if you count the nanny!'

Although continuing this superficial chat, Anthony was fighting an instinct to flee, having no desire to hear about Thomas's success, Thomas's promotion, or – worse – the prowess of the savvy young genius who had taken over his own job. Besides, they were clearly blocking the entrance – impatient customers struggling to squeeze past – so why not use that as an excuse to get away?

'Have you time for a drink? There's a nice pub around the corner.'

Anthony had no choice but to let himself be steered into a typical 'Thomas' pub – spacious and stylish, with leather sofas, antique mirrors, and a well-groomed clientele. But, once they were seated with their pints at a quiet corner table and continuing the small talk, he cursed himself for not having gone straight home after his interview. Then, all at once, Thomas leaned forward and said in a more serious tone, 'I can't tell you, Anthony, how glad I am to have run in to you. I've been feeling rotten, all this time, about not having been in touch.'

'That's okay.'

'No, it's *not* okay. I know I should have contacted you, but I was in a state of shock. We *all* were – and all horrified on your account – and we did have several discussions about what we ought to do. But the general consensus was that any show of sympathy might only make things worse. You might regard it as an intrusion, or even feel we were probing for salacious details.'

Anthony sipped his beer, pleased to hear that he hadn't been vilified and brutally cut off, as he had always feared, indeed believed. In point of fact, he hadn't actually expected any friendly overtures, given the "tact" and caution of his circle – the unwritten rule that one didn't pry, but kept a certain distance. And he had been as bad, of course, failing to offer any help or support when Thomas was struggling with the arrival of his first-born and with Beth's protracted depression. Back then, he hadn't realised that friendship demanded candour and unselfishness – probably the reason he had avoided it so long. It was Betty and Darren who had taught him the value of human warmth and sympathy, so couldn't he break the habit of a lifetime and open up to Thomas now? After all, most of his former colleagues must already know the gist of the story, if only from court reports and titbits in the tabloids, so pointless to try to suppress it. Draining his glass for courage, he gave Thomas a brief resumé of the last two shameful years, especially the indignities of prison.

To his intense relief, Thomas reacted with obvious sympathy. 'It sounds absolutely appalling! I can't imagine how you endured it.'

Anthony forced a laugh. 'I didn't have much choice.'

'But how are things *now*? Are you back on your feet and working again?'

It took another inward struggle for him to admit the nature of his current servile job.

Again, Thomas seemed horrified. 'But that's a total waste of your talents! Surely you can find something better.'

Having briefly explained the problem of his criminal conviction, Anthony returned to the bar to buy his round, feeling a strange combination of lightness and anxiety in having dropped his mask – and guilt was added to the mix when, coming back to the table, he found Thomas on the phone.

'Lord, I'm sorry,' he said, the minute Thomas had rung off. 'I'm taking up your time, when you're probably needed at home to lend a hand with the baby chores.'

'To be perfectly frank, it's a relief to be away from all that mayhem! And, anyway, I may be able to help you with a job. I've just been on the phone to an accountant friend of mine who set up a recruitment agency a year or two ago – one of those boutique affairs, specialising in top accountancy jobs. It's been remarkably successful – so much so that Hugh's now struggling to cope single-handed and is looking for a researcher to assist him. I know for a fact that he hasn't yet seen anyone who's quite the right fit, which is why I rang him just now. I didn't mention your name, of course.' Thomas stretched his hand towards him, in a gesture of reassurance. 'I wouldn't dream of betraying your confidence until you'd given me permission to tell him the whole story. But, first, I needed to sound him out, in case he simply turned you down point-blank. Far from it! He seemed really keen on meeting you – as soon as possible, he said. So I promised to ring him back once I'd discussed it with you and knew you were okay with the idea. It goes without saying I praised you to the skies – your skills, your efficiency, your sheer dedication – and told him I was sure he wouldn't regret it if he took you on.'

Deeply touched, Anthony muttered his embarrassed thanks.

'And there'll only be the two of you, so you needn't worry about anyone else knowing your private business. Hugh's a single guy who works from home – although I'm afraid he happens to live in Claygate, which would be quite a trek for you.'

That was of little concern, since he already had a long journey to work. What mattered was the importance of making a new start.

'His parents left him their house, you see. They'd taken early retirement and relocated to France and, as their only child, *he* got the spoils! The place is really too big for a guy on his own and I know he planned to sell it and move somewhere much more central, but he seems too busy ever to get round to that. But at least there'll be plenty of room for another desk, or even a separate office. And I'm pretty sure, Anthony, that once he's had time to see your talents for himself, he'll give you more responsibility – maybe even make you a consultant.'

After another half an hour discussing the nature of Hugh's business, as well as Thomas's news, Anthony felt distinctly cheered at having cemented a new friendship. And the thought of landing a worthwhile job, with decent pay and the prospect of promotion, had undoubtedly lifted his spirits. Indeed, having taken leave of Thomas, he positively bounded into Harrods, set on buying Mary the most lavish gift in the store.

CHAPTER 26

'Mary, it's me!' Anthony lowered his voice to avoid disturbing the lone man at the next table, although, with the café half-empty, he could talk without distraction. 'Darling, I'm in a Starbucks near Hugh's and I just had to ring and tell you that he's taken me on and I start exactly a month from today!'

'Oh, that's fantastic! Congratulations! Didn't I say there was nothing to worry about?'

'Yes, but when he insisted on seeing me twice, I felt he might have serious doubts about my lack of experience. But it turned out that he was just up to his ears at the time of our first interview and needed things to calm down a bit before we discussed his proposal in detail. And now that we've had a really long session, I have to say it does sound really promising. I'll start as a researcher, but even at that stage, he's offered me a pretty generous salary and, once I've been there a month or so, there should be commission and bonuses on top – and more responsibility, I hope.' He nodded his thanks to the waiter, who had just brought his macchiato. 'Obviously, I'll have to do my homework first and also get to know the business hands-on, but if it all goes well, he said he'll let me phone-screen certain clients before he sees them in person. And, eventually, I'll be able to conduct some of the interviews myself.'

'It sounds really great! And of course you'll do well. He's jolly lucky to have you.'

Although touched by her never-failing belief in him, he realised he was interrupting her work. 'But, look, I'd better ring off and let you get back to the coalface!'

'No, you phoned at the perfect time. Mr Edwardes is lunching with a client. He didn't leave till half-past one and it'll be a long lunch, he said, so I'm not expecting him back yet.'

'Good! Because I want to take you out tomorrow to celebrate, so we need to make the arrangements.' The man at the next table was also on his phone now and thus unlikely to eavesdrop – not that he was saying anything private; he just detested people listening in.

'But we're meeting Josie tomorrow. Surely you haven't forgotten.'

He *had* forgotten, dammit, despite his pleasure in the fact that Mary seemed so keen to "show him off" to her best friend. 'Sorry … course we are. Well, how about the Saturday after ?'

'Perfect! But *I'll* lay on the celebration. It's your birthday the following week, remember, so I'll cook you a nice birthday dinner.'

'No, darling, this is on me. I want to take you somewhere really special, to make up for New Year's Eve.' No way could he admit it, but it had been galling stuck indoors on the giddiest night of the year. The cat was to blame, as usual, because with Mrs Murray-Wood visiting her new-born grandson in Cheltenham, Mary was seriously concerned about Anton's firework phobia. So he'd had little option but to stay in with her and try to soothe the wretched creature. Left to himself, he would have dosed the phobic with Valium then gone out on the tiles, but Mary felt duty-bound to lay on cuddles and cat-treats in person.

'But you've already spoilt me rotten with that fabulous Christmas present. I can't imagine what it cost!'

Any amount of expense was justified by Mary's delight in the solid-silver charm-bracelet. His natural inclination, in Harrods jewellery department, had been to choose the sort of restrained and stylish bracelet Deborah would have liked – until he saw the cat-charms: ten different felines, each beautifully crafted and surprisingly realistic, and an additional related charm, inscribed with one word, "PURR". Deborah would have spurned it as intolerable schmaltz, but Mary's exuberant joy in the gift when she opened it on Christmas Eve morning, half-an-hour before leaving for Lancashire, had irradiated his Christmas. And in one sense she hadn't been absent, on account of her frequent phone calls, expressing extremes of gratitude for both the bracelet and his cat-sitting.

'Hold on a minute, Mary. The espresso machine's just gone into overdrive, so I missed what you last said.'

'That I'd feel really bad about you spending another penny on me.'

'Listen, I'll soon be earning much more and I have savings anyway. But tell you what, let's make it just a small-scale celebration, so long as it's something you'd really enjoy?'

'Well, there is one thing …' She broke off, always bashful about stating any wish – in marked contrast to Deborah's strong sense of entitlement.

'Yes, come on … tell me, darling.'

'Well, I'd adore to have a cocktail. I've never had one in my life but, a few months ago, Josie went to this amazing Hawaiian-themed place and said it's like you've arrived at a tropical beach, with real sand and palm trees and even recorded tropical birdsong – and all that in the East End!'

Involuntarily, he grimaced. If he had to go to a cocktail bar, then he would opt for Dukes or the Connaught and stick to gin-martinis, rather than indulge in the garish, ultra-sweet concoctions served at dodgy-sounding Hawaiian joints.

'And, honestly, it won't be expensive, even given all that décor. It's in an unfashionable area, you see, and Josie said the prices were unbelievably low. And, anyway, if we restrict ourselves to just one cocktail each, we could then go back to my place and …. Oh, shit!' she exclaimed, her voice changing in mid-sentence from excitement to consternation. 'I haven't a thing to wear! It may be cheap, but it's dressy, and Josie wore a sleeveless party frock. I won't have time to make a dress because – well, that's a secret, connected with your birthday.'

'Sounds exciting,' he said, 'but don't worry about the dress. We'll go out on the Saturday morning and I'll buy you one. I'd love us to choose it together.'

'Absolutely not! I won't hear of—'

'The sales are all on,' he interrupted, 'so we can pick up a real bargain. And, if you still object, it can be your birthday present.'

'But my birthday's not till June.'

'Not another word, Mary! I've just finalised our plan for Saturday week: Oxford Street in the morning, then an evening in tropical paradise.'

*

'I just can't tell you how wonderful it's been – the best evening of my life!'

Mary's enthusiasm was so overarching, he tried to ignore his own discomfort at sitting in a murky gloom, surrounded by tacky paper palm trees and people half his age, festooned with a garish flower-garland, and having to raise his voice above the raucous music. Both vocalist and ukulele were trying to out-shriek each other, while an off-stage parakeet added its own disharmonious note.

'Just the names of the cocktails are so poetic! I can't wait to tell Josie I've had a Blue Hawaii, a Hula Girl and a Moby Dick Sazerac.'

In point of fact, the drinks were violently coloured and freighted with such a surplus of fruit, foliage and paper parasols, he could barely slide his straw down amidst the soggy debris. And to him their names were more lustful than poetic: Pirate's Passion, Lava Flow, Torch-Lighter, Missionary's Downfall – all expressed his mounting excitement at seeing Mary with bare arms and throat and a most enticing cleavage, instead of muffled up in her usual winter jerseys. And she was wearing sheer filmy tights instead of thick black leggings, so he could admire the sheeny length of her legs beneath the short, swirly skirt. One thing was for sure – he didn't need *his* torch lit.

'I shouldn't have had so many, though. I think they've gone to my head!' Mary gave a delightfully girlish giggle as she drained the blaze-blue, syrupy dregs from her glass.

'They're mainly fruit-juice, darling, so I reckon you're high on the atmosphere. And, anyway, we've had lots of food to mop up any alcohol there was.'

'Oh, yes, I loved that, too. Those shrimp-and-mango skewers were out of this world! And what was that other thing I liked?'

'Coconut scallop ceviche.' His eyes kept straying back to her tantalising flesh. It was he who had insisted on a low-necked style of dress, overriding her preference for something more "covered up", but, when they found the ideal frock marked down to half-price in a bargain bin, Mary's fear of extravagance fortunately outweighed her fear of immodesty.

'Josie didn't even tell me they served food here. Actually I still feel guilty about not having cooked you dinner at my place – though I couldn't eat another thing, could you?'

He could most definitely eat *her* and was having to exert extreme self-control to restrain his hand from reaching out and running down inside that inviting neckline. 'Tell you what – let's go back to my place for a coffee. And if you don't fancy coffee so late on in the evening, my new Nespresso machine makes a pretty mean hot chocolate!'

'But what about Anton?'

'He's probably fast asleep on Mrs Murray-Wood's lap.' He might know little about pets, but he had never heard of anyone having to rush back for their cat, as they would for a human baby. But Anton *was* her baby, he had to keep reminding himself, when her cat-obsession began to test his patience. 'Just ten minutes, okay? Then I'll put you in a taxi home and you can spend the rest of the night with Anton.' No wonder he was jealous when the cat shared her bed, her pad, her life, even perched on the edge of the bath when she was soaping her glorious body.

He waited till Mary had vanished into the Ladies before he paid the bill, not wanting her to fret about the expense. He kept remembering how she'd told him that, when she first moved to Seven Sisters and was saving up to pay the backlog of her rent, she had ventured out each evening in the cold and dark to one particular supermarket that sold food half-price after midnight. How pitiful it seemed for her to be saddled with that extra burden so soon after giving birth, just to save a paltry few pounds. But 'paltry' was his arrogance talking: for her – even more so for Darren – those few pounds could be crucial.

'Oh, Anthony!' she exclaimed, emerging wreathed in smiles. 'You should just see those loos! You're greeted by a cut-out cardboard couple wearing not a stitch except a grass skirt and a flower garland, and they're standing underneath a huge cut-out palm tree, with loads of little coconuts clustered around the trunk.'

Never mind the coconuts – it was the thought of Mary wearing nothing but a grass skirt and flower garland that was dangerously inflammatory. He had to take things slowly, of course, but, once they were in his flat, who knew what might happen? The sheer depth of her appreciation had drawn them even closer and, for once, she was supremely relaxed, even a little tiddly, if only on the atmosphere. And it would be so much better for their first full-on encounter to be at his place, not hers. For one thing he had a king-size bed, not a cramped divan, and there'd be no risk of Anton jumping up to join them, or of Mrs Murray-Wood listening in from upstairs. He was even tempted to lace her hot chocolate with vodka, to undermine her defences – except that he must never, ever take advantage of her naiveté and trust. That way lay disaster.

*

'This hot chocolate's really gorgeous – so rich and sweet and creamy!'

Like *her*, he thought, watching her spoon up the froth, her full, willing lips closing round the spoon in a way that drove him wild. So far, however, she had permitted nothing more than a few kisses and when he had tried to slip his hand inside her dress she had resisted vehemently. He was still mystified as to why. She couldn't be scared of conceiving since he'd already explained that he couldn't make her pregnant – an anguished conversation due to his fear of her reaction, assuming, as he had, that a young Catholic woman from a family of nine would welcome at least a few kids. Yet to his great relief she had told him in her turn that she had no desire for even one more baby, in case, again, she felt no shred of love for it. She actually believed she didn't deserve a child and had resolved to save all her love for cats, especially rescue-cats in dire need of affection.

As he continued to gaze at her greedily, she reached out to put her cup down on the coffee table and, misjudging the distance, gave a cry of horror as the dark brown liquid splashed all over her dress.

'Shit, it's hot!' she exclaimed, making a dash for the bathroom.

Take the dress *off*, he ached to say, not just to save her being burned, but to have her naked in his flat, at last. But he dared not say a word, let alone go after her. Instead he sat in silence, listening to the noise of running water while erotic fantasies ran riot in his head.

At last, he called out, 'Are you okay? Not scalded?'

'No, it's just the dress – it's ruined!'

'I'm sure it isn't – it's polyester, not silk, remember, so it should wash out quite easily.' He resented the closed door and the fact he had to raise his voice, instead of pressing close to her and whispering sweet nothings. 'But I suggest you soak it straight away, to stop the stain taking hold. Borrow my dressing-gown – it's on the back of the door.'

Now he could hear rustling noises – again dangerously inflammatory – yet he knew he must stay put, ironically aware that although the situation had played right into his hands, no way could he exploit it – or her.

A few tense minutes ticked by, then she put her head out of the bathroom door, holding the now wet dress. 'Anthony, be an angel and fetch me a hanger, then I can hang this over the bath to dry. Oh, and perhaps you'd bring me one of your sweaters, too, so I can make myself at least halfway decent.'

The last thing he wanted was for to be even halfway decent. The provocative sight of her clad only in his dressing-gown was already fatally undermining his so-far iron control. When he returned with the hanger and jersey, however, he found her slumped on the sofa, silent tears sliding down her face. 'What's wrong, my darling? What is it?'

'I feel such a clumsy oaf, ruining the evening.'

'Of course you haven't ruined it. We had a magical time and no way could you spoil it through one tiny little mishap.'

'But you'd never do a stupid thing like that. In fact, compared with you, I'm beginning to feel pretty useless altogether. I mean, you're much cleverer than me and know loads more about the world and politics and stuff. And you buy me all these lovely things, which I could never do for you. And this ... this dressing-gown ...' The words were sobbing to a halt.

'What's wrong with it?' he asked, sitting close beside her. 'Is it too rough against your burned skin?'

'No, nothing like that. You see, it's a dressing-gown I'm making for your birthday – a lightweight summer one. It's meant to be a secret, but now I've spoiled that, too, I may as well tell you that *it's* gone wrong, as well. It started off quite promisingly, because I found this length of shot-silk in a car-boot sale, which looked really rather nice and was your favourite slatey-blue colour ...'

His own dressing-gown was workaday white towelling, but shot-silk seemed the perfect phrase for his present state of mind: shot to pieces by tempestuous emotions, glittery with hope, yet fraught with the risk of driving her away. What, for pity's sake, had happened to the old controlled and stolid Anthony – practical and boring like his dressing-gown – now superseded by some frenzied adolescent?

'But when I got home and unfolded it, it had all these streaks and patches where the colour had faded or gone a nasty murky shade. I've been doing my best to cut out those substandard bits, but that's made me short of material and now it'll end up far too skimpy. So it seems everything I do for you is crap, whereas what you do for me is always great.'

'You're completely, utterly wrong, darling. The things you do take time and dedication, so how on earth can you call them 'crap'? It's easy for me to buy you a dress – all I have to do is flash my credit card – but it requires much more effort on your part to get yourself to a car-boot sale and battle through the crowds there, then sit up night after night wrestling with faulty fabric some heartless shyster sold you. That's true devotion, Mary, and I'm the luckiest man in the world to be the object of it. No one's ever made me a dressing-gown before – or made me *any* clothes, or cakes. In fact, I've never met a woman with all your different skills: sewing, cooking, upholstering, baking … I wouldn't change you for the world.'

'You're just saying that to cheer me up.'

'I'm not – I'm really not! I can't tell you how much you mean to me and how totally special you are.' As he took her in his arms; he was aware of his erection, terrified she would feel it through his clothes and then all the trust between them would be lost. Desperately seeking distraction, he began playing mental chess: queen to knight four, pawn to bishop three, bishop to …

Useless. Even the thought of a bishop couldn't seem to stop his hand from sliding between the lapels of the dressing-gown. As it encountered naked flesh, he tensed in expectation of a furious rebuff, but, unfathomably, miraculously, she didn't appear to be resisting, but was actually pushing the towelling off her shoulders. Now, at last, he could see her breasts, every bit as beautiful as he had imagined in his fantasies. Yet how could this be happening, when, mere minutes ago, she'd been accusing herself and sobbing, seemingly in no mood for even the most innocuous advance?

Still torn between restraint and lust, he slowly reached his mouth towards those breasts, at first hesitant and tentative as he gently traced their outline with his tongue, before finally daring to kiss the nipples. The gasping cry she made seemed to startle the whole flat – no way a cry of protest, but sounding almost wanton. Then, all at once, she threw off the gown completely, revealing her rounded, rosy body in its provocative entirety. Transfixed by her bush, he could only stare at the exuberantly curly mass, glinting coppery like her hair, a few rebellious wisps and strands overflowing the rest, in total tinder-box contrast to Deborah's waxed barrenness.

How could he control himself? Confronted with such a sight, his lips were moving inexorably down, encountering the rough tease of that hair, his tongue exploring the secret softness it shielded. Mary's second cry was so unrestrainedly passionate, his former doubts and agonising vanished at a stroke. He no longer even *had* a mind. Both he and Mary were now – utterly and only – one thrusting, plunging, audacious, reckless body.

CHAPTER 27

Mary took a bite of her doughnut, tonguing up a drool of jam from her lip. 'Don't forget, it's Valentine's Day next Saturday.'

'I could hardly forget' – Anthony was captivated by her mouth, its mobility, expressiveness – 'when every shop and restaurant is trumpeting the fact! But don't worry – it's all in hand.'

'Anthony, if you're planning to buy me anything or take me anywhere, I totally forbid it. You'll spoil me rotten if you keep showering me with treats – and my Dad strongly disapproves of people being indulged!'

He tensed at the mention of her father. Keen for him to meet her family, she had suggested a weekend away, staying at their home in the tiny Lancashire village of Dutton. What he hadn't yet told her, though, was that Probation wouldn't permit the visit unless her parents had been informed about his crime; any couple aghast at the prospect of an unbaptized baby would hardly welcome a murderer in their midst. 'Well, that's a shame,' he said, forcing his mind back to the conversation, 'because I've already booked a rather romantic little restaurant.'

'That's sweet of you, darling, but could you possibly *un*book it? You see, I've planned a special Valentine's dinner at my place. You've no idea how many recipes there are online – Love Buns, meringue kisses, pink-champagne sorbet, passionfruit soufflé, and anything and everything in the shape of a heart. I've decided on the first two courses and, for dessert, I'll probably settle for the heart-shaped mocha mousse cake. And, if you fancy that, I can spell out our names on top with crystallised rose petals. Oh, and I've invented a Cupid's Cocktail for us!'

'Lord! All that'll far outshine any restaurant I've ever been to, so it's dinner *Chez Marie* – just as long as we spend the rest of the evening in bed!' He squeezed her hand suggestively, running his little finger in slow, teasing circles around the inside of her palm.

'Like we did last weekend?'

'Are you saying you don't want a repeat?'

'No! I do! I do! Just thinking about it makes me tingle all over. You know, until this last month, I simply hadn't realised the amazing things two bodies can do together.'

'Not *any* two bodies – yours and mine. I reckon we're made for each other.'

'Definitely! I know I'm inexperienced, but I'm pretty sure you're the best lover in the world.'

Were he Anton, he would have purred. Indeed, he'd been purring more or less non-stop since their first post-Hawaiian-cocktail-bar encounter. Deborah had always made him feel inadequate in bed, yet in Mary's eyes he was Adonis, Romeo and Byron, all mixed up. Indeed, since that enchanted night, he felt they were on permanent honeymoon, and today they were playing at being a well-established married couple, since they had done the Saturday shop together and were now relaxing in the supermarket café.

'More coffee?' he asked, although with so many things to celebrate it should really be champagne. Sex with Mary came top of the celebratory list, of course – her joyous, impassioned, and sometimes sweetly shy response. But he had also enjoyed a challenging first week with Hugh, relieved to be using his professional skills again and to have ditched the dreaded cleaner's uniform. True, the journey to Claygate was somewhat tedious, but he put it to good use by working on the train, and had bought the latest iPhone to mark his change in status. In addition, his forty-second birthday had infinitely surpassed his fortieth and forty-first, even the shot-silk dressing-gown proving only the tiniest bit skimpy. Best of all, Barbara had at last okayed his bid to move in with Mary, so they could embark on a new life together.

Returning with two more coffees, he slipped his hand unobtrusively under the table and let his fingers stray along her thigh. The vivid purple sweater she was wearing and the crazy blue flower in her hair – inspired, no doubt, by the cocktail bar – seemed to symbolise the new radiance in his life, used as he was to Deborah's neutral tones. There was only one real aggravation – and one totally his fault – that he had gone through all the rigmarole of arranging the move to her bedsit without realising there were other options (which only went to show that he had indeed become the frisky adolescent Mary had awakened, in strong contrast to his usual efficient self who thought things out in advance, rather than acting on impulse). Admittedly, *wherever* he lived with Mary, the place would have to be inspected, to ensure it complied with minimum Home Office standards, and Mary herself interviewed, to check she was fully cognisant of his past, but at least Mrs Murray-Wood wouldn't have been involved. In point of fact, the old lady had made no objection. 'Of course, Mary dear. Anthony's a real gentleman'. But then she hadn't needed to be told, thank God, about the 'gentleman's' descent into criminality.

Nonetheless, he was annoyed with himself for coming up with a much better idea only late last night – not too late to change plan, though, and he was determined to use his persuasive powers on Mary. 'Darling, there's something I want to discuss with you.'

'About Valentine's Day, you mean?'

'No, about our future.' That 'future' was fraught with problems. He was not only on licence for almost another fifteen months, with all its attendant restrictions, he also happened to be already married, however much he and Mary might be playing at man and wife. In the continued absence of any communication from Deborah, he had considered initiating divorce proceedings himself, yet the thought of further acrimony blighting his rare and new-found happiness made the prospect anathema. So, for the moment at least, he must remove his "missing" wife from the equation and concentrate on Mary. 'Listen, my love, because of the ban on pets at my flat, we've both simply taken it for granted that we'll move to *your* place. But actually there's nothing to stop us looking for a new flat – one with more room, to start with, and a nice little garden for Anton.'

Mary's face expressed instant dismay. 'Oh, I couldn't leave Mrs Murray-Wood – not when she's been so kind. And, anyway, she'd be terribly lonely without me and I'm not even sure she could manage all the chores without my help. Besides, she's only just agreed to you moving in. I mean, she was really decent about it and also quite excited, so how can we possibly tell her the whole thing's off? And don't forget her son's coming to stay next month, with his wife and the new baby, and she's dying for us both to meet them.'

Anthony said nothing, though inwardly fuming that his and Mary's future comfort should be sacrificed for an eighty-two-year-old widow and some unknown son and his family.

'And we couldn't possibly move Anton. Cats are territorial, you see, and more strongly bonded to places even than to people, which means my pad is now his main source of security. Rescue cats always tend to be more sensitive, because they may have been seriously traumatised, so even tiny changes can be terribly upsetting.'

Hadn't *he* had been seriously traumatised, for God's sake, by two years in an unspeakable gaol? 'I'm sure he'd settle, given time,' he said, with admittedly spurious authority, 'especially with a lovely new garden to explore.'

'But who'd look after him when we're both at work?'

'The whole point of cats, from what I can gather, is they don't need much looking after. And, even if I'm wrong, surely there are paid, professional cat-sitters.'

Mary looked so aghast, he might have been King Herod about to slaughter the Innocents. 'I wouldn't touch such people with a bargepole! They're often not vetted properly and some of them are just in it for the money and hardly care about their charges.'

Although even more disgruntled that a mere cat should dictate their living arrangements, he controlled his irritation, recalling Deborah's accusations of selfishness and dominance. Whatever happened, he must avoid a repeat of that.

'I really hate to say no, my sweet' – she slipped her hand into his, with a fond, beseeching look – 'but I just don't see how we can risk Anton's health and happiness.'

'Okay, I understand.' After all, he would still have this beguiling girl – and her deliciously curvy body – wherever they were living. Nor would the dratted cat live for ever, so *one* day they could start afresh.

'I knew you would, my love. After all, you're almost as close to Anton as I am.'

Hardly, when he'd just been anticipating with relish the wretched creature's demise. But Mary so adored him to cosset and cuddle her "baby", he had learned to do it automatically, just to see her fond, maternal smile. And she was smiling so entrancingly, the last of his resentment drained away.

'We'd better get back for him now,' she said, 'and, once we've put these groceries away, we need to rearrange the bedsit, to make more room for *your* things.'

He rose eagerly to his feet. His things could wait; he had other, better plans for the afternoon.

CHAPTER 28

'Great to see you, Darren! It's been ages.'

Anthony was enfolded in a bear-hug, once Darren had let him into the flat and, seconds later, Carol-Ann appeared, teetering towards him on her usual high heels. And her usual mask of make-up was also, of course, in place, which he couldn't help comparing to Mary's natural, country-girl look – infinitely more appealing.

'Come in and sit down. And do forgive the mess.'

In fact, the flat was exceptionally tidy and more spacious than his and Mary's place, with a proper separate sitting room. However, from what he'd seen so far, this particular area of Lewisham was little better than Tottenham.

'Coffee?' Carol-Ann asked. 'The kettle's on already.'

'Yes, please. Black, no sugar.'

'I know you boys will want a good long natter,' she said, returning with a tray of cups. 'But, I won't be in your way – don't worry. I've arranged to go shopping with my friend, Nikki, to look at wedding dresses.'

'Yes, now you've fixed the date' – Anthony perched on the sofa with his cup – 'I suppose there's masses to do.'

'Too sodding right, mate!' Darren joked. 'But just try and stop Carol-Ann making this the wedding of the year!'

'In that case,' Anthony said, unzipping his leather suit-carrier, 'we need her expert opinion on your outfit. I had a good look through my suits and decided these two were the best. My own preference is for this one, because the colour and the style give it the look of proper morning dress.'

As he shook it out, Carol-Ann went into transports over the designer label. 'Lord, it's ever so posh!'

'Yes, it is a good one – that I can guarantee. In fact, it's a bit too dressy for the office, so I've only worn it once. But you may prefer this Hugo Boss. It's a wool-and-mohair blend, so it doesn't crease, and the colour's rather subtle, don't you think – what they call Anthracite.'

'They're both absolutely smashing, Tony, but I definitely prefer the grey. It looks real classy, don't it? Go and try it on, Darren.'

Ten minutes later, Darren reappeared, now totally transformed. 'Blimey!' he said, stealing a glance at himself in the mirror over the mantelpiece. 'I'm a toff now, same as you, mate.'

Anthony nodded, amazed at the metamorphosis. The sleek cut of the trousers flattered Darren's slender build, and the waistcoat looked particularly impressive, with its real bone buttons and paler dove-grey stripe.

'I can't believe it fits you so well,' Carol-Ann exclaimed, 'like it was made for you special by one of them ritzy tailors.'

'Well, it was always a fraction too tight on me, whereas Darren's just that bit slimmer. I doubt if I'll ever wear it again, to be honest, so do feel free to keep it, Darren.'

'No way, mate! It must have cost a bleeding bomb!'

'All the less reason then to leave it unworn and unloved.' It had actually been in storage, since one of the major disadvantages of living in a bedsit was the lack of wardrobe space – the lack of space, full-stop.

'And here are a few extra bits and pieces,' he added, trying to interrupt Darren's effusions of gratitude. 'Belt, shirt, tie, cufflinks.' He had purchased them new as part of Darren's wedding present, although, as he unpacked them from the side pockets of the carrier, he pretended they were just on loan, to circumvent more embarrassing thanks.

Carol-Ann picked up each item with something close to reverence, as she lighted on more designer labels: Aquascutum, Gucci, Thomas Pink. 'I wish you dressed like that every day,' she sighed, once she had buckled the belt around Darren's waist and fastened the satin-silk grey tie.

'While I shovel crap, you mean, and lug sodding great bags of cement round the site?' Despite the jocular tone, Darren was turning this way and that as he glanced surreptitiously at his reflection in the mirror with a mixture of pride and disbelief.

'Thanks a million, Tony,' Carol-Ann enthused. 'And I see I'll have to buy a pretty snazzy dress to be worthy of my bridegroom! Which reminds me – I'd better dash off now or Nikki will go mad. She hates to be kept waiting.'

Having seen her off with several smoochy kisses, Darren immediately went to change out of his suit, as if unable to believe that such a creation could actually be his to wear.

'Honest, mate, I'm choked,' he said, returning to the sofa in his former shabby jeans and sweatshirt. 'No one ain't ever been so sodding kind – not in me whole life. I was in your debt before this, but now I owe you big time.'

'We're friends, Darren, aren't we, so it's not a question of debts.' It never failed to strike him how unlikely it was that he and Darren should have become so close when in his former life he would never have contemplated a friendship with someone so profoundly different in social and educational terms. Such snobbish, judgemental thinking now made him distinctly uncomfortable, and only proved how segregated his world had been, upholding something not far off a racism of class. Yet Darren's unwavering loyalty and deep concern for his welfare had been sadly lacking amongst his mainly upper-class FFC associates.

'But I want to hear about *you* now, Tony. How's things with Mary, for starters?'

'Pretty damned fantastic! Although I have to admit I'm finding it a bit of a strain, the two of us crammed into one room – or three of us, I should say, as the bloody cat has its own play area, would you believe, despite space being at such a premium.'

'So she's still besotted with the creature?'

'More so – if that's possible!' Anton's worst habit was his insistence on sharing their bed, a practice endorsed by Mary, who claimed that now he'd established the habit it would be cruel to turf him out. There was barely room for the two of them, let alone a restless cat, who changed position several times a night and seemed to take an unholy pleasure in paddling about on top of the duvet.

'And how's the new job?' Darren asked, gulping his now-cold coffee.

'Busy! It's a huge improvement on office cleaning, but hugely more demanding, too. I know how lucky I am to have landed it at all, but I have to say the journey's a bit of a nightmare. I always leave well after the rush-hour, yet the trains still seem to be jam-packed.'

'It sounds like you're back to all the old pressures, mate.'

Yes, he thought: staying late every evening, fielding endless emails and more or less cemented to his computer screen: researching markets;

finding clients; thinking up advertisements to go online or in the broadsheets to promote Hugh Henry Harvard. Hugh's actual surname was Petit and his second name Timothy, but, presumably, "Harvard" added cachet to the boutique agency's name, whilst Henry provided a nice alliterative touch. The real-life Hugh Petit assumed his new recruit was endlessly available, even at weekends. In fact, if he hadn't deliberately switched his phone off at Lewisham station, his imperious boss would probably be ringing him right now.

'You watch it, Tony! You don't want to risk losing Mary. Our women need to see us regular.'

'I do see her,' he retorted, uneasily aware that it was Darren he was neglecting more than Mary. He simply didn't have the time now to continue with the postal tuition or lay on supplies of books.

'Don't get me wrong, mate. I'm dead proud of you – same as you of me – but ain't there a risk of burnout?'

'Look, things will probably quieten down, given time. This early stage is bound to be hectic while I'm learning the ropes and trying to prove my worth to Hugh.' And, once they did abate, he was determined to reinstate Darren's mentoring. The lad was naturally bright and as hungry for learning as Anton was for cod-in-cream, and if he had only been at Pembridge, instead of a sink comprehensive, would have gone far in life,

'You look tired, mate. You need a break. Tell you what, why don't you and Mary come with us to Clacton over Easter? Carol-Ann's parents are pushing off for a week in Lanzarote, so we'll have their house to ourselves. Okay, Clacton ain't exactly Lanzarote, but at least the weather's bucking up a bit, now we're almost into April.'

'I'd love to, Darren, but Mary won't leave the cat on its own, and her landlady will be in Cheltenham again, visiting her grandson.' Now he had actually *met* the grandson – a chubby little bruiser with a pair of lungs that could out-shriek Maria Callas on an off-day – he felt even less sympathetic to Mrs Murray-Wood's now frequent absences. On the plus side, though, his and Mary's lovemaking was infinitely more relaxed with the old lady out of the house. However much he delighted in Mary's new vocal repertoire of passionate moans and cries, he feared they must be dismayingly audible to anyone upstairs.

'Shame!' Darren said, spooning the dregs of sugar from the bottom of his cup, as if trying to stave off hunger pangs.

Anthony, too, was distinctly peckish and, again, he thought of Mary – the delicious home-made cakes she always served with tea or coffee. Carol-Ann hadn't brought them so much as a ginger nut.

'We'd have had us-selves a ball at the seaside and, anyways, I'm dead keen to show you the parents' house. Honest, I don't know how they ever coughed up for that swanky place. Mind you, her mum rakes in a fortune just in tips.'

'How are you getting on with her now?'

Darren shrugged. 'She still thinks her only daughter could do miles better for herself than marry a loser like me.'

'Darren, you're not a loser! How many times do I have to tell you?' What he couldn't say, however, was that Carol-Ann did seem several cuts above her fiancé, in terms of her job, accent and general demeanour. Relationships were puzzling, though – there was so much one didn't know about that went on between a couple, or why they were together at all.

'And what's happened with your ex?' Darren was now attacking the sugar bowl, spooning up its contents with famished concentration.

'She's *not* an ex – that's the problem.'

'You mean you still ain't heard a dicky-bird?'

'No, nothing. But, quite frankly, I think far less about her, now I have Mary in my life.' From what he could gather from his father, he and Deborah seemed to spend a lot of time together, as if she were gradually becoming more his child than *he* was. At least that spared him the obligation of making frequent visits himself – a definite advantage, since his father's grief and continuing disapproval roused a tide of curdled pity and anger in the permanently "branded-as-criminal" son.

'And what about Mary's family? I know you're not allowed to stay with them, but …'

'Well, her sister, Sharon, came down to London recently on one of those weekend packages – you know, hotel, rail fare and a show thrown in as well – so we took her out to dinner on the Friday.'

'*And?*'

Impossible to explain to Darren that he'd found Sharon rather uncouth, with a much stronger Lancashire accent than Mary's, and a less refined manner altogether. Despite his earlier self-rebuke about having been a snob, there was no denying he *was* still a snob at some level. Indeed, he had been wondering since that Friday evening what on earth had made the difference between boorish Sharon and gracious Mary – maybe the latter's genteel boss, Mr Edwardes, or the surprisingly well-spoken Josie.

Josie herself had posed a different problem: in no way boorish, but distinctly cool towards him when they'd met. Perhaps she disapproved of the age gap, or resented the fact that Mary had relayed to him the whole grim saga of the baby, when formerly she was the only one in the know. Since the complexities of female psychology were still something of a mystery to him, he simply had to accept that, however great his love for Mary, he had signally failed to hit it off with her best friend.

'You ain't said a word, mate. So did you like this Sharon bod?'

'Stuff Sharon!' Anthony said, suddenly jumping to his feet. 'I've a better idea, Let's pop out to your local and have ourselves a pie and a pint.'

'Yeah, fine with me. I'm famished!'

As the two of them left for the pub, Anthony couldn't help reflecting that Mary would have prepared a three-course, home-cooked meal for any visitor, and would never dream of leaving anybody 'famished'. He ran through in his mind again all her attributes and talents – ample compensation for any minor problems or annoyances. And, as for the ecstatic heights they reached at night, that was the mouth-wateringly luscious icing on the cake.

He swung along the road with Darren, smiling like the proverbial foolish lover and feeling doubly blessed to have such a perfect woman and so good and loyal a friend.

CHAPTER 29

"We are sorry to announce that the 20.03 to London, Waterloo, has been cancelled. This is due to a shortage of drivers. South-West Trains apologise for any inconvenience caused."

Anthony muttered a string of curses, not just furious with South-West Trains – and annoyed with Hugh for keeping him so late, again – but even angered by the unseasonably lousy weather. They were into May, for God's sake, so why was it belting down with rain – not benevolent April showers, these, but lacerating downpours? His clothes were sodden from the long walk to the station and he was also starving hungry after a particularly hectic day, with no time to grab so much as a snack. Hugh, apparently, could exist on air, coupled with relentless work, but he himself was merely mortal and needed sustenance. Not that there was any hope of finding any on this godforsaken station, which didn't have so much as a vending machine, let alone a refreshment bar. Even the waiting room was locked. However, perching on the distinctly uncomfortable wooden-slatted bench, he gave grudging thanks that at least the station overhang sheltered him from the rain.

He tried ringing Mary – fourth time – but her phone was still switched off and she had still failed to respond to his text messages. She was nearly always home at this hour, preparing his and Anton's supper and, even if Mr Edwardes had kept her late – a pretty rare occurrence – she would have rung to let him know. So where the hell could she be?

He unfolded his soggy wet *Standard*, but the news was obsessed with the General Election, now only three days away. That posed another problem in that, having mixed with the so-called underclass in prison, he was now increasingly concerned with the whole issue of social justice and thus wondering if he should he break with his lifelong habit of voting Conservative – a habit shared by his parents and grandparents. On the other hand, decent welfare was only affordable with good economic management, which the other parties seemed unlikely to deliver. Perhaps, for once, he wouldn't vote at all. At least it would save a trek to the polling station and, in his present overburdened state, even the smallest chore was unwelcome, already lumbered as he was with visits to Probation. Thank God those were only monthly now, not weekly, and Barbara had kindly arranged evening appointments, aware of the demands of his new job. Nonetheless, he was beginning to tire of the same reiterated questions: 'Are you now, or have you ever been on illegal substances?' How many more times did he have to tell them *no*? His only drugs, apart from a nightly glass of claret, were handfuls of aspirin for tension headaches and a daily excess of caffeine.

'Do you feel there's any danger of repeating your offence?' Yes! At this very moment, he was contemplating a double murder: first the head of South-West Trains, followed closely by this morning's weather forecaster, who had blithely predicted dry weather all day – the reason for his lack of an umbrella.

Braving the rain, he jumped up from the bench and began pacing along the platform, as if his own activity could somehow expedite the train, although his thoughts continued to circle around Probation. Despite his high opinion of Barbara, the visits seemed a waste of time – hers as much as his, since surely she should concentrate her efforts on her psychotic, junkie or otherwise addicted clients. And, last month, when she was on leave-of-absence, his session had been a total washout. He'd seen some limply useless fellow, with the unlikely name of Thaddeus, whose first bumbling utterance was hardly likely to inspire confidence: 'I'm afraid I haven't done this before. It's my first day in the job, Mr Bowman'.

Forced to read from a crib-sheet, Thaddeus went right back to square one: 'Where are you living at present?' 'Are you married, or in a relationship?' 'Do you have children and, if so, how many?' 'Are you currently in work?'

Couldn't they keep records, for heaven's sake?

He stopped a moment to watch a couple of squirrels chase each other up the wooden fence bordering the platform. Hugh's fondness for Claygate's wildlife and semi-rural atmosphere probably accounted for his tardiness in moving back to Central London, which he'd been planning to do for years. But how could any amount of flora or fauna compensate for living in this benighted suburban backwater with slow, infrequent, unreliable trains?

The half-hour wait seemed endless, although eventually when the train came meandering in at least he could sit in the warm and dry in a relatively uncrowded carriage – one advantage of leaving work so late.

Having tried Mary again – still no joy – he set to reflecting on their somewhat unfestive Easter. When she wasn't in church, she'd spent most of the time knitting him a sweater, making him a simnel cake and crafting new playthings for Anton. Her latest idea – a cardboard box filled with small, light-as-air plastic balls – had proved a huge hit with the cat, who loved burrowing deep into them, rolling them around with his paw, or just lying sprawled on top of them.

'Oh, isn't he adorable?' Mary kept exclaiming – a sentiment he found hard to share. *She* was adorable, no question, and he relished the way she cossetted him with clothes, cakes and cuddles. Sometimes, though, in the course of that long weekend, he had felt stifled by domestic claustrophobia and envied Darren and Carol-Ann their wider horizons in Clacton.

Suddenly aware that he had wasted the last three-quarters of an hour doing nothing but fume and speculate, he opened his laptop and set to work on the latest task assigned to him by Hugh: trying to source an exceptionally high-powered candidate for an exceptionally demanding job. However, it did prove therapeutic, since the train no longer seemed to dawdle, but appeared to put on a spurt and reach Vauxhall in record time despite stopping at every godforsaken station in between.

Changing to the Victoria Line, he was surprised to see a crush of people standing five-deep on the platform, those in front being pushed dangerously close to the platform edge by the impatient mob behind. True the line was often crowded, but this great solid phalanx of passengers was unprecedented at nine o'clock in the evening. The explanation wasn't long in coming, though, as a disembodied voice boomed across the station: "*Transport for London apologise for the further delay to your service. This is due to a passenger incident at Oxford Circus ...*"

If 'incident' was a euphemism for suicide, the delay could last till kingdom come, so maybe best to cut his losses and take a taxi home – except that his exit was blocked by the heaving mass of people continuing to build up. Frankly, he lacked the energy to fight his way through them and out, so he resigned himself to a long, frustrating wait.

When, at last, he heard the rumble of a train and an announcement that the service was now restored, the ensuing scrum was a test of strength and character. The earlier arrivals obviously took precedence, yet people were shamelessly pushing and shoving on all sides. Desisting from such behaviour, he waited for the next train and somehow managed to cram himself into the carriage as the very last person in. Standing wedged between a bloke with an unsociably jabbing rucksack and a woman who'd clearly never heard of deodorant, he was all but ejected at the next station, Victoria, by those pouring out of the carriage, only to be squeezed still further by an even larger crowd struggling to get in.

Nevertheless, he tried to make some use of the time by continuing to think out new avenues for tracking down that super-perfect candidate needed by the end of the month. It didn't help that he was lurching on his feet as the train jolted on its rackety way, but at least there was no danger of falling over in these sardine-tin conditions. What mattered was they were moving – fast – and had already passed Oxford Circus.

Yet, just at that moment, the train juddered to a halt and the dreaded voice announced: "*We apologise for the further delay to this train. We are being held at a red light due to a problem with the train ahead. Transport for London apologise ...*"

Two apologies this time, he noted – perhaps to cover the fact that they hadn't stopped at a station, but in the no-man's-land of a tunnel, the firmly closed tube doors making it impossible to nip out of the carriage, ditch the tube and hail a cab.

As the delay continued, he struggled to get a grip on himself, rather than give way to more pointless irritation, consoling himself with the thought that Mary was bound to be home by now, ready to give him her usual hero's welcome. And, having never been a hero to anyone before, the experience was shamefully gratifying. Closing his eyes, he kicked Hugh assignments from his mind and concentrated instead on Mary's luscious body.

*

'Mary!' he called, as he let himself into the flat. No reply. No sign of her whatever. And the scene that met his eyes increased his fears tenfold. The place looked ransacked – the bedspread ripped, ornaments knocked over, sofa cushions scattered on the floor, along with the entire boxful of Anton's plastic balls, some of which had rolled into odd corners. Worse, the whole room reeked of a pungent shitty smell. Had there been a burglary and the thief deliberately defecated, before making off with the loot – a not uncommon practice, according to Darren? But, if that were the case, what had happened to Mary, for Christ's sake? Was she injured? Had she fled?

Suddenly, he heard a peculiar yowling noise coming from the bathroom and burst in to investigate, stopping in his tracks as he discovered Mary alive, thank God, but crouching fully clothed in the empty bathtub with a cat struggling in her arms – not the now plumply placid Anton, but some skeletally thin creature, with patchy, balding fur and wild, green staring eyes. Mary's face was scored with scratch-marks, her hair dishevelled, her clothes stained with cat-piss, and worse. Horrified, he rushed to her aid, only to be attacked in his turn by the vicious beast.

'Ssshh! Keep quiet,' she whispered. 'He'll calm down in a moment, so long as we keep calm ourselves. I've given him half a Valium and it should work pretty soon.'

Valium? How could the normally tranquil Mary be in possession of tranquilisers?

'I just hope they're not too old to be effective. The doctor prescribed them years back, after I'd lost the baby. Of course, I kept that totally secret – just pretended I was suffering from stress.'

Her words were drowned by further shrill cries from the still belligerent animal.

'I thought I'd contain him in here,' Mary continued, ignoring the noise as she gently stroked the cat and murmured words of comfort into its ear, 'until the tablet takes effect' — you know, to stop him doing further damage, or terrifying Anton even more. The poor darling's taken refuge in the garden, where he'll get thoroughly soaked to the skin.'

As *I* am, Anthony refrained from saying, aware that all available sympathy was being lavished on this unspeakable intruder. At least Mary's lulling and soothing appeared to have succeeded – unless it was the Valium – since the cat finally subsided on to the makeshift bed she had made for it in the bath. Having checked it was safely asleep, she clambered out, gave herself a quick clean-up, then led him to the stinking sofa and sat beside him with a sigh of profound exhaustion.

'What the hell's going on?' he asked, every word of her explanation only deepening his dismay: another rescue-cat, for pity's sake – one she'd found on a nearby council estate being tortured by a gang of thugs, and now near-hysterical after, she suspected, a whole lifetime of abuse.

'But, once I've showered him with love and affection, darling, that'll give him a sense of security and he'll improve out of all recognition.'

'You mean you intend to *keep* the crazy creature?' Mixed fury and incredulity made his voice as shrill as the cat's.

'Oh, we haven't any choice, darling. If we don't offer him a home, he'll either be killed by those barbarians or be put down by the vet.'

'You say "*we*", Mary' – his tone was now more measured, although icy cold – 'but you actually mean "*you*". When it comes to me, I simply won't countenance housing a second cat.' He glanced around the chaotic room, closing his nostrils against the stink of cat-shit. Mary couldn't comprehend how threatened he felt by such rank mess and disorder. Throughout his life he had needed things to be neat and under control, so this present shambles was very nearly intolerable.

Mary slipped her arm around his waist. 'You love Anton, my sweet,' she pleaded, 'and *he* was pretty frantic when we found him, so, given time and patience, I'm sure we'll have the same result – a happy, settled kitty.'

'Time and patience, Mary, are non-existent in my life right now. Besides, no way do we have room here for two cats. And, anyway, I'm more concerned about those scratches on your face and hands than about some feral monster. Shouldn't you see a doctor – maybe get a tetanus jab?'

'I had one only a few years ago, when Smokey went through a bit of a wild stage. Don't worry, darling, I'll disinfect the scratches in a sec, but first we need to talk about our new arrival.'

'He's not "*our*" – I told you. And, I'm sorry, Mary, but I'm so damned hungry, I can't concentrate on anything else. I haven't eaten since breakfast, a good fifteen hours ago.'

'Lord!' she exclaimed, glancing at her watch. 'I can't believe it's ten past ten. I must have lost all track of time. No wonder you're starving, you poor love. I'll go straight out to the kitchen and rustle up some supper for the four of us.'

So it was a foregone conclusion, was it, that the ferocious beast was here to stay? 'Fish and chips will be quicker,' he said curtly, turning on his heel 'I'll fetch them now, okay?' Fish and chips for *three*, though. And if Mary dared to share her portion with this odious interloper, he hoped it bloody well choked to death on a bone.

CHAPTER 30

'Get lost, you fucking animal, before you drive me over the edge!'

Anthony all but kicked the cat, but he had met his match in Sheehan, who continued hissing, baring his teeth and clawing savagely at his hands. In the last three weeks, he personally had become the chief target of attack, and clearly Sheehan detested the very sight and smell of him – a mutual detestation, needless to say. Mary kept assuring him that he mustn't take it to heart, and that the cat was probably wary of the entire male sex, having been abused non-stop by males. So did she expect him to change his gender, on top of everything else?

In fact, she never saw the situation at its worst, because when he and she were together in the bedsit, Sheehan was better behaved – at least to some degree – saving his murderous ire for him, the hated male.

'Back off, Sheehan!' he shouted, wincing at the new red weal on his already sore, scratched hands. Sheehan! What a name – meaning 'little peaceful one" and chosen by Mary in the desperate hope that the cat would become serene.

Disobeying her instructions, he went to fetch the cat-carrier that he himself had chosen in place of the battered cardboard affair Mary had owned since Smokey's era. This new one was made of the strongest steel and strongly resembled a cage, so, first, he'd had to overcome her objections to its use. 'It's for Anton's sake,' he'd impressed on her, 'to save him from attack. When Sheehan's hell-bent on savagery we need to confine him or he might seek to oust his rival.' Mary, unconvinced, frequently engaged in a struggle to keep the peace between the two warring felines, although it was patently impossible to make Sheehan feel wanted and happily "'at home", whilst preventing Anton from suffering any sense of exclusion, let alone any wounds. Mary, though, clearly believed in the impossible, despite the fact that Anton now spent most of his time seeking refuge in the garden shed, cowering pathetically in a corner, ears flattened against his head. Anthony was sometimes tempted to join him, not just to escape the obnoxious Sheehan but to get some light and air. On this particular morning, though, he had promised not to set a foot outside the bedsit until Mary returned from church.

At the risk of serious injury, he managed to capture Sheehan, force him into the carrier and deposit cat and cage in the bath. Slamming the door on the monster, he marched over to the stereo and switched off the pet relaxation CD that had been playing almost every minute, with no noticeable effect. That facile, so-called soothing music drove him to distraction, as did the album's formal dedication to "The Divinity in Cats". Sheehan *divine*? Attila the Hun was more like it.

He put on his favourite Bach, instead, playing it as loudly as he dared, to drown the aggressive yowls echoing from the bathroom. If the din disturbed Mrs Murray-Wood's son (who was staying with his mother, together with his wife and baby, on a maddeningly extended visit), then that was simple recompense for the bawling of the infant, Robin – another ill-chosen name. Robin sang melodiously, didn't screech the place down.

He glanced at his watch: 10.20am. Well, at least he had a period of grace before he was obliged to release the cat, to prevent Mary coming back to find her 'sweet new kitty' in captivity – and not, on this occasion, to save Anton from attack since the poor whimpering wretch had made himself scarce at the crack of dawn this morning. The ten o'clock Mass lasted a good hour-and-a half, what with the long Sunday sermon and the tea and biscuits afterwards, so he was mercifully cat-free for a sorely needed respite. The whole Catholic thing, to be honest, was another source of conflict and he found himself resenting Mary's simplistic faith, and her frequent acts of idolatry that left him holding the fort with the cat from Hell.

He stared grimly at his laptop screen, annoyed he had made no progress on his work. Now that he'd been with Hugh four months, his responsibilities had enormously increased and he was now regularly preparing Value Propositions for briefing potential candidates, and also writing up job-specs for clients. But those assignments he'd promised to do at home seemed to founder in a scum of feline noise and disturbance. Apart from anything else, today's stifling heat had turned the bedsit into an oven, which shot his concentration to pieces. The temperature outside well exceeded the late-May average and intensified the smells – all *Sheehan* smells, of course: his piss, his shit, his disgusting cat-food with its stomach-churning fishy smell. As for hygiene, that was out of the question. The creature was still not house-trained since Mary claimed the process was too traumatic at present for so bewildered a kitty. Bewildered? He had more venomous adjectives.

He peered out of the window, although there was little in the way of view, just the glare of gloating sunlight. On a Bank Holiday weekend like this, he and Mary should be strolling by the sea, or at least enjoying the cool of one of the London parks, not imprisoned in a claustrophobic basement.

Slumping back on the sofa, he snapped his laptop shut, resentful not just of Sheehan, but of the huge demands imposed on him by Hugh – not far short of exploitation. His boss could work him into the ground with no redress, knowing full well that any ex-offender was highly unlikely to land a good professional-type job. In some ways, he envied Hugh: the single life, with no dependents, no distractions, and the bonus of a sizeable house. True, he drove himself as relentlessly as he did his new researcher; nonetheless, he didn't lack for company or sex. Indeed, with three girlfriends on the go, all ignorant of the other's existence, he could flit blithely from Jean to Ruth to Katy, avoiding all ties and commitment.

His love-life, in contrast, had been seriously curtailed, not just by the Murray-Wood crew (whom Mary seemed to imagine had nothing else to do than listen in to any intimate sounds from downstairs), but also by the insufferable Sheehan. Mary worried that, if the new cat was present in the room whilst they were making love, he might well be frightened or upset, given his mercurial state, by sights and sounds he didn't understand.

'Well, get him *out* of the room!' he'd snapped on one occasion, all but driven to breaking point. But she deplored the thought of shutting her precious pet in the bathroom, unless it was imperative for Anton's sake, and she dared not let him loose in the garden, for fear he might never return – an outcome he most fervently desired.

Okay, to give her credit, she was aware of his feelings and did do her utmost to compensate, but the one and only thing that would help – to turf out the intruder once and for all – she refused to countenance, claiming 'the poor defenceless cat' would meet a certain death.

But what about his demise – a slow death from ever-escalating tension?

'So how's he been?' Mary asked, the minute she returned from church.

His usual loathsome self, he bit back. She looked so girlishly beguiling, in her full-skirted summer dress and flower-encircled hat, he couldn't help but relent. Her arms were bare, her legs were bare, the frock was flimsy and low-necked – an open invitation for him to strip her naked and lay claim to her again.

'Fine,' he lied, knowing any hint of trouble would send her rushing to Sheehan's aid. Thank God the creature couldn't blab about the unendurable hour he'd spent howling in a carrier, with no chance of either comfort or escape. The only plus side of that mounting agitation was it appeared to have worn him out, and, once released, ten minutes ago, the delinquent had collapsed onto his bed. From what he could gather, most cats didn't have beds – and certainly not the luxurious creations Mary crafted – but of course, in her view, animals ranked way above humans, on a par with angels and, yes, gods.

'And how about our gorgeous Anton?' she asked next, tossing her hat and handbag onto the table.

'He's fine, too.' Another lie. Whilst trying to gobble his creamed chicken mousse, Anton had been assaulted by the predatory Sheehan – pure perversity on the latter's part, since he detested Mary's home-cooked kitty delicacies and refused to touch anything except one malodorous brand of cat-food – surely ridiculously fussy behaviour for a once-starving refugee

'He polished off your mousse, Mary' – he was becoming a serial liar – 'and he's just strolled out to the garden again. It's such lovely weather, he's probably sunbathing!' Licking his wounds, more likely – wounds both literal and metaphorical.

'Oh, darling, you are clever! You've obviously done a brilliant job of coping with them both. I just knew that would happen once he got more used to you, so I reckon this could mark an important change.'

Riled by her optimism, he refrained from a reply.

'I'll make a start on *our* lunch now.' She slipped an affectionate arm around his waist. 'You must be getting hungry.'

'I don't want lunch.' Taking advantage of her proximity, he kissed her full on the mouth. Yet already she was tensing in his embrace. Did she imagine that the uncharacteristically comatose Sheehan would object to the merest kiss? Unwilling to be side-tracked, he whispered into her cloud of curls, 'I want us to make love – right now.'

'Let's wait till this afternoon, my sweet. I heard Robin crying when I came in, so the family can't have gone out yet. I know they're planning an expedition to Hampton Court, so why don't we hang on till the coast's clear?'

Furious, he pulled away. 'Mary, it's absolutely nonsensical to let them rule our lives! At this rate, we'll lose all autonomy.' And he didn't add that, by the time the Murray-Wood brigade did eventually go out, Sheehan was bound to have woken and would be causing his usual mayhem.

'But what about lunch?'

'Bugger lunch! I'm starving for your body, not your beef casserole.'

She gazed at him with genuine compunction, as if the idea of anyone being hungry for anything was deeply painful to her – although not painful enough, for God's sake, to make her change her obstinate stance.

'I'm really sorry, darling, but I find it so hard to relax, knowing we'll be overheard from upstairs – not to mention Sheehan getting so desperately upset.'

'Listen, Mary' – he tried to moderate his voice – 'we simply have to move. We can't go on like this, or it'll drive us both insane. We need a flat at least three times the size, and one that's self-contained and sound-proofed, to give us space and privacy.'

'But we can't possibly inflict a house-move on Sheehan when he's still so agitated.'

'Look here, Mary, I only agreed to give him house-room because you assured me he'd settle down pretty soon and be eating out of our hands by now, and I was stupid enough to believe you.'

'Okay, I admit it's taking much longer than I hoped, but, don't you see, that only proves how terribly he must have suffered. So how can we be cruel enough to condemn him to yet more trauma?'

'Easily,' Anthony muttered, determined, for once, not to let her overrule him. His sweet, submissive Mary had a streak of iron running through her veins when it came to ill-treated creatures. Well, he himself was an abused, ill-treated creature, denied not just peace and space, but any semblance of a sex-life.

Clamping his arms around her again, he half-led, half-forced her over to the bed. 'Anton's outside,' he whispered, 'Sheehan's asleep and, if we make love really quietly, no one's going to hear us from upstairs.'

She continued to look unconvinced, so he simply tugged her zip down, the filmy dress cooperating by flopping limply to the floor. On account of the heat, she wasn't wearing a bra, and the sight of her voluptuous breasts was so inflammatory, he pushed her almost roughly on to the bed, tore off her wisp of pants and began thrusting into her with greedy desperation. He had promised not to make a sound – he didn't – sounds were immaterial now that he had her where he wanted. His brute male self was taking over, so she hardly even existed for him, except as a body he *had* to have – now, this instant, without delay. And, totally fixated on his own furious lust and longing, he exploded, within seconds, in a silent, savage, shuddering release.

CHAPTER 31

He strode blindly on in the blistering heat. No idea where – too much turmoil in his head. He'd all but raped her, for Christ's sake, forced himself upon her, as nothing more than a receptacle for his long-pent-up sexual greed. Yet his shame and guilt were curdled with a seething residue of anger. Hadn't she driven him to this, with her ridiculous fixation on her cats? He ranked well below them – that was obvious.

He stopped a moment, thrown by the churning maelstrom of contradictory feelings. This was the girl he cherished and adored, even hoped to marry, so why the dirty tide of recrimination and resentment? Had he ever truly loved her, he hardly dared to ask, or just lusted for her body, that firm, glowing, youthful flesh? Had he ever truly loved anyone, or was he constitutionally incapable of love?

In an effort to dispel so perturbing an idea, he pounded on again, blundering like an automaton along the sweltering streets and aware of other people only if he happened to bump into them. His mind refused to quieten, though, now thinking back to the man he'd been three years ago – successful and self-satisfied, incapable of sexual violence, let alone of murder – a good man, he'd assumed, and deserving all his advantages on account of his hard work and application. What arrogance! And as much of an illusion as his ill-conceived passion for Mary.

Only now did he see that it *had* been ill-conceived. Their backgrounds, world-view, politics, religion, meant they had almost nothing in common. Mary didn't have a world-view and lamentably little political nous. He had conceived an instant passion for her, literally at first sight, enchanted by the sweet, young damsel in distress who had praised him as a hero, needed him and trusted him. Submissive women were something of a rarity, yet here was one who seemed perfectly content to idolise and spoil him, defer to him in most things. No one could doubt her virtues – compassion, kindness, gentleness (all of which he lacked himself) – but basically she was an uneducated country girl who would never really understand the sophisticated, privileged world he simply took for granted, partly his own fault since he had concealed the greater part of it, just as he had from Darren. Yet it was the unsophisticated, unprivileged Darren who had seen the situation much more clearly, even tried to warn him that he and Mary were ill-matched. He had opted to follow his cock, though, rather than his reason, allowed his pathetic need for cosseting and admiration to blind him to the facts. And, on top of everything else, he'd landed up in the wrong job – one that could have been a life-saver but in fact threatened him with burnout because of his despotically slave-driving boss.

As he passed a recreation ground, he suddenly doubled back and squeezed his way through the gang of kids loitering by its gate, heading for a lone mutilated tree, overhanging a patch of scuffed and scruffy grass. Desperate for shade, he flung himself down beneath it, cursing the crowd of children shrieking on the seesaw, or being pushed on the swings by doting parents – a reminder of his failures as a failed parent and failed family man.

'Piss off!' he snapped as a mangy dog came bounding up to him. The "NO DOGS" notice was apparently ignored here, since two other unkempt mongrels were picking a fight by the fence, prompting unwelcome thoughts of Sheehan and Anton.

Despite having rested barely a moment, he jumped to his feet, needing to keep on the move and, anyway, if he wanted shade, why didn't he head for the green space of Finsbury Park? Okay, it was quite a trek in the scorching heat, but who cared?

However, out in the unkind streets again, he was reminded of the day of his release – another baking hot Bank Holiday when he'd felt similarly out of tune with the weather and the general mood of leisure and relaxation. Barbara might be full of praise for his "progress" during those last nine months, but him it seemed just a string of wrong decisions.

He was careering along at such a lick, the park was already in sight, though he was sweating so profusely his shirt was sticking to his skin. So, when a double-decker bus with Hampstead on its destination-plate happened to lumber past he raced towards the bus-stop and jumped on board. The Heath, with its wealth of trees, would be considerably cooler than Finsbury Park and, being three or four times the size might offer a greater chance of peace and solitude.

However, the bus was as hot and crowded as everywhere else, and any prospect of peace unlikely since his mind had now switched to Deborah and his total ignorance of her present life. His father, always grudging with any information, had given him her new address in Belsize Park, but imparted little else in the way of solid facts. To be honest, he hadn't minded much of late, because his involvement with Mary meant that Deborah had faded in importance. Now, though, he was stricken by the thought of her being "lost" to him entirely, which only proved how disloyal and superficial he must be, switching his affections from one to the other in a matter of mere hours. Nonetheless, he still yearned to see his wife and, if nothing else, was curious as to why she had moved to North London when it entailed a longer journey to her office – unless she had a new job.

On impulse, he got up from his seat and lurched along to the front of the bus. 'Do you go anywhere near Belsize Park?' he asked the driver, jolted by his sudden longing to re-engage with her.

'The tube's your better bet, gov. Get off at the next stop, walk back to Finsbury Park, take the Victoria Line to ...'

Storing the instructions in his head, he alighted from the bus and began jogging back the way it had come. Okay, he was acting irrationally again; he could hardly call on his ex unannounced, after all this time, but at least this was his chance to suss out where she lived. She was unlikely to be there in fact, since as an inveterate sun-lover she'd probably be out with Jonathan, perhaps at the zoo or a theme-park, or wherever parents took their kids on Bank Holiday weekends – which meant there was little risk of her spotting him.

He negotiated the tube journey almost automatically as he continued to think about his wife. And, in less than half an hour, he was turning into her street, concealing himself behind the tree outside her flat, so he could take a good look at the place without arousing suspicion from the neighbours. The elegant period building was freshly stuccoed and newly painted – a contrast to Mrs Murray-Wood's house, with its air of neglect and far less genteel surroundings. Deborah's was the ground-floor flat, which looked light and airy and spacious with its wide frontage and tall windows – again strikingly different from Mary's gloomy basement. He dared to venture a few yards from the tree, feeling ridiculously nervous, like a burglar or a stalker, but wanting to peer more closely at the place and check there wasn't a sign of anyone at home. Why didn't he simply leave a note, saying he happened to be in the area and could she kindly get in touch? They were still husband and wife, for God's sake, so he had a perfect right to know her future plans.

Forced to tramp back to the newsagent to buy some writing materials, he hastily scribbled a message and was about to creep up to her flat again and slip it through the letterbox when a sudden knocking on the main front window made him freeze in embarrassment. Too late now to flee. Deborah was framed in the pane, looking her svelte and slender self, and elegantly dressed in crisply tailored white linen slacks and a stylish navy top. For a moment, they stared at each other, then she pushed the window open and invited him in.

Fazed by this unexpected welcome, he stepped into the cool, marble-floored hall to see her emerging from the doorway of her flat, her signature-scent of Guerlain *Idylle* wafting in the air.

'Anthony!' she exclaimed. 'I was just about to email you, and suddenly you appear in the flesh!'

So why was she about to email – to dun him for cash, or state her terms for the most punitive of divorces?

'But we can talk about that later. You'd better come in and sit down. You look absolutely exhausted.'

A total wreck, she meant. He had come out in a tearing rush, desperate to escape Mary's pitiful sobs, and simply pulling on any old clothes that came to hand. And, ever since, he'd been racing about and was now perspiring so profusely he must smell disgustingly rank. Indeed, as she ushered him in to sitting room and he perched on her ivory sofa, he felt like a pollutant in her impeccable flat.

'What on earth have you been doing to get yourself so hot and flustered? There's some prosecco in the fridge, so how about a spritzer to cool you down?'

Far from hostile, she seemed positively gracious and once she had slipped out to the kitchen he took the chance to scrutinise her surroundings. What struck him first was the absence of any mess or clutter, as if had stepped from one world into another and was breathing fresh new air. No cat-hairs, or scratching-posts, or cat-playthings underfoot. No damage to furniture or furnishings from vicious, unsheathed claws, and the stink of litter-trays now replaced by the swooningly sweet scent of Madonna lilies and a lingering trace of *Idylle*. Yet how strange that the flat was so orderly and neat, with a toddler living here. There was none of the usual evidence of children: a pushchair in the hall, perhaps; or grubby finger-marks on the glass-topped coffee-table; or toys scattered on the floor. Perhaps Jonathan *didn't* live here. Although shocked by the idea, he was troublingly aware that the last time he'd seen Deborah, she'd been patently unable to cope with the burden of motherhood and, if things had grown steadily worse since then, might she actually have decided to have the child adopted? A huge wrench for any mother, of course, but might it not explain why she had taken no action in initiating a divorce?

'I wasn't sure if you'd eaten,' she said, returning with a tray, 'so I've brought a few little nibbles.'

He glanced at the assortment of delicacies: smoked salmon, stuffed olives, shitake mushrooms, fresh asparagus spears – typical Deborah fare. Indeed, as he took a long draught of his spritzer, he had a definite sense of coming home – to fine wine, fine china, gourmet food. 'Exactly what I needed!' he said, the frisky bubbles tingling on his tongue.

'Well, if you will gallivant around on the hottest day of the year!'

Her jocular, even affectionate tone released some of his racking tension and he dared to relax a little as she seated herself opposite and asked him what he was doing and where he lived?

As the safest option, he gave her a brief resume of his job. 'It's been quite a challenge learning a completely new business, but things are going pretty well – apart from the very long hours. I need constantly to communicate with potential candidates, who are only available after their normal working day, so I rarely leave the office till late evening. And the journey from Claygate makes me later still, although actually I may be moving.'

What in God's name was he saying? He had made no conscious decision and, anyway, if he wanted to stay with Barbara at the same Probation Office, any future house-move would be severely limited in scope, since her office covered only certain postcodes. 'But how about *you*?' he asked, trying to suppress his own confusion. 'Are you still at Maddison Carruthers?'

'Oh, absolutely! I've had a promotion, actually, and a pretty hefty pay-rise.'

'Congratulations!' If his hunch about the adoption had been right, then, perhaps, without the burden of a child, she had become again the successful, super-creative woman he had married.

'And I owe that to Jonathan,' she added, with a laugh. 'You see, I was put in charge of a major account for a new baby-teething product, and just at the time Jonathan was cutting his own first teeth. So it was a piece of cake to come up with a really convincing idea for a campaign, since I was writing from the heart and knew first-hand the strain it put on mothers – the broken nights and constant crying – and the pain it caused the babies themselves. Well, it turned out to be a runaway success and won several industry awards. And, on the back of all that, the agency's profile was raised and we landed two big new accounts within a matter of weeks.'

As she reached out for an olive, he was distracted by a sudden thought of Sheehan, who would have jumped up on the table and started sniffing and licking Deborah's tray of snacks, if only to reject them in favour of his Whiskas. Mary's disregard for hygiene must contravene all the basic Health and Safety laws, he realised with a shudder.

'And I became the go-to person for all things baby' Deborah continued, delicately nibbling on her olive, 'which was a bit of a hoot, considering how overwrought I'd been – in fact, pretty crap at motherhood altogether. But things improved enormously once I managed to get hold of an absolutely A1 nanny when Jonathan was six months old. She's so calm and genuinely motherly, she had a quite magical influence on him, and that helped *me*, of course. And she's moved with me here and now lives in, which has truly been a life-saver. I can't introduce you, I'm afraid, because Sunday's her day off.'

He had no desire to meet any nanny – super-motherly or otherwise – but he did finally dare ask where Jonathan himself was.

'Oh, he's with this new friend of mine, Louise. She's also on her own with a toddler, so we came up with this plan to look after each other's children on alternate Sundays. And it's working really well, because it gives us each …. But, look, you don't want to hear all these domestic details. And I have to say you still look frightfully hot and bothered. How about another spritzer?'

When she returned with the drinks, he made an effort to rally himself and converse in a normal fashion. Yet, beneath their genial exchanges, he was reflecting on the gulf between them: she radiant with health, gold-plated with success, and with all her childcare worries solved; he exhausted, run down and totally unsure of his future direction. Nonetheless, it was a definite relief to discuss subjects unrelated to cats. Mary's outrage at any cruelty to animals, her indignation over "celebrity cats" and her worry about the growing trend for Cat Cafés, were hardly topics of burning interest.

He knew Deborah must be busy, though, on her one precious child-free day, so he was determined not to outstay his welcome. However, as he was about to make his farewells, something completely different issued from his mouth, something entirely unpremeditated. 'Deborah, listen, I've missed you terribly.' His own voice shook him to the core – a torrent of words racing ahead of his mind and arising from some impulse he hadn't even been aware of. 'We belong together, don't we, after all these years? Okay, we've both been through our separate traumas, but that could be a new bond between us. And don't forget it was you who originally suggested we should patch up our differences and start anew on a different basis, with you earning the money and me looking after Jonathan. Oh, I know I dismissed the idea out of hand, but that was an age ago and I'm beginning to think it might actually work. Admittedly, things are very different now – you have the perfect nanny, and I have a good job – but both those could work in our favour if we decided to make a go of it together.'

'Anthony, I can't believe what I'm hearing!' Deborah sprang to her feet in indignation. 'You told me at the time I was more or less insane to come up with so unworkable a plan – said you couldn't possibly live with a child whose father you'd bumped off. And if you think you can change the brute fact of that killing, well, you're seriously deluded. I can see how it might suit you, of course, to come waltzing back now that I'm a far better prospect – not just my nice fat salary, but a live-in nanny laid on, so you wouldn't have to lift a finger when it comes to Jonathan. Or perhaps you imagine you could bribe the girl to take the brat out of your hair, whenever you happen to be at home.'

'That's totally unfair!' He, too, jumped up, so that they were facing each other like combatants. 'I distinctly remember all you said then about how your parents and mine had made you realise how precious a long marriage could be. Well, we've clocked up twenty years together, which surely counts for something.'

'In point of fact,' she said, coldly, 'we've been separated for the last two-and-a-half years, and married for just eleven before that.'

'Twenty since we first met,' he insisted.

'For God's sake, Anthony, let's not split hairs! The very reason I was about to get in touch with you – which we haven't even mentioned yet – is that I'm suing for divorce.'

He seemed to reel on his feet, tried frantically to fight back. 'Well, why the hell didn't you mention it, instead of leading me on and—'

'Leading you on? What's that supposed to mean?'

'Well, pretending you were so pleased to see me, and telling me you were on your own, and—'

'I never said such a thing!'

'I'm sorry, Deborah, but when you were talking about your friend, Louise, you said loud and clear that she was on her own, like you.'

'Yes, she is – and so was I, back then. But, if you really want to know, I met someone else, a few months ago, and we plan to move in together.'

Although doubly shocked now, he refused to let her see how crushed he felt. 'Isn't that rather premature?' he asked, recalling his own initial feelings for Mary. 'How can you know anyone in depth after just a few months?'

'I don't need a lecture on my private life, thanks! I know Peter through and through and, in fact, and we're going to get married the minute I'm free.'

Free. So *he* was her encumbrance. He slumped back on the sofa, deeply mortified as he recalled his crass proposals at the very point she was discarding him; resurrecting the idea of their getting back together, which he had vehemently gunned down when *she* was the one suggesting it. And, despite the fact he'd been secretly hoping that Jonathan had been adopted, a mere thirty minutes later he'd offered to look after him full-time. Worse, he had completely ignored his entanglement with Mary, still sharing her bed and home, still lusting for her body, and bonded by their both being "secret criminals". His twenty months in prison must have affected him so radically it had destroyed all his former common sense and cogent decision-making.

'Perhaps I ought to put you in the picture,' Deborah said in a slightly less hostile tone. 'Peter's a highly successful architect and a fair bit older than me, which actually suits me very well. You see, with three grown-up children of his own, he's had loads of hands-on experience and is absolutely wonderful with Jonathan. And he's so keen on being a step-father and starting again as a family man he's having extensive renovations done on his house to make it safe for a toddler. He lives nearby, in Primrose Hill – an area I've come to love. It's nice here, of course, but Primrose Hill is a real gem, being so close to Regents Park and with all the green space of the Hill itself. And, talking of green space, Peter has a pretty decent garden of his own. It's a bit of a jungle at present, but he's putting that to rights along with the house, clearing out the undergrowth, even getting rid of the pond, so Jonathan can't fall in. The place was once his family home, but after his wife died he let it go a bit – understandably.'

Anthony seemed to be shrinking and dwindling in contrast to this paragon: the 'highly successful', thoughtful, fatherly widower, and the owner of a house and garden in one of the most exclusive areas of London. There must be a downside, surely. 'But does he know about Jonathan's conception and about … about …? He could barely pronounce Craig's name and, if Deborah felt the same, perhaps she had kept her wonder-man in the dark.

'Of course he knows! But it only made him more determined to be there for the kid.'

Anthony stared down at the solid oak parquet floor. How could he compare, severely lacking in such good-heartedness and with no property, no experience of children and, in Deborah's eyes, devoid of any assets whatsoever? 'Well, I'd better get out of your hair,' he said, barging towards the door.

'Hold on a minute, Anthony, now you're here, we ought to get down to business and discuss the logistics of the divorce.'

'I'm sorry, but I'm leaving. And, if you're so keen on breaking everything up, ask your solicitor to send me a letter.' And, with that, he stormed into the hall and slammed the front door behind him.

CHAPTER 32

'A double Scotch, please.'

It was all he could do to say 'please', having queued so long at the bar, jostled by a noisy crowd intent only on enjoying their Bank Holiday weekend. Even getting into the pub had entailed squeezing through dozens of worse-for-wear drinkers overflowing onto the pavement.

But where else could he go? The brutal truth was he no longer belonged anywhere, now that his relationship with Deborah was finally extinct. And, as for Mary, having left her in such distress, he could hardly go crawling back for comfort and reassurance. Yet, the fact he wanted that comfort, despite realising how unsuited they were, left him still more confused. Besides, it would be difficult to break the ties when they were already living as a couple – one sanctioned by Probation – his clothes and possessions still ensconced in her bedsit. The thought of Probation brought only further disquiet, as he imagined Barbara's reaction were she ever to hear he had forced himself on Mary.

He took his drink to a free table at the back and sat pondering a still more intractable problem: how to excuse his sexual violence to Mary herself. Perhaps he could pretend that Deborah had dropped the bombshell of the divorce early this morning, rather than just now. Although a lie in terms of timing, it might at least assuage some of Mary's dismay if he explained he'd been so shaken by the news he had acted out of character. Indeed, it might even be the kindest way to end things altogether – which probably had to happen since there was clearly little future for the pair of them. He could say that his unexpected grief and agitation had showed him he was still emotionally entangled with his wife, so it was hardly fair to continue living with Mary. Yet that might be a bombshell for *her*, and no way could he just callously walk out on her, bonded as they were not only by being lovers, but by them both being secret "criminals".

Unless *she* decided she no longer wanted to live with him. The prospect, perversely, cut him like a knife.

'Mind if I sit here?' A well-dressed guy was approaching his table, a pint of Guinness in one hand, a mobile in the other. 'It's the only free chair in the place!'

'Go ahead.' Anthony grabbed the menu and studied it, to prevent the fellow striking up a "friendly" conversation. Instead, his neighbour's *Imperial March* ringtone reminded him that his own phone had been switched off for the last two hours. Wearily, he reached for it, checked a couple of texts, then, having noted three private-number missed calls, tapped his answerphone, alarmed to hear Darren's voice, sounding increasingly frantic with each message:

"I'm in dead trouble, mate. I just have to talk to you!" ... *"Tony, where are you? I've lost all sodding hope and no one else can help."* ... *"For fuck's sake, switch on your phone, Tony. I'm in the shit and can't fucking stand it no longer."*

Anthony sat paralysed, vaguely aware of his neighbour still cackling into his mobile. What the hell could he do? Impossible to ring back on a withheld number, so he dialled Darren's mobile only to get an "OUT OF SERVICE" voice message – and the same when he rang Carol-Ann and, finally, her parents. Deeply troubled, he checked the time of Darren's three calls, relieved to see they'd all been made in the last half-hour, so – please God – the lad would try again. He pushed his drink away. It was imperative to remain clear-headed if Darren needed urgent help, and he now regretted the two earlier spritzers. To distract himself, he picked up the menu again, yet the dishes failed to register as he muttered, over and over, 'Ring again, for Christ's sake!'

After what seemed an aeon, his phone did ring and, before he'd even had a chance to say hello, Darren's frenzied voice resounded in his ear.

'Oh, thank God, thank God! I was scared you'd done a runner, mate, and you're the only one who—'

'But what's happened?' he cut in.

'It's too long to explain – my sodding credit's running out. Fuck these prison phones! They're—'

'Prison?' Anthony prayed that he'd misheard.

'Yeah, I'm in the nick again. Chelmsford, this time. I'm desperate, Tony, but I ain't got no time to go into it. We'll be cut off any minute!'

'Quick, before we are, promise you'll apply for a Visiting Order, then I can come and see you.'

'No, you won't never want to see me again once you know what I've done. And, anyways, it's a hell of a trek.'

'Not another word, Darren! I'm coming and that's the end of it. Just fill in a VO request form and I'll move heaven and earth to be with you in person the day after I receive it.'

And, with that, he drained his glass – although not even a large Scotch could assuage his sense of deep foreboding.

CHAPTER 33

Finally, Anthony arrived at Chelmsford Prison, the journey – involving long delays, bus- replacement services and listless Sunday trains – having taken over two hours. Yet standing outside, just looking at the oppressive walls topped with razor-wire, made him want to turn tail and flee. He stood his ground, however, fighting a wave of claustrophobic panic, followed by nightmare flashbacks, including full colour close-ups of Craig's prostrate body bleeding on to the sheepskin rug. If he set foot within this dreaded place, suppose he were never let out again, but faded and shrivelled like those Wandsworth lifers who lost heart, weight, identity and purpose with each successive year in custody?

But he was here for Darren, he reminded himself, not to indulge in such ludicrous fears – although he still had no idea why the lad should be in an Essex gaol, indeed why back in gaol at all. The Visiting Order had taken a whole twelve days to arrive, despite his own efforts to expedite the process with a spate of emails and phone messages, all ignored. Eventually he had resorted to the post, and also written personally to Darren, enclosing a sheet of first-class stamps and a substantial postal order to top up the lad's phone-credit, but there had been no call or letter in reply – just the formal VO itself.

Pondering Darren's silence, he forced himself to approach the Visitors' Entrance, following a motley crew of mainly women and children – wives and girlfriends and their offspring, he assumed. Such family groups reignited the dejection he had felt two days earlier on receiving from Deborah's solicitor the first formal notification of the divorce. And she remained on his mind as he reached the check-in area and was subjected to the indignities she herself had described when visiting him in prison: the sniffer-dogs; the thorough-going body-search, including a metal-detector; and the probing questions by insolent screws who seemed to regard all visitors as potential criminals.

When, at last, he made his way to the Visits Hall, his agitation mounted at moving further into the prison system. In his mind, he was being ordered to swap chairs with Darren and put on the shiny red tabard that distinguished inmates from visitors, knowing that, after a brief hour or two, he would be hauled back to his cell.

However, the sight of Darren himself removed all other thoughts from his mind. The lad was skeletally thin, parchment-pale and sitting hunched at the table with an expression of total despair. And he was wearing prison clothes, which meant he must already have been convicted, and not just on remand.

He sprang to his feet as Anthony approached, and they dared a wary hug, both conscious of the hawk-eyed officers patrolling the hall, ready to pounce on any out-of-line behaviour.

'Thank God you're here, mate! I was shit scared you'd change your mind.'

'But didn't you get my letter?'

'What letter?'

Anthony shook his head in frustration, knowing how letters could be confiscated in prison, or go astray, or simply be held up in the labyrinthine system. 'Well, you'll get it in due course, I hope. But for God's sake, Darren, tell me why you're here – unless ...' he added, noticing the snack bar further down the hall, '... you'd like some food and drink first.'

'No. I can't eat nothing. I'm still in shock, see, and feel sick as a pig the whole time. But what really freaks me out is the thought of you giving up on me, once you know what I've done.'

'Well, unless you tell me, I never will know, will I?'

In the ensuing silence, Darren grew visibly more tense: fists clenched, brow furrowed, mouth so tight his lips all but disappeared. Then, suddenly, he blurted out in a breathless rush: 'I broke into Carol-Ann's parents' house – stole her mum's diamond ring. Planned on selling it, see, and using the cash to buy Carol-Ann this wedding dress – one she'd set her heart on, with lace and frills and beads and stuff. Her parents had promised to pay for the dress, along with a load of other stuff, but the bills was mounting up and up, so they called a halt, see – just like that – said she had to keep within their budget and choose something much less pricey. Carol-Ann was in tears, mate, and I was really pissed off. I mean, they're made of money, I swear. Even the ring I nicked was worth three grand.'

Profoundly shocked, Anthony was straining every nerve and muscle to conceal his appalled reaction to such complete and utter folly. 'So you managed to sell it?' he said, tersely.

'No. I was dead unlucky, mate – went down to Clacton when they was meant to be away, but Rita – that's the mum – came back unexpectedly and caught me red-handed. I took to me heels and fled – straight into the arms of their fucking next door neighbour, a giant of a bloke who overpowered me easy, and rang the cops there and then. So I was banged up in the cop-shop for the night, taken to court next morning and charged with aggravated burglary.'

Anthony was still barely able to credit that Darren should have robbed his own parents-in-law-to-be. However, he tried to discount his personal feelings and focus on the facts. 'I thought aggravated burglary entailed carrying an offensive weapon?'

'Yeah, it do. And all I had was a sodding screwdriver – you know, just to force the lock on the jewellery box. But Rita swore blind I was waving it about in her face and even threatening to kill her. That's a lie, Tony, I swear to God. Okay, I ain't no saint, but never in me life have I laid a finger on no one. But she's always had it in for me, and this was her big chance to land me in the shit, cancel the wedding and bar me from their house. The cops went to see her that same day and when I was interviewed later the DCs told me all the crap she'd said about me being, like, real vicious. But it was her word against mine, see, so I didn't have a dog's chance. I mean, she's posher than me and speaks nice, and that stuff makes a difference. And her neighbour was also interviewed and told the cops that "the lovely lady next door" was fucking Mother Teresa and no one in the street had a word to say against her! I didn't have a leg to stand on, 'cause the DCs kept repeating that breaking into someone's house with a screwdriver was proof of bad intent. But the way I grew up, a screwdriver's just a tool of the trade.'

Anthony winced, still making a supreme effort not to judge or condemn. Wasn't he himself at least partially to blame? As he'd become more involved with Mary and increasingly busy with Hugh's work, he had let his mentoring lapse. And part of that mentoring had involved financial management skills, so, if he had only persevered with them, Darren might have learned to live within his budget and not resort to crime again.

As he struggled between self-reproach, and mixed pity and blame for Darren, the large crowded hall seemed to blur and recede. Even the buzz of conversation, the tramp of the screws' prowling feet and the cries from restive children were all fading into silence. He was conscious only of Darren: his predicament, his future, the note of genuine anguish in his voice.

'I just want me life back, Tony – except I aint got no life any more. This place is a right head-fuck, yet I can't see no way out.'

'But didn't you get any proper legal advice?' Anthony asked, at last.

'Yeah, saw the Duty Solicitor.'

'And?'

'He told me to say nothing at me recorded interview. But I couldn't just sit silent and let that shit of a Rita get away with a pack of lies. He also told me to plead not-guilty in court, but I took no notice of that neither.'

'But why, for heaven's sake, when you knew it wasn't aggravated burglary?'

''Cause in their eyes I was a liar and a thug. A sergeant in the cop-shop actually called me a low-down piece of scum, so if that's how they saw me …'

Anthony, too, was beginning to feel like a piece of scum: back with the criminal class, his every movement scrutinised by suspicious, surly screws who would be only too happy to march him out of the room for the slightest infringement of the rules. His other self – Hugh's professional researcher – belonged to a different life entirely.

'And, anyways, at least a not-guilty plea means the whole thing's over and done with much more quick. Instead of hanging about for three or four months before me trial came up, I was in the Crown Court just sixteen days later. Besides,' Darren shrugged, 'I'd have probably been found guilty whatever I fucking pleaded – just wasted all that time going out of me mind every time I thought of Carol-Ann. You need to understand, see, that till I met her, I never had nothing to lose – okay, loads of one-night-stands, maybe, but never no one who wanted to set up home with me and have me kids and everything. Way back, when we first met, I told you me whole story about never having no family or nothing, and now I've ruined me one chance. I mean, what's the point of anything now I've lost me girl?'

Anthony tensed at the sound of sobbing from the woman at the adjoining table. Whatever Darren's crass stupidity in risking all he had for the sake of some damned dress, the sheer sadness of his story made him, too, want to weep.

'And, see, the other reason I pleaded guilty was I couldn't bear the thought of her sitting in the gallery in court, listening to every word. And me having to call her parents liars, not just in front of her, but with them there, too, most like sneering and gloating and—'

'But why didn't you contact me ages ago – the minute you landed in here, before you ever went to court? I could have visited you straight away, while you were on remand, and wouldn't even have needed a Visiting Order.'

Darren stared down at his hands, the nails bitten to the quick. 'I was too ashamed, mate – couldn't tell you I'd fucked up the wedding when you was going to be best man and lent me that posh suit and everything. And, anyways, I kept hoping I wouldn't be convicted.'

'How on earth could you think that, with all that weight of evidence against you? Okay, a lot of it was false, but you knew they'd see it as gospel.'

'I weren't thinking mate – just kidding meself along. I had to hang on to something, see, or I'd have gone ahead and topped meself. I'm still tempted, if you want to know. The judge gave me five sodding years – on account of all me previous, see – so I reckon I'd be better off ending it all, like tomorrow, than having to rot here all that—'

'Darren, I absolutely forbid you to talk like that! I'm here for you now, and I'll visit as often as I possibly can, just to stop you losing hope. But it's vital that you see this as a wake-up call and use the time in the most positive way you can, rather than giving way to despair. And you'll only serve half, remember. Okay, even two-and-a-half years seems like an eternity – I know that all too well – but you have to make an effort to keep busy and engaged: sign up for Education, take any courses on offer.'

Darren shook his head despondently. 'With all them cuts and stuff, I'm not allowed to at this early stage. You have to wait, like, months.'

'Well, we'll return to the postal lessons, then,' Anthony said, furious at a system that let prisoners waste their time and drift into abject depression rather than insist they keep busy and improve themselves.

'I'll set you assignments and you can send them back, like you did before.' However hard it might prove to fit in postal tuition on top of his demanding job, not to mention regular visits to Chelmsford, he had to make some compensation for his shaming negligence.

'But why the hell should you, Tony, when I've fucked up so bad?'

'Because I'm absolutely determined that, from this minute on, you're going to make the best of yourself – push to be Enhanced, see the Education Officer.'

'I already seen him, mate, told him I didn't want no Education, at no stage. You can't have forgot, Tony, it pays far less than jobs like wing-cleaner.'

'Bugger the cost! I'll make up the difference. I'm earning a lot at present – bonuses and commission on top of my basic salary. Hugh may be a slave-driver, but he's a very generous one, so for God's sake let me help you in any way I can. I've already sent a postal order, which should turn up in a day or so, and I'll continue sending money – and books, and food, and anything else you want. But I need to know how you are, Darren, so you must top up your phone-credit and ring me every few days.'

Darren seemed too choked to reply. 'You're sounding like me … me *dad*,' he stuttered, finally.

'I hope not! You don't want a dad who's been in nick!'

Anthony's attempt to lighten the atmosphere seemed useless. Darren still looked utterly wretched and was still refusing to meet his eyes.

'I ain't treated you right today, Tony. You come all this sodding way and I ain't asked you a single thing about your life.'

'But I'm here to talk about *you*, Darren. I needed to hear the whole story.'

'Well, you've heard it now, so tell me about Mary – how she is and everything.'

'She's fine,' he lied. True, they had made their peace, partly through some tender, gentle lovemaking, to compensate for his abrupt, one-sided, almost brutish assault, but things were still tense between them. And, just last week, there had been another blow: Mrs Murray-Wood announced, with profuse apologies, that her son and his wife had invited her to live with them in Cheltenham to provide hands-on baby-care, so she intended to sell her London house. Mary had been devastated, not only because of the close bond with her landlady, but because she knew how unlikely it was ever to find another place as convenient and cheap, and one willing to accept two warring cats. He just hadn't had the callousness to tell her that no way could he start again, in any new location, with her and the monstrous Sheehan, and thus the whole matter of their future still posed enormous problems. The last thing he wanted, however, was to burden Darren with such dilemmas. 'I'll tell you more on my next visit, but this is your time, Darren, and there isn't much of it left, so let's hear about your cellmate and what it's like here in general.'

'Don't mention me cellmate! He smashed up the whole cell last week, starting with his bunk – ripped the sheets to bits, tried to tear the mattress apart, even pissed on the bed-clothes and ...'

As Darren continued recounting prison horrors – the gangster, Todge ('He'd slit me throat for a Mars Bar!'), the blackmailing bully, Ron ('Gimme twenty quid, Darren, and I'll see you come to no harm. Otherwise ...'), the mind-blowing boredom of twenty-three-hour lock-up, with no job, no activities, no access to the gym – Anthony became increasingly conscious of how blessed he was in comparison. Okay, his ties with Deborah were broken, any future with Mary impossible, his daily pressures about to increase exponentially, yet he was still free from confinement, free from bullying and violence, free to go outside and feel the bright June sun on his face.

When Darren was released, the weather would be dark and cold. He did some quick calculations in his head: if the lad kept to the straight and narrow to ensure his sentence wasn't increased, he should be out early in November 2018 – yes, an eternity, for God's sake, for his poor, despairing friend.

PART FOUR - 6th December 2015

CHAPTER 34

No way, he thought, with a quick glance at his watch, could he turn up thirty minutes early for an engagement he was dreading. So, walking on from the tube to Primrose Hill village, with its crop of chichi little cafés, he stopped at the first, squeezing his way through the youngish crowd queuing at the counter for takeaway cakes and home-made bread. Subsiding at a table near the back, he glanced at the groups and couples all around him, feeling out of tune with the general convivial mood of those relaxing, laughing and leafing through the papers. His apprehension about meeting Peter – not to mention Jonathan – was increasing by the minute, especially as he had no idea *why* Deborah should have invited him to their house for Sunday-morning drinks. It was certainly not divorce-related because, just a matter of days earlier, he had received the Decree Absolute – a document that spelled shame and failure as far as he was concerned. To give his ex-wife credit, though, she had insisted on an amicable, non-recriminatory divorce, with recourse to lawyers kept to the absolute minimum, and he was forced to admit that the whole business had proved far less painful, protracted and expensive than he had ever dared to hope.

'What can I get you, sir?'

The waitress's coppery hair reminded him of Mary, bringing a pang of loss and lust, along with his usual sense of hurt pride that she should be quite so content without him. There was no denying she had landed on her feet – thanks to Hugh, of all people.

Thoughts of Hugh reminded him that his ever-demanding boss had already texted him twice this morning, so, having ordered a coffee, he checked his phone again. The tone of the two new messages made it clear that Hugh was annoyed he'd been "gadding about" – and thus largely unavailable – on both the weekend days. Yesterday's visit to Darren in prison was hardly gadding about and, as for today, there would be not the slightest pleasure in watching Deborah and Peter play out their loving-couple role.

As the waitress retuned with his coffee, he mentally undressed her, laid her on the table, clad only in her skimpy white frilled apron, and—

'Sure you don't want anything to eat?'

Just you, he thought, aware that with no wife or girlfriend, or any time to do internet dating, the prospect of sex seemed increasingly unlikely. And things were little more cheering on the Darren front, since the lad's efforts to sign up for the prison education programme had foundered in a quagmire of red tape and inefficiency, or been frustrated by a shortage of staff. He did now have a job, but only of the most mindless kind, packing breakfast items into plastic bags. He had also been Enhanced, which meant more privileges but, having been at Chelmsford over six months, he was clearly losing hope of learning some specific trade or furthering his education. And that made his own frequent visits and postal assignments all the more essential. He had even contacted Betty at one point to see if she could help. It pleased him that they had stayed in touch over such a long stretch of time, if only very sporadically. And after their phone call he had found himself drifting back to boyhood and imagining her as his fond, easy-going mother, one who eschewed improving museum visits or tours of dreary ruins, in favour of rackety funfairs and indulgent ice-cream parlours. A cruel irony, it struck him, that while his education had clawed its relentless tentacles into every so-called "holiday", Darren's had been deplorably neglected.

Once he'd finished his coffee and paid the bill, he emerged from the fug of the café into the churlish winter air. The recent change of weather – the loss of light and shorter days, the falling leaves and near-naked trees – seemed to symbolise his personal descent into a bleak and lonely future. As he approached Peter's imposing mansion, however, he resolved to suppress such thoughts. It was imperative for his own self-respect that he shouldn't appear crushed by the divorce. And, pausing a moment on the flight of grand stone steps leading up to the house, he let the glittery Christmas tree sparkling in the front window serve as an exemplar: even a sombre fir could put on a bright façade.

*

His smile was securely in place as Deborah let him in, despite his conflicting emotions: deep dejection that she was now an 'ex'; and an unsettling seethe of desire prompted by her long slender legs and seductively high heels.

'Come in and get warm,' she said, sounding genuinely welcoming.

As Peter followed her into the hall, Anthony was completely unprepared for the solidly built, comfy-looking man of middling height, with a lined but pleasant face and neatly cut grey hair, wearing a faded bluish sweater and unremarkable grey trousers. He had conjured up someone entirely different: a thin, arty type in dark glasses and black polo-neck, dauntingly tall and with dramatic, Craig-like colouring.

'So good to meet you, Anthony. I've heard so much about you.'

What had Peter heard: that his fiancée's discarded husband was a murderer, a jailbird, a selfish, dominating monster? Hastily remembering his manners, he returned the man's warm handshake, then, as he was ushered into the sitting room, expressed his admiration for the house. Again, he had pictured it quite wrongly. Instead of ultra-modern minimalism, there were brightly coloured Persian rugs, a collection of antique clocks, several patrician-looking pieces of Edwardian furniture, and a general air of old-fashioned comfort.

'Yes, we love it here,' Peter said, motioning Anthony to the sofa.

'We' was as painful a word as 'ex' and, despite his genial exterior, Anthony was coiled like a spring, expecting Jonathan to appear at any moment. How could he lay eyes on a child whom he personally had made fatherless? And, when he added Craig's other three children to the lives he'd irreparably damaged, his guilt and remorse quadrupled. Guilt was, indeed, a constant nagging sore, and he envied those who could simply take their innocence for granted and weren't compelled to live in endless fear that their past would be discovered.

'What can I get you?' Peter asked, juggling bottles on the heavy-shouldered sideboard. 'If you happen to be a whisky drinker, I have a rather fine single malt.'

'Sounds just the job!' At least it would take the edge off his distress at being no more than a casual visitor to the woman who had once shared his life and bed.

Once the three of them were settled with their drinks, Peter leaned forward, obviously playing the role of perfect host, as *he* was playing perfect guest. 'Do tell me about your work, Anthony. Deborah says you're in the recruitment business.'

Anthony complied with a brief and highly edited account, having no intention of mentioning the pressures dictated by his subordinate position as the ex-con "leper" unable to find any other professional job.

And, when Deborah asked if he was enjoying his new flat in Finsbury Park, he concealed the fact that, being still on licence, he'd had little choice as to where he could move if he wished to continue seeing Barbara at Landsdowne Road. It was only four months, in fact, until his licence period expired but, although that would spell new freedom, it also brought a certain dread, because however much he begrudged the time for appointments, Barbara did provide empathetic support. And rather to his own surprise, he had come to admire her profound desire to improve the lives and chances of what he once would have condescendingly called the dregs of society – a vocation in total contrast to Deborah's career, with its emphasis on wealth, status and prestige. Indeed, his ex-wife's expensive necklace – emeralds and pearls, by the looks of it – would have been far beyond Barbara's meagre pay.

He and his hosts continued batting various subjects about, maintaining the charade of an amiable encounter. Inside, though, he was struggling to quash hideous images of Peter and Deborah in bed.

'What a magnificent tree!' he exclaimed to fill a sudden awkward lull in the conversation.

'Yes,' Deborah agreed, 'it is rather stunning, isn't it? I decorated it ridiculously early. Most of my friends leave it till Christmas Eve, but Jonathan saw the baubles I'd bought and the tinsel and strings of lights and kept begging me to put them on!'

Anthony tensed at the name, still unable to bring himself to ask if the child was actually here, although soon the talk moved on to Christmas in general – their plans and his own. He muttered something noncommittal about meeting up with friends, having already heard from Deborah that his father was spending the festive week ensconced here in the bosom of his new "family". In the absence of any other relatives – except for Deborah's parents for whom he was anathema – his Christmas was, frankly, a non-starter. As for Mary, although he was still in contact with her, she was hardly likely to invite him down to Hampshire to spend Christmas with her fifty charges. At least there was Darren, whom he had promised to visit on Christmas Eve, but visits were forbidden on Christmas Day itself, so there would still be that aching void to fill.

Fortunately, the subject changed to the floods in the North, but, just at that moment, there was a series of vociferous cries from upstairs. 'That's Jonathan,' Deborah said, fondly, rising to her feet. 'He always makes his presence felt when he wakes up from his lunchtime nap! Excuse me a second, Anthony.'

He would excuse her all damned afternoon, if she only kept the child away. But in less than ten minutes she re-entered the room, slowing her pace to that of the toddler beside her. Anthony forced himself to look at the sturdy little boy, in miniature designer jeans and trainers, his solemn face topped with a thatch of Craig-dark hair. Could the red-faced, bawling infant he'd met previously at the prison visit be this self-same child?

'Say hello to Anthony,' Deborah instructed.

Anthony sat ramrod-tense, expecting Jonathan to shun him, maybe even scream hysterically, as if sensing at some instinctive level that this stranger was an evil killer. But, to his complete astonishment, the child rushed eagerly towards him, reaching out both arms, his serious expression transformed by a radiant smile.

'That really is extraordinary,' Deborah remarked. 'Normally he's extremely shy and especially wary of strangers.'

Far from seeming shy, Jonathan darted over to the door to retrieve the cuddly toy he'd dropped, raced back to the "stranger" and plonked it on his lap. 'This is Ferdinand,' he said, in his high-pitched lisping voice, tweaking the black plush cat by the ear.

'Well, you've definitely made a hit!' Peter exclaimed, with a laugh. 'Ferdinand is his absolute top favourite, and no one else is ever allowed to hold him – not even me.'

Anthony sat cradling the furry black body, fighting off painful reminders of Mary – not to mention Anton and Sheehan. Nonetheless, he was touched by Jonathan's trust in him, having expected mutual detestation. The little boy was actually pressing close to his knees as he fondled and stroked the cat, and tried to guide the "stranger's" hand to Ferdinand's back, to encourage him to do the same.

'He has a complete fixation on cats,' Debora explained, 'and just can't keep away from our next-door-neighbour's rather gorgeous tabby. Fortunately, she's a kindly soul and invites Jonathan round to see Tigger almost every day. He's now desperately keen to have a cat of his own, and I've promised him he can, but I just haven't had a minute to look into it, what with the upheaval of the house-move.'

He was jolted by Deborah's change of heart, since never before had she shown the slightest interest in owning any sort of pet. She appeared to have mellowed altogether, though, and was far less tense and spiky, presumably due to Peter's influence. Her new husband-to-be seemed enviably laid-back – perhaps the man she should have married from the start, rather than an equally tense, equally ambitious, equally competitive partner.

Jonathan trotted out to the kitchen and returned with a few more toys, all of which he placed on Anthony's lap: a model sports car; a wooden jigsaw; and an ugly red-nosed clown puppet.

'Well, he's obviously smitten,' Peter said, with a smile, 'bestowing all his treasures on you!'

Anthony's scant experience of children left him tongue-tied, but Jonathan himself continued to talk – although in the somewhat effortful, hesitant way he assumed was common to most toddlers – about his toys, his nanny and, yes, the next-door cat. He noticed Deborah and Peter exchange a glance, then Peter went over to Jonathan and tried to remove the toys from Anthony's lap.

'No!' Jonathan objected, doggedly replacing them.

'But it's Tigger's lunchtime,' Peter cajoled, 'so we need to go round to Mrs Pearson and help her feed him.'

'I want *him* to come,' the child insisted, clinging to Anthony's hand.

'He'll join us in a little while, okay? But first Mummy wants to talk to him.'

Anthony froze. What now? Deborah was looking suddenly more strained, so it was bound to be an awkward conversation. And, as Peter disappeared with the child, she got up and stood by the mantelpiece.

'Anthony, there's something we want to ask you. It was Peter's idea, in fact, and to be honest I was appalled when he suggested it. But what you need to know first,' she added, walking over to join him on the sofa, 'is that I'm expecting another baby'

'Congratulations!' It was all he could do to make it sound sincere. Peter had obviously wasted no time, clearly had super-fertile sperm.

'He – and it is a he – is not due till latish May, but we wondered if you might consider being his godfather.'

'*Godfather!*' The word came out as an explosion. How could the murderer of this new baby's elder brother possibly assume the responsible, indeed honourable role of godfather? Deborah's parents would be totally outraged and, as for attending any christening ceremony in which *he* played a part, they would simply refuse point-blank. 'But … but…' he stammered, 'I'm not religious, as you know perfectly well.'

'Oh, we don't mean in that sense,' Deborah explained. 'Just a private, unofficial sort of arrangement. There won't be a church ceremony and no promises or formal responsibilities. I admit it does sound incongruous – if not to say downright off-beam – and I said exactly that to Peter at the time. But what you have to understand, Anthony, is that he's a truly good man who sees the best in everyone and wants the best for them. And because he comes from a big family, with sisters, brothers, aunts, uncles, cousins – you name it – he's very much aware that you have none of that.'

Anthony fumed in silence. So this was pity on Peter's part: the big-hearted paragon with a large, devoted family, bestowing his largesse on the poor emasculated loner.

'I mean, even your father seems to have come over to our tribe. I suppose because he's now quite pally with my parents, he feels a tug of loyalties about seeing you at all.'

Did he pick up a hint of blame, now? He'd neglected his only relative, left Deborah to do all the visiting and caring, so the lonely widower had been forced to seek solace elsewhere.

'Peter and I both feel you've suffered enough. In fact, I've come to see – perhaps rather late in the day – that you paid a much higher price for what was as much my fault as yours.'

An apology, for God's sake – one he had never expected.

'I did pressurise you to have a baby – I admit that now – and I couldn't really empathise with your horror of a sperm-donor. So I went ahead and took matters into my own hands, which, of course, had disastrous consequences for you as well as Craig. I didn't intend that for a moment, but what I did intend was to pass off someone else's child as yours, and that was undoubtedly wrong. So Peter feels we owe you a gesture of forgiveness – not just for the deception, but for all you've lost and all you've been through.'

Oh, magnanimous Peter, dreaming up this preposterous godfather notion as less an act of pity than one of compensation – a form of compensation he most emphatically didn't want.

'To tell the truth, I'd have probably gone for a clean break had Peter not persuaded me to see things from your viewpoint. I was certainly relieved that the divorce was so quick and hassle-free but, weirdly, when the whole thing was finalised, I did feel quite a pang, much to my surprise. I kept remembering how romantic our first meeting was, and all the years we had together and ...'

Now embarrassment was added to his toxic mix of resentment and annoyance. Such sentimental nostalgia was surely not just tactless but unfair to Peter, however infuriatingly saintly the guy appeared to be.

'Don't get me wrong, Anthony. I'm happier than I've ever been. Peter and I are so utterly right for each other, and he's wonderful with Jonathan, and thrilled about the new baby. And this pregnancy is heaven, compared with that ghastly non-stop vomiting I suffered with the first one. I was completely unable to function then, whereas these last three months I've hardly felt sick at all. And I'm far less stressed in general, because I only work-part time now and still have my fantastic nanny as well as all Peter's support.'

Pausing for breath, she flashed him a look of concern. 'But when I think how busy you are and presumably isolated, as well, since you're living on your own, it all seems a bit unfair. I mean, I'm about to marry into a whole new loving circle, whereas you seem a bit adrift, if you don't mind me saying so. It may sound dreadfully corny, but Peter and I want to share a bit of our happiness and we thought that being involved with a child might give you something precious, too.'

Precious? Had she forgotten that he had never really wanted a child, let alone someone else's?

'Oh, I know you're not keen on babies, so there's no need to be involved at this stage. But maybe when the new arrival's older – say four or five or so – you might enjoy taking him to the zoo, or out for a pizza, or to a puppet show or some such. And that would allow us to maintain some sort of contact, rather than severing all ties and becoming strangers to each other, or, worse, enemies.'

So the supremely happy Deborah wanted to sweep everyone – even the killer of her first-born's father – into the golden circle of her radiant new tribe. 'Look, I … I need to think about all this. Frankly, it's a bit of a shock.'

'Of course. I understand entirely. And it goes without saying that if you don't like the idea, that's the end of the matter. But Peter said we should at least suggest it and then let you decide.'

'Okay, I will, but not right now. In fact, I … I think I'd better be going. I have things to do back home.'

'Oh, do stay a little longer. In fact, why not join us for lunch?'

'No, really, I—'

'Well, I insist you come and meet Tigger – if only for five minutes, otherwise Jonathan will be terribly disappointed. I want you to know that it truly was a first for him to take to someone so quickly and unreservedly, as he did with you just now. And, as for talking to a stranger quite so freely, that's utterly unheard of. With almost all our visitors, he hangs back, completely silent, and hides his face in my skirts.'

Deborah was certainly playing her cards: pity, compensation, blame and now flattery. He could hardly disappear, however, without saying goodbye to Peter, at least, so reluctantly he let himself be led into the adjoining house. If only, he thought, re-applying his polite but rigid smile, Mary were here to wax ecstatic over Tigger, so he could slip away unnoticed back to his child-free, cat-free life.

CHAPTER 35

'Oh, Mary, it's absolutely nothing like I imagined!' Anthony surveyed the landscaped garden, its profusion of trees and shrubs providing an attractive background to the Swiss-style wooden chalets set amongst them. 'I thought a cattery would be, frankly, a bit of a dump, with ugly cages and wire-netting and an overpowering smell!'

Mary gave a charming giggle. 'Well, you can see how wrong you were. And, by the way, don't call it a "cattery" in front of Lady Lawson. It's the Pampered Paws Cat Hotel – and extremely exclusive, I might tell you! Her aim in setting it up was to make it a real home-from-home, with every guest treated like a member of the family. And she never has more than twenty, so she can cater to their individual needs – a special diet, maybe, or extra heating for the elderly, even extra cuddles if the cat's a nervous type, or missing its owner a lot.'

'I bet you're good at the cuddles.' He felt a sudden vain longing for her to cuddle *him*. She looked as delectable as ever, even in her work clothes.

'You bet! In fact, come and see Tabitha. She's one who needs lots of attention. And, anyway, we ought to get out of the cold.'

She led him along the conifer-bordered path into one of the chalets, where a small white cat was curled up on a bed that looked comfier than his own.

'Meet Tabitha,' she said, picking up the creature and, much to his envy, snuggling it close against her breasts. 'The poor darling was abused as a kitten and this is the first time she's been away from home since she was adopted. Her owners were distraught at having to board her, but they were going to Dubai on business so they didn't have much choice. But they're fine about it now, because we Skype them every day so they can see for themselves how well their baby's settling in.'

'I'm tempted to book a chalet myself,' he joked, surprised by the spaciousness of the pens, their cleanliness and cosy warmth.

'Well, if you fancy a scratch-post, a sit-box and a sun-shelf, please feel free! We lay on all mod cons, of course, and loads of different cat-toys.'

Not to mention Christmas decorations, he observed, noting the miniature Christmas trees, hung with cat-treats rather than baubles.

With a final loving stroke, Mary laid Tabitha back in her bed. 'I'll show you just one more – our gorgeous Siamese, Oscar. It's his birthday today, so we're making a special fuss of him.'

Anthony gazed at the sinuous creature with its snooty expression and joltingly blue eyes.

'He's very inquisitive by nature, so he'll sit in his run and watch me working, or keep an eye on the wildlife. We have lots of squirrels here, and we put bird-feeders outside each enclosure, to prevent the cats getting bored – although that's not very likely because they're all visited at least five times a day, including a late-evening round to make sure they're settled for the night.'

'Do you ever get any sleep, Mary?'

'Oh yes! And I have plenty of help in the daytime. Jane and Simon come in Monday to Saturday, and Lady Lawson does a fair bit herself. But she's eighty-one next year and getting a bit doddery – which is why she's so relieved to have me living in. You see, all the cat-monitor-screens (2 hyphens inserted) are set up in my personal quarters, so I'm alerted to any emergency, day and night. In fact, I'll show you my place now. I've finished work for the moment and I'm sure you could do with a coffee.'

As they walked across the gardens, he yearned to take her hand, even press himself against her, and had to keep reminding himself that there was no future in their relationship. Indeed, seeing her in this extraordinary new setting made it even more apparent that they inhabited worlds a million miles apart, and the fact he still lusted for her body was partly because he had no other woman in his life – and was unlikely to find one when there was so little time to socialise.

'I have my own kitchen and bathroom,' she said, ushering him into the annexe adjoining the main house. 'And a separate bedroom, at last. And it's completely self-contained, so I can do my own thing when I'm off-duty, cook my own meals, and—'

There was a sudden loud mew and a black cat wandered in, sniffed the air a moment, then made a beeline for him, purring in happy recognition. 'Anton!' he exclaimed, touched by the cat's welcome.

'He's so thrilled to see you – isn't that lovely! Lady Lawson lets me keep him here, just like she keeps her cats at home in the main house.'

Anton was still rubbing himself against his legs, so he sat on the sofa and settled the cat on his lap, if only to please Mary.

'Just listen to him purring! You stay there and make a fuss of him, and I'll go and put the kettle on. I've made you your favourite flapjacks, by the way – oh, and before I forget, I also made you a Christmas cake, so remind me to give it to you before you leave.'

What he loved about Mary was that she never held grudges, or harboured resentments about what he couldn't be or hadn't done. Despite their break-up, here she was cossetting him again, and he was comforted to think that, however infrequently they might meet, they would probably remain good friends. She had certainly gone up in the world, he thought, glanced around the surprisingly large sitting room – not just working for a wealthy aristocrat, but living in much greater style than her former cramped and smelly bedsit.

'Well, there's no doubt you've come up trumps,' he said when she returned with the coffee and flapjacks and sat companionably beside him.

'Oh, Anthony, this is my absolute dream-job! In fact, I can hardly believe I'm here, especially having been in such depths of despair. You were pretty low yourself, remember, what with us two splitting up, then Mrs Murray-Wood disappearing, so we lost our home as well. And, when Mr Edwardes decided to take retirement, it just seemed the final blow – except there was worse to come, of course, when Sheehan got run over. I still feel guilty about him, actually.'

'Look, it wasn't your fault, Mary. The fact he got through such a sturdy fence shows he was determined to escape and, with no road-sense, he was just asking for trouble.' He, too, had felt guilty at Sheehan's demise, but only because his reaction was more one of relief than distress. Sheehan's very wildness threatened his fundamental need for order and control and – still more unsettling – the cat's violence seemed an echo of his own. Having grown up to regard himself as high-principled and virtuous, it was as if Sheehan were a reminder of his detestable dark side.

'Yes, Lady Lawson said feral cats are almost impossible to domesticate and, however careful their owners are, often run into danger, so she told me not to blame myself. We lit a grief-candle together and she even let me make him a memorial garden in part of the grounds, and we performed a little ceremony for him there. And, in the end,' she added, passing him his coffee, 'it all worked out for the best, because if I hadn't been in such a dreadful state, I doubt if you'd have had that talk with Hugh.'

Certainly, only his deep concern for Mary had made him ask his boss if there was the slightest chance he knew anyone, amongst his literally hundreds of contacts, who might offer her live-in work, preferably with animals. Being a country girl at heart, she had decided not to continue with secretarial work, and also refused his offer of paying the rent on a new flat for her. 'Though I have to say, Mary, I was utterly amazed when he came up with the goods. He's not exactly the soul of human kindness, so I assumed he'd just say no and tell me to get cracking on his work!' In point of fact, Hugh had risen to the challenge not for Mary's sake, but as a favour for one of VIP clients, Ivor Lawson. Ivor was worried about his mother, who, desperate for help in her Hampshire cat hotel, was so stringent in her requirements that she had rejected literally scores of applicants. The successful candidate had to be female, single, childless, well-mannered and respectful, willing to live on the premises and work unsociable hours, and have a total dedication to cats – Mary, to a T.

Mary gave a long, contented sigh. 'I'm just so relieved she took me on and that I got through my initial trial period. And, thank the Lord, she's really pleased with me now and seems to want me to stay for ever!' She passed him the plate of moist, raisin-studded flapjacks, then sat back against the sofa cushions. 'If only you could find your dream job. I know things are okay-ish at Hugh's – like they were for me at Mr Edwardes'. But it wasn't until he bowed out that I realised the job wasn't "me" – and never had been. Even as a kid, I imagined myself working at Battersea Dogs' Home, or helping out at a cat-refuge. Did you have a childhood dream, Anthony – maybe want to be a missionary in Africa, or the next Sean Connery?'

He suppressed a smile at the thought of his ambitious, high-powered father allowing his only son to "waste his life converting heathens", let alone embark on the uncertain career of actor. Childhood dreams were to be rooted out at source, the son in question not permitted the dangerous option of choosing for himself some unsound or wayward path, but forced like a hothouse plant towards the light and air of wealth, power and status. 'To be honest, Mary, even if I were free to choose my ideal job right now, I'm not sure what it would be. And, although I've saved a lot, thanks to Hugh's hefty bonuses, I've no burning desire to spend that cash, as I used to in the past, on expensive clothes and meals and suchlike. I'm very muddled at the moment, not sure who I am or where I belong.'

He paused a moment, reflecting of all the recent financial scandals – rigging of foreign exchange markets, bribery and corruption, money laundering, mortgage scams, fraudulent payment protection schemes – which now made him feel increasingly uneasy, especially the subject of tax-avoidance. Some of his fellow employees at FFC had been the very accountants who dreamed up canny wheezes for minimising their clients' tax. And the bloated multinationals were still more devious, depriving the Treasury of a cool ten billion a year and, he reckoned, costing the European countries combined a tax shortfall of some hundred-and-fifty billion. Back then, he had simply accepted such practices as a normal, legal and, indeed, sensible method of "tax-optimising", as he and his colleagues preferred to call it. Yet his twenty months in gaol had made him see the injustice of a system in which small-time benefits-cheats were banged up in a prison cell while the fat cats got off scot free, receiving, as opposed to punishment, huge bonuses, lucrative consultancies and sometimes even peerages. And the bankers were worse still. Only this last Monday, the government admitted it was watering down the rules intended to hold them to account, despite the cost to the tax-payer of a veritable fortune in bailouts. 'I'm much more aware now of social and financial inequality. I suppose I used to regard it as the natural order of things, however awful that sounds.'

'Actually, so did I' – Mary gave a wry smile – 'but from the opposite end of the scale. Where I grew up, there were people with grand houses and stables full of thoroughbreds, while Dad was out in all weathers, repairing their fences, and poor Mum took in sewing to help feed and clothe us all.'

'How are your parents?' he enquired, embarrassed by this further evidence of the unbridgeable gulf between their families.

'Well, the floods have hit them badly, of course, and they're also disappointed about me giving up my "proper job", since it was Dad who originally persuaded me to do a secretarial course. And they can't help feeling that if I wanted to work in the country, why didn't I return to Lancashire and live much closer to them.'

'Well, I know why – you're scared they'll somehow ferret out the fact you've had a baby, if you see too much of them – although I must say, Mary, it does seem highly unlikely.'

'I'm not so sure. I spent a couple of weekends with them, helping clear up the flood-damage, before I moved down here, and Mum kept making pointed references to some local girl who'd "gone to the bad", so I was terribly on edge wondering if she *knew*. But let's not even talk about it!' She gave a dramatic shudder. 'By the way, going back to the inequality thing, I do feel rather guilty working with such cosseted cats. Their owners are all well-heeled and pay a fortune for them to stay here, and it seems wrong that I'm not devoting myself to more deserving kitties who have nothing and no one in their lives. But I'd need money to do that and, anyway, where would I live?'

Perhaps, he pondered, if he continued to earn well, he could he set her up one day in her own refuge for the Darrens of the cat-world. In fact, Darren was on his mind since the lad's phone call yesterday, saying he was about to be transferred from Chelmsford to Coldingley Prison, in Bisley. The latter, being C-Category, might with luck mean a single cell and more time out of it, and perhaps a better chance of enrolling in some educational courses. Yet poor Darren had sounded highly apprehensive, dreading the prospect of spending the unfestive prison Christmas in a completely new environment, with no familiar faces. As for his own promised visit on Christmas Eve, it would have to be re-negotiated for an entirely different prison in a matter of mere days – and so was almost certainly out of the question.

Suddenly aware that Mary was still awaiting some response, he dragged his mind from Coldingley back to the cat hotel. 'Well, at least you're getting masses of hands-on experience here.'

'Yes, absolutely, But I'd much rather talk about you. Do you intend continuing to work for Hugh?'

'I don't have much alternative, although I feel out-of-sync now with that world and even with Hugh himself. I can't share his passion for all that high-tech stuff – smartwatches, and fitness-trackers and auto-IQ coffee-machines. Oh, I admit I was just the same, once, craving all the latest executive toys, but,' he shrugged, 'I don't know what I want these days – certainly not a swanky house like Deborah and Peter's, which I definitely would have envied in the past.'

'Hey, talking of Deborah and Peter, I still don't understand why you went there in the first place. I know Deborah wants a cat for her child, but it does seem a bit peculiar that you should be getting it for her, now you're divorced and everything'

Undoubtedly peculiar, he silently agreed. Deliberately, he hadn't told Mary the whole story. Apart from the fact that he rang her only sporadically and, on account of his long working-hours, kept their phone calls brief, he'd also been totally confused about the issue. 'Well, what you don't know, Mary, is that Deborah asked me to be godfather to the new baby she's expecting.'

'Oh, how lovely, Anthony – that's an honour! And it means she can't be hostile. Perhaps it's her way of healing the rifts.'

'Maybe so, but I can't possibly accept. And, even if I wanted to – which I most emphatically don't – Probation are utterly opposed to the idea. My session with Barbara was due the following Tuesday, so I had a chance to discuss it and she seemed quite concerned that I'd gone to see my ex at all. She pointed out that, if I continued doing so, I might build up further resentments about her affair with Craig and all its disastrous consequences, and might even be tempted to resort to violence again. And she was still more worried for Jonathan – said what an impossibly difficult situation it would be for both of us and how dangerous it could be for the child's whole welfare and future development. She even suggested that Deborah's pregnancy hormones might be influencing her a bit – you know, making her euphoric and unrealistic, and that, once she'd given birth, she could well regret the whole godfather idea.'

Mary took some time digesting these new facts and sat frowning over her coffee. 'Well,' she said, at last, 'if Barbara's right – which I suppose she must be, as the expert – why on earth are you going back to Deborah's to deliver the cat – why getting the cat at *all*?'

'Barbara doesn't know about that, to be honest. Besides, I intend to make it the quickest possible visit, just in and out.'

Mary looked alarmed. 'But, Anthony, you must stay until the poor cat's settled. I mean, he may well be very nervous after the long car journey and leaving his mum and everything.'

Hastily, he reassured her, before explaining a little further. 'If you really want to know, the whole cat thing was prompted by guilt. Not only was I declining the role of godfather, but I'd been horribly ungracious when they first suggested it and even dashed off very rudely, leaving Jonathan in tears. I was dying to get away, you see, but for some unknown reason the kid had taken a shine to me and insisted on showing me the neighbour's cat, and after that he wanted me to go up to his bedroom to see his rocking-horse. But I'm ashamed to say I refused point-blank and left him in an awful state, poor child. And he *is* a poor child, Mary, despite his many material advantages. All the money in the world can't do away with the fact that his father's dead, his half-siblings probably hate his guts and when he's older he'll have to live with the constant fear of the whole story coming out.' As I do myself, he added, under his breath. 'Anyway, by the time I got round to phoning Deborah, later on that week, I'd had a chance to reflect on my behaviour, and realised at base I was jealous. I suppose seeing Peter and Deborah so ecstatically in love meant—'

Awkwardly, he broke off, aware that love was a tactless subject to discuss with Mary. 'I knew I had to do something to make up, so when Deborah started telling me how Jonathan kept begging to have his cat in time for Christmas Day – which seemed more or less impossible with less than a fortnight to go – I decided to ring you straight away. I mean, there was Deborah knowing nothing about cats or how on earth to get one, while you were working for someone who actually bred Egyptian Maus.'

'Well, it was perfect timing, Anthony. The kittens are now four-and-a-half months old, which is the best and safest age for them to leave for their new homes. They've all been vaccinated and dosed for worms and they're all completely house-trained, so Deborah won't need to bother with any of that. And Lady Lawson has picked out the perfect one for Jonathan – an exceptionally gentle, affectionate kitty, who's already very well socialised, so he'll take easily to strangers. I suppose her three great-grandchildren have made her aware that even the kindest of toddlers tend to rough-handle their cats. Oh, and, as I explained on the phone, you're not allowed to use Rameses for breeding, so he's already been neutered, which you said Deborah would want in any case.'

He nodded, finding it impossible to imagine his career-oriented ex-wife becoming an enthusiastic cat-breeder.

'We'd better keep an eye on the time,' Mary added, looking up at the clock. 'Lady Lawson has invited us for sherry at noon and it's already quarter to. It's a blessing you got here so early, which gave us the chance to chat a bit.'

'Well, it was a pretty easy run on Sunday morning and that hire-car is definitely a goer!'

'You broke the speed limit, you mean!'

'Yes, probably. But that's your fault, Mary,' he laughed, 'for insisting I deliver the cat today, which means not turning up too late and disturbing Peter and Deborah.'

'Never mind them! It's Rameses I'm concerned about. It's far better for him to go straight to his new home rather than you keeping him at your flat overnight. Two different places will only confuse him and make it harder for him to settle. Anyway, finish your coffee, then we'll make a move. I only wish I could invite you back here afterwards for lunch but I'll need to return to work I'm afraid. Don't worry, though, I'll wave you off first. I intend to give Rameses a special goodbye kiss!'

Not him, he noted – only the damned cat.

*

'This is my friend, Anthony,' Mary said shyly, as Lady Lawson came hobbling to the door of her large, rambling, converted farmhouse.

He glanced at the tall, stooping woman, her baggy cords and scuffed lace-up shoes topped incongruously by an expensive-looking silk blouse and matching multi-coloured turban. Her lined, weather-beaten face was dominated by eagle-sharp eyes of deep, unfaded brown – the eyes of a younger woman.

She ushered them in to a large, cosy sitting room, in which a grand piano rubbed shoulders with a clutch of round, fleece-lined cat-beds, which she appeared to have made herself, since there were offcuts of the same fabric and a sewing-box nearby. No actual cat, however, was anywhere to be seen.

Once the pleasantries were over and she had poured generous measures of sherry, she said, with obvious concern, 'Before I show you Rameses, I need to be absolutely sure he's going to a good, loving home.'

He reassured her that Deborah and Peter were utterly reliable, owned an extensive garden, and had promised never to leave Jonathan unsupervised with the cat, at least at this early stage.

She nodded in relief, before asking if he was familiar with the breed.

'I'm ashamed to admit that I'd never even heard of an Egyptian Mau, until Mary mentioned yours.'

'They're quite simply the finest cats in the world.' The old lady's tone brooked no contradiction. 'And the ones *I* breed have an outstanding reputation. For this particular litter, I went all the way up to Edinburgh for my stud-cat, which is quite a trek at my age but well worth it, I assure you, since Osiris is a Grand Champion and in great demand from breeders. You may not realise, Mr Beaumont, but there are only six approved stud-cats in the whole of the UK.'

No, he hadn't realised; what he did know was that all cat-lovers seemed extraordinarily obsessional.

'Rameses' mother, my beloved Kiya, is also a Grand Champion. In fact, along with the kitten himself, I'll be giving you certain documents, including a CGCF Registration Certificate, and a guarantee of his pedigree going back five generations to his great-great-great-grandparents. You'll see it lists by name all the Champions and Grand Champions in his lineage.'

Which must account for the kitten's high price, he assumed – on a par with a new designer suit – which made it perfect for Deborah, who, if not an out-and-out snob, had a definite predilection for things prestigious and superior.

'Well, shall we go and see them?' her Ladyship suggested.

As Mary sprang to her feet to lend her a supportive arm, he noticed the look of genuine warmth exchanged between the two women. Her Ladyship's daunting exterior, he guessed, concealed a kindly heart so how fortuitous that Mary should have a found a second elderly lady supplying, as had Mrs Murray-Wood, accommodation, company, affection and a shared passion for cats.

'I keep them in the old dairy,' Lady Lawson explained, 'which has been part of the house since we knocked through the dividing walls.'

As she led the way into a bright, airy room, with green-tiled walls and floor, he tried to take in all the clutter: a confusing array of cat-beds, cat-toys and litter trays, and what he assumed was an activity-centre, with a tree for the cats to climb, an obstacle course to divert them, and a length of rubber tubing through which four excitable kittens were boisterously chasing each other.

Kiya rushed up to her owner, sniffing at her trousers, presumably knowing there were cat-treats concealed in the capacious pockets.

'What an exquisite cat!' he exclaimed, with genuine admiration. Used as he was to common-or-garden black moggies, this mother-cat was truly distinctive, its fur warm bronze in colour, spotted strikingly with black, its eyes an intense gooseberry-green, How could Deborah not approve of so rare, exotic and aesthetically appealing a creature?

Having finished feeding Kiya, Lady Lawson pointed out the prettiest of the kittens, its spotted fur an exact copy of its mother's, although the eyes were bluey-grey.

'That's Rameses,' she said, adding, as if she had intuited his thoughts, 'At about six or seven months, his eyes should turn a deep vivid green. I'll give him to you to hold in a sec, but first he needs to get used to your presence and your smell.'

He tensed at the prospect of having the kitten in his arms. Cats probably had a way of sussing out their fans from their detractors, so suppose it started howling in distaste? However, when, at last Lady Lawson entrusted the kitten to him, Rameses snuggled trustingly against him and even started to purr. Aware that both women were anxiously watching this bonding process, he gave thanks to any Egyptian god who might have ensured its favourable outcome. He had better be on his guard, though, or her Ladyship would encourage him to choose a second kitten for himself.

Instead, she busied herself fetching all the cat accoutrements Deborah would need: a cat-carrier, a litter tray, one of the round, fleece-lined beds, together with various types of kitten food and Rameses' favourite toys. As the things piled up, he began to wish he'd hired a ten-ton truck rather than a modest-sized BMW 325i.

'I've made a few notes for your friend' – Lady Lawson brandished a couple of pages, written in her expressive hand – 'instructions on feeding and suchlike, and the best kind of litter tray. And please tell her to keep the kitten confined to just one room – preferably the kitchen – at least for the first day or two. Put all his things there, especially the cat-bed. That's important because it smells of mum and home.'

Once Mary had packed the items into a strong, capacious canvas bag, she took the kitten from his arms and coaxed it into the carrier. 'I suggest you get off straight away,' she said, 'so that he reaches his new home as soon as possible. He may be a bit upset en route, but just press on and reassure him in a gentle, soothing voice. And, if you're careful not to drive too fast, with any luck, he'll fall asleep.'

He was suddenly reminded of his parents driving him to boarding school when *he* was still a kitten, although with no bedding that smelt of home, no gentle, soothing reassurance, only lectures on the perils of idleness, and how second-best was never, ever good enough.

As the two women came out to the driveway to help him load the car, he couldn't help reflecting that everyone but him seemed to have a proper home: Rameses about to join his new happy family; Lady Lawson with her beloved cats and tribe of children and grandchildren; Mary clearly in her element, responsible for twenty "guests". Would he ever find his own niche, he wondered?

But further thoughts of Darren quelled any such self-pity. The online reports of bullying and staff shortages at Coldingley that he'd laboured through last night, added to accounts recalled from Wandsworth inmates about some C-Category prisons being actually *worse* than B-Categories, made Darren's fate and future a matter of the deepest concern.

So, as he drove away, he resolutely fixed his mind on what else he could possibly do to temper his friend's ordeal at least a fraction.

CHAPTER 36

'Honest, Tony, I ain't never been more proud of meself in me life!'

'And I'm proud, Darren.' Indeed, Anthony was tempted to jump to his feet and give the lad a congratulatory hug – impossible with so many vigilant officers patrolling the Visitors' Hall. 'And all the more so when I know how hard it was.'

'Dead right, mate! I was shaking like a jelly when I had to say me piece. Kaleem, our Team Co-ordinator, got up and announced, all formal like, "And now one of our team is going to give a personal testimony of his life." The whole room went quiet and I was so shit-scared it was all I could do not to bolt straight back to me cell.'

'But you've been rehearsing it for ages, you said. I mean, all this time, you've talked of little else! And, just last week, you told me you'd practised it so often you could almost do it in your sleep. Anyway, didn't you write it all out and—?'

'Yeah,' Darren interrupted, 'but even all that practice don't prepare you for standing up in front of a bunch of hard-boiled kids and telling them your life-story. Most of them was offenders theirselves – the youngest barely thirteen and the oldest only seventeen, yet they still had this tough-guy swagger, like they believed they could get away with murder. But what I done was focus on just one lad – Ryan he were called – my buddy for the workshop. See, each of us prisoners on the team are matched with one of the kids whose offences aren't that different from ours. Ryan had been shoplifting, see, and nicking stuff from school. And it were really weird, mate, he even looked like me at that age – a bit of a titch with this shit-awful acne. Well, you won't believe this, Tony, but he seemed to be drinking in me every word. And, once I got into me stride, I realised they was *all* listening, like what I'd said had really made them think.'

Darren's enthusiastic tone was a marked contrast to his terror and reluctance when he had first signed up for the Crime Diversion Scheme, KEEPOUT. In truth, he had only done so after weeks of nagging on his own part and a final ultimatum. On that particular day, he'd gone down with a throat infection, but still struggled all the way to Bisley, knowing Darren would be gutted if he cancelled his promised visit. Yet, finding him still obstinately defeatist, his patience had run out and he'd shouted at the lad that, if he didn't at least apply to be accepted for the training, he would give up on him and stop visiting. Although obviously shaken, Darren had continued to object: he would never get through the security checks demanded, let alone the long, scary, formal interview and, anyway, he would feel a total sham signing up for a programme called KEEPOUT, when most of his life he had never managed to keep out of nick himself.

'But that's the whole point,' Anthony had retorted. 'Only inmates like you can tell it how it is and warn the youngsters off.' The youngsters had, in fact, been less his concern than Darren, who, since his transfer to Coldingley, had refused to enrol in Education, take any vocational courses, or even consider KEEPOUT, despite the latter providing proper professional training and – most important – a better chance of staying out of gaol.

Thank God his ultimatum had succeeded, but, although Darren had been involved now for the last two-and-a-half months, he had remained continually fearful that he would never make the grade and 'couldn't tell no one nothing'. Thus his exuberance today was all the more unexpected and, as he detailed his performance, he sounded positively triumphant.

'The personal testimony always includes three elements, see, and, long before we stand up in front of the kids, we're taught how to apply them to our own lives and offences. But the kids ain't had that training, so they wouldn't think out all that stuff theirselves and need *us* to point it out.'

Darren had already told him about the three elements – indeed, about every other aspect of KEEPOUT – during all the visits and phone-calls since mid-January, although never with this present air of confidence.

'First off, I had to say, "Don't feel sorry for me, 'cause I was responsible for me crime" – you know, to make them realise *they* was also responsible for whatever wrong they done. See, they was all from the Youth Offending Team, so some had been nicked for breaking into premises, or carrying a knife, or being drunk and disorderly and stuff. So I told them how, when I were first banged up in Chelmsford, all I could do was feel sorry for meself and blame that right cow, Rita. But then I had to explain that blame don't get us nowhere and that I brought the whole thing on meself. Which leads on to the second thing – spelling out the consequences of me action. I felt really choked, mate, telling them how I'd lost me girl – the best relationship I ever had – lost me job, lost me freedom. And the third bit of the testimony was naming all the victims. That were a real stretch for me, 'cause before I started the training, I'd been kidding meself that Carol-Ann were the only victim. But the team forced me to see her parents were, as well, *and* her grandparents, and the next-door neighbour and his doddery old mum, who's a right bag of nerves already. And there was also all the victims of me earlier offences, like shops I robbed, or people I scared shitless. And even you're a victim, Tony, now.'

As Anthony opened his mouth to object, Darren rattled on again, as if he had an overwhelming need to restate all he'd learned. 'I mean, letting you down when you was decent enough to say you'd be me best man. And all them Sundays you slogged out to sodding Chelmsford, just to stop me losing hope. And then schlepping here, week after week – the first time on New Year's Eve, for fuck's sake, when you could have been out on the town. Okay, Bisley's a shorter journey, but it's still a hell of a trek. And you must have been close to freaking out when I didn't take no notice of what you kept on saying about bucking up and doing something positive – or not till you gave me that … What were it called?'

'Ultimatum.'

'Yeah. That got me off me arse, though I were dead sure they'd never accept me on the programme. And, even when they *had* done, and were saying I was doing well, I thought they was just kidding. But yesterday was me breakthrough, Tony. You should've heard me speaking to all them people like I were fucking David Cameron or something! Then, when I'd finished me spiel, saying as cool as a cucumber, "Any questions, ask me at the lunch-break."'

'And did they?'

'I couldn't get away! Ryan were sitting next to me and he'd been in care, see, same as me – had no one in his life to give a shit about him, or teach him right from wrong. So he knew I weren't just someone from outside who'd always had a proper home and everything and took all that for granted, but had struggled to survive, like him. And two other lads had been packed off from one foster-mum to the next, like they was an unwanted parcel or something. One were moved eleven times in thirteen years and, just as he were settling into some new pad, they'd turf him out again, so he felt he didn't belong nowhere. Yet when he first strutted into the workshop he were this right little tough guy who knew it all, didn't he? By the end of the day, though, he actually started blubbing – told me no one gave a shit about him, so he'd learned not to give a shit about no one else, but he were beginning to see how wrong that were.'

Although delighted by Darren's progress, Anthony found it hard to concentrate, given the usual distractions of the Visitors' Hall – bored, restless children arguing and grizzling, and the accusing voice of a brassy blonde shrilling from the adjoining table. Yet Darren's word 'triumph' refocused his attention.

'Then, after lunch I had me second triumph – playing the main character in this role-play called Peer Pressure.'

'But you told me distinctly, a month ago, that you couldn't act for toffee and would rather cut your throat than perform a part in public!'

'Yeah, but the funny thing were, Tony, once I were in the role, with a proper audience and stuff, it just seemed, well, like natural. I reckon all them drama skills they teach us must have got through me thick skull in the end. See, I played this young lad, Bob, who's bullied by two older boys, one a drug-dealer, and Bob ends up drunk and stoned, then, when he's off his head, they give him a knife and dare him to steal this posh bloke's phone, so he ends up being nicked. Well, that were exactly what happened to me, when I were Bob's age, and I landed up in Feltham, didn't I? So it were dead easy to act the part, 'cause I'd been that lad meself. And why we do it for the kids, see, is to warn them not to let the bully-boys talk them into doing stuff that could screw up their whole life.'

Darren paused to wolf down the last knob-end of his pasty, one of the many little treats Anthony had brought him from the snack bar. Last week he'd been complaining about tepid, greasy prison food, served in such tiny portions 'you could put it in me eye'.

'And when we'd finished the performance, everyone started clapping, like we was proper actors on a stage. That were a first for me, Tony! In all me twenty-four years, I ain't never been applauded. And I ain't never set foot in a theatre – thought they was only for toffs like you.' Darren now unwrapped his Crunchie bar, snapped it in two and offered half to Anthony.

He took it gratefully, having skipped lunch altogether. Due to engineering works, the train had been unconscionably slow, although at least he'd managed to grab a taxi at Woking and even succeeded in relaxing on the pleasant drive through shady woods. This prison itself had its share of trees and even a bit of garden, so, despite its ugly buildings (once a comprehensive school), it was far less grim than Wandsworth.

'But wait, there's something better!' Darren took a large bite of Crunchie, swallowing it in seconds. 'At the end of the workshop, Ryan came up to me, all bashful-like, and told me what I'd said had made a real impression and he'd decided there and then to change his ways. I felt dead chuffed, mate. I mean, just to stop one kid from landing up in nick … Tell you the truth, I was so overcome I blubbed meself when I got back to me cell. See, once the kids and the Youth Offending Team had left, all me mates on the programme crowded round and told me I'd done great. And Lorna – she's our Operations Manager – said it were one of the most moving testimonies she'd ever heard and I were a better actor than some real-life ones on telly!'

'Congratulations, Darren. That's fantastic!'

Barely stopping to acknowledge the compliment, Darren raced on again. 'And another thing – this work's made me see that me own life weren't nothing like as bad as some of me team-mates'. Kaleem and Akuchi was in these violent gangs, see, and was stabbed so many times soon they was carrying blades theirselves. And, when Kaleem were only a nipper, he were asked to carry drugs and started using himself before he were fourteen. And, a few years down the line, he began sweating and shaking and seeing things that wasn't there, 'cause he'd developed paranoia, see.'

Darren broke off to say proudly, 'I can *spell* that word now, Tony, and loads of others we're learning on the course. But I ain't forgot, mate, that you was the one who first taught me to read and write, and told me I were talented and stuff. I thought you was just being kind, 'cause we was mates and everything, and it weren't till all them pros started spouting the same thing, I reckon it sunk in, at last.' He suddenly leaned forward and reached his hand across the table. 'But I owe everything to *you*, mate. If you hadn't kept on at me non-stop, I'd still be pushing a broom round all day. And to think I'm better paid for doing the programme than I ever was in any prison job I done before!'

'I did try to tell you, Darren, but you can be a stubborn bastard, you know!'

'Yeah, but I were convinced back then I were on the scrapheap and nothing were never going to change. And all that stuff you kept saying about the scheme giving me support and companionship and whatever, didn't mean nothing at that point. But you was right, as usual, 'cause me and me six team-mates are all there for each other now.' The lad looked up, held his gaze. 'But don't think I can do without you, Tony, 'cause you're special and I can't. Even when I were at real rock-bottom, it was you who got me through. I used to think of you watching over me, almost like you was an angel.'

'An angel with a criminal conviction!'

'Still an angel, mate. All them nights, when I were in a real dark place, I'd get out every letter you ever wrote me and read them over and over to meself. Honest, I'd have topped meself if you wasn't there to write and visit and just keep me going from week to week. And that wake-up call – I bloody needed it, or I'd never have pulled meself together and had me big triumph yesterday. So all your nagging paid off, mate, and now I'm doing stuff for other people, like you always done for me. And, believe you me, some of them kids have been through much worse shit than mine – beaten to a pulp, or buggered by some creepy "uncle" in the Children's Home, or already hooked on booze or worse. But I had the same lousy start, see, and made all the wrong choices and fucked up me whole future, same as they done, so they could relate to me, like I was one of them.'

Darren paused for a second, as if running out of breath. Weirdly, the shrewish woman's voice fell silent at the exact same moment, to be replaced by loud, incongruous giggling from a child at the table behind. Darren, however, seemed completely unaware both of his surroundings and the noise.

'What I ain't told you yet is, in six weeks' time, I start working for a course in Peer Education. It's a new B-Tec Level 2 they just set up as part of KEEPOUT, and the training I already done counts towards it, see – youth work and running groups and stuff – so it should only take three months. Then there'll be this ceremony, when some VIP comes in from outside and hands us our certificates. And get this, Tony – they're recognised in the workplace as a proper qualification – you know, like GCSEs!'

And that must mean as much to Darren, Anthony guessed, as his own Cambridge degree. Indeed, he had felt more a sense of shame, back then, in failing to get the First expected by his parents, than any trace of Darren's cock-a-hoop pride.

'So it'll be easier to get a job, see, once I'm out of here. And Lorna said they might even let me work as a volunteer with the Youth Offending Service. But, long before me release date, I can do more training here and won't be written off as a thickie, like always in the past. I mean, one of our team were expelled from three different schools and told he'd never amount to nothing, yet he's about to start an Open University course! And, 'cause he's serving a twelve-year sentence, he'll probably get his degree while he's still banged up, so there's hope for me, as well, Tony. Just give me time and I'll be a real clever-clogs!'

'Of course there's hope for you, Darren. I've been saying that since …'
He left the sentence hanging as another officer prowled past. Several had been monitoring their table, alerted by the lad's excitable tone. Presumably, in any prison, excitement and violence might be only a hair's-breadth apart.

Although Darren lowered his voice, his elation was still palpable. 'Last night I wore me KEEP-OUT T-shirt to bed, 'cause I didn't never want to take it off. But I were on such a high, I couldn't sleep a wink. So, to calm meself, I imagined you was me dad and that I lived with you in, like, a proper family. And you'd just come back from work and went straight upstairs and sat on me bed – without even taking off your coat or kissing mum or nothing – and you said in a real proud voice, "You done brilliant, son!"'

Too embarrassed to reply, Anthony sat reflecting on the daunting, lifelong role of fatherhood. Would he ever have the courage and commitment to embrace it in Darren's case? After what seemed like an eternity, he decided to shelve the question and contented himself with, 'You've done brilliantly, Darren!'

*

'I'm sorry, folks, but there's still a bit of a hold-up. We're dealing with an incident, as I told you earlier, and we're rather short-staffed at present, so we need all hands on deck. But there's nothing to worry about. Just be patient a bit longer, and we should be able to let you through.'

The jaunty voice booming through the Tannoy only increased Anthony's annoyance. Since an 'incident' could cover anything from a suicide to an assault, 'a bit longer' might well stretch to an hour. They had already been confined in this stuffy waiting room for over twenty minutes, having been corralled from the Visitors' Centre into the "holding area"– a term he knew from his own spell inside, although the connotations of restraint were anything but welcome. As for being short-staffed, there probably wasn't a gaol in the country that didn't have a dearth of officers struggling to control a glut of inmates, which invariably resulted in abuses and inefficiency.

He checked his watch – again. Little hope now of making a start this evening on Hugh's demanding new project. His unreasonable boss still had no compunction about expecting him to put in great chunks of homework on a Sunday, regardless of 'footling' prior commitments such as prison visits.

As he fidgeted on the uncomfortable metal seat, he was further vexed by the gargantuan woman beside him, overlapping his space and breathing so laboriously she appeared to have chronic asthma. Her child was similarly obese and twice as noisy, as she continually harangued her mother for yet more sweets and crisps.

He shifted his thoughts to Darren, uneasily aware that the lad was far more compassionate than he was and would never damn people for their weight or eating-habits. He was also much further forward in taking responsibility for his crime, whereas *he* was still tempted to blame Deborah, or Craig, or the gastroenteritis that had forced him to leave work on that fateful day a lifetime ago. During this afternoon's visit, Darren had even expressed a desire to compensate Carol-Ann's once-hated parents and, although he'd no idea as to how to go about it, the highly commendable instinct and ideal put his own attitude to shame. If anyone cried out for compensation, it was Craig's bereaved family and Hazel and her children, but even the briefest consideration of restorative justice brought such a surge of guilt, he invariably buried his head in the sand. His more conscientious mate could clearly teach him a thing or two.

'Mum, I want them Monster Munch!' The child's mouth was already crammed with crisps, whilst she dunned her mother for more. Half-masticated particles were spraying in his direction, and the tang of salt-and-vinegar conflicted with the reek of the woman's overpowering floral scent, and the faint smell of prison bleach wafting from the floor.

His mind remained on Darren as he sat re-checking his watch. For all the lad's good qualities and his remarkable new confidence, he would still face a raft of problems on release, not least his rough accent and bad grammar. However unfair it was that a well-spoken public-school chap devoid of any drive or skill was more likely to succeed than a talented working-class bloke, it remained a fact of life. He had, on one occasion, attempted to correct the lad's accent, but Darren had looked so hurt and embarrassed, he'd never again been so tactless, nor continued trying to straighten out his grammar. Maybe grammar was part of accent, so long-established and deeply engrained, it was more resistant to change than were reading and writing, in both of which Darren had made huge advances.

He unfolded his *Sunday Times*, skimming through yet more coverage of last week's Budget, and then a piece about the poorest, most disadvantaged kids usually being landed with the least qualified and least experienced teachers – as in Darren's case. There was also further comment on the recent financial scandals, which reminded him that one of Darren's team-mates was serving a two-year sentence for minor fraud. It seemed a travesty of justice that many of the gilt-edged corporate fraudsters, guilty of far worse, remained securely in their privileged positions and kept their snouts smugly in the trough.

As for his own future, it was less than four weeks now until his Licence expired on 22 April, after which he would be free to apply for any job he desired, without being answerable to Probation. A hollow freedom in fact, since, however many jobs he might "desire", he was most unlikely to be offered them, with that indelible stain on his past. Any potential employer could easily check his criminal record online, be it spent or not. And the stain itself was a lifelong impediment not just to securing fulfilling, well-paid, work, but to ever feeling guilt-free, or free from the constant fear of someone stumbling on the truth. Even the other post-Licence freedoms of being able to travel abroad and live wherever he wanted seemed out of the question at present. With Hugh laying claim to so much of his time, how could he jet off to foreign climes, or devote himself to the taxing chore of flat-hunting?

He was reminded of the flat he had once hoped to share with Mary – the sensuous little love-nest of his dreams. He still phoned her every now and then with a sort of desperate lust – all the more unwarranted since she had recently let slip she was dating one of the helpers at the cattery. Apart from plunging him into an oil-slick of irrational jealousy, the news had highlighted his own lack of any "date". With no social life, he was unlikely to meet a new female, yet he couldn't live like a monk forever, for God's sake!

He stuffed his paper back into his briefcase. His concentration was shot to pieces – not helped by this noisy, crowded room. Instead, he skim-read the tattered posters on the walls, warning of the dangers of drink and drugs, or spelling out the penalties inflicted on those smuggling in banned items. Despite such draconian punishments, an extraordinary amount of contraband seemed to land up within prison walls. According to Darren, it was easier to get drugs in gaol than to get a bar of soap.

All at once, a baby in the seat behind started wailing inconsolably, competing with the sudden boom of the Tannoy.

'Okay, folks, it's okay for you to leave now. We do apologise again and we thank you for your patience. An officer will escort you to the outside gate and please remember to take your belongings with …'

Notwithstanding the baby's screams, most people had picked up the gist of the announcement and were pushing and shoving in their haste to escape the confining, malodorous room. Anthony stood back to let the harassed mothers past and those hampered by heavy bags or baby-buggies, who soon caused a bottleneck in the corridor outside. There was further jostling and complaining while the escorting officer took his time unlocking yet another door with what seemed five different keys. But, at last, Anthony felt the fresh March breeze on his face as the door led outside to a narrow, fenced-off walkway and he could now see the main Visitors' Gate. Once safely through it, he strode ahead of the waddling Mmums, dawdling kids and tottery old folk, hoping he might find a taxi with as much ease as earlier and thus avoid the slow, infrequent bus-service that meandered its way to Woking station and often failed to link up with a fast train.

He wheeled round in surprise as a voice behind him called his name – a triumphant '*Anthony*!'

A well-dressed man about his age was dashing towards him with a smile of apparent recognition. But who *was* he, for heaven's sake? Anthony searched his mind for clues, but the stranger lacked any distinguishing characteristics that might have made him easier to place, being of middling height, with brownish hair and greyish eyes.

'You don't recognise me, do you?' the guy said with a laugh, just as Anthony was wondering if he should fake a cheery greeting.

'Er, no.'

'Marcus Rutherford – Trinity Squash Club!'

'Marcus – of course!' Anthony now recalled their relentlessly competitive games whilst inwardly cursing this unexpected encounter. The bloke was bound to ask what he'd been doing in the two decades since Cambridge, and such questions made him invariably uneasy.

'How extraordinary to bump into you here, of all places!' Marcus exclaimed, falling into step beside him.

''I've been visiting a friend,' Anthony explained tersely, aware that most of Marcus's circle were unlikely to have friends in gaol. 'What about you?' he added, hoping to switch the focus to his fellow alumnus's probably impeccable career.

'Oh, I've just come from a meeting with the Governor. I'm involved in an organisation called Blue Sky – a name we took from Oscar Wilde's *Ballad of Reading Gaol*. I'm sure you recognise the quote: "I never saw a man that looked with such a wistful eye upon that little tent of blue which prisoners call the sky". We try to help with prisoner rehabilitation and provide loads of support on release – finding them jobs and so on.'

Anthony had no wish to extend this conversation. However much he might admire such ideals – and indeed those of KEEPOUT, both outfits aiming to remedy the shaky prospect of ex-cons – the subject was too uncomfortably close to the bone. Besides, with the exception of Betty and Barbara, do-gooders had never really been his type.

'I need to liaise with the Governor every now and then, because the guys in the print-workshop here produce our main directory. You might even be interested in becoming one of our supporters,' Marcus suggested. 'But, that apart, we simply must catch up with each other's news. I remember you so well at Cambridge – dedicated, single-minded, and usually trouncing me on the squash court!'

Anthony forced a smile. At this particular moment, he felt far from being a victor.

'Let's have a drink, okay? There's The Hen and Chickens, close by, or a really cool gastro-pub in Knaphill. I have my car here, so either's fine.'

'Actually, I'm, er, a bit tied up this evening.'

'Oh, just a quickie, Anthony! It's such a coincidence for us to meet and we have masses to discuss after all this time.'

Too much, Anthony thought, wondering how he could refuse without sounding thoroughly ungracious.

'And I'd like to tell you more about Blue Sky. I'm so passionate about it, I can probably bore for Britain!'

Please don't, Anthony bit back. It would be tricky, if not nerve-wracking, to discuss the prospects of ex-prisoners without admitting he was one of them.

Did you drive here, too, by the way? If so, no problem – we can take both cars and meet in the bar.'

'No, I came by train.'

'In that case, I can run you back to the station once we've had our drink.' The maddeningly persistent Marcus was already steering him towards the car park.

It seemed he had no option, although he was determined to keep the conversation focused on their squash games and on Trinity in general, restrict himself to one brief drink, then plead a prior engagement and nip back safely home.

CHAPTER 37

'As you know, Anthony, this will be our last meeting.' Barbara's desk was as neat as always, the folder four-square on to it, three pens lined up in readiness,

He nodded, confused by his mix of relief and apprehension. Although often resentful of these time-consuming appointments, he did value Barbara's interest in his life, her praise of his "progress" and desperate wish for him to succeed. Without Mary's constant company and concern for him, such things were non-existent in his personal life, except to some degree from Darren, of course.

'Before I sign you off officially' – Barbara picked up one of the pens – 'we have to complete your self-assessment form, in conformity with NOMS requirements, which means asking you the usual questions.'

'Yes, please go ahead.'

'Are you currently taking any drugs?'

He had answered 'no' a score of times, but presumably drugs were an ever-present risk for many of Barbara's clients.

'Have you recently been tempted to commit a crime?'

'*No!*' he said, emphatically. The continuous flashbacks to his original crime were enough in themselves to guard against a repeat.

'During the last year, have you mixed with any known criminals?'

'Only Darren.'

'And are you still seeing Darren regularly?'

'Yes, and he seems to have turned the corner at last, thank God.' Having given her a brief account of KEEPOUT, he added the lad's most recent achievements, chief of which was being appointed Team Co-Ordinator – a truly demanding role that involved him taking centre-stage for much of every workshop. 'He's also started teaching a young guy to read and write – someone he met in the gym who missed huge amounts of schooling. Darren's recycling all the books and lessons I've given him in the past, and says soon he'll be teaching *me*!'

'That's great news, Anthony, especially as I know he was close to despair, not that long ago.'

'Apparently, he said to his pupil, "Stop being a hitman and get stuck into a book, mate". I had to laugh, remembering that when I first met him he didn't know his basic ABC!'

Barbara nodded approvingly before resuming her questions. 'Are you still living alone?'

As she continued ticking boxes on her paperwork, Anthony recalled how many Wandsworth inmates had rubbished the Probation Service – some with no good reason except spite, but others whose experience had been pretty damned appalling – so he was blessed in having Barbara.

'And still working for the Hugh Henry Harvard Agency?'

'Well, currently I am, but I've just given in my notice.'

Barbara raised a quizzical eyebrow. 'Do you have another job lined up?'

He hesitated. 'Not exactly lined up, but I'm about to embark on a complete change of direction. It's very much in the embryo stage at present, but I'd love to discuss it with you – if you have the time.'

She glanced at the clock on the dingy, yellowing wall. 'Well, if you prefer, we can carry on with the questionnaire a little later in the session. And since you're my last appointment, we can run over, if needs be.'

He wondered, as so often, if she had no husband to rush home for, no kids to feed and put to bed? Throughout his twenty months with her, she remained an unknown quantity, despite her intimate knowledge of *his* life.

'So what's this new project, Anthony?'

How the hell could he précis the whole challenging turmoil of the last four weeks into a coherent whole? 'Well, last month,' he said, trying to organise his thoughts, 'I ran into an old Cambridge friend. To be honest, I was desperate to get away, but after a couple of beers, I began to relax and enjoy his company so we went on for a meal together, and over dinner we more or less swapped life-stories since we'd last met in our twenties – jobs, marriage, children, the whole shebang. Marcus said he used to be in marketing, but is now the MD of Blue Sky, which I'm sure you must have heard of, because it helps rehabilitate ex-prisoners by offering them employment.'

'Only vaguely,' Barbara admitted, putting down her pen.

'When it was *my* turn to talk about work, I was extremely careful not to say a word about my conviction, but I did tell Marcus how pressured I was at Hugh's and how I resented his demands. And that led him to mention a current Blue Sky vacancy for a Business Development Manager, and he suggested I apply if I was so fed up with my present job. Well, I tried to change the subject, convinced they wouldn't consider an ex-con, but he continued to enthuse about how I'd fit the position to a T, with my specific skills and years of experience. Then, suddenly – and I blame the wine – I blurted out the fact that I myself had been in prison. To my surprise, he didn't turn a hair – in fact, he assured me that in an outfit like Blue Sky it could well be an advantage, rather than a bar.'

'Because of the empathy you'd have,' Barbara said, nodding in agreement, 'with the ex-offenders you'd be working with.'

'Well, that apart, it would be a huge relief for me personally not to have to hush up my past and live in fear of discovery. But I was still very dubious about making such a major move, and also very loth to let Hugh down. And Thomas might be miffed, as well, since it was he who first put me on to Hugh. More important still, I needed to find out far more about Blue Sky before taking a step I might subsequently regret. So the next morning I stood up to Hugh, for once, and told him in no uncertain terms that I wanted the whole following weekend free. Fortunately, Darren had already suggested me having that Sunday off because he could see my weekly visits were taking quite a toll on me. He's always been an empathetic type, and the KEEPOUT thing is increasing that, I reckon.'

'*And?*' Barbara prompted, clearly aware that he was rambling.

He sat in silence for a moment, considering how to cut through all the detail. There was certainly no need to explain the extent of his researches that weekend – not just Blue Sky but the whole concept of social enterprises in general. Nor would he reveal his contradictory reasons for wanting a new start – the obvious one, of course, of trying to play some tiny part in reducing the re-offending rate, but selfish reasons, too, not least an end to the daily trek to Claygate and his mortifying subjection to Hugh. There was also his secret shame in that, Darren apart, he had never lifted a finger to help the disadvantaged in society, having been trained from early childhood to consider only his own success and self-development. Both he and his parents had been completely unaware of the gross unfairness of a system in which those dealt the grimmest cards in life made up the bulk of the prison population, while those cossetted through a golden pipeline from the top prep-schools to the top positions in society basked in their warm pool of prosperity and privilege. He'd been equally ignorant of the hand-to-mouth existence of menial workers like those at Fabuclean and, indeed, the latter's straitened circumstances now made him feel a distinct unease about still working for and with the super-rich – all the more so when, just last week, one of Hugh's clients had casually mentioned shelling out three-thousand pounds for the pruning of just two trees in his garden. In Darren's eyes, that would be an obscenity. And, as for the seventy-two grand another client had paid for his pre-order of the upcoming Tesla Model X, the lad would barely credit such extravagance.

'Well, tell me what you've decided,' Barbara urged, 'then we can move on to a general review of your case – which is the main purpose of this session.'

Not for him, it wasn't. He had no desire to review the last twenty months, was more intent on the future and utilising Barbara's knowledge to help him map it out. 'It wasn't an easy decision, mainly because my various goals seem to be in conflict. No way am I a bleeding heart – and never will be. I still believe in profit, still expect a decent salary and comfortable way of life.' Barbara herself might be prepared to work for peanuts and accept her cramped and shabby office with its threadbare carpet and cheap utility furniture, but however much he admired her dedication, such austerity appalled him. 'It's probably hard for you to understand, because you're a total idealist.'

'We're discussing *you*, not me, Anthony, and our time together is limited,'

'Sorry – I'll be quick!' he said, registering the veiled rebuke. 'First, I arranged to meet Thomas over a drink, to sound him out about Hugh's reaction if I left, but he assured me I'd worked wonders for the agency – increased its turnover, brought in a wealth of new business, even taken over the running of the finances. So Hugh couldn't reasonably expect any more and, if I wanted to quit, he'd simply have to lump it.'

Far from 'lumping it', his boss had been downright nasty, with accusations of 'gross ingratitude', and an insistence that he worked out each and every day of the official three months' notice.

'Fine,' he'd replied, through gritted teeth, 'but only from nine to five. No more overtime, and no more home assignments ...'

'So have you applied for the Blue Sky vacancy or not?' Barbara's "get-to-the-point" chiding interrupted his reverie.

'Yes, and already had two interviews. But just this last Monday, everything changed, so I'm actually hoping they *don't* offer me the job. You see, I was late into work that day – some signalling problem held up all the trains – but although I stayed till ten in the evening, to make up, Hugh was particularly vicious and got at me non-stop. And, all at once, I felt my rage explode and vowed I'd never take the risk again of being landed with an unpleasant boss. I wanted to be my *own* boss and do things *my* way. But not just that – I've changed so much these last few years, I feel an urge to do the sort of work that's some damned use in the world.' His constant guilt about having failed to compensate Hazel and her children had partly influenced his decision, in that he knew he needed to make some form of restitution, however indirect. 'Anyway, as I sat fuming on the train back home, it suddenly occurred to me that I could set up a mini-Blue Sky myself and run it on my own terms.'

'But you'd need huge funds for such a scheme,' Barbara instantly objected.

'Actually, I'm pretty sure I could get them. I was so enthused by the idea, I stayed up all that night, trying to work out whether it was do-able and practical, and how Community Interest Companies apply for grants and loans and suchlike. There was reams of stuff about it all and the more I read, the more I realised how much I didn't know, and how many decisions I'd have to make further down the line – what sort of company to go for, one with a board of directors, or trustees, or did I set up as sole trader. Soon, my mind was simply buzzing with ideas and, when I did some brainstorming on possible investors, I saw that—'

The sound of loud, resentful voices suddenly echoed from an adjoining room, reminding him that Barbara put up not just with rotten pay, but with anger and abuse from many of her clients. At least *he* had never been uncivil, although right now he was guilty of taking up her time. 'Well, as the hours ticked on,' he continued, 'it became clear that I'd definitely need colleagues and employment agency staff – people who'd share my vision and be passionate about my plan. And, talking of plans' – he allowed himself a grin – 'I began drawing up a business plan there and then, sprawled on the sofa at four o'clock in the morning!'

Barbara, however, was frowning. 'Anthony, I don't want to dampen your enthusiasm, but I can see a lot of problems ahead. For one thing, you'll be in competition with Blue Sky itself, not to mention all the prison charities.'

'A lot of those are tiny, though, and run by people who lack my solid business grounding. I applaud their ideals, of course, but frankly half of them are offering little real meat. I intend to set up a full-scale recruitment agency, and that in itself would make me different from Blue Sky. You see, they take ex-prisoners directly onto their own books and so act as the employer, whereas *I* shall be the broker. And the great thing is that all the experience I've had with Hugh in recruitment and consultancy is exactly what I need for my new enterprise. It's also provided loads of contacts, some of whom I can approach for funds. And I might even interest their leisured, well-heeled wives in becoming volunteers – maybe train them as mentors, or persuade them to use their charms on local employers and point out the advantages of taking on ex-offenders. As I don't need to tell you, Barbara, that can enhance a company's reputation and give it definite kudos. And, even in the corporate world there's quite a buzz about social responsibility and doing one's bit for the have-nots. Young people in particular tend to seek greater meaning in their work these days and—'

'You've obviously thought this through,' she interrupted, 'and I don't doubt your proficiency – far from it.' She leaned down to ease her shoe, an elegant high heel in a different class entirely from her colleagues' well-worn trainers. Yet, for all her smart attire, she looked weary, short of sleep. 'I'm no expert on the corporate world, but I feel I ought to warn you there's a general reluctance to donate to prison charities, or even volunteer for them. I blame the tabloids, frankly – the almost gleeful way they condemn any sort of law-breaker. And that in turn ties the government's hands when it comes to prison reform, because if they're hoping for re-election, they can't be seen as soft on crime. You know all that, of course, but what you may not realise is that, as an ex-offender yourself, you may find great difficulty in getting access to prisons and prisoners, let alone finding a bank and an insurer willing to back your company.'

He did, in fact, realise all those problems, as well as the challenge involved in building up relationships with local councils, contractors, and prospective employers – all essential if he wanted to offer the widest range of jobs to his ex-con clients. But meeting challenges was simply part of the task and, in any case, Marcus might be willing to share his expertise. They had met twice more and established a genuine bond, even agreeing to future squash games. Admittedly, his new friend would be disappointed that he'd decided not to join Blue Sky, but surely he wouldn't object to him setting up his *own* scheme.

'And, anyway' – Barbara tapped her pen impatiently on the desk – 'a good half of all prisoners lack the skills required by the vast majority of jobs. And many are incapable of working in any capacity, because they're dyslexic, or illiterate, or hooked on drugs, or unable to fill in basic application forms or accept any kind of settled working routine. And, of course, a lot of them have mental health problems.'

'Yes, I've seen that for myself,' he countered, but—'

'*And,*' she cut in, 'most who did have jobs outside will probably lose them permanently just by going into custody. And, even when they're released, they're statistically more likely to re-offend than be offered a second chance.'

'All the more reason for me to offer them that second chance! And forgive me contradicting you Barbara, but a lot of them do have skills. Some of the fraudsters I met inside could easily have set up their own successful businesses or been an asset to a big financial company. I also met construction workers, roofers, drivers, gardeners, chefs – you name it – and quite a few in retail, including two senior managers. And since there are serious staff shortages in most of those sectors, surely it makes sense to match the prisoners' skills to the needs of the companies crying out for labour – once the guys are released, of course. I mean, why let all that talent go to waste? It used to really bug me seeing people with potential mouldering in their cells watching the Jeremy Kyle Show and assuming they'd never work again.'

Aware Barbara was shaking her head, he quickly aborted her response. 'Okay, I admit that most need training and enthusing – apart from the few natural-born entrepreneurs – but once they're secure in a job and have a reason to get up in the morning and a basic shape and structure to their day, they're likely to be extremely committed.'

'I'm afraid quite a few simply prefer to vegetate.' Barbara leaned back in her chair, as if signalling they should soon call a halt to the discussion.

'Only because they can't see any viable alternative. Take Darren, for example. For ages he just sat moping in his cell, but once he was given definite goals and a sense of purpose, he's become a different person. I don't think it's ever struck him before that he could be a positive force in society, rather than a destructive one.'

'Darren's a case apart, though, because he's had *you* as his personal mentor, but the vast majority just won't relate to such airy-fairy concepts, especially not the hard core of persistent offenders, let alone the psychopaths.'

He, too, shook his head – and with definite irritation. "Airy-fairy" was the sort of damning term he would have expected from his parents, not from Barbara. If his father could hear him now, he, too, would be listing all the risks, pointing out that flaky notions such as trying to "make a difference to the world" or "being a positive force in society" had to be backed by a rigorous business plan – exactly what he intended, in fact. 'Barbara, if nothing else, it makes perfect sense economically, when you think of the huge cost of re-offending – not far off eleven billion, I reckon, not to mention the human cost.'

'In *this* job I'm hardly likely to forget either! I might see a client just after his release and he's back inside within a matter of days. And, depressing as it sounds, a considerable number of ex-offenders actually want to stay in prison, or can't wait to be reconvicted. For them it's the easy option – free board and lodging and no responsibilities.'

'It's not like you to be so cynical!'

'It's not cynicism – it's realism. And another harsh fact that may affect your enterprise is the recent savage cuts. Just the prison Education budget alone has—'

'People blame the cuts for everything,' he interrupted, 'but from what I witnessed in Wandsworth, it's more the utter inefficiency and bureaucratic inertia stifling all initiative that are at the root of the problem. I can't stand inefficiency and I *do* have initiative, which is why I feel I need to take some action, on however small a scale.'

'You just told me you weren't an idealist' – Barbara gave a grudging smile. 'And, actually, I admire your new ideals, but I'm afraid the very bureaucracy you criticise may stifle any venture you set up. But' – she glanced at the clock again – 'we've digressed quite long enough, Anthony, so it's back to the paperwork!'

As she began firing more standard questions at him, he nursed a sense of bitter disappointment. Having expected her encouragement, he'd received instead a sack-load of objections.

'Are you still living in your Finsbury Park flat?' Her pen hovered, ready to tick.

He nodded. In fact, he'd intended to run his business from there, until her crushing negativity had forced him to re-think the whole project

Once she had completed his general case review, Barbara rose to her feet and shook him warmly by the hand. 'It's been a pleasure working with you, Anthony. And I wish you all possible success in the future.'

A shade ironic in light of the fact she had done her best to quash that future while it was still a fragile embryo. Yet as he left her office and walked out on to the street, he had to admit she might be right about the sheer unfeasibility of his scheme. After all, she knew far more about ex-cons than *he* did, having worked with them all her life.

Unwilling to go tamely home with so much on his mind, he headed for Bruce Castle Park, where there would be some peace and quiet to think. And, strolling along a shady path, he passed a makeshift stall set up by two small boys, selling their discarded toys at vastly inflated prices. Sadly, there were no takers – and dusk was falling anyway – but he couldn't help but admire their entrepreneurial streak, reminded as he was of his own similar exploits. His most ingenious scheme at prep-school had involved hollowing out a copy of the Shorter Oxford English Dictionary and using it to conceal a small transistor-radio. Since all radios were strictly forbidden, many prepubescent customers flocked to borrow his "musical dictionary" for an hour, or a whole evening, paying him in sweets or comics – also strictly banned, but smuggled in regardless.

His most lucrative customer, Cameron, was the son of mega-rich tax-exiles living in the Bahamas who, notwithstanding their personal excesses, believed in the rigour of the Pembridge education system – which had indeed cracked down hard when his transactions eventually came to light. The school had even summoned his parents who, along with the scandalised headmaster, were determined to put a stop to such precocious business dealings. And, years later, at FFC, despite its apparent encouragement of entrepreneurship, there had in actuality been little real scope for taking more than moderate risks, or following any personal agenda not supported by his senior colleagues, because of the emphasis on teamwork and general consensus. Nonetheless, his entrepreneurial spirit was still alive and well, and during these past few weeks, he'd felt galvanised, even liberated, by the prospect of setting up his own "baby" and being the one in charge.

He dodged a football kicked in his direction by a group of teenage boys, envying them their physical activity whilst *he* was stuck in his mind, his former excitement now doused by Barbara's warnings and misgivings. Even the weather seemed downcast, despite it being latish April: grey and murky, with an oppressively leaden sky.

He veered left between the trees, losing all sense of time as he wrestled with the conflict: did he go ahead and establish his new company, or ditch the whole notion to avoid the risk of failure? And, when he finally turned his steps towards the tube, he was still weighing up the pros and cons – until the shrilling of his mobile roused him from introspection.

Lord! He'd totally forgotten Darren's promised phone call this evening – all the more shaming since the lad was ringing specifically to wish him luck for this new post-Licence period, and had probably had to queue during the whole of Association to use the phone at all.

'Well, mate, how did it go?'

'Okay,' he said, deciding not to elaborate, for fear Darren's precious phone-credit might run out. Besides, he hadn't breathed a word yet about either Blue Sky or any possible new venture, in case neither materialised.

'That's not much of an answer, mate! Come on – tell me how it feels to be free of all them restrictions.'

In fact, Barbara's downbeat talk seemed to have lumbered him with *new* restrictions. He'd been fool enough to imagine that she would back him up to the hilt, even put him in touch with various supportive professionals. 'A bit daunted, to be honest, Darren.'

'Now, just you listen to me, Tony.' Darren's voice was urgent, almost peremptory. 'You got to sodding well believe in yourself, like you're always telling me. This is your new start, mate, a chance to change, like I done.'

Change – the very word he'd used to Barbara. So why, for pity's sake, was he allowing her to pour cold water on what for him could be a turning-point? She mostly dealt with clients who lacked his own expertise – or lacked any skills at all – so obviously she'd be duty-bound to steer them away from impractical hopes and dreams. But his was a different case entirely. With all his business acumen, he was hardly likely to set up a company on shaky foundations and inadequately researched.

He stumbled to a halt as he realised with a jolt that, almost from the cradle, he had relied on other people to dictate his next step in life: his parents selecting the finest schools and the most prestigious college; the Careers Advisor directing him to the top accountancy firm; the senior members of that firm providing a template for his whole subsequent career. Why in God's name had he been so passive, allowed these various 'minders' to steer and mould him in the conventionally approved direction, instead of branching out on his own individual odyssey, or becoming a downright maverick? And how the hell could he have been blind to it so long, even at this very moment putting store by Barbara's advice, when she knew next to nothing about the business world? Besides, whatever happened, he wouldn't exactly starve. The sound investments he'd made earlier in his career were still reasonably intact, having been earmarked for an exorbitantly expensive divorce that turned out to be low-cost. He had also saved a decent sum from his long hours working for Hugh – more than enough to keep him afloat, even allow him to take a second "perilous" risk, if the first one proved unviable.

'Tony, are you still there, mate?'

'Sorry – just got a bit distracted.'

'Distracted' was too weak a word. He felt shaken to the core by his sudden shaming insight – indeed, contemptuous of himself for having been a sleeping-partner in his own life, the indulged, feather-bedded puppet-son, with every advantage except the chance to be himself. And, even now, for pity's sake, at the advanced age of forty-three, he didn't know who he was, because his true self had been so long encrusted by a thick carapace of what he *should* and *must* be. One thing was clear, at last, though. The old Anthony was obsolete, and had to be reconstructed, with a little help from Darren.

'You're right!' he exclaimed. 'In fact, you've hit the nail on the head. I do need to believe in myself, and I do intend to change. And actually I've come up with an idea for a complete new start.'

'Brilliant, Tony! So spill the beans.'

'No, I can't explain on the phone – it's just too complicated – but I'll tell you about it on Sunday, okay? All I'll say at the moment is that it's going to be one hell of a challenge, but absolutely no one's going to stop me!'

'Excuse me!' barked a peevish voice, as a woman with two ferocious-looking dogs endeavoured to push past.

Chastened, he stood aside, totally unaware he'd been causing an obstruction. 'Listen, Darren,' he said, once the trio had grumbled their way past, 'I want you to keep this date free: November the seventh, 2018.'

'Me release date!'

'Exactly. You see, I intend coming to the prison gate and escorting you home.'

'I ain't got no home – or have you forgot?'

'No, I haven't forgotten, but you're going to stay with me, at least until you've found your feet. The second bedroom in my flat's just gathering dust at the moment, so you can dust it in lieu of rent! And we're going out that same evening for a double celebration – of *your* release and *my* new venture.' In another eighteen months, his fledgling company could already be well-established, given hard graft and determination on his part. 'First, we'll have a slap-up meal, then we're going on to the theatre.'

'The *theatre*?'

'Well, you said you've never set foot in one, and surely that's all wrong now you're something of an actor yourself.'

'Sodding heck, mate!' Darren gave a hooting laugh. 'Except I ain't got a thing to wear for a posh do like that. I told you, Tony, ages ago, Rita must have cleared out all me stuff once I were banged up, including that snazzy suit you gave me.'

'Don't worry – I have plenty more suits.'

Before Darren could say thank you, another thought flashed into his mind: if the Finsbury Park flat was to be the new company premises, and where Darren would eventually be living, couldn't the lad take on some actual role in the business? His youth would be an asset, as well as his first-hand experience of many different prisons and his struggles, post-release, to find any kind of work. And his natural rapport with ex-offender clients – a rapport he himself lacked, as an over-privileged toff

– would be another bonus. In fact, strange as it might seem, this once 'thickie' and 'bricktop', to use Darren's own terminology, could turn out to be a valuable co-worker. His recent training in group-work and leadership was exactly what the new project required and, by the time of his release, he would have learned a whole lot more, developed greater confidence, and honed his various skills. At present he was studying drug-abuse, gang culture, and anger-management – all pertinent to a company intending to find employment for ex-cons. And his ever-increasing ability to manage the kids attending his workshops – some of them downright bolshie – and to assess their needs and states of mind, would certainly be a plus point.

Meanwhile, he and Darren could use part of each weekly visit as another sort of training session – to initiate his new recruit into the aims and structure of the company and encourage him to come up with his own ideas. And, once they were actually working together, Darren would no longer have to worry about accommodation or finances – probably for the first time in his life – so would be free to devote his time and energy to the enterprise.

The lad's effusive thanks intruded into his speculations, followed by his habitual question. 'But why the hell should you do all this for me?'

'Isn't it what *fathers* do?' Embarrassed, as usual, by his own sentimental words, Anthony also felt a hypocrite, knowing he was rubbish at love of any sort, paternal or romantic. Besides, for all his buoyant optimism with Barbara, there were, in fact, risks all along the line – the risks of love itself, Darren's own inexperience of any such employment and whether he would even have initiative or staying-power, not to mention the whole question of how they would hit it off as flatmates. He might long to have the place to himself, or be driven mad by Darren's music, habits – anything. So be it. He simply had to accept full-on the whole uncertain future, including sharing his home with someone he hardly knew in some respects, yet who clearly had a deep need of him as mentor, provider and, yes, father.

'Fucking hell!' the lad expostulated. 'Me credit's running out.'

'Quick – before you're cut off, tell me you're on for our theatre date.'

'Wouldn't miss it for the world, mate!'

Anthony snapped off his phone as the line went dead, and continued down the dark and shadowy street. No moon, no stars, just the harsh stare of the lampposts shedding incongruous lustre on the sullen drizzle now spattering his suit. Yet as he approached the underground, he felt the ghost of a smile daring to take shape on his lips: an almost-hopeful, not-quite-optimistic, but definitely go-for-it smile.

And, striding into the entrance to the tube, he murmured as much to himself as to Darren, 'Just give us time and we'll sodding well show 'em, son!'

ACKNOWLEDGEMENTS

I owe a huge debt of gratitude to all those patient and generous people who helped me research *The Tender Murderer*. Chief of these was David Zinzan, former Deputy Chief Constable of Devon and Cornwall, and, before that, former Head of Serious and Organised Crime at the Met, and Area Commander, SE London. Despite his eminence, he was never too busy to answer my questions on all aspects of policing, and even read the entire typescript to ensure I'd got things right.

Equally generous were the criminal barristers Sam Thomas and Beth O'Riley, who, notwithstanding their pressured lives, spent patient hours explaining the complexities of the legal system, and also conducted me on personal tours of various courtrooms, including the Old Bailey. Beth even let me watch her in action and was truly impressive!

As for the prison sections, I couldn't have written them without the help of many ex-offenders who were kind enough to tell me their personal stories and provide vivid and often troubling details of life inside. The most distinguished of these, Jonathan Aitken, now works tirelessly for prison reform and helped me plan the final part of the novel, as did Peter Stanford, a personal friend and Director of the Longford Trust. Both men introduced me to several organisations that share their aims and ideals: Tempus Novo, the St Giles Trust, Blue Sky, Only Connect, and Prosper4 – the latter's CEO, Michael Corrigan, proving doubly helpful as a former ex-offender, and currently the driving force behind a range of social enterprises that find work for serving prisoners and ex-offenders. And, having worked for 10 years at Deloittes, he was also an invaluable source of information on Anthony's former career in Corporate Finance.

Another Antony – Antony Harper – was my go-to-man in the field of specialist recruitment agencies, patiently explaining the demands and challenges of this type of work, so that when *my* Anthony eventually finds employment in this field, I could describe the job with more confidence and conviction.

Equally assiduous was Lady Dusha Bateson, who introduced me to Egyptian Maus, sharing both her passion for and extensive experience of this distinctive and strikingly beautiful breed, one of the very few naturally spotted domesticated cats.

Thanks are also due to my good friends, Beth Galvin and Lorna Fowler, for providing details of Lancashire life and landscape; to Mary Sparrow, whose name I purloined (with her permission, I hasten to add!); to Aisling Carson and Ollie Davies for help on a million matters from Marylebone Village to Hedge Funds; to award-winning radio producer, Piers Plowright, who provided invaluable advice on my typescript, and to my maths-wizard brother, Dr Robert Brech, who checked all the dates, figures and timings in the novel.

Last, but very much not least, I want to pay tribute to the men at Coldingley Prison, who gave me one of the most memorable and moving days of my life, by allowing me to witness their highly professional and impressive performance as part of the KEEPOUT Crime Prevention Scheme.

19602613R00187

Printed in Poland
by Amazon Fulfillment
Poland Sp. z o.o., Wrocław